MW01600466

From the Start

QUIBLINGS: BOOK 1

KATIE DUGGAN

Copyright © 2023 by Katie Duggan

All rights reserved.

No part of this publication may be reproduced, distributed, or transmitted in any form or by any means, including photocopying, recording, or other electronic or mechanical methods, without the prior written permission of the publisher, except as permitted by U.S. copyright law. For permission requests, contact Katie Duggan (KatieDuggan.Writes@gmail.com)

The story, all names, characters, and incidents portrayed in this production are fictitious. No identification with actual persons (living or deceased), places, buildings, and products is intended or should be inferred.

Cover Illustration & Design by Paige Moreland

Edited by Cheyenne Duhon & Paige Moreland

Buttercup Illustration by Paige Moreland

Scene Break Illustration by Emily B. Rose

2nd edition 2024

Originally published 2023

Paperback: 979-8-9906598-3-4

Ebook: 979-8-9906598-2-7

Contents

Content Warnings

While *From the Start* is, at its heart, a romantic comedy, serious topics are included as well. Life is funny, and life is tragic, and I hope I was able to marry these two facts.

From the Start features consensual open-door sex, terminal cancer, the death of a family member (off page), PTSD symptoms (specifically nightmares), and graphic autistic meltdowns.

There is also mention of past trauma including: death of family members by drunk driving, fatphobia, bullying, ableism, and religious trauma.

While it is my biggest hope that *From the Start* brings joy and healing to its readers, I understand that may not be the case for everyone. If you think it may be too much, please take care of yourself and your brain first.

If you have thoughts that are overwhelming and need someone to talk to, please call 988 if you are in the U.S.

Love,
Katie

KATIE DUGGAN

Dicktionary

For readers like me, who search specific keywords on their e-reader to get to the good parts sometimes: I hope this makes it easier on you.

Smut can be found in the following chapters:

- Chapter 10

- Chapter 11

- Chapter 14

- Chapter 16

- Chapter 17

And for those who want to avoid the smut: please know that while the following chapters are the ones with graphic intimate scenes, sex and pleasure is discussed frequently and graphically in *From the Start*.

Playlist

While writing I curated a playlist of songs that related to Nic, Josh, and their love story. The lyrics may not always directly apply, and listening to the playlist is not necessary for the enjoyment of *From the Start*.

Songs are listed at the beginning of each chapter, and you can scan the QR code below to be taken directly to the Spotify playlist.

You can also find the playlist "From the Start by Katie Duggan (Quiblings #1)" on my profile, Katie Duggan.

For those who are trying to figure out how to fight for what they want and deserve in life: I promise we'll get there, and I'm so proud of us for fighting.

And for Mom, who always knew this would happen, even when I stopped believing. Now put the book down before I traumatize you back.

KATIE DUGGAN

"Here we go again."
-Mamma Mia (2008)

KATIE DUGGAN

Chapter 1

Nic

Playlist: "Clever," Beartooth

> **Mom:** I love you!

> **Mom:** Have a safe trip, text me when you get home?

Seen by Nic at 7:55pm.

I hate my family.

Okay, maybe that's a little extreme, but if you were autistic with seven siblings and parents who thrive on chaos and noise, you would get it.

Every Sunday, my family, at least those who still live in the area, gather at our parents' house for dinner. Despite the exhaustion and two and a half hour ride on the Metro North, I'm a frequent attendee.

Groaning, I stretch my arms over my head and lean against the back of my seat. The train back to the city is pretty empty tonight, thankfully, so I was able to snag a six-seater in order to spread myself out. I pull my headphones and tablet out of my tote bag and put the headphones over my ears, opening up the Apple TV+ app to press play on my favorite *Ted Lasso* episode.

I've watched the series several times and will probably watch it several more, as the familiarity is comforting to me. As the sound of dialogue fills my ears, it quiets the sound of the train on the tracks and my ruminating thoughts about my family. I love them, but I don't know how to set the boundaries necessary for a healthy relationship with them.

As I watch the episode, I become hyper focused and the world around me is less overwhelming.

Until someone puts their bag on the end seat. I feel it immediately, the shift in pressure on the vinyl seats. When I glare up, I see some wannabe lumberjack talking at me. I'm short, the shortest woman in my family, so everyone always feels tall to me. But this guy? He's actually tall. He's easily over six feet with broad shoulders and a big body, effortlessly taking up space, physically and metaphorically. The lights in the car are off, so I can't see him very clearly, but I am able to make out a short, well-groomed beard.

All he needs is a flannel shirt and an ax and he'd go from *wannabe* lumberjack to *actual* lumberjack.

Despite the noise-canceling headphones over my ears, he's still talking, unbothered by my lack of a response, or the fact I don't know what the fuck he's saying.

I give up.

Irritated, I tear my headphones off. "What?" I snap, not bothering to mask my feelings.

"Whoa," he says, putting his hands in the air, as if I was the one to take him by surprise. "Easy there, Buttercup. I was just asking if it would be okay if I sat here."

I scowl at him, placing my iPad on my lap. "Why? Is it because the train is *so* crowded and you can't find any other seats?" I ask, voice dripping with sarcasm. I'm not being polite, I know this. But I'm burnt out, and masking is too much effort for this guy. "And my name is *not* Buttercup."

He clears his throat, and it feels like he's trying not to laugh at me, like I'm a joke. I clench my fists in my lap, my nails digging into my palms causing a welcome sting of pain. "I didn't mean that your name is Buttercup. It's just a common term of endearment."

I wrinkle my nose. "I am *not* endearing," I spit, releasing my fists and picking up my iPad. And they say I'm bad at reading subtext in social situations. Why isn't this guy getting the hint?

"Yes, I see that now." He coughs into his fist. "Can I sit here? I promise I won't bother you."

How can he say that when he's been bothering me relentlessly for the past ninety seconds? "My guy, you and I are the only ones in this car. There's no reason you should want to sit here."

He sighs, "Can I be real with you? I've had a long day, and I walked four cars looking for a six-seater. This is the only one I've seen with less than five people sitting in it. I'd *really* like to put my feet up, and you've probably noticed I'm a big guy…"

"Fine," I snap, leaning across to grab my tote bag from the seat across from me, tucking my knees under me so that he can put his feet up. I *never* want to hear that I'm not a kind-hearted person. "But *please* don't talk to me."

I'm not exactly known as the friendliest person in the world, especially after being subjected to an overstimulating day with my overwhelming family. I'm certain that's what he's thinking, but I don't have the energy to care or be self-conscious about it. I just want to get the fuck out of Connecticut and back to the apartment I share with my younger sister, Jo, in Williamsburg. I just want to watch my comfort show and not have Bigfoot himself–themself? I'm unsure of Bigfoot's gender identity–trying to interact with me on a goddamned train with no escape. There has to be a horror movie like this.

When I glance up again, he's slowly lowering his body to the end seat on the other side from me. A confused expression flashes on his face, illuminated by the passing lights outside. "Do I know you from somewhere?"

I sigh heavily and shoot him yet another glare. "And here I was saying please and everything."

He clicks his tongue and cocks his head, putting his feet up on the seat across from him. "You're going to have to beg better than that, Buttercup."

"My name still isn't Buttercup," I grumble.

"Well, considering I don't know your name, what else am I supposed to call you?" I hear smugness in his voice, and I fight the impulse to smack him.

"Nic. My name is Nic," I sigh.

"Is Nic short for Nicole?"

I'm used to this question. It makes sense, and in a way, this random man acting predictably is comforting.

"Nicoletta," I say reluctantly, crossing my arms across my chest and lowering my gaze. "But I go by Nic. Not Nicoletta, and most definitely not Buttercup."

I see the Yeti uncross his legs and lean forward in my peripheral vision, his elbows resting atop his knees. "No way! I went to elementary school with a Nicoletta. It's not a very common name, is it?"

My eyes snap back to him. He's right. It's not a particularly common name, and usually I'm the first and only Nicoletta people know. "What station did you get on?" I ask nervously, a sense of dread slowly spreading through my body like a dark, heavy fog.

"Port Haven, why?" he says, squinting his eyes as he looks at me. His eyes widen, and he gasps, "Holy shit. Nicoletta Quinn?"

I nod apprehensively. I most definitely went to school with this man, and while I didn't keep in contact with any of my classmates, knowing my luck, he's the last person I want to see.

In the dark, I can just make out a grin spreading across his furry, Yeti-like face as he leans back against his seat.

I recognize that smile. The smile that still haunts some of my worst memories. It chased me out of my hometown and across state lines.

"Holy shit. Nicoletta fucking Quinn. It's Josh Henry."

Chapter 2

Josh

Playlist: "Cold Caller," Julia Jacklin

Well. This isn't how I saw the night going.

How the hell was I supposed to know I would run into Nic Quinn for the first time in over a decade, all because I just had to sit in a six-seater tonight?

Sure, I wanted to put my feet up after a physically and emotionally draining day, but I really could have sat anywhere.

It wasn't that complicated.

But, here we are: Nic's eyes shooting lasers, and me knowing full well that she could kill me if she wanted to.

I laugh nervously and shift in my seat. "Funny running into you here."

"What the *fuck*?" she replies, and I'm surprised that steam isn't blowing out her ears, like an old-timey cartoon.

I swallow thickly, suddenly feeling like I'm ten-years-old again. Growing up in Nic Quinn's orbit was difficult, to put it mildly. She was whip smart, and honestly, the entire Quinn family was intimidating. They were a big, well respected family in Port Haven, with Nic's parents being prominent lawyers in the community. We were in the same grade, and though she was quiet and kept to herself, it always felt like there was an unsettling power about her.

Obviously she hasn't changed a bit.

"It's good to see you," I offer cautiously.

"Fuck off," she snaps. "I moved to the city to get the hell away from you, Josh Henry."

I wince. I had done the same, honestly, but maybe less vehemently. Despite going to different high schools, it still felt like Nic was a part of my life. I only remember actually seeing her once after we were in high school, but she was never going to be completely out of my life as long as I lived in Port Haven.

I moved to the city for undergrad and my advanced degrees, happy to finally be able to start fresh without bringing my childhood baggage with me. Most of the time, you can avoid people you don't want to see in the city, but now it feels like I've continued to exist in Nic Quinn's orbit without even realizing it.

"Uh, I actually have been living in the city for almost ten years. I went to NYU for undergrad and got my Ph.D. at Columbia." I smile shakily, hoping she can't sense the fear I'm feeling. "Sorry." I'm not sure why I'm apologizing, it's not like I did anything wrong, but I still feel like, by moving to the same metropolis as her, I've somehow inconvenienced her.

She groans and lets her head flop against the window with a heavy *thud*. "And I went to Columbia for undergrad and NYU for my Ph.D."

"Well, rats. We just missed each other." I joke in an attempt to lighten the mood.

Nic's murderous expression informs me my attempt falls flat.

She's examining me, her gaze going up and down my torso, and I protectively cross my arms over my chest. I'm a big guy, tall and fat, and I take up a lot of space. Most of the time, I'm absolutely fine with my body, but the way she's looking at me right now makes me want to hide myself.

"What do you do?" I ask awkwardly.

Her eyes snap to mine, then quickly look away. "I'm a psychologist," she mumbles so quietly I almost can't hear it.

I wait for her to elaborate, maybe ask what I do, but she doesn't. Instead she puts her headphones on and picks her tablet back up, completely ignoring me.

Well. I know she hated me, but Jesus, we're in our late twenties.

I lean over and tap her foot. She jumps and drops her feet to the ground. "Seriously?" she pulls her headphones off violently. "Don't fucking touch me without my consent. Actually, don't fucking touch *anyone* without their consent."

I flush, embarrassed because, goddammit, she's absolutely right. "Fair. I just...are you going to ask me about what I do?"

She looks honestly baffled. "Why would I do that?"

I bark out a disbelieving laugh. "Because it's the polite thing to do? Because I asked you about what you do, and you give and take in a conversation?"

She at least has the grace to look sheepish. "Oh. Um. Yeah. I did tell you I don't want to talk, though," she reminds me.

"You really hate me that much?" I ask, my anger bubbling steadily inside me. I think I'm a pretty likable guy, but my god, is she making it hard to remain that way. I don't know why I want to talk to her so badly, but I do.

"Of course I hate you," she spits. "You made my childhood a living hell."

It feels like she's slapped me. I made *her* childhood hell?

"You know, I always thought the same about you. But I grew the hell up," I say with a cold, disbelieving laugh as I gather up my things.

"Oh, now you leave."

"Yeah. Because honestly, I don't want to be around your negative ass energy."

"Fuck off," she says as she leans forward, hands balled into fists. "If you're trying to prove to me you've changed, that you're not someone worth hating, you're failing spectacularly."

I stand from the seat and bow dramatically. "Pleased to be able to prove you right. Have a great night, Buttercup," I yell as I walk away, knowing the nickname bothers her.

"Fuck off. Again!" she yells back. I've lost track of how many times she's told me to do that.

I stomp through the car and into the next one. There's no six-seater, but being as far away from that...that *menace* is honestly my top priority.

I don't understand why she's acting like this. Sure we weren't friends as kids, but unlike her, I was nice. Hell, she was my first crush, despite her aloofness, despite her always acting like she didn't like me. Yet, somehow, I'm the bad guy because I thought, not having seen each other in ten years, she might have matured past our childhood animosity.

I throw my small duffel and messenger bag into the rack above an empty row. Once I'm seated, I pull out my phone and text my cousin, Tara, to let her know I'm on the train.

I sigh and lean back against the seat, feeling completely drained after today. I should grade papers, but after that little reunion, I need to relax. I pull a copy of an Adriana Herrera historical romance from my bag, opening it up to where I left off, allowing the story to distract me for most of the ride.

"Excuse me, sir. Grand Central's next." I jump as the conductor hovers over me. That was fast.

"Thanks," I mumble, closing the book and sliding it back in my bag.

As I exit the train, someone plows into me, and I stagger back from the impact. This isn't an unusual occurrence in the city, but it is unusual that the person who almost had me sprawled on my ass is a good foot shorter than me.

"Oof!" the human wrecking ball says as I try to steady myself. "Sorry."

Two hours ago I wouldn't have recognized that voice. Now? It's like fingernails on a chalkboard.

"Had to ruin my night even more, Buttercup?" I ask.

Nic's shoulders stiffen and she slowly lifts her head, eyes narrowing as she takes me in. Her headphones are on, and I realize she might not be able to hear me, so I repeat myself.

"I heard you the first time, asshole," she snaps. "And you're one to talk." She stomps away, and I definitely don't notice how curvy her ass and legs look in the leggings she wears.

I swallow as I watch her go, waiting until she's far enough away so I can avoid her.

After a few moments, I slowly make my way through the station. It's late, so all of the shops and restaurants are closed, but there's still a handful of tourists gathered in the main concourse, staring up at the ornate ceiling in wonder. When I first moved to the city, I would stop every time I took the train home and admire the artwork too.

The first time I didn't do that, I knew I was a real New Yorker.

Granted, earlier that day I had also physically fought a rat over a bagel with lox from my favorite bakery.

Real New Yorker.

I walk to the subway concourse, swipe my Metrocard, and take the escalator down to the 4 track.

And of course, who is standing there on the platform waiting for the same train, in all her noise-canceling headphone glory? I go over a decade without seeing Nic fucking Quinn, and now I have to deal with seeing her *thrice* in one night?

Unbelievable.

She doesn't see me at first as I walk down the platform, and I'm hoping it stays that way. But just as I'm passing her, her shoulders tense and her head shoots up, like a predator sensing its prey.

When she looks my way, I get a very pissed off middle finger, but considering everything else I had to put up from her, this is *nothing*. I smile tightly at her, which causes her frown to deepen.

I might get some sick satisfaction out of that. Until a few minutes later, when we both get off at Union Square.

She does a double take seeing me this time, and if it were anyone but her, I'd laugh as we both stood waiting for the L. Maybe make a joke about kismet.

The city's too damn big for this.

When I *finally* get off my final stop of the night...so does she.

"No way," she says disbelievingly, tearing her headphones off her head, messing up her short curls in the process. "No fucking way." She looks disgusted, like she stepped in dog shit.

I can't help but smirk. She's just so pissed. "Looks like we're neighbors, Buttercup. Need me to walk you home?"

She takes a step toward me, standing on her tiptoes to try and reduce the height difference between us. It's a little bit funny, because she doesn't realize it doesn't make much of a difference.

"Listen here, Josh Henry." A delicate hint of lavender wafts from her. For such a fucking terror, it's disorienting that she smells so nice.

Jesus Christ, focus, Joshua.

"Tonight was a blip in the Matrix—the worst of all blips. I'm going to walk home. *Alone*. The same way I do every night, and you're going to start the very long descent back to hell."

I can't help it. I laugh, and she glares at me, sticking her chest out. "Don't you dare laugh at me," she growls.

"Sorry. That was funny," I say reluctantly. It *was* funny; I can recognize and appreciate a good joke.

She blinks, a baffled expression on her face. "It was?" she says, her voice a strange tone. "I'm not really funny."

"Well, considering all I really know about this version of you is your astonishing ability to verbally abuse someone, I can't say if you're funny or not. But it was a clever joke."

Her face contorts, and for a moment, I think she's going to cry. For some reason I refuse to process, I absolutely hate the idea of that. But just as suddenly as the blazing hatred was gone, it's back, her brown eyes flaming. "Well. Whatever. You're going to wait five minutes to leave so we never have to see each other again. Deal?"

"Deal."

"Great. Have a fantastic fucking life, Josh Henry," she says as she turns and walks away, flipping her middle finger at me over her shoulder.

For some reason, I do as she asks, standing in the tunnel staring at my phone before leaving the station.

It's only a ten minute walk to my house, a brownstone in Williamsburg I've owned since I turned eighteen.

I love it here: it's big and quiet when I'm alone, but I love hosting and because of the extra space, my friends and family visiting from out of town always have a place to stay.

It's home.

When I step into the foyer, I flip the lights on as I go to the kitchen, mind wandering as I make a mug of tea and grab a banana. I head up to my office on the third floor to grade the essays I assigned my Shakespearean Tragedies class at the beginning of the week. I'd asked students to analyze a soliloquy of their choice from any of the works we'd studied this semester. Since finals are next week, it was supposed to be a quick, easy assignment that I could grade quickly.

"Supposed to" being the key phrase.

I've been in Port Haven the past few days after Tara called me Thursday afternoon to tell me Grandma was back in the hospital. She's been fighting lung cancer for the past year, and it's been a rollercoaster. When I got the call, I canceled my Friday classes to take the train home and stayed through the weekend. After receiving some pretty bad news, I wasn't sure if I'd be able to make it back in time for class tomorrow, but Grandma insisted I return to the city.

I like my life. When I'm lonely, I have my friends, family, and dating apps to remedy that. But I always feel a little more hollow after spending extended time in Connecticut, especially with Grandma being so sick.

I don't know how I'd *want* to spend a Sunday night, but right now, with my mug of English Breakfast tea, sitting alone in my four-story home doing the job that I worked hard for and *love*, I know this isn't it.

Chapter 3

Nic

Playlist: "You're On Your Own, Kid," Taylor Swift

"Shit," I curse, the contents of my reusable shopping bag tumbling to the ground around my feet.

After fuming over the existence of Josh Henry all day, I went to Summit Stone, the local climbing gym I'm a member at. When climbing incredibly high didn't eradicate him, I made a run to the store to grab a pint of Ben & Jerry's for myself and a package of Jo's favorite chocolate-covered raisins. I also grabbed a sugar-free gelato she adores, knowing that sometimes her blood sugar is unpredictable.

Chocolate should fix everything, but I don't know that it can erase the absolute gall of this man to live in not just New York, but Brooklyn.

I hurriedly shove my food items back into my tote and straighten, shoving my key into the lock and pushing the door open.

"JoJo!" I sing in that annoying tone all sisters are gifted once a younger sibling is born. "I brought snacks home and checked your Google Calendar. *Miss Congeniality* is back on Netflix and I think-"

I stop mid sentence when I look around the living room, my stomach plummeting.

"Uh, hey Jo," I say, slowly lowering the bag to the counter. Any sudden movements could startle her. "What's happening here?"

Jo lowers the side of the green velvet couch she's attempting to drag across the room to the floor. She glances over at me, her face red and covered with a sheen of sweat. Her dark hair is thrown up in a messy ponytail, and she's wearing a cropped tank top and leggings. "Great, you're back. I need your help moving this. Who knew couches were this heavy?"

I hold in a deep sigh and the urge to tell her that every-one knows that couches are heavy. I don't do well when my plans unexpectedly change. Unlike me, Jo loves surprises, so I'd planned on us having an easy-going movie night, something we haven't been able to do in months.

But Jo is obviously out of her depth and I feel like I should help with rearranging. It's not like I have anything better to do.

While I'm certain my family has noticed my hate of change over my twenty-nine years of existence, they don't know why. They just think I'm particular.

"Okay," I sigh, resigned to my fate. Sometimes, it's just easier to go along with things and cope with them afterward instead of saying anything. "Where do you want it to go?"

"I was thinking it would be nice if we could enjoy the view while sitting on the couch!"

I turn my head and look out the single window in the living room, making sure our view of the neighboring building's fire escape hasn't magically changed since I left for work this morning.

It hasn't.

"Uh, okay," I agree reluctantly, moving toward the opposite end of the couch.

"You're home late," Jo huffs, attempting to blow a piece of curly hair away from her face.

"I went to the gym," I tell her as we scoot the couch toward her chosen spot.

"Don't you usually climb in the morning?"

"Yeah, I went twice today," I admit, a flush covering my cheeks. "Lots of pent-up energy to get out."

Jo shudders. "Ugh, I don't understand how you can deal with climbing that high. You're out of your mind."

Jo is one of my seven siblings. She's the third oldest, after Kat and me, and Jo's the most daring of any of us. Except maybe our baby brother, Leo, but he's still a reckless teenager. Growing up, Jo would chase Kat—our oldest sister—and I around cackling whenever she found a garter snake in Nonna's garden during the summers. She was the one sneaking into the room Kat and I shared to terrify us with ghost stories *way* after our bedtime. To an anxious little girl who felt out of place in the world, Jo seemed fearless.

Except when it came to climbing trees or anything else involving heights. Which is hilarious, considering she works for Coffey & Co, a prominent event planning firm in midtown with an office on the twenty-fifth floor. She did, however, manage to snag an office without a window, which probably helps.

I shrug. "It clears my mind. And my mind needs clearing right now."

"Hey, if it works, it works. I just..." She shudders again. "No. Not for me."

"Then why do you want to move the couch to face the window when we live on the third floor?"

Jo stops moving so suddenly that it feels like a freeze frame in a movie. "I-damn. I didn't think about that." She walks around the side of the couch and collapses onto it. "That's probably why we had it against the window to begin with, right?"

Well, that and our view is ugly as fuck.

"It's easier to watch the TV the way it was," I say in what I hope is a soothing tone as I sit next to her. "Remember when we had weekly movie nights? Before you dated Kelsey? I was actually hoping we could start those up again, if you wanted to..." I trail off.

Jo groans and scrubs at her eyes with the heels of her hands. "Fuck."

"What's going on?" I ask. "You're acting weird."

"You think everyone acts weird," she reminds me.

She's not wrong, people are strange. "Okay, you're acting weirder than *usual*, Giovanna."

She turns her head to look at me. "I didn't get the promotion," she says in a defeated tone, dropping her head back against the couch

I stare at her. "What? You're their top rated planner and have the highest percentage of repeat clients and vendors! You had this in the bag. Did Daniel get it?" Daniel is what Jo jokingly refers to as 'the token straight, white guy' of the firm. Coffey & Co is renowned throughout the tri-state area for their focus on the LGBTQIA+ community and inclusive events. It's why Jo wanted to work there so badly.

"Kelsey got it," she murmurs, looking away from me.

My jaw drops. "Kelsey *Williams,* Kelsey? Your ex-fianceé Kelsey? *That* Kelsey?"

"That Kelsey," Jo confirms glumly.

Kelsey started working at Coffey & Co as a junior planner just under a year ago, and Jo, well, Jo fell. Hard. She was the last of my siblings I expected to jump into a relationship so suddenly, and with a colleague at that. Kelsey pretty much moved in after their first date, and Jo proposed three months later. After four months and thousands of dollars in deposits later, just as suddenly as she'd moved in, Kelsey moved out. Jo came home from work one night to see she'd moved her stuff out of our place, leaving Jo nothing but a note on her dresser along with her engagement ring. Jo never told me what the note said, but the past few months have been understandably tough for her.

"Fuck, I didn't know she was qualified."

"You and me, both. She basically jumped right from being a planning assistant to a senior coordinator," Jo mutters. "And—get this–I think she's fucking Becky."

My jaw drops. "Becky? Becky *Coffey* Becky?" Becky Coffey is Jo's boss and the owner of Coffey & Co. "I thought she was straight?"

"'Straight-ish' is the term she uses," Jo says. "I'm sure they won't go public for a few more months because otherwise it looks sketchy as fuck. But Becky butt-dialed Daniel last week, and he swore he heard her and Kelsey moaning each other's names, over and over." She pauses and bites her lip. "I didn't believe him, and I don't want to...but what if it's true, Nic?" She slumps further into the couch, a defeated expression on her face.

"I'm sorry," I say sincerely. I'm not really sure what to do or say in this situation, so I just prop my chin on her shoulder. "That really sucks."

She rests her head on top of mine, inhaling deeply. "It's not your fault."

"I know, but it's still a shitty situation you have to deal with."

"Yeah," Jo answers quietly. "It really is." She lifts her head up. "Wait, what were you saying about *Miss Congeniality*?"

Thirty minutes later, we're watching Jo's favorite movie, both of us happily eating our snacks while I'm burrowed in my weighted blanket.

"Are you going to tell me why you went to the gym twice? You're a creature of habit, and that's a weird-ass thing for you to—ah, shit." Jo twists her shoulder and licks a drop of sugar-free gelato that had dripped onto her arm, right above her

CGM—continuous glucose monitor. Jo has Type 1 Diabetes and wears a CGM so she can easily access her blood sugar levels.

I sigh and shake my head. "Long story."

"Oh, that's fine," Jo says. "I spill my guts, but you keep your secrets. You know you feel better when you talk about it."

I scowl at my pint of Phish Food, violently stabbing my spoon repeatedly into the melting ice cream. "Fine. Do you remember Josh Henry? He was in my class in elementary school."

I can almost hear her blinking at me. "Should I?" she asks nervously.

"No. And you're lucky–he ruined my life."

"Wait. This isn't that guy we saw at that party we crashed that one summer?"

I wince at the memory; of loud music and voices, of making eye contact with none other than Josh Henry on the beach.

Of him coming over to me, despite me actively trying to avoid him, and spilling his cheap-ass beer all over me.

Which, of course, prompted me to throw my wine cooler on him.

Jo cackles. "Oh my god, you were so mad."

My cheeks redden. "I was wearing a white t-shirt and smelled like cheap beer." She doesn't know how, after I left the party, I went home and had what I now know was a meltdown, over-whelmed by the entire experience.

"Okay, okay, so this dude ruined your life in high school and-"

"It wasn't just that night. He was in my class in elementary school and has always been terrible. He beat me in the spelling bee I spent months studying for, and when I was being bullied he just let it happen, Jo. He never said anything." I choke out the last part, clenching and unclenching my hands.

Memories of myself as a kid play in my mind. Everyone insisted on calling me 'Nicoletta,' despite my requests to be called Nic like I was at home. I ate lunch in a classroom or office most days because I didn't have anyone to eat with. I would play alone during recess. Kids would whisper when I asked to go back inside when the sun was too bright or when everyone was too loud–which was often.

Then there was Josh Henry, in all his perfect blond hair and blue eyed glory, who was universally adored. Josh Henry, who never gave a shit that, on a daily basis, I sat alone on the bus crying the whole way home. It's been decades since that happened, but sometimes I still feel like that little girl who nobody quite understood.

"He made fun of my name," I continue, still clenching and unclenching my fists to ground myself. "He said it sounded like Nutella."

"Nicoletta...Nutella," Jo says, her mouth slightly twitching, and honestly, I have to give her credit for not laughing. "That's why you've always hated being called Nicoletta?"

I shrug. "Nobody at home really called me Nicoletta unless I was in trouble, so it never felt like *me*. I wanted to be taken seriously, even as a kid, and I just wasn't."

"And seeing him on the train brought all of that hurt back to the surface," Jo says softly. I think about how she has to see Kelsey every day at work, how it must make her feel.

"Yeah–I'm sorry. This is so inconsequential compared to-"

"Uh-uh," she says sternly. "No comparing our hurts. My sister who's a psychologist says that's a trap."

I smile shakily. "She sounds annoying."

Jo gently elbows me. "She's not. *You're* not, Nicky. It's okay that you feel the way you do."

"Thanks, JoJo."

It doesn't fix everything. I'm still angry and hurt, but sometimes, it's good to be reminded of what I already know.

Chapter 4

Josh

Playlist: "Oh No," Andrew Bird

You can tell it's the first week in May because not even my most active participants are making a sound in class. I can't blame them. I feel that itch for a break from classes, too, even though I know I only have one week before the first summer term, when I'm teaching a writing intensive course.

I sigh and close my copy of *Hamlet*, looking out at the lecture hall full of students. "You know what, everyone, let's call it a day. Don't forget on Thursday we're preparing for the final. Class is optional, but I'd come if I had any concerns or questions."

I have no idea if they heard me or not. Despite *Hamlet* being my favorite play, it apparently wasn't theirs, because as soon as the words are out of my mouth, eighty English majors are out of their seats and collecting their shit.

In less than a minute, they've all funneled out, leaving me alone in the lecture hall. I pack up my bag before starting the twenty minute trek back to my office. I'm done with classes for the day, but I have a meeting with an advisee in an hour, and I still have to finish grading those damn monologue papers.

Sometimes, I think about how lucky I am, that I get to geek out and talk about how cool Shakespeare is and get paid for it. Honestly, I love every part of my job.

Despite that, lately I've been feeling like something's missing.

Even worse than the empty feeling that's swirling in my chest is the fact I can't stop thinking about Nic fucking Quinn.

Because she pissed me off so much, obviously. I can't stop thinking about the way she spat at me, the way her calves flexed, and her leggings clung to her curves as she stood on tiptoe to try to match my height.

Of all the other ways I could make her eyes flash with passion.

Fuck, I need to get laid. Unfortunately, Tinder and Grindr have both been fruitless, and I'm an anonymous, one-time hookup kind of guy. Lube and my hand have been pulling their weight lately.

When I get back to my office, I set up my laptop and, for a reason I can't explain and won't rationalize, search Nic Quinn on Facebook.

Her account is pretty private, and her profile picture is at least a few years old. She is giving whoever took the picture some *serious* side eye. I wonder what the photographer did to get on her bad side. Her hair is long, past her shoulders, unlike the pixie cut she sports now. Her untamed chestnut curls are the same, despite the length difference.

There's no information about her workplace or where she lives, and I don't know why I'm disappointed.

I don't like her, and she certainly doesn't like me.

So why do I find myself searching for her sister's name?

Nic is one of like…a thousand kids, which is useful for my current goal: creepily stalk her.

When I search for people with the last name 'Quinn' in Port Haven, I come across a Ren Quinn, who I infer is Nic's younger brother. He has dark wavy hair, mossy green eyes, and a beard a little shorter than mine. I remember him being a few years younger than Nic, and according to Facebook, he still lives in Port Haven and teaches at the elementary school. A quick glance through Ren's friends list leads me to Katerina Quinn Holt's profile.

She was married fairly recently, and her post for her mom's birthday last month is complete with a family portrait from the wedding. A quick count reveals that there are eight Quinn offspring in total.

Nic sticks out like a sore thumb in the picture. She and her sisters, excluding the bride, wear floor-length mauve chiffon bridesmaid dresses, and her hair is long, straightened and pulled back from her face.

What really gets me is her *smile*. You can tell she's trying, but god, it looks like she's fighting back pain. I can't help but laugh at her expression.

For some reason, I remember how she told me how she hates being laughed at, and my laughter dies off. Which is ridiculous, of course. She's not here. She has no idea I'm laughing at her.

But it still feels wrong. Like I'm just another asshole who laughs at her and makes her feel small.

Like she could be right about me.

"Henry!" My best friend and coworker, Nellie, raps her knuckles on my door. "Welcome back."

I quickly close my tabs, the way I did back in highschool when Grandma opened my bedroom door without knocking. "Hey, Nell, thanks."

"Are you doing okay, buddy?" she asks gently, placing her hand on my shoulder.

My heart sinks. With how much Nic is occupying my mind, I've barely thought about Grandma and the conversation we'd had with her care team this weekend.

How treatment is no longer shrinking the tumors, and they've found new ones. How Grandma made the decision to stop treatment and enter hospice. How Tara and I packed up her hospital room, all the flowers and cards, and moved Grandma back into my childhood home, not knowing how much longer she has.

And I've barely even thought about her, instead dedicating time thinking about a woman who hates me. Shame creeps up within me, filling every crevice of my body.

I shrug. "I mean, I guess as well as I can be. She's dying, and it doesn't feel real. It all–it happened so suddenly, you know? But she wanted me to come back, to work and to live normally. That's always been important to her." I clear my throat, desperately trying to swallow the overwhelming wave of emotion snaking up my throat.

Nellie frowns and squeezes my shoulder. "You're allowed to hurt, but you're also allowed to enjoy life when you can. Myrtle wants that for you, and so do the rest of the people who love you." She pauses for a moment. "Do you think I could go visit her?

This makes me laugh, and I lean back in my chair, crossing my arms over my chest. "You know she'll just ask why we're not married yet, right?" While Grandma is extremely accepting of my sexuality, she's wanted me to marry Nellie since the first time the two of them met.

"Hmmm...do you think she'll accept 'engaged to my fiance' as an excuse?" Nellie says casually, lifting her left hand, where a startlingly big diamond sits on her finger.

I leap out of my chair. "Holy shit! Why didn't you say anything?" I wrap my arms around her, enveloping her in a bear hug. She squeals as her feet leave the ground, hugging me back.

"It happened Friday night! And I didn't want to tell you until you could hug me!"

"Ugh, only acceptable excuse," I tease as I lower her back to the ground. "Holy shit, Nellie. I just–fuck I'm so happy for you."

"It's weird though, right? Me having this when you're going through...everything."

I force a smile, but she's right. I've lived with grief and loss for over two decades, but I've never been quite able to balance the hurt and joy of life, instead numbing it in various ways.

"I can still be happy for you, Nell. And I am. I'm so, so happy for you and Ty."

"I'm happy, too," she says, grabbing my hand and squeezing it. "But enough about me. What do you want to do for your birthday this year?"

I blink at her. "My birthday?"

She sighs heavily. "Dammit, Josh. You do this every year. And every year, two weeks before your birthday, I remind you your birthday is in two weeks and that the Friday before your birthday is reserved for your birthday party."

"Okay but can we not do it at Franzino's again? The pasta was terrible."

"Yeah, it was," Nellie agrees, wrinkling her nose. "You'd think with such an Italian name they'd at least know how to make a good pasta dish. Let's just do a chill night with the usuals at your place? Mocktails and charcuterie boards?" She nudges my side with her elbow, wiggling her eyebrows.

My parents were killed in an accident caused by an intoxicated driver when I was little, something Grandma reminded me time and time again in high school and college. I never got my driver's license because of it, but I still leaned on alcohol to cope with uncomfortable emotions for years. Four years ago, I woke up one morning and had no idea how I got home. After that, I made the decision to stop drinking. When I told Nellie, she immediately learned to make dozens of mocktails to accommodate me at parties, and I love her for it.

"I am a slut for a good charcuterie board," I admit. "That sounds good. Low key. I don't want anything too exciting."

She pumps her fist. "Fuck yeah. Tyler's gonna be so excited. They've been wanting to try this new almond torte recipe."

Tyler, Nellie's now-fiancé, is a pastry chef at an exclusive restaurant uptown. They also like me enough that their delicious baked goods are frequently on my kitchen counter or in my office at school.

I smile at her, and for the first time in days, Nic Quinn isn't the main thought occupying my mind.

Chapter 5

Nic

Playlist: "Pompeii," Bastille

I woke up this morning sweaty, my limbs heavy, and my nipples peaked. It's been almost three weeks since Joshua Henry stumbled back into, and consequently ruined, my life, and last night, I had a dream of his beard scraping against the inside of my thighs as he moaned my name. At first, I didn't realize it was him. Then he looked up at me, and those sky blue eyes met mine with an unmistakable look of longing and hunger in them.

I jolted awake because what the *fuck*?

I breathe heavily as the sun leaks through the blinds, the dream playing on a loop in my head. I work from home on

Fridays, and though the benefits of teleworking are plentiful, today it means I can stay in bed a little longer and take care of at least one problem Josh Henry is the root of.

It's fast and hot, desperate and hard, and I definitely don't picture the duke from the latest historical romance Jo forced on me as a big, hulking giant with dark blond hair and blue eyes too beautiful to belong to an evil goblin.

I'm not a big reader, but Jo's always begging me to read these books with swooning women whose boobs are popping out of their dresses and men with ridiculously perfect hair on the cover. I have to hand it to her–they're great to keep on my reading app for times like this.

After I toast a couple of frozen waffles for breakfast, I sit at my desk in our spare room. It's an all-purpose room of sorts, one I primarily use as an office and Jo uses as a library.

As I wait for my computer to boot up, my phone *dings* with a notification from Tinder. A couple of days ago, I decided enough was enough with this, "*Hey is it just me or is Josh Henry hot as fuck now?*" bullshit my brain kept bringing up, so I went back on the apps, swiping desperately for a hookup.

Enter Bryce. Bryce is cute, all blond waves and clean shaven. He does something on Wall Street, which is gross, but he thinks I'm cute–or at least cute enough to get drinks with. Drinks that will hopefully end with a quick fuck at his place, my place, or, hell, even against the bathroom door at the bar.

Then we'll never talk again, and for a few days I'll ruminate on being sexually broken instead of having my thoughts consumed by someone who most definitely should not be taking up *any* real estate in my mind.

> **Bryce:**
> looking forward to tonight, cutie.
> <winking emoji>

I read the text a few times and feel nothing. Despite knowing exactly how tonight will end, and that ending being exactly what I want...I don't feel anything.

No jolt of excitement, just numbness.

How the fuck does a damn sex dream with the person I hate most in this world turn me on more than the idea of actually being fucked by a real live person?

Sex has never been simple for me. I know it's supposed to be enjoyable, and I have no difficulties enjoying time alone, but whenever I've fucked someone else, I can't come. I've slept with a handful of people and it's never been memorable. It always ended with me faking it to spare my partner's feelings.

When I don't react to their touches, partners have asked what I like, but I don't know how to answer that question, or even what the right answer is. I have no idea what I like to do with a partner, or what I don't, and I've never been able to express that lack of knowledge, either.

Hooking up with Bryce won't rock my world, I'm certain, but it will get Josh out of my head. Even if I'm overthinking the entire time, at least I won't be thinking about him.

> **Nic:** me too <smiling emoji> see you at 8?

> **Bryce:** yep! i love lace. <winking emoji>

He loves lace? I have no idea why he said that or how to reply to that.

I simply decide to not answer his message, and instead start my work day.

The day drags by, but I show up to the bar on time and wait for Bryce to show up. Forty-five minutes later, he is nowhere to be seen. Which I don't care about. It's fine. It's no big deal if he stands me up. I have no emotional investment in the night or him.

But I do hate having plans fucked up.

Five minutes later, Bryce glides through the door, a smile plastered on his clean shaven, conventionally attractive face.

"It's great to meet you," Bryce says, flashing me a megawatt grin as he hops onto the barstool next to me. "I've been thinking about you all week." He places his hand on my bare knee.

I force a tight smile. I know we're both expecting to end the night by fucking, but this still feels forward and uncomfortable. I fight the impulse to jerk away from his touch, instead pinching the skin on the back of my hand to distract me from my discomfort. "Yeah, same," I lie. "How was work?" First dates suck, but at least there's an expected social script to follow.

He ignores me, instead hollering at the bartender. The sudden noise makes me jump and wince. My earplugs are in my purse, but I don't want to make a show of getting them out. I pinch my hand again. "We'll take six tequila shots."

"You're taking six tequila shots?" I ask, startled by the sheer amount of alcohol he's just ordered.

He laughs. "Christ no. What am I, a frat boy?" I laugh nervously. "No, three for each of us."

I swallow hard. To be fair, I definitely wanted to be tipsy before we fuck, but I'm already drinking a Dark and Stormy. That plus tequila shots? I don't know if I'll be able to walk straight.

"I don't like tequila," I lie again, stirring my cocktail with a straw. "Bad experience in college." A bad experience with tequila in college seems like a universal experience according to movies.

Bryce huffs as the bartender delivers the six tequila shots to us. She shoots him a nasty look, and I don't blame her one bit. I eye the shots uneasily. I saw them being poured, so I know she didn't spit in them, but I would have if I were her.

"You're really not going to take the shots I'm buying for you?" Bryce says, tapping his fingers impatiently on the bartop.

"I didn't ask you to buy them."

"That's really fucking rude of you. I thought you were different." I fist the hem of my skirt, squeezing tight until I feel my nails digging into my palm through the fabric.

I wore a pushup bra for this asshole.

"Fine," I say through gritted teeth. I grab a shot glass and salt shaker then quickly lick the back of my hand and shake salt on it. I lick the salt off and tip my head back, the tequila burning my throat as I shoot it back. I can feel Bryce staring at me as I bite into the lime wedge, but I keep my gaze down.

I want to go home. Crawl into bed and call one of my siblings...I certainly have enough to pick from.

But I can't bring myself to leave.

"Fuck, Nic. You're so fucking hot," Bryce says, his voice low and husky.

I don't respond, instead beginning the ritual of taking a second tequila shot.

I'm not naive. I know I'm being manipulated. I just don't know how to *stop* it.

We're silent as we finish the remaining shots, and as he finishes his last one, he slams the empty glass on the bartop. "Let's get out of here."

I'm filled with relief. Despite my lack of skill in social situations, this probably means one of two things. One: he wants us to get out of here *separately* and I can go home, or two: we're going to get out of here *together*, and I'll at least complete my goal of having bad sex tonight.

"Yes," I agree.

"Great. My friend's friend is having a party. Let's go there."

Or neither of those things will happen and instead I'll be invited to some random person's party.

Say no. My brain urges me, *Say no, go home, eat the pint of Phish Food you have in the freezer. Do anything but agree.*

"Sounds good," I respond airily.

For fuck's sake.

Bryce throws down enough cash to cover the shots and an extraordinarily small tip. I wait until he's not looking to slide an extra twenty toward the bartender before hopping off the barstool and following him out of the building.

Luckily, the party is only six blocks from the bar. However, as we walk, I realize I am quite tipsy and certainly not walking straight, as I'd predicted. I'm wearing heeled lace-up ankle boots with my black sundress, and of course I have bike shorts under to prevent the miserable sensation of my thighs rubbing together. At least I can stagger around comfortably.

Bryce is silent while we walk, except for that awkward moment when, while staring at my chest, he blurted out, "nice tits," while we waited at a crosswalk.

Thank you, push-up bra.

Our destination is a brownstone, the kind of house that makes a millennial cry just by being in its vicinity. We walk up the front steps, and Bryce knocks on the door. A beautiful, tall woman opens it, her face brightening when she sees us.

"Babe! You're here!" she squeals, throwing her arms around Bryce's neck. She presses her lips to Bryce's, who returns her energy with a very loud, sloppy kiss.

What. The. *Fuck*.

My mouth is hanging open as they break apart and she turns toward me. "Come in, come in! Did you guys have enough to drink? I forgot Josh doesn't drink, so it's a dry party." She grabs our wrists and drags us through the doorway. Holy hell, she's as strong as whatever tequila Bryce ordered at the bar. "We only have to stay for a little while, and then we'll get going."

"Uh, I'm sorry. Who are you?" I hear myself slurring my words and want to kick myself.

"Oh, has Bryce not told you yet?" She turns to Bryce and smacks his shoulder playfully. "Babe! I told you to tell them before you take them to a secondary location!"

I can hear people talking and laughing further inside the house, and I hope they have food. I could really use food. I need to sober up, quickly.

"They don't like it when I tell them," Bryce whines, rubbing his shoulder.

The woman rolls her eyes and turns back to me. "I'm sorry about him. He's such a dumbass sometimes." She sticks her hand out to me. "I'm Maddie, Bryce's girlfriend."

Girlfriend? My head pivots between them. "Oh my god, I'm so sorry, I had no idea-"

Maddie laughs. "Don't worry, he's not cheating. We want you to be our third!"

"What?" I shift my gaze to Bryce, who is very pointedly not looking at me. "Bryce never said anything like that to me."

"Oh yeah," Maddie waves her hand, as if she's telling me it's not a big deal. "Nobody takes it well if you put that in your profile, but we swipe through Tinder and choose our matches together. You were just too pretty to pass up." She strokes my arm.

Oh my god.

Oh my *god*.

I was just Unicorn Hunted.

Fuck. I don't even know what to say–I don't *want* to have a threesome. That sounds twice as terrible as sex with one person.

"Is there food here?" I blurt out instead of dealing with this disastrous date.

Maddie blinks. "Um, yeah. In the kitchen. I need to mingle a little more, but then we can get out of here, yeah?" She winks at me, and my stomach violently churns.

This is when not being able to stand up for myself bites me in the ass, when I'm drunk off tequila and apparently about to have my first threesome.

Awesome. Love that journey for me.

Maddie leads us further into the house, past a living and dining room, where a good amount of people are mingling. She walks us into the kitchen, where several charcuterie boards are spread out on the island.

Score.

I eagerly grab a small plate and begin piling on food, hoping it will soak up the excess tequila. Despite my food aversions, I'm pleased that they have Italian meats I'm familiar with from my upbringing, as well as my favorite crackers.

"Maddie! You didn't tell me Bryce was coming!" I look up to see a woman giving me a strange look out of the corner of her eye, despite obviously addressing Maddie.

I get it. I'd be giving me a strange look if I wasn't me, too.

"Oh, yeah. Sorry," Maddie responds, not sounding sorry at all. "And this is our friend..." She looks at me. "Shit. What's your name again?" For fuck's fucking sake.

"Nic," I mumble, stuffing salami into my mouth.

"Right. Nic," Maddie says.

"Maddie, we've talked about this. You've got to stop bringing your unsuspecting Tinder matches to parties," the other woman says, looking and sounding a special kind of fed up.

Maddie begins to argue with her, and I take the opportunity to slip out of the kitchen and into the adjoining living room, desperate for respite.

Apparently in this specific situation, respite equals being in a room with at least a dozen strangers.

I find an empty spot against the wall and lean against it, happily munching on a cracker.

"Yeah, Josh and I fucked one night in our junior year after studying for finals."

My ears perk up. I don't know anyone here, but that doesn't mean the tea isn't interesting.

"Oh my god, yeah. We fucked that year too. That was the hardest I've ever come."

Damn, this is the most interesting thing I've heard in a *long* time. "Oh, me too," the taller of the two women says, fanning herself with her empty plate. "He did this thing with his tongue-"

"Oh my god, that mouth," the other woman moans. "God, I still dream about him going down on me. I've tried to teach Tony how to do it, but god, it's not the same."

"And his cock? Fucking *huge*. It didn't look like it was curved, but it felt like it."

"I wonder if he did something with his hips."

"Whatever he did, I had ten orgasms that night. Ten!"

I choke on my prosciutto. Women are out here having ten orgasms with some guy, and talking about it, while my running average is *zero*. And since Maddie and Bryce expect me to go home with them, I may drop into the negatives. Considering how the night is going, that feels possible.

The shorter woman sighs wistfully, apparently not concerned with the fact I could be very likely choking to death next to her. "No one has ever fucked me the way Josh Henry did."

Somehow, the shock I feel following her words dislodges the meat from my windpipe.

Josh Henry?

I scan the room again, and there he is, in a white button-up shirt. The sleeves rolled up to right below his elbow and enough buttons undone to expose a scattering of chest hair. Black tattoos cover his exposed skin, which surprises me. He doesn't seem like a tattoo guy.

Oh no. He's *hot*.

Fuck, I need to get out of here.

I turn to go back into the kitchen determined to make up some excuse to Bryce and Maddie, but my toe snags on the floor and my charcuterie goes flying into the air as I fall to the ground.

Chapter 6

Josh

Playlist: "Do You Really Wanna Know?" Sea Girls

A loud *thud* echoes through the living room, interrupting my conversation with a former classmate from undergrad. "Sorry, I'll be right back," I tell them before walking toward the other side of the room, where a woman in a black dress with short, curly brown hair is sprawled out with charcuterie scattered around her.

My heart stutters, immediately thinking of Nicoletta Quinn and her unruly locks, before telling myself that it can't be her. I can't see the woman's face, and from this angle, I don't recognize her. I'm not sure why someone would crash a dry birthday party, but apparently they did.

"Are you okay?" I ask her, crouching down next to her head.

"Oh my God," Rosie, another classmate from undergrad, says, twirling her hair around her finger and pouting. "She just, like, went flying, Joshy."

I ignore her, as the short-haired woman clambers to her feet. "I'm fine," she says, staring at her skirt as she pulls it down. "I'll clean-"

"Oh my god, Nora!" Maddie, Nellie's roommate from grad school comes careening into the room with her boyfriend Bryce behind her. They're both such tools. I don't know why we continue to invite them. She grabs the woman's arm roughly, causing her to stumble into Maddie. "I'm sorry, Joshy. She's ours."

"Wait," I scowl. "*Yours*? For fuck's sake, did you guys bring your Tinder match again?"

Nellie, who came in behind Bryce, throws her hands in the air. "That's what I said!"

"If it helps, she didn't know she was going to be our third until we got here," Bryce offers.

That does *not* help. It actually makes it much worse. She wasn't given the opportunity to say no if she wanted to, and I suddenly feel extremely protective of this person.

"Hey." I bend down to finally look into her face and immediately jerk back when the warm brown eyes that have been haunting me meet mine.

"Hello. Sorry for dropping food all over the floor," Nic mumbles, looking much less surprised to see me than I am to see her. I can smell the tequila wafting off of her.

I glare at Maddie and Bryce, who at least have the decency to look guilty. "Is she drunk?"

"She wanted to drink," Bryce whines. "And how was I supposed to get her here without her being drunk?"

I see red.

"Alright, you two, get out," Nellie interrupts, reading my mind. She grabs Maddie and Bryce by their arms. "Tyler!" she shouts to her fiance across the room. "Come play security guard with me."

Bryce and Maddie protest as Nellie and Tyler, who's only a few inches shorter than me, shove both of them toward the front door.

Nic is quiet, and I gently nudge her. "Kitchen," I say simply. If the smell is anything to go by, she's wasted, so simple phrases seem like the best way to communicate.

She obliges, following me out of the room. She walks to the island, pressing her hands to the surface and leaning over it as she exhales slowly.

"Do you need water?" I ask, already grabbing a cup and pouring her some.

"No," she mumbles, her head drooped low. "I didn't know this was your party."

I place the cup of water in front of her. "Okay."

She looks up, her eyes red and watery. "No, really. I didn't. I didn't know anything. I didn't know he had a girlfriend or that they wanted a threesome..."

I swallow hard. She looks so sad and dejected, and my heart hurts, against my better judgment. "Are you okay?"

She nods her head, lifting a trembling hand to pick up the cup. "Yeah, I just want to go home."

"I think you know I can't let you leave like this," I say softly.

She sniffles and wipes her nose with the back of her hand. "We matched on Tinder this week. I wouldn't have gone out with him if he'd mentioned a girlfriend or a threesome. He bought so many shots, and I–I fucked up, Josh Henry. I fucked up spectacularly."

"Did he hurt you?" I ask tersely, clenching my fists.

She shakes her head and takes another sip of water. "No, not like that. I just–please. I want to go home."

"I'll take you home," I offer.

Her head snaps up to me. "Absolutely not."

"You're drunk. It's not safe, Nic."

"I know I'm drunk. I know it's not safe. But I don't want *you* to know where I live." She eyes me suspiciously.

It's strange, but this small glimpse of the Nic I saw a few weeks ago on the train makes me feel a little better.

"I'll ask Tyler to take you. They'll make sure you get home safe. Okay? They're way less terrible than me, and they won't tell me where you live. Promise."

She squints her eyes at me, then sighs. "Did I crash your birthday party?"

I grimace and rub the back of my neck. "Yeah."

She groans, grinding the heels of her hands into her eyes. "I can't believe I feel bad about ruining your birthday. I should be thrilled."

There she is.

I talk to Tyler, who agrees to take an Uber with Nic to make sure she gets home safely.

"Wait, so you *know* Maddie and Bryce's third?" Nellie asks as we follow Tyler and Nic, who are already chatting like old friends, down the front stairs.

"She and I went to school together as kids," I say.

"He's an evil goblin," Nic hisses over her shoulder to Nellie. She trips, and I reflexively reach out to catch her, though she ends up just falling against Tyler's side.

She bursts into loud laughter, and I try to ignore how lovely it sounds. "For fuck's sake, Nicoletta," I sigh.

Her laughter stops as suddenly as it started, and she spins around, pointing her index finger in my face. "Evil goblin! You're still making fun of my name!"

Tyler gently turns her around, but not before she can give me a last dirty look and both middle fingers. The Uber pulls up just a few seconds after we reach the sidewalk, and Nellie and I watch as Tyler helps Nic into the backseat before blowing Nellie a kiss and climbing in after Nic.

"Evil goblin, huh?" Nellie asks as we watch the Uber drive away.

I sigh. "We may have not gotten along as kids."

She snickers. "Wow. You know what, next time you see her, thank her for me. I will be exclusively referring to you as Evil Goblin Boy from now on."

I roll my eyes as we turn and walk back toward the house. "I will *not* be seeing Nic Quinn again."

She snickers and gently bumps her shoulder against me. "You know, I have a feeling you may be wrong about that, Evil Goblin Boy."

Chapter 7

Nic

Playlist: "Big Bird In A Small Cage," Patrick Watson

The Irish genes I inherited from my father betray me when I wake up this morning. Normally, I consider it a blessing I can drink copious amounts of alcohol and not black out or be hungover. Right now, unfortunately, it means I remember everything from last night.

Everything.

How I was strong-armed into those tequila shots and was almost pressured into a threesome I didn't want to have.

How I fell back into Josh Henry's life, literally.

How I was so drunk, his friend had to make sure I made it home safe because there was no way in hell I was letting Josh know where I lived.

I groan and prop myself against the headboard, pulling my knees to my chest, wrapping my arms around my legs.

All of those memories are so vivid, and while I was definitely taken advantage of, I hate that I didn't leave the first moment I felt uncomfortable. I hate how trapped I felt, like I didn't have a choice.

I need to change–I just don't know how.

Eventually I get up and throw on a sports bra and bike shorts, my go-to gym outfit. Climbing always helps when I feel over-whelmed, and is preventative for me as well, so I try to climb most days when possible. When I go to grab a couple of my favorite granola bars for breakfast, I bump into Jo. She was home last night when Tyler brought me home and was able to help me get me to bed.

"Good morning," she gives me a sympathetic look over her mug of Earl Grey tea. "How're you feeling?"

I shrug as I open the pantry. "I mean, grateful to not be hungover, and humiliated to remember every last minute of last night."

Jo winces as I pour myself a glass of iced coffee. "The Quinn genes are truly a blessing and a curse," I grunt in agreement.

"Tyler seemed nice. Are they a friend of yours?" she asks, setting her mug on the counter.

"We met last night at Josh's party. Josh didn't want me trying to make my way home alone last night, and I didn't want Josh knowing where I live."

"Ah, yes. Of course," Jo nods sagely, like this makes any sense. "And who is Josh? The Tinder guy?"

I unwrap a granola bar and take a bite. "Fuck, Jo. Brace yourself for this: the Tinder guy brought me to Josh Henry's goddamned birthday party."

Jo gasps with the perfect amount of drama. "Josh Henry? Your arch-nemesis Josh Henry?"

"Yes! Bryce, the Tinder guy, got me drunk and brought me to Josh's house so I would have a threesome with him and his girlfriend."

"Fucking *low*," Jo says as she dunks her teabag in her mug. "So wait, you drunkenly crashed Josh's party with your date and then he was a douchebag?"

"No," I sigh, taking another bite of my granola bar. "Worse. He made sure I was okay and safe and ensured I got home safely."

"That *asshole*," Jo replies, her mouth twitching. "Truly the worst of the worst."

"Stop," I groan. Jo snickers, pulling out her phone. She taps on the screen, probably checking her blood sugar, for a moment before shrugging and reaching across the counter to steal one of my granola bars. "And it gets worse," I continue. "Apparently he's some sort of renowned sex god. I overheard these women talking about how good he is in bed."

"Huh." Jo's a lesbian, so I think she has trouble with the idea of men as sexual at all.

"Now that I think about it, there were rumors when I was in high school." I frown as memories come back to me. "He went to St. Michael's, but he partied a lot with people from Port Haven High."

I overheard classmates whispering about how surprising it was that he rocked their world and everyone wanted to hook up with him. I was annoyed for several reasons: first, ew, Josh Henry is an evil goblin. Second, people made it clear they found it surprising because he was fat, which is so gross and fatphobic. Though I hate Josh Henry, it has nothing to do with the size of his body. The fact that people judged him because of it pissed me off.

Jo raises her eyebrow. "Damn. Maybe I'll look him up." She shudders. "No, I can't even joke about that."

The gears in my head are turning, though, and I'm not sure I like it. But Josh took control last night when everything went to shit. He made sure I was safe and comfortable, even though I was in his home uninvited. He took care of me. Took care of several other women at that party at some point too, apparently. What if that's my problem? What if I've been sleeping with the wrong people? What if—

I try to shake the absolutely unhinged thought process from my mind. "I'm going to the gym. I'll see you tonight?"

"Yeah. Are you going home for dinner tomorrow?" Jo asks as I walk toward the door.

I grimace. "No. I–no. I can't handle it right now."

I leave the apartment and begin my walk to the gym, a very, very bad idea formulating in my mind.

Standing on Josh Henry's doorstep for the second time in less than twenty four hours is probably the most deranged thing I've ever done. Climbing helps clear my head, and it also helps me make decisions, work through problems.

The problem plaguing me was that I found myself in a deeply terrifying situation last night, a situation that could have caused permanent damage. A situation where I felt trapped.

I never want to feel the way I felt last night again. I want to feel in control of my life, of my body. I want to be able to vocalize my needs, to enjoy sex, and to set boundaries with my family and work and simply not feel...like this.

Which somehow led me back to his doorstep.

I didn't bother changing or showering after my climb, knowing if I did anything before doing this, I would chicken out. So here I am, in all my sweaty glory. I take a deep breath and ring the doorbell. There's no answer at first, so I impatiently press down on the button with my finger again. And again. And again. It takes a few more moments, but I finally hear footsteps approaching the door and the click of a lock.

Josh's eyes widen, and he freezes after opening the door. "Nic?"

"Hi. Can I come in?" I ask, bouncing on my toes, like it's not at all weird for me to be standing on the stoop of his brownstone after drunkenly crashing his party and calling him an evil goblin the previous night.

"What are you–" he begins to ask.

"Thanks!" I cut him off mid-sentence, ducking beneath his arm and into the foyer.

I hear him muttering under his breath as he closes and locks the door behind me. I look around and find that it all looks different when I'm not intoxicated and blindsided by a threesome.

"How do you know where I live?" Josh asks, stepping around me. I eye him as he moves.

"Really? You don't remember? Damn, Henry. I thought *I* was drunk last night," I tease, hoping to cover up the anxiety.

He sighs and runs his fingers through his hair, which looks messy, like he recently rolled out of bed. And *maddeningly* soft. Dammit.

"I don't drink," he says. "So trust me, I remember last night quite well." He runs his eyes down my body, and I'm impressed they don't linger on my chest, where I know my nipples are visible through the unlined bra. The evil goblin is apparently quite the gentleman. "I'm simply surprised you remember."

I shrug, unaffected. "I'm half-Irish. To make up for freckles and sunburns, the genetics gods decided I don't have to deal with blackouts or hangovers."

Josh's eye twitches. "Nice."

"Anyway," I say, steepling my fingers in front of my face like a conniving supervillain. "I heard some *very* interesting information about you at your shindig last night."

He raises his brow and crosses his arms over his broad chest as he leans against the wall. He's wearing gray sweatpants and a white tank top. His torso and arms are covered with the tattoos I got a peek of last night, florals on his left arm, and–surprisingly–a Lion King tattoo on his right. "What?" Josh asks. "Did you hear it's my birthday today?"

Wait, *what?*

"Hold on–I thought your birthday was last night?"

He shakes his head, a strand of his dark blond hair falling across his forehead. It's annoying to see it so obviously out of place, and my hands twitch as I fight the urge to push it out of his face. If I could even reach it, the man is tall as fuck.

"No, my birthday party was last night; My twenty-ninth birthday is today."

Fuck. I'm embarrassed. I didn't know it was his birthday today, and if I had...what? I honestly doubt it would've changed my mind. But more importantly, why do I care?

He walks past me and further into the house, where I remember the living room and kitchen are located. "Do you want something to drink?" he calls over his shoulder. "I can make chocolate milk. That was your favorite, wasn't it?"

I eye his retreating body. "How do you know that?"

His shoulders tense, but he keeps walking, not looking back at me. "Chocolate milk is every second grader's favorite."

I shuffle after him, looking at the framed pictures on the wall. Most of them are of Josh and his grandma, a sweet lady who goes to church with my parents. A few photos show a blond toddler with baby blue eyes, a dark haired man, and a blonde woman. His parents, I assume. One shows the same man and woman at a very early 90's looking wedding. In another, the tiny menace I remember from childhood is missing his front teeth at a Mets game with his grandma. Josh grows up before my eyes at his various graduations, his grandma proudly grasping his arm at each one. Josh and a girl–

I freeze and narrow my eyes. She's pretty. *Really* fucking pretty. Tall and curvy and perfectly white teeth, long wavy blond hair swaying. Josh's arms are wrapped around her, and they're both doubled over in laughter.

"Nic?" Josh calls from the kitchen. "Do you want that chocolate milk?

I move away from the picture, pushing the strange feeling in my chest way, way down. It's not that I'm jealous. I'm not, but if Josh has a girlfriend, I might have to rethink my plan.

"Okay," I sigh, making my way into the kitchen. Josh is frowning into the refrigerator, his face scrunched in a way I would find adorable if it were anyone else.

Josh pulls out a carton from the fridge and holds it out to-ward me without looking at me. "Is oat milk okay?"

"Yeah, that's fine. Thanks." I look around the kitchen. It's big and an open concept, like one of those kitchens you'd see on HGTV. "Nice place you have here, Henry. Who'd you kill to be able to afford it?" I say, attempting a joke.

Josh's face as he turns from the refrigerator immediately in-forms me I failed–miserably. "I—uh. It belonged to my parents. They died when I was a kid."

Oh my fucking god.

"Oh my fucking god." My face is so red-hot you could cook pancakes on it. "Fuck, I was trying to make a joke. I'm so sorry. I forgot—"

"It's okay, Nic. It's been over two decades."

"I wasn't trying to insinuate you killed your parents," I tell him, my voice small.

"I know, Buttercup." I wince at the nickname, and I swear, this douche-canoe fights back a smile. "I'm going to make your chocolate milk now."

I need to ask him. Before I lose my nerve or say something worse than what I already have. While climbing this morning, I thought about it, the pros and cons of what I want to do...and for once, I know what I want.

It's just a matter of expressing myself, and it was my inability to do just that which landed me here in the first place.

I watch Josh bustle about the kitchen, getting a glass from a cabinet and scooping something from a mason jar into it before pouring the oat milk on top, mixing it all together. I'm looking at what he's doing. Not his ass, which doesn't look perfectly grabbable.

I realize in the silence, I'm licking my lips like a fucking weirdo.

I'm not particularly proficient at social cues and decorum, but I do know leering at the ass of the person you hate most while licking your lip probably isn't a social norm.

"Uh. Happy birthday," I offer helpfully, attempting to break the awkward silence between us.

Josh turns toward me, extending his arm to hand me the glass of chocolate milk. I gratefully take it from him. "Thanks," he answers, eyeing me with a look I think is benevolent curiosity? It's hard to tell most of the time. He's almost a full foot taller than me, but the expression on his face somehow makes him look like a bamboozled puppy. It isn't adorable. Not at all. "I've gotta be honest," he continues. "I didn't expect to spend the day making chocolate milk for you."

"Everyone has to have their worst birthday at some point," I say, attempting another joke.

He doesn't laugh.

I sigh, tapping my fingernails on the glass. "Sorry. I have a tendency to say stuff without thinking."

He doesn't respond.

I can feel the word vomit crawling up my throat, and despite desperately wanting to keep it down, it doesn't feel like there's anything I can do to prevent the inevitable. "I have issues with social cues and stuff," I blurt out. "So sometimes I just say shit, and I don't realize it's not something I should say until everyone's staring at me and sometimes I don't even know what I said wrong–just that I broke some social rule and I'm sorry I keep doing this and—"

"Nic," Josh interrupts. "It's okay."

I draw in a ragged breath, winded from verbally vomiting on him. "Sorry."

"Unless you're apologizing for basically breaking and entering into my home, there's no need for apologies."

"There was no breaking involved," I grumble, taking a sip of chocolate oat milk. I don't know exactly what it is, but something about the flavor and the texture combined is a damn dream. I moan and close my eyes from the pleasure I feel, lowering the cup from my lips. He chuckles, and it almost sounds sweet. Almost. "What did you put in this?" I ask before raising the glass to my mouth again.

"It's good, right?"

"Mmm," I agree, my mouth full.

"It's the vanilla oat milk." I open my eyes to see his eyes on my mouth. Self-consciously, I dart my tongue between my lips to lick up any wayward liquid. He clears his throat and blinks rapidly, raising his eyes to meet mine. I look down at the floor. "It makes a huge difference," he continues. "That and homemade chocolate sauce."

I scoff, "Overachiever."

"But the secret ingredient is cyanide. It really adds a kick, don't you think?"

I gasp, and my neck snaps up to look at Josh, who's shaking with silent laughter. "You're joking?"

"Yes, Buttercup." He chuckles and bites his lip. "I'm joking. Your chocolate milk is cyanide-free."

I put my glass down on the island and groan, scrubbing my face with my hands. "Sorry, sometimes it's just hard for me to tell—"

"Hey, it's okay." He's standing across from me and leaning his ass against the counter, his legs extended out and crossed at the ankle. "Tell me what you heard about me last night."

I blurt it out before I can lose my nerve. "These women were saying you're really good at fucking."

Of course it's just as he takes a sip of the can of sparkling water he had gotten himself. He chokes and starts sputtering, his eyes misty and skin flushing.

"*What*?" he manages to gasp out.

"They also said you have, like, a massive dick," I offer helpfully. Men like to hear they have big dicks, right? Shockingly, my words don't seem to help. He's thumping at his chest as he coughs, and I try to wait for him to stop choking, the damn fool.

I've never played the waiting game well.

"Is there really a curve, or is it something you do with your hips when thrusting?" I ask him loudly over his hacking coughs. "They said it didn't look like it was curved, but it felt like it—"

"Please," he wheezes, looking distressed. "Please, stop talking and give me a second." He's hunched over, gasping, and it kind of looks like he's in pain, so I indulge his request, tapping my sneakered foot impatiently on the tiled floor. Finally, Josh starts breathing enough to speak. "Sorry," he gasps. "Sorry, I must have misheard you. I thought you were asking extremely invasive questions about my sex life after showing up uninvited on my fucking *birthday*."

I blink at him blankly. Is he being sarcastic? Besides talking to Jo and going to the gym, that's literally everything I've done today.

He sighs and takes another sip from his can of sparkling water before speaking. "Fine. You win. It's something I do with my hips. Now, will you pretty, pretty please explain why you showed up at my home to interrogate me about my sex life?"

I raise an eyebrow, curious. "So, what, you like, tilt your hips or something?"

He nods, staring me dead in the eye. I'm intrigued, and for once I don't want to hide my eyes. "Yes, Nicoletta. I tilt my hips or something."

I finally look away, my face heating. "And it feels good? For your partner?"

"That's what they tell me," he pauses. "And apparently what they tell random strangers, too."

"Huh," I muse, taking another sip of the annoyingly delicious chocolate oat milk.

I see Josh rubbing his temples out of the corner of my eye. "Listen, Nic, as delightful as this little reunion has been, I have to go to Port Haven and-"

"I want to have sex with you," I blurt out, hoping I come across as braver and more confident than I feel at the moment.

He blinks, his expression shifting, but still unreadable to me. "You...what?"

My face reddens even more, heat spreading across my cheeks. "Those women last night sounded like they liked it. Having sex. With you. And I–uh, I haven't particularly liked having sex with anyone before, so I thought we could maybe try to–" I trail off.

Josh is staring at me, his mouth agape.

"Can you say something, please?" I suddenly feel naked, raw. I'm twisting my hands as the silence continues, as I get more and more unsure, more overwhelmed. I'm flushed and anxious, and I know the red flags: the shame I feel for saying the wrong things has triggered a meltdown. I need him to say something so I can get out of here and under my weighted blanket—

"I have no idea what to say to that," he finally says, after what feels like a million years.

Fuck.

Fuck.

I begin rocking back and forth on my toes. My heart is pounding too hard in my chest, the beat echoing in my ears. "I— uh, you're right. This was a bad idea, I'm probably still drunk or something," I stammer as I straighten, my eyes stinging with tears I'm desperate to keep hidden. "I'm gonna go, and we'll pretend this never happened and never see each other again. Happy birthday. Sorry I asked for sex. Bye."

I start to purposefully walk toward the front door, trying to steady my breath with the deep breaths Maria, my therapist, told me to take when I feel this way. My heart is pounding, and my hands are shaking as I reach for the doorknob. I'm so close. I can do this, I just have to make it home and—

"Nic!" Josh calls my name loudly from behind me, and everything inside of me explodes. It feels like I lose strength in my legs, falling on my shoulder into the door. I cry out and cover my ears, the dam breaking, any hope of making it home before falling apart long gone. My limbs shake like tree branches in a storm as I slide down the door, my legs folding beneath me.

"Jesus Christ–are you okay?" Josh is somehow right in front of me, dropping to his haunches. He begins to reach out to me but seemingly thinks better of it, retracting his hand.

"Too close," I manage to whimper, unable to express myself any more articulately. He seems to understand, though, and scoots back far enough that I don't feel cornered. My heart is pounding, and tears are running down my cheeks. A million thoughts run through my head, and not one of them is discernible at this moment. "I'm okay," I gasp, wrapping my arms around my torso and squeezing as tightly as I can.

"You don't look okay," Josh says softly.

I hate this part, how worried and freaked out people get whenever this happens. I know what's going on: my nervous system is overwhelmed, overstimulated, but it will be over soon. Most people don't understand, and nobody really seems to know what to do with a fully grown woman rocking and sobbing on the floor.

I don't answer him. I *can't* answer him. It's too much. Everything is too much. I can feel every thread in the fabric touching my skin, and the lights in this foyer are too damn bright.

Meltdowns are hard and embarrassing, even more so when they happen in front of someone you hate, who you also just asked to engage in casual coitus with you.

It can't be more than a few minutes before my breathing finally slows, and I'm able to regulate again. I look up, meeting Josh's gaze. He's sitting back on his heels, his hands on his thighs and the expression on his face still undecipherable.

"Sorry," I sniff, wiping my nose with the back of my hand. I move to get up. "I'm gonna go now."

"Nic, what the hell just happened?" Josh asks. His voice is clear and steady, the opposite of how I feel.

"Nothing," I say, looking down to avoid his gaze as I shakily get to my feet.

He stands too, his stature towering over me. "That didn't look like—"

I stare at the ground. "I had a meltdown, okay? I'm autistic. Sometimes they happen when I get overstimulated or over-whelmed."

It occurs to me that this is the first time I've ever told someone I'm autistic, and I don't know what to expect from him. My stomach sinks at the uncertainty I feel throughout my body.

"Okay," Josh says slowly. "What helps you feel better after a meltdown?"

I blink, surprised at his response. If I were home, I'd strip off all my clothes, wrap myself in my weighted blanket, and put on some comfort episodes of *Ted Lasso*.

"I'm just–I'm gonna go home now," I reply awkwardly, turning to open the door.

"Nic," his voice is soft. "I know you hate me, but I just want to make sure that you're okay."

Tears well up in my eyes again. What is even happening right now? "I'm a big girl, Josh Henry. I can take care of myself."

"I know you can, but you look tired and I have a comfortable couch and chocolate milk. You don't have to stay long, just until you're feeling a little better."

I eye him. This feels...safe. But it shouldn't.

Right?

I find myself nodding, even while internally kicking myself.

This must be how people end up making deals with the devil.

Chapter 8

Josh

Playlist: "New Perspective," Panic! At the Disco

Nicoletta Quinn is in my house. On my couch. Wrapped in a blanket and drinking her third glass of chocolate oat milk.

This is decidedly not how I expected to spend my birthday.

Nic insisted she could leave and would be fine, but I didn't want her to be alone right after her meltdown.

I don't know much about autism, but I know she was hurting and what she experienced couldn't have been easy. No one should have to go through that alone.

She's barely said anything since her meltdown, except for asking for another glass of chocolate milk. But, surprisingly, the quiet hasn't been uncomfortable.

"Are you doing okay over there?" I ask her.

Nic makes an affirmative noise from her cocoon. I can't see her face, but I can hear her slurping from the straw I'd given her for the chocolate milk, to make it easier for her to drink while wrapped in a blanket. She mentioned tight pressure helps after meltdowns, as she helped herself to the throw blanket I keep on the back of the couch. She then wrapped herself in it so tightly I genuinely worried for her circulatory system.

She pokes her face from the blanket a tiny bit and I try, and fail, to fight back a smile. Christ, she's beautiful when she's not harassing me. Her big brown eyes are heavy lidded and puffy from crying, and I hadn't noticed before, but she still has a scattering of freckles across the bridge of her nose. One day, in second grade, I remember she furiously tried to erase them until our teacher sent her to the principal when she refused to stop. We'd thought it was funny, Nic and her hatred for her freckles. She was a funny, strange kid.

Now, I can't help but notice they look like the stars you can't see in Brooklyn.

My hand twitches. An odd desire builds in me to run my finger over each and every freckle I can see, and maybe the ones I can't see, too.

"Is there any way..." Nic asks bashfully, breaking my freckle-induced haze.

I smile. "Another glass?"

"Yes please." Her smile is small, a barely-there upturn of those pretty pink lips.

But it's there.

After I bring her fourth glass of chocolate oat milk from the kitchen, she decides to talk.

"So," she says.

"So," I echo.

"I bet you're wondering why I asked you to have sex with me."

"I sure am," I reply, leaning against the back of the loveseat I'm sitting in, crossing my left leg over my right thigh.

She's quiet for a moment before speaking. "It sounds–it sounds like you're good at it," Nic says, her voice wavering like she's not quite sure about what she's saying. "And it sounds like people enjoy sleeping with you."

I shrug my shoulders nonchalantly. "I have sex, and I enjoy it. I like to make sure my partners enjoy it, too."

"One of them said you made her come ten times in one night."

My face flushes. An unexpected consequence of continuing this conversation is that Nic saying the word "come" has my dick hardening.

In my gray sweatpants.

I casually reach down the couch for a throw pillow and place it on my lap in a very cool, very chill manner.

"She said you do this thing with your tongue-" Nic continues.

"Yes, I, uh—I do things with my tongue," I interrupt, suddenly embarrassed. I'm not ashamed of my sex life or averse to talking about it, but when Nic Quinn is gazing curiously at me, all wrapped up in her blanket burrito, I feel bashful.

She's quiet, and I wonder if I've made her uncomfortable. Her parents go to the same church as Grandma, and I wonder if she subscribes to their church's teachings regarding sex.

Is it something she sees as wrong? Dirty?

"I don't like having sex," she finally says, interrupting my train of thought. "I like the idea of it, but I've just never been able to *enjoy* it. To get there, if you know what I mean."

"You've never orgasmed?" I clarify, wanting to confirm before losing my mind over the fact this terrifying and beautiful woman across from me has never experienced an orgasm.

"No, no, I have. Alone. Never with a partner, though. When I'm with someone else, it feels like I have expectations I have to meet, something to prove. It's a performance, trying to act and move just right, and then there's so much sensation. It's easier to just use my vibrator alone, in a controlled environment," she pauses, taking a deep breath. "But I *want* to enjoy sex with someone else."

She's rambling, and I can see her knee bouncing beneath the blanket. I've noticed she rambles and moves some part of her body whenever she's nervous. I don't want her to feel nervous with me.

"Nic, breathe," I say, hoping that's an okay thing to say to her right now. She takes a deep breath, though, and it doesn't seem to upset her. "What exactly are you saying?"

"I feel like something's wrong with me," she says, looking deeply ashamed. "I logically know there isn't, that this isn't an abnormal thing for people with vaginas, being able to make yourself come yet struggling with a partner. But I want to be able to express what I want and what feels good for me. Whenever I've had a new partner and they ask me how I like to be touched, I can't answer because I don't know. I'm so hyper focused on making sure I'm doing the right things during sex that I've never been present enough to be able to identify what feels good, never been able to give direction or ask for what I need. And I want to learn to do that. As much as I hate saying this, I think you can help me. I mean...there's no risk of feelings fucking things up. You hate me. I hate you. And I won't worry about hurting your feelings by speaking up and asking for something, or letting you know when something isn't working."

When she finally stops talking, the room goes quiet.

I stare at her.

She stares back.

I should say no–right? There's a reason I stick to one night stands. There are no strings. No expectations. But she looks so hopeful, over there all wrapped in my blanket.

I should definitely say no.

"Okay," I hear myself say.

She gasps. "Really?"

No, dumbass. "Yeah. I'll help you out."

For fuck's sake, Henry.

"Oh my god. Wow, okay. Um, so should I just get naked now?" she asks, eagerly peeling the blanket off of her body.

My eyes widen, and even though my dick thinks she is a genius and that this is the very best idea, I have to keep at least some of my wits about me. "Okay, uh. No. I can't today. I really do have to go to Connecticut. And we need to discuss what this is going to look like for us."

She scrunches her nose. "Are there terms and conditions I have to pretend to read, too?"

I roll my eyes. "We need to have defined boundaries and limits before we jump into a sexual relationship."

She eyes me warily. "Is that normal?"

"For me it is. There's always an upfront discussion about expectations and boundaries."

"Huh," Nic says, looking thoughtful.

"I'll text you more about it," I say, holding my hand out. "Can I see your phone?"

She laughs, loud and sharp. "So you can put a virus on it? I don't think so."

"So you trust me enough to sleep with me, but not enough to let me touch your phone?" I ask.

She looks at me like this is not at all baffling and actually quite obvious. "Yes?"

"Noted," I say, nodding my head. She gives me her number, and I enter it into my phone, sending her a quick text with a link.

She looks at me skeptically. "What's this link for?" she asks.

I shrug my shoulders. "Dunno. You should probably open it."

"It's a virus, isn't it," she says like a statement.

"I'm an English professor, Buttercup. I can barely run a virtual class."

Seconds later, the opening bars of "Never Gonna Give You Up" by Rick Astley play from her speakers.

I bite my fist, shaking with laughter as she scowls down at her phone. "I hate you," she mutters without looking up.

"I guess I earned that."

She sighs and stands up, stretching her arms above her head. She's wearing a longline bra, so a sliver of her belly was already exposed, but it rides up a little higher now. I can't help but notice the few dark freckles scattered across her midriff. I swallow hard. What noises would she make while I traced those smooth markings with my tongue? Would she gasp? Moan? Whimper and pull at my hair?

Holy fuck. I'll eventually get to find out.

"Well, this was fun," I blurt out. "You're good to go home?"

She nods. "Yeah, thanks for..." She looks at me, an intense look on her face that makes me shift under the pillow my cock is currently trying to launch off my lap. "This. This was very out of character for an evil goblin."

I shrug. "Even evil goblins take their birthday off."

"Okay. Uh. You'll text me?" she asks. She's fidgeting nervously, and I just want to take her hands in mine and—

Well. We're not going *there*.

"Yes," I confirm. "I'll text you, and we'll discuss everything further."

"Cool. Cool, cool, cool. I'm going to leave," she says, shooting finger guns at me.

"Okay. Bye," I say, hoping I sound cool and not like someone who's desperately trying to hide his erection under a throw pillow.

"Bye."

I wait until I hear the door close before violently throwing the pillow across the room and moving as quickly as I can to the front door. I turn the locks and sprint upstairs to continue imagining how she'll react to me licking her soft skin, fucking my hand all the while.

Chapter 9

Nic

Playlist: "The Woman I Am," AURORA

Quiblings Group Chat

Kat: when is izzy's birthday?

Leo: the same day as my birthday.

Kat: you're useless.

Izzy: august 19th. why?

Kat: i need a password and i've used every other sibling's birthday, so it's your turn.

Ren: did you not use leo's birthday already? which is also izzy's birthday?

Millie: lmaoooo kat did you forget they're twins

Kat: i was BARELY around by the time mom had them how is this my fault.

Alex: since i live on the west coast and am barely around, do i have an excuse to forget all of your birthdays?

Jo: no.

Kat: no.

Nic: no.

Izzy: august. 19th.

Leo: what she said.

Ren: i actually don't care.

Millie: Lorenzo shut UP. this isn't about you.

Ren: <middle finger emoji>

Josh doesn't text me until Monday evening, while I'm curled up in my weighted blanket after work, watching an episode of *Ted Lasso*.

Josh: Hi, Nic. This is Josh Henry. -J.H.

Josh: I worked on this over the weekend and thought it might be a good place to start. -J.H.

Josh: [link]

I scowl at my phone as I text him back.

Nic: i'm not falling for that again, ass-hole.

Josh: Falling for what? -J.H.

Nic: despite what the song says, you have to give it up.

Josh: LOL. I'm not Rickrolling you, I made a survey for you to fill out. -J.H.

I raise my eyebrows, and despite not fully believing him, I click on the link.

It's a Google Spreadsheet, with a list of dozens of sexual activities–some I've heard of, some I haven't. At the bottom, it looks like Josh has edited it to include some pretty basic positions, like missionary, cowgirl, spooning, doggy...

I blush and bite my lower lip, my thumbs dancing across my phone screen..

Nic: this seems thorough.

Josh: I personalized it for our arrangement, of course, but this is pretty much the discussion I have with sexual partners on paper. -J.H.

Nic: with all of your partners?

Josh: Yes. -J.H.

Nic: every time?

Josh: Yes, Buttercup. -J.H.

I scroll through the list, which starts with bondage and suspension. Specifically, blindfolds.

Huh. I've never thought about what it might be like to be blindfolded during sex.

Josh: I'm getting tested for STIs this week; are you willing to do the same? -J.H.

Nic: I actually went to the clinic after I left your place on Saturday and everything came back negative. Do you want me to send you the results?

Josh: That would be great, thanks. Are you on birth control? -J.H.

Nic: i'm on the pill. but i still only fuck with condoms. protection should be an equal responsibility.

Josh: Damn Straight. I also always use condoms. -J.H.

> **Nic:** so, how do i fill this out?

> **Josh:** See how there are three columns for each item listed? The first column is for you to select your experience and/or interest. The second column is for any limits you have. The last is if you'd be interested in giving, receiving, neither, or both.

> **Josh:** Have fun, Buttercup. <winking emoji>

> **Josh:** -J.H.

I sigh, swipe up on my messaging app, and open the spreadsheet.

Blindfolding: No experience, want to try, give & receive.

There's something about the idea of straddling Josh's hips while he can't see me, running my fingernails up and down his soft body.

Fuck.

Yeah, definitely curious about that.

My answers are the same for light bondage and shibari. Chains are a no-go. Same with multi-day bondage, gags, hooks, and, after Googling the term, mummification.

I move on to the next section, which is impact play.

Spanking: Some experience, want to try, receive.

Hair pulling: No experience, want to try, give & receive.

Josh's hair just looks so fucking soft, and I'd love to see his face when I–

Wow. Weird.

But it's just Josh. Maybe he likes that too.

The rest of the items in impact sound far too painful for now, so I go to the next section, titled "sexual activity."

It starts with fellatio and cunnilingus, which I'm able to fill out relatively quickly. I've both given and received head, and I've never really enjoyed either. But as far as I know, I don't really enjoy anything. Since this is about figuring myself out, I'm up for trying new things and trying old things again.

Fellatio: Experienced, want to try, give.

Cunnilingus: Experienced (didn't enjoy), curious, receive.

I make a note that I don't like cum in my mouth, shuddering at the memory of how I had gagged and rinsed with mouthwash the first and only time a guy came in my mouth. The taste and texture had almost triggered a meltdown, and he yelled something about me being disrespectful as he got dressed and left my dorm.

Unlike some other things I've tried and not enjoyed, this is one of the things I have no desire to try again.

Cumming on partner: Experienced (receiving), willing to try, give & receive.

Masturbation: Experienced (solo), curious, give & receive.

Vibrators: Experienced (solo), curious, give & receive.

Orgasm control: No experience, curious, give & receive.

Sensation play is the next section, and as someone who is both sensory avoidant and sensory seeking, I'm intrigued by all the different ways one can experience sensation during sex.

Scratching: Experienced (give), want to do, give.

Biting: No experience, want to try, give & receive.

Kissing: Some experience, want to try, give & receive.

When I finish this section, I move on to "breath play." I have almost no interest in that. Except for one thing.

Light choking: No experience, want to try, give & receive.

I put "no interest" for everything in the "Humiliation" section, but when I get to "Service and Restrictive Behaviors," there's an undeniable ache at the apex of my thighs.

Kneeling. Begging. Why can I imagine kneeling and looking up at Josh? Why can I imagine Josh kneeling and looking up at me?

Worse, why is that hot?

Kneeling: No experience, curious, give & receive.

Begging: No experience, curious, give & receive.

> **Nic:** done.

Josh: Someone's eager. That was fast. -J.H.

> **Nic:** things your first girlfriend said?

Josh: Wouldn't you like to know, Buttercup? -J.H

> **Nic:** yes. that's why i asked.

Josh doesn't reply, and I feel antsy. I decide to go on a run, throwing on activewear and my sneakers. Fifteen seconds into my run I remember I fucking hate running and go back home, choosing to wash dishes and scrub the shower instead.

After an hour, Josh finally texts back.

> **Josh:** Interesting. -J.H.

That's it? I express complete honesty in my secret sexual fantasies, and it's *interesting?*

"Fuck!" I swear, slamming my phone on the counter. I don't realize Jo is walking into the apartment until she speaks.

"It's good to see you, too," Jo says, eyeing me cautiously as she shuts the door behind her and puts her bag on the counter.

"Sorry," I groan. "Today's been weird."

Jo nods. "I mean, as long as you don't start screaming like that in the middle of the night or anything."

Guess that means Josh and I will be staying at his place if he does his job right.

I pick up my phone to see if he's said anything else.

> **Josh:** How did it feel to think about all of this? To fill this out? -J.H.

Hot. Exciting. Terrifying. Everything.

Nic: wouldn't you like to know.

Josh: You're not funny. -J.H.

Nic: it was intense.

Josh: How so? -JH

Nic: i don't know. when i realized i didn't want to try a lot of things, there was this voice inside me insisting you might and i should be willing to do it if you wanted to. but i remembered that you told me i had to be honest about this so…

The little dots pop up to show Josh is typing, and then disappear. And then pop up again and disappear again.

Can he tell I omitted how much thinking about the things I was interested in had me aching to learn all he could teach me?

Josh: You're not being fair to yourself. You have every right to express your desires, wants, needs, etcetera without thinking about someone else. Especially in our situation. -J.H.

Nic: that's easier said than done. i'm not good at asserting myself.

Josh: I understand. -J.H.

Josh: Thanks for filling this out, it's really helpful. Work is crazy the next few days, but would you want to come over at six on Thursday to finalize things? -J .H.

Nic: and fuck?

Josh: ... -J.H

Nic: your enthusiasm is flattering, really.

Josh: Nic, trust me. I very much want to fuck you. -J.H.

Josh: But first and foremost I want to fuck you in a way that's safe physically and emotionally for us both. -J.H.

I'm taken aback. I've never had a partner be so thorough before having sex. It usually was just kissing and asking about protection before we just...did it.

I don't know how I feel about Josh taking it so seriously. In one way, it's good to know he cares about my safety. In another, it's strange because *I* don't care this much about my own safety.

Something else to process in therapy.

Nic: okay. so i just… come over thursday night?

Josh: You just come over on Thursday night. -J.H.

Nic: do i bring anything? Or wear anything in particular?

Josh: Whatever makes you comfortable. I don't have any expectations for the night beyond discussing our lessons. -J.H.

Josh: An orientation, if you will. -J.H.

Nic: okay. cool.

Nic: see you thursday, i guess.

Josh: See you Thursday, Nic. -J.H.

Nic: You really don't have to add your initials to the end of every text you send, you know.

Josh: I do know, thanks.

Josh: -J.H.

I spend the rest of the night beneath my weighted blanket as my mind spirals. What if this is a terrible idea? What if I mess up or do something wrong? What if it turns out to be a giant prank? Or he decided he can't sleep with me because I'm autistic? None of my previous partners knew about my diagnosis, and I didn't even mean for him to know. I do some deep breathing exercises and remind myself of the way Josh emphasized the importance of open and honest communication between us. If he expects and trusts me to be honest, I think I can expect the same from him, too.

I hope so, at least.

The next two days drag by, and the moment I arrive at work Thursday morning, I want to turn around and go home.

I oversee three colleagues who come in and work together every day, meaning they've bonded and have inside jokes and little quirks with each other I don't understand.

No one I work with is aware of my autism diagnosis. The organization I work for is a suicide prevention non-profit, so mental health is talked about frequently. But my diagnosis is new, and autism is still highly stigmatized, which makes me wary of disclosing it to people.

My family doesn't know. Not even Jo, and we live together. Getting diagnosed didn't change me, and they've always known I was quirky and quick to anger.

It's just easier this way.

I think.

Brooks, one of my coworkers, comes into my office and asks if I watched whatever reality dating show has new episodes on Fridays.

I actually was busy getting smashed and ruining my least favorite person's birthday party while trying to avoid a threesome.

"No," I say awkwardly instead. "I missed it. What happened?"

Something I've learned along the way is people like it when you show interest in things they like. While this is probably something most people know intuitively, it's something I have to be cognizant of.

He and my other coworkers, Danny and Alyssa, immediately tell me everything I missed.

They're nice enough, but when the workday comes to an end, I hear them whispering about happy hour. And just like usual, they didn't invite me.

I don't need friends at work, but it'd be nice to not feel like I'm always the outsider. Like I was an equal, just as capable and funny as the rest of them. Because I can be capable, funny, and autistic.

It's probably for the best that they didn't invite me because I would have declined.

I have class tonight.

Chapter 10

Josh

Playlist: "Mr. Brightside," Boyce Avenue

"Shit," I swear, pulling the smoking roasted vegetables from the oven. I lost track of time, stirring the sauce and making sure the pasta didn't boil over.

It didn't hit me until after I'd already begun cooking how ridiculous of me it was to attempt to make boxed spaghetti with frozen meatballs and jarred sauce for someone whose Italian heritage was notorious in our hometown.

But I wanted to cook for her. I like cooking, and because my last meeting ran late, I wasn't able to make the shepherd's pie I'd planned on. But I was able to swing pasta and roasted veggies.

Maybe I can pretend the vegetables are blackened on purpose?

I just want to make sure she's comfortable. I made a full pitcher of chocolate oat milk so she can drink as much as she wants.

I didn't have any classes today. Instead my calendar was packed with meetings discussing curriculum and shit, yet all I could think about was her and everything I'd learned about her over the past few days, sexually and not.

She's driving me fucking wild.

Of course she is. She's never *not* fucked with my head.

When I hear the doorbell ring, I freeze, like I don't know what I'm supposed to do in this situation.

Finally, I move to the door and open it.

God, she's so damn pretty. Her curls are parted to one side, and she's wearing a white button-up top that's rolled up to her elbows with black paper bag pants that show off the soft silhouette of her waist and hips.

I'm so fucked.

I clear my throat. "Hey."

"Hi," she says, looking into her tote bag as she rifles through it. She pulls out a bottle of wine and smiles. "I brought this. Is this a good host gift? I'm not really good at stuff like this."

I swallow. "This is so thoughtful, thank you. But for future reference, I don't drink."

Her brow furrows until her eyes widen with remembrance. "Oh, my god. You literally told me this."

"In passing. It's fine."

She snatches the bottle out of my hands. "What the fuck? Don't lie. It's not okay," she yelps, smashing the bottle on the stoop. We both stare down at the broken glass and spilt red wine for a moment before she speaks again. "I may have panicked," she admits.

I can't help the laugh that bubbles out of me. "A little bit."

"I'm really sorry, Josh," she says, wringing her hands. The distress on her face evaporates my urge to laugh at the chaos.

"Hey," I say. "It's okay, I promise. You forgot. And you took care of the problem. A bit dramatically, but that was sweet of you."

She groans. "You must think I'm such an ass."

"I think a lot of things about you, Buttercup, but not one of them is that you're an ass."

"Oh, God," Nic sniffles. "Does the smell trigger you?"

"Nic, I'm okay. It's not the first time since I've been sober that I've smelled or been around alcohol, and it definitely won't be the last. Please come inside."

She reluctantly steps through the doorway. "You promise you're okay?" Her eyes are so big, and she looks like she's about to cry. I definitely shouldn't find this endearing, but I do.

"I'm okay," I confirm. "I made dinner if you want to grab something to eat while I clean this up, okay?"

"You're not going to relapse if I leave you alone?"

I sigh. "Nic. Go eat."

She shuffles into the kitchen, and I grab a paper bag and broom from the front closet, making quick work of cleaning up the broken glass. When I finish, I throw the bag away in the trash can and go back inside. I find Nic sitting on my kitchen counter, sipping chocolate oat milk and reading the papers she definitely wasn't supposed to see yet. She'd slipped off her white low-top Converse while I was outside, revealing pink ankle socks with little soccer balls all over them.

"So," she says, putting her glass down on the counter and peering at me over the papers. "What's this?"

"Do you–do you want something to eat?" I wheeze, my face reddening at the knowledge of what she was reading.

She looks embarrassed. "I'm a really picky eater and ate before coming over."

"Ah," I say, trying not to show any hurt. She doesn't have to eat my food. Hell, it's not even good food. It's just boxed pasta with store-bought tomato sauce and overly roasted vegetables.

"I have food aversions, due to my sensory issues," she continues. "I make sure to eat before I go anywhere." She digs through her tote and pulls out a plastic baggie with Goldfish. "And I brought a snack in case I get hungry. I have safe foods I take when I go places."

Safe foods. I'd done some research after she told me she was autistic and talked to my cousin Tara's wife, Belen, who is an occupational therapist that works with autistic adults. She gave me a list of content creators and resources and drilled into me that some charities are actually hate groups.

One TikTok creator Belen recommended said in a video that sensory issues are common autistic traits, but they vary from person to person.

I wonder if that's impacted Nic's experience with sex?

"I have a pint of Ben & Jerry's in the freezer, if you like that?" I offer as I scoop food for myself into a bowl, deciding the vegetables most definitely cannot pass as intentionally blackened. "It's Phish Food."

"That's my favorite flavor! But this chocolate milk is perfect right now." She picks up the glass and takes another sip.

Once I've served myself, I begin to eat and lean against the island, our positions from Saturday reversed.

"So," she says, putting down her glass and flipping through the papers again. "What exactly is this, and why is my name on it?"

I clear my throat. "I made a syllabus. For us."

"A syllabus?" she asks incredulously. "You made a *sex* syllabus?"

I blush, staring into my bowl. "I'm a teacher. This is how I do things. And I thought it might be helpful having everything written out." I omit that in my research on autism, I discovered many autistic people feel most comfortable with routines and plans. I thought this might be helpful for her.

"Huh," she says, pursing her lips. "This is...thorough."

I'd spent an unbelievable amount of time after getting her answers back organizing and planning out a course of sorts.

"I mean, you obviously have a say in everything," I say, rubbing the back of my neck awkwardly. "And either of us can stop, skip, or change anything for any reason."

She doesn't say anything, and it's disconcerting.

"Is it okay?" I prompt.

"Wow," she says, looking up and meeting my gaze. "This is actually really great." I let out a sigh of relief. "But Jesus fucking Christ, Joshua. Could you be more of a fucking nerd?"

I scowl and reach over to her, swiping the syllabus from her hands. "Okay I think you've had enough time to look this over. Let's talk about it—" Nic opens her mouth, "*without* you insulting me." She promptly closes her mouth.

"The first few pages have the expectations, limits, and boundaries, both my own and the ones you expressed in your survey. For example, for my own mental health and well being, I don't do sleepovers. I'm game for anything I've listed, but, unless there's some sort of emergency, you've gotta go home when we're done, okay?"

"Okay," she agrees easily.

"Another boundary I have is alcohol consumption. I take consent extremely seriously, and I'm not comfortable having sex with anyone who isn't sober."

"Fair."

"Also, if you have other sexual partners, that's fine by me. But we need to communicate with each other about it, and routinely get tested and use condoms. That's pretty much it for me. Everything in the syllabus is stuff we both are comfortable trying, according to your survey answers, but if there's something you really want to try that isn't included, we can absolutely discuss it. Do you have any—"

"No kissing," she blurts out before I can finish my sentence. "No kissing."

I blink at her, a little stunned. I shake my head and flip through the syllabus. "I thought I saw kissing on your survey as high interest? I included kissing at the beginning of our lessons."

"Kissing's fine," she shrugs. "You can kiss me wherever you want, as long as it's not on my lips."

"Um, okay?" I say, confused.

She shrugs. "I don't like you. So I don't want to kiss you."

I scowl at her yet again. "Delightful. For what it's worth, I don't have a humiliation kink."

Although, considering how much she's turning me on and how mean she is to me, maybe I do.

"Ha ha," she says humorlessly. "Okay, so is there like...a sex schedule in this little syllabus of yours?"

"Not a schedule, but I grouped together different activities in a way that builds, so we can see what you like. I was planning on spending time just touching and kissing to start. But since you're not comfortable with that, there's room for spontaneity and creativity."

"So, technically what you had planned for tonight isn't applicable anymore?"

"Technically not," I answer.

"What happens tonight?" Nic asks.

"We can talk about—"

"Do you want me to go down on you?"

"Oh so we're just...we're just going for it then?"

She swings her legs and hops off the countertop, walking forward until we're only inches apart. "I can see your hard-on through your jeans, Henry. I don't think you're in any position to not want to just go for it."

Fuck.

"Couch?" she asks, taking my hand in hers. I'm dazed but somehow manage a feeble nod as she leads me into the living room.

Then she shoves me, and I fall back on the couch. She climbs onto my lap, her thighs framing mine. Her mouth and tongue are on my neck, and it's so all so fast.

"Uh," I manage to say.

"Shut up, and let me make you come," she breathes into my jaw before scraping her teeth along my beard.

This feels like a dream, her straddling me, grinding her core over me. This is everything I've wanted...but it feels wrong.

Really wrong.

As Nic begins to unbutton my shirt, I feel it. Her hands are trembling.

"Nic, stop," I say, covering her hands with mine. "Slow down."

"I'm gonna give you a hickey. It'll be really funny," she says, a tremor in her voice.

"Jesus Christ, you're fucking shaking," I say, gently lifting her off my lap and depositing her on the couch.

She groans. "I just wanted-"

"I know, Buttercup. But you have to know after everything you've told me about your experiences with sex, seeing you shaking isn't going to fly."

"I'm sorry," she says, her voice quivering as she presses the heels of her hands into her eyes. "I'm so sorry."

"You're okay," I say gently. She's still shaking, and I'm worried that she'll spiral into something more intense. "Do you want a weighted blanket and some chocolate oat milk? Let's slow down."

Nic peers at me through her fingers. "You have a weighted blanket?"

I'd ordered one the moment she left on Saturday because I wanted to make sure she had one if she got overwhelmed again. It was at my door when I came home from Port Haven Sunday night.

I shrug in what I hope is a nonchalant fashion. "Yeah, you mentioned you find them comforting, and I wanted to see what the fuss was about."

"That would be really helpful."

I go upstairs to get the blanket and then make a pit stop to get her a glass of chocolate milk. When I come back into the living room, Nic has her eyes squeezed shut and is hugging her knees to her chest.

"Here," I say, putting the blanket next to her on the couch and setting the glass on the coffee table. "Is there anything else I can do?"

"No, this is good," she says, pulling the blanket over her. "Thank you."

I sit on the couch and pick up the remote. "Do you have a favorite movie I can turn on? TV show?"

Nic cheeks turn a spectacular shade of pink. "Have you seen *Ted Lasso*?"

"No, I haven't."

Yes, I have.

"It's on Apple TV+. It's my favorite show," she says.

"What's it about?"

Nic begins to relax as she tells me all about the history of the show and the characters, specifically how hot Rebecca and Roy Kent are, which I definitely agree with her on.

Watching her talk so passionately mesmerizes me, and I completely ignore the show, staring at her instead.

"Is it okay if I take my shirt off?" Nic asks suddenly halfway through the first episode.

I swallow hard. "Uh-"

"Sorry, this shirt has a tag that's just really-"

"That's fine," I wheeze, squeezing my eyes shut and not wondering if, like her belly and face, her cleavage is scattered with freckles. "I won't look."

"Thanks."

I had most definitely been looking forward to taking that shirt off *for* her, running my fingers up her sides and making her shiver as—

"Ok, I'm good," she says and I open my eyes. She's still wrapped in her blanket, but a tan bra folded on top of her blouse catches my eye. She's *topless* topless. Like *braless* topless. Like right now the weighted blanket is brushing against the breasts I can't stop imagining. What the hell, am I jealous of a weighted blanket?

We watch the show in silence for a few minutes, and the next time I look over, her eyes are still glued to the screen, but the blanket has fallen off her shoulder. A whole scattering of freckles covers her collarbone and shoulder.

She must feel me looking at her, because she looks over at me, and our eyes meet. "Um, hi?"

"Hello," I say.

"Can I help you?" she asks sarcastically.

I shake my head, feeling my cheeks heat. "No, sorry, it's just—your freckles—very pretty." Great work Joshua, very Shakespearean scholar-level of eloquence.

She blinks at me and looks down at her shoulder. "I've always hated them."

"They look like stars," I tell her. "I—I want to touch them. Can I? You can say no." Though I might cry if she does.

"You want to touch my freckles?"

"Only if it's alright with you, Buttercup."

"Okay," she answers.

I reach out and softly brush my fingers over the cluster of freckles right where her neck meets her right shoulder. Her breath hitches.

"Is this okay?" I murmur.

"Yes," she breathes.

I let my fingers explore her freckles. There are so many, like markings on a map decorating her body. "Can I kiss them?"

She nods, her eyes on my mouth.

"I need your verbal consent, Nic."

"Yes," she affirms. "You can kiss my freckles."

I move closer to her and press my lips to a specific freckle on the front side of her shoulder I've already grown quite attached to. I kiss the other freckles I can see, paying close attention to her reactions. Her breath is shallow, and when I meet her gaze, her pupils are dilated.

I let one of my hands settle on her waist over the blanket. "Do you have a lot of freckles?"

I feel her nod her head. "Nobody's ever called them pretty before."

I scoff. "That's silly. They're lovely. I want to kiss all of your freckles and show you how pretty I think they are."

"All of them?" she squeaks.

"Whichever ones you like me kissing."

"I—" Nic clears her throat. "I have them all over. Everywhere."

I trace the shape of a freckle at the base of her neck with my tongue, and she lets out the sweetest little whimper. "Coincidentally, I'd very much like to kiss all over your body. Is that okay?"

"Yes," she gasps.

I pull away from her and gently push the blanket from her shoulders. *Sweet fucking Jesus.*

Her breasts are small and round, and though they look similar to how I imagined, there was no way my imagination could ever do her loveliness justice. There's a freckle adjacent to her left nipple, which is tightened to a peak and begging for my mouth.

I wrap an arm around her waist again and pull her into me, leaning down to press my lips to a particularly enticing freckle on her cleavage. "So beautiful," I murmur against her, placing my other hand on her upper thigh and gently massaging it. "How does this feel?" I ask her before moving my lips to another freckle that's just begging for my attention.

"It feels good," she gasps. She's moving her hips, and I know she's trying to find friction to ease the ache between her thighs.

"Lie back for me," I murmur. Together we move her body so she's stretched out on the couch, and I'm on my knees between her splayed legs, leaning over her. I cup one breast in my hand and dip my head down to kiss a freckle on the underside. "Did you know you have a freckle on your left areola?"

She raises her head. "I do?"

I smile against her soft skin. "Mmhmm."

"You can kiss that one, too. If—if you want." she stammers.

I press my lips to that pretty little freckle and softly run my thumb over her taut nipple, and fuck, I want to taste her. She gasps loudly, and her hips jerk. I lift my eyes and meet hers, bright and blazing.

"Please," she whispers. I swirl my tongue around her nipple and she moans in response to my touch. Her head falling back against the armrest, hands tangling in my hair.

"That's perfect, Nic," I praise. "Show me what you like." I run a hand up her thigh and cup her hip. "You taste so sweet. Do you taste this good everywhere, pretty girl?"

"I don't know," she squeaks.

I kiss her other nipple and let my hand run over her stomach, inching lower and lower until I'm flirting with her waistband. "Can I touch your pussy, Nic?" I ask.

"God, yes," she groans, her thighs opening wider. "Let me take off my pants."

She lifts her hips, and together we shimmy her pants off. She's so tantalizing, lying on my couch in her yellow cotton panties with little flowers all over them. Her entire body is flushed pink, and I toy with the edge of the fabric.

"I like these," I murmur.

She frowns. "Don't tease. I don't really have any sexy underwear that isn't painful to wear, so I wore my confidence underwear. These helped me get my job, you know."

"I'm not teasing," I assure her, my voice rough. "I promise." I can't stop staring at her panties. I just know her pussy is wet and swollen and as pink as the rest of her body.

I lean over her and press my lips to her neck, moving one hand down to slip beneath the fabric between her thighs.

"Fuck me," I groan into her neck, my fingers running through the curls beneath her panties. "You have curly hair everywhere."

"Is that okay?" she asks tentatively, her thighs squeezing against my hand. "I know some people don't like—"

"Whatever is right for you and your body is perfect, Nic. But knowing there's even more of those maddening curls of yours on your pussy is thrilling to me."

She whimpers as I tentatively stroke her, peppering her neck with wet, open-mouthed kisses and spreading her with my fingers.

"Good girl," I groan. "You're doing so fucking good, Nic."

"I'm not going to tell you you're doing a good job, if that's what you're fishing for," she grumbles.

I roll my eyes. "No, I'm just praising you, dumbass."

She shoves my shoulder. "Hey!"

I jump, my hand jerking upward, and the heel of my hand unintentionally grinds against her clit.

Nic gasps as her hips jolt. We both freeze and stare at each other, wide-eyed.

"You started it," I say, trying to defend myself.

"Seems fair for you to finish it, then," she growls, grabbing a handful of my shirt in her fist and pulling herself closer into me.

I lift my eyebrow and try to ignore the way my cock jumps at the rasp in her voice. "Oh, so that's what Nic Quinn likes." I firmly press the pad of my thumb just above her bundle of nerves.

The sounds she makes as I circle her clit are incredible, breathy gasps and moans of "please" and "more."

"Do you want my fingers inside you?" I ask, pushing myself off of her.

She loosens her grip on my shirt. "I think so?" she says, so unsure sounding that a strange feeling blooms in my chest, knowing this is the first time someone's given her the attention she needs to connect with her body.

The whiplash this she-devil gives me.

I slowly push my middle finger into her, her muscles tensing as she adjusts to me.

"Yes," she breathes, her eyes fluttering closed and her head rolling back against the arm-rest as I curl my finger, finding that spot that makes her breath hitch in a brand new way. I want to collect her sounds like memories, keep them locked in my mind and replay them whenever I can.

"Tell me when it's good. Just like that," I grit out, adjusting myself so my free hand is next to her head. "Do you want another finger?"

"Please," she breathes.

"Tell me."

"I want another finger."

I growl, pressing my ring finger into her. She wraps one of her legs around my hip, and I feel an unexpected sense of pride toward her for doing that without prompting.

I circle her clit and curl my fingers inside of her, and *Christ*. For someone who seems determined to make my life hell, the way her pussy grips my fingers really does feel like heaven.

Her breaths are shallow, and I can tell she's close.

"You're doing so good, Nic. Can you come for me?"

"I'm trying," she whimpers, squeezing her eyes closed. "I'm—"

I still my movements, sitting back on my heels. Her eyes fly open, and she jackknifes up.

"What the fuck, Henry?" she seethes. "I said I was *trying*."

"If you have to try, you're not going to get there, Buttercup," I say simply.

"So you just stopped?"

"Nic," I grab her hand, and she immediately tries to pull away, but I'm not letting go. "I wasn't touching you the way you needed to be touched, and you weren't giving me any feedback on how to make it better."

"My feedback is that I like you a lot better when you're touching my clit than when you stop touching my clit."

My fingers are literally still inside her, and she's sitting up, all furious at me.

It's hot as fuck.

"Show me how you touch your clit," I tell her, moving our hands so they're placed over her panties. "When you're alone, how do you make yourself come? Show me, so I know. Please."

She softens a bit. "You were doing fine," she says, voice small.

"Yeah. I was. But you deserve better than fine. That's what this is all about. I want to give you good, great even. But I need your help to be able to do that."

She swallows. "I'm embarrassed." She averts her eyes.

"Please don't be. You're in a vulnerable state right now. Sex and intimacy are vulnerable, and that's okay."

"You don't think I'm weird?"

"I don't." I pause. "Have you ever come in front of someone before?"

She blushes and shakes her head. "I've gotten close, but then I always lose it."

"Let's try this together. And if you feel comfortable, I want you to talk to me, to tell me how you feel and what you need. We're doing this because you don't care about hurting my feelings, remember?"

She nods. "Yeah."

She takes a deep breath and reclines to a lying position as she lowers her hand to her panties. My cock twitches when I notice she's so wet, there's a spot on her panties. She slides the fabric to the side and uses her other hand to spread her curls. I can't help my moan as I take in where she's glistening. "Your fingers are still in me," she whispers.

"Do you want me to take them out?"

"No, can you...can you do that thing you did before?"

"This?" I curl my fingers into her, and her mouth falls open as a breathy gasp leaves her lips.

"God, that's really good." She uses two fingers to firmly circle her clit. I can't stop staring at her as she touches herself.

"Do you want to touch your tits?" I ask her.

She nods in response.

"Do it."

She squeezes her breast, clasping her nipple between her thumb and forefinger.

"Tell me if you don't like something, okay?" I remind her.

"Okay," she agrees. Our heavy breathing speaks for us as she touches herself, our hands grazing as I thrust into her. I can't stop staring at her cunt, how she plays with her clit. Circular motions around, then up and down, then back to circular again. As I try to memorize each movement, I can feel her tightening around me.

"Can you—can you talk?" she asks. "Like you were before?"

Jesus Christ.

"You like it when I tell you how pretty you are, Nic?" She whimpers. "You want to hear how tight, how fucking wet your pussy is around my fingers? How I can't stop thinking about how good you'll taste when I get my mouth on you?"

"Oh, God," she chokes out, her movements against her clit becoming more frantic, harder. I follow her rhythm, my thrusts quickening, growing a little rougher. "Oh, God."

"That's it. Let go, pretty girl. You're absolutely perfect," I grit out, my teeth clenched.

"Josh, Josh. I'm—" she chokes out. Her back arches off of the couch, and she cries out as she comes, pulsing around my fingers. Fuck, I almost come from just watching her let herself go. Her hand falls from her clit, and I still my hand, selfishly not wanting to leave her empty just yet.

Her eyes flutter open, and fuck, they're so warm and bright when she's satiated and not threatening me. She's positively glowing in the wake of her orgasm.

"I'm not broken," she murmurs, lifting her hand from her breast to push a strand of hair out of my face before quickly jerking back.

The softness of the action surprises me, and I lift my eyes to meet hers. She immediately averts her gaze.

The corner of my mouth raises in a half smile. "You could never be broken, Buttercup." I lean over her and press my lips to her forehead. Some of her curls are plastered to her forehead, wet with sweat.

And I hate the way I want to stay this way forever, her hand over mine and my fingers inside her.

Chapter 11

Nic

Playlist: "Pretty Please," Dua Lipa

I feel like I've been cracked open. Like everything I've worked so hard to lock away from the world is spilling out around me.

I don't like it.

I especially don't like feeling this way with Josh Henry's fingers inside my damn vagina.

I shift awkwardly as he sits back and pulls his fingers out of me. I am suddenly very aware I'm lying naked, except for my confidence underwear, on his couch while he's still wearing his chinos and green button up.

"You're staring at me," he murmurs. He's looking at his fingers, which are coated in the evidence of how hard I just came.

Oh god. I came. On him.

I swallow. This is good. This is what I wanted, right? And it was good, but I have no idea how I looked, if I was okay. Did I do it right? Did I fuck up? Did I–

"Nic," he says, in a tone that's both firm and gentle, soothing and annoying as fuck. What a good way to describe this damn man when he's between my legs. "What's going through your head right now?"

I shift beneath him again, my knee moving against him as he hisses between his teeth.

Oh.

Oh.

"Is that your dick?" I blurt out, sitting up to look, and yup. He's big and straining against his pants. "Can I see?"

He raises a brow.

"I'm literally almost naked, and you're fully clothed. I want to see."

"It's a pretty standard dick," he says, flushing.

"According to the women at your party, it might as well have super powers."

"For fuck's sake," Josh grumbles, hastily untucking his shirt and unbuckling his belt. "Fine, I'll show you. And then we cuddle and finish that episode of *Ted Lasso* or whatever you need, and you'll be nice to me for five minutes while we do it, and then you go home, okay?"

"Uh-huh," I reply, only half listening. Instead I'm focused on Josh's fingers, still glistening with my release, as he unfastens his pants. He shoves them down over his hips to mid-thigh, pushing his briefs down after them.

Oh my god.

I've seen a few dicks. And yeah, I guess it's a pretty standard dick. Proud, kind of angry looking, because why wouldn't male genitalia look aggressive? There's also a big tattoo of a human skull on his left thigh that almost—but not quite—distracts me from his impressive length. "That's a nice penis you've got there, Henry."

"Uh, thank—"

"No wonder you're such a dick—look at that thing! You're like ninety percent cock."

He scowls at me, wrapping his hand around the base. "You're done." He moves to pull his briefs back up.

"No, no, sorry. I'm just nervous," I admit, internally kicking myself for admitting that to him. "You're really hard."

"Yes, Buttercup. When someone is aroused, their blood goes to their genitals and—"

"Why are you aroused?" I tilt my head and force myself to make eye contact with him. It's already hard for me most of the time, but even more so when his cock is in my peripheral vision. And now I'm back to staring at his cock.

He scoffs, sounding almost disbelieving, squeezing his hand around himself and stroking upward. "I don't know if you missed it, but you were just writhing on my fingers."

"That turned you on?" I ask, finally meeting his eyes. His gaze is intense, like he can see right through me. "Me coming?"

"My god, Nic. Of course it did. You felt incredible. *You're* incredible."

It almost feels like there are butterflies in my stomach, but that can't be right. Joshua Henry *cannot* be giving me butterflies. Must be fruit flies.

"Really?"

"Mhmmm. I want to see it again. And feel it on my fingers again, then on my tongue, on my cock."

I swallow.

"You're blushing," he murmurs.

"I want that, too," I admit breathily.

"Now?" he asks, and I nod. He groans. "Can I touch you?"

"Please."

His hand slips back into my underwear, going straight to my center. He pulls his hand out, glistening and covered in the evidence of how much he turns me on.

Then he fists his cock and uses my wetness to lubricate his firm strokes, from base to tip.

"Oh my god," I choke out, impossibly more turned on by this.

"Touch your clit, Buttercup. Make yourself come for me," he chokes out, his voice strained. I notice how he rotates his wrist as he jerks himself, how his grip tightens on the upstroke.

I slide my hand down my body and into my underwear, spreading myself and moaning when I feel my clit, still swollen and sensitive from my first orgasm.

"Good girl," he grunts, shifting and lowering himself over me, so close I can feel his hand stroking himself against my belly.

"I want you to come, too," I say breathlessly, entranced by the feeling of us touching ourselves against each other.

"Christ, Nic. I've gotta," he grunts. "I've gotta come for you." The only sounds for a moment are the squeaking of the couch cushions, our sounds as we pleasure ourselves. "I'm close," he grunts, his pace quickening. "So fucking close."

"Me too," I whimper. I can't take my eyes off his Adam's apple, the way it bobs and curves, and I reach a hand up to touch it, running my fingers over it. I want to dream of it, the way it looks when he feels this pleasure.

"Can I come on you, pretty girl?"

"Yes," I respond, so close to the edge my vision's blurred.

He moans, and I feel the elastic that's been stretching within me snap, the first waves of my orgasm violently crashing over me. I squeeze my eyes closed as garbled, unintelligible noises come out of my mouth.

"Nic, look at me. Please," he whimpers.

I force my eyes open, and when our eyes meet, I don't want to look away. He's looking at me like...I don't know. Nobody's ever looked at me like this before. He presses his forehead to mine and closes his eyes as a shudder ripples through his body. He comes on my stomach, moaning my name as his nose nuzzles mine. I wrap my arms around his big body, running my hands up his shirt and over the planes of his back, over his ass and the back of his thighs, his muscles tensing at my touch.

"Fuck," he gasps, and the arm supporting his weight buckles, his heavy body falling on mine.

Oh my god.

"Shit," Josh says, scrambling and pushing off of me. "Fuck, are you okay? I'm so—what the hell are you doing?"

I wrap my arms around his shoulders and pull him back onto me, his body pressing mine into the cushions. "Don't. Move," I hiss, my body feeling like a balloon deflating from the pressure of his body on mine.

This almost feels better than the orgasm.

"Nic—I have to clean you up."

"Leave it. Stay," I demand. "You feel good."

His body starts to relax into mine. "I weigh a lot. I don't want to hurt you," he murmurs, his voice muffled next to me.

"You won't. You're like a weighted blanket, only better."

"I'm gonna crush you."

"No you're not. I can still talk. I'm breathing fine. Please just...let me have this?"

He's quiet for a moment before speaking, "Promise I'm not hurting you?" He sounds nervous, and I don't know how to express just how much he's doing the opposite of hurting me.

"Promise," I say, wrapping my arms around his center. "I'll say something if it hurts."

We stay there, his large, beautiful body soothing my keyed-up nervous system.

Maybe this wasn't such a bad idea after all.

Chapter 12

Josh

Playlist: "Mountain To Move," Nick Mulvey

I came on Nic Quinn's stomach last night. And her confidence panties. I didn't notice until she was ready to go home. When I got up, I noticed I'd smeared my cum all over her freckled belly and her pretty little panties.

I went into the kitchen to clean myself off with a paper towel, and she shuffled into the guest bathroom, her clothes in her arms and the weighted blanket dragging behind her like a cape.

When she came back out, fully clothed, she stood on her tiptoes, kissed my cheek, firmly thumped my shoulder, and shoved something into my pocket.

"You can wash these for me," she said sweetly, batting her eyelashes.

After she'd left, I'd groaned as I pulled out her confidence panties that now were covered in our arousal. If she didn't specifically call them her confidence panties, I wouldn't be washing these, and she wouldn't be getting them back.

But she did.

However, she never has to know how I made myself come one last time that night, fisting my cock with them.

I've *never* been like this before, but it doesn't surprise me. Knowing Nicoletta Quinn, she's probably out to ruin my entire life.

"Josh!" Nellie snaps her fingers in my face. "Did you hear me?"

"Yes," I lie.

"So that works for you?"

"Yes. Wait, what?"

Nellie scowls and takes a sip of her iced chai latte. "What's going on today? It's like you're not really here."

I *feel* like I'm not really here. I feel like my head is still with Nic. I haven't heard from her since she texted me to let me know she got home safe last night, after I made her promise to do so. I haven't texted her, either, because what do I say? *Hey Nic, got any more of those panties I can fuck?*

"Sorry," I say guiltily. "I'm just—"

"Do you need to get laid?" she interrupts. Nellie is one of the few people in my life I haven't slept with, and that's been very much on purpose. Our feelings have always been platonic, and Nellie is demisexual, only having sex with an emotional connection. Meanwhile, emotionless sex is the only kind I have.

She knows what a big role sex plays in my life, but I haven't told her about Nic and me. How do I explain that? It doesn't even make sense to me.

"I *need* this summer session to go by quickly. I'm over it already," I grumble. I'm teaching an online Intro to Shakespeare Course, which is probably my least favorite course to teach. It's an elective taken by mostly freshmen and sophomores who aren't looking to major in English but are getting their humanities requirements over with.

"How's Nic?" Nellie asks, making me choke on my sparkling water. She smirks. "Tyler said she was really funny and has a cute sister she lives with." She waggles her eyebrows. "You should get the sister's number. Bet she'll help you get out of this funk before the wedding."

I blink at her. I have no idea what she's talking about. "What wedding?"

"My wedding that I literally just gave you the date for, and which you agreed to officiate? Jesus Christ, Joshua. What's going on?"

I look around, like there could be someone else or a camera hiding in Nellie's tiny office. "Nic and I fucked last night," I whisper.

Nellie screams.

"Shut the fuck up," I hiss.

"I knew there was something between you, I *knew* it."

"Yes, it's called hatred," I inform her. "We detest each other, but she asked me to help her with sex. So we're like...having sex.

Together. Lessons," I say. I know I'm not making much sense, but the situation doesn't make sense.

She blinks at me. "So it wasn't just a hookup?"

"It's an ongoing hookup. "

"Have you ever slept with the same person more than once?" She tilts her head, and I feel like she's trying to therapize me.

"No," I admit.

"Hmm. Interesting," Nellie muses. "Maybe you should bring her as your date to the wedding in November."

I scoff. "You know I don't date."

She waves her hand at me dismissively. "Bring her as your enemy with benefits, then. She'll make things interesting."

Make things interesting she does.

"I'll think about it," I compromise. "But I don't know if she'd even want to go, or if we'll still be spending time together in November. She was involuntarily dragged to my party, and I don't think parties are really her scene." I don't tell her about Nic's autism or what I've learned from her and my research so far.

"So when are you two 'hanging out' again?" Nellie asks, using finger quotes.

"I don't know; we haven't talked since last night."

"You didn't text her today?" Nellie's eyes widen as she leans forward. "Wow, you must really hate her."

I stare at her, not understanding what that has to do with anything.

"Check in with her! See if she's doing okay!" Nellie exclaims, slamming her to-go cup down on her desk. "I know you don't do repeats, so you don't do check-ins, or text to say you had fun, but you should text her. Stop acting like a fuck-boy."

"What do I say?"

She rolls her eyes and holds her hand out. "Give me your phone, Joshua."

I oblige, and she holds my phone up to my face to unlock it before tapping on the screen.

We're silent as she types, and I expect her to show it to me, but when she speaks, it's to let me know she sent it.

"Nellie, what the fuck?" I exclaim, reaching for my phone, but she jerks it away.

"Shut up, she texted back."

"What did she say?"

Nellie ignores me as her eyes scan the screen before laughing and typing out another message.

"Penelope," I groan, drawing out the last syllable.

"I'm talking to your girl," she says, not looking at me.

"She's not my girl," I grumble, slumping back in the chair and crossing my arms over my chest.

Nellie doesn't say anything for the next few minutes, and I've just about given up. I'm weighing the pros and cons of walking to the Apple Store and getting myself a new phone when she finally speaks again.

"Here." Nellie slides the phone across the desk.

I look at her warily. "What did you do?"

She waves her hand at me dismissively. "Don't worry about it."

"I'm worrying about it."

She stands up. "I'm grabbing lunch. See you tonight, bestie."

"Why would I see you tonight?" Nellie doesn't answer, just winks and ruffles my hair before leaving me alone in her office without saying a word.

It's not until I grab a sandwich from a nearby shop and am back at my desk that I realize I can just look at Nellie's texts to Nic.

Josh: hey nic! i just wanted to check in after last night <smiling emoji> how are you feeling?

Nic: who is this?

Josh: it's josh henry?

Nic: no it's not. josh texts like a grandpa who's used to carrier pigeons.

Nic: did you kill him and steal his phone? i won't tell anyone.

Nic: i don't care.

Josh: omg. wow. i'm impressed.

Josh: this is josh's friend nellie, we met at his birthday party! tyler is my fiancé?

Nic: i knew it wasn't josh, he texts with proper punctuation and capitalization and always signs his initials.

Josh: does he really? what a fuckin nerd.

Nic: right??

Josh: he told me he was waiting to hear from you and that dumbass gave me a little backstory on what happened last night (no judgment at all! he's a cutie, you're a cutie, glad y'all got it on). but i told him HE should text first because he hosted so here we are.

Nic: lmao men are clueless.

Josh: amen. you doing ok? do i need to kick his ass?

Nic: i'm fine, but please feel free to kick his ass.

Nic: just because.

Josh: will do. are you shacking up again tonight?

Nic: no, i overslept so i'm going to the gym after work.

Josh: wait what gym do you go to?

Nic: i go to a climbing gym a few blocks from my apartment.

Josh: you fucking rock climb? bad ass bitch. i've always wanted to try it.

Josh: you are way too cool for him.

Josh: please don't tell him i said that.

Nic: lol i won't.

Nic: i actually have a platinum membership and i can bring an unlimited number of guests. you and tyler should come with me some time.

Josh: omg seriously?

Josh: what about tonight?

Nic: sure! i'll send you the info

Nic: shit, i forgot that this is josh's phone lmao.

Nic: what's your number?

Josh: stfu i did too wow lmao he's sitting across from me at my desk all panicky because i haven't given it back lmao

Josh: wait, can he come too? since this is his phone and he'll probably see our conversation.

Nic: yeah, but tell him he has to pay $20 for the pass or something.

Josh: duh.

Josh: ok i just sent your contact to myself, so i'll text you from there. you're the coolest, can't wait to climb some rocks tonight.

Nic: okay!

I roll my eyes as I read the end of their conversation, and just as I'm about to put my phone back in my pocket, I get another text.

> **Nellie:** hey, you me and ty are going to try a new climbing gym tonight at 6 ok? passes are $20, cash only. here's the link, wear something comfy!

Nellie is always at least fifteen minutes late, so I arrive ten minutes late. I don't want to be alone with Nic for too long, primarily because she definitely doesn't want to be near me for too long—unless she's coming.

However, being alone with Nic would have been preferable to walking into the gym and seeing not only Nic, but Nellie, Tyler, and another woman I don't recognize standing and talking like old friends. Nic's back is to me, and she's wearing the same style of bike shorts and longline sports bra she'd worn to my place Saturday morning, only this time they're black. And I know what she looks like underneath.

My shorts are mercifully pretty baggy, but I still do a quick check to see if my newly acquired erection is visible.

It is.

Tyler and I make eye contact over Nic's head, and they clear their throat, nodding in greeting. Every single head turns my way. Nic is laughing and smiling, but as soon as she sees me, the levity melts off her face, and the usual scowl she has for me when she's clothed is back in place.

"Joshua Charles Henry! You're late!" Nellie yells, scowling at me. "And we're using Nic's guest passes, way to be disrespect-ful."

"I lost track of time," I lie.

Nic sighs loudly. "It's $35 for a guest pass."

I frown at her. "Nellie told me it was $20." I stopped at an ATM to get cash out, even though I knew they were fucking with me.

"Right," Nellie agrees. "But that's before taxes and service fees."

Nic snickers, and Nellie shoots her an amused eyebrow wag-gle.

I glare at them but take out my wallet and hand two twenties to Nic, who snatches them from me and slips them into her bra. "Aren't you going to pay and get my change?"

"Well, you were late, so I'll pay after. And I don't have any cash on me," she says cooly, crossing her arms in a way that pushes her breasts out. My hands twitch as I struggle to not look at her protruding nipples. "They know me here, it's fine. You have to sign a waiver with Joey, and then he's going to give you a rundown," she motions to the front desk with her head.

I sign the waiver, and even ask Joey about the fee. He confirms that because of Nic's level of membership, she is able to bring an unlimited number of guests to the gym free of charge.

Great. I don't know how I feel about Nellie helping Nic scam me.

When I return to the group, I introduce myself to the woman I don't recognize.

"Oh, I know who you are, Josh Henry," she says, her tone and cheery smile deceptively bright. "Hurt my sister and you'll wish you were never born. Our dad's an ex-seminarian, so I was raised with a healthy disregard for order and the rules. Keep that in mind." She squeezes my hand. "I'm Jo, by the way."

Nic's sister. I remember her from the family picture I found on Facebook. They have matching brown eyes, and Jo has dark brown, almost black, wavy hair that flows over her shoulders. She throws her hair behind one shoulder, exposing a patch of some sort on her arm. I notice her nails are long, except for her left ring and middle fingers, and painted a deep red. Her nail color choice definitely represents the blood she'll draw when she gouges my eyeballs out of my skull.

Joey comes over to us and gives a quick orientation, explaining the different levels of walls and safe climbing instructions. When he talks about the auto-belay system available on most walls, I feel my heart in my throat. At my size, I'm definitely over the weight limit for the device. After the orientation, Nic walks toward the back of the gym, where the more advanced walls are. She stops at one with small holds continuing onto the ceiling and clips into a harness. My dick jumps at the way it highlights her already spectacular ass.

"Where do you think you're going?" Nellie asks when I start to follow her, Tyler, and Jo to the beginner-friendly walls.

"Uh, to rock climb," I lie. I have every intention of staying on the ground, considering the device most definitely can't hold my weight.

She elbows me sharply in the side. "Why don't you keep Nic company? The three of us are just going to be talking about wedding logistics anyway."

I look between the three of them. "Why?"

Nellie grins at Tyler. "Jo works for one of the most sought-after event planning firms in the tri-state area. We weren't even going to try to book them, but then Nic mentioned Jo and connected us, so she's going to plan our wedding!" Nellie is bouncing on the balls of her feet and smacking Tyler's arm with excitement. Tyler looks down at her with bemused pride. "Now, go climb with Nic," she says, pushing me away.

I glare at her. "You're literally the one who invited *me*."

"Right. Before this became a business meeting. Now shoo, Joshua."

I sigh and walk toward the wall which Nic's already scaling like some weird lizard. She glares down at me. "This is a 5.10 route, Henry."

"I don't know what that means," I interject.

She glares at me. "It's not an easy wall. The kiddie walls are that way." She motions over toward Nellie, Tyler, and Jo with her head.

I scowl. "I was sort of forced over here." I clip myself into the harness, praying the automatic belayer will hold my weight because I don't feel comfortable asking anyone to belay for me. Then I stare at the wall.

Because how the fuck are you supposed to do this?

I hear a very loud, very melodramatic exhalation of air from somewhere above me, and then Nic is pushing herself down the wall until she lands next to me. "Need help?" she says coolly.

"Nope," I say in what I hope disguises the panicked way I feel.

"Have you ever climbed before?" she asks, her voice softening a little.

I swallow and look into her eyes; they're a soft caramel brown with flecks of gold. Her head is tilted to the side, her curls flopping to that same side, and she seems relatively harmless at the moment. "No," I admit, finally.

"Does Nellie know that?" she asks.

"Yup," I say.

Nic looks over her shoulder to where Nellie and Tyler are now climbing a much more approachable wall while Jo chats with them from the floor. "I think Nellie's trying to force us to spend time together," she whispers.

"Oh, I *know* Nellie's trying to force us to spend time together," I chuckle, running a hand through my hair. I feel her eyes lift and follow the movement.

"Do you have a secret crush on me or something, Henry?" she asks teasingly.

"I wouldn't dare, Buttercup," I lie. "No, I made the mistake of mentioning our plan, and now she wants us to get married and have babies, probably."

"Gross," Nic says flatly, unclipping herself from the auto-belay system and then reaching to unclip me. I feel my entire body heating at her hand's close proximity to my aching cock, but she doesn't seem to notice as she grabs my wrist. "Come on, this way."

She drags me through the gym to another wall toward the back, away from the rest of our group. "This one's a 5.6 wall, so one step above the least complicated, but it's fun," she says, standing back and looking up with her hands on her hips. "It's the one that made me fall in love with climbing." A soft smile spreads across her face, and it's so fucking enchanting, I can't look away.

Or maybe I just don't want to.

"Do you think I can handle it?"

"I wouldn't bring you over here if I didn't think so," she says, and for some reason that warms me to my core. "You might not be able to reach the top the first time, but that's not the only way to be a successful climber. If, as you climb, you feel good and sure of yourself, that's a good climb in my book."

She looks so reflective and peaceful while talking about climbing, displaying a confidence I haven't seen in her before, and it takes my breath away, seeing what lights a fire in her.

"How do I start?" I ask.

"That's the beauty of it, Joshua," she says, smirking at me. "There are a million different ways to climb this wall, and the way that works for me might not work for you. The journey is personal." She clips herself in and stands on her tiptoes, grabbing onto a hold. I marvel at the way her back and shoulder muscles flex as she pulls herself up.

"You okay?" she asks, not looking at me, her abs tensing as she moves her foot to a hold.

"Uh—"

She looks at me. "Joshua! If you want to climb, you gotta climb."

I swallow, my anxiety about the auto-belay increasing. "I think I need to tell you something."

She tilts her head to the side. "Okay?"

"I, uh. I weigh more than the auto-belay's weight limit" I admit, shame washing over me and filling every part of my body. I'm not ashamed of my body, but sometimes I'm ashamed of how it feels like it can inconvenience other people.

She blinks at me a few times. "I didn't think about that. I'm sorry," She pushes herself down the wall and lands back on the ground. "I'll belay for you."

She says it easily, like my body isn't inconvenient.

"Are you sure?"

"Yeah. Let me grab a sandbag."

Nic unclips from her harness and goes toward the front. She comes back a few minutes later holding a sandbag that looks as big as her.

After a few minutes, I'm ready to climb, and she's set up to belay. I feel better knowing we've taken the proper safety precautions that will allow me to climb safely, but I'm still a little anxious. Any sort of new physical activity is anxiety-inducing because I don't exactly know how my body will look while doing it, or what it's capable of.

I take a deep breath and begin to climb.

When I look down at her over my shoulder, she beams up at me, a smile so bright and toothy and the complete opposite of what I've seen of Nic and somehow, it's the most Nic thing I've ever seen.

Chapter 13

Nic

Playlist: "Walk Me Home," P!nk

"Try the purple one to your right; no, your *other* right," I instruct Josh as I belay from the ground. He's about six feet up, and this is his third attempt. I thought I'd hate this, but I don't.

Probably because he's terrible at climbing and not because he keeps looking for me for instruction and reassurance and *not* because he looks cute when he's nervous.

Absolutely not that.

Josh's hand slips and for the third time, I carefully lower him to the ground. He immediately falls to his ass.

He looks up at me. "How do you not hate this?"

I smirk. "I certainly didn't love it the first time I tried it, either. It's taken practice and time."

He groans and lies back, covering his eyes dramatically with the backs of his hands. *Why* do I want to know if he'd let me sit on his face right now?

Maybe I'll ask him about adding it to the syllabus. Some extra credit, if you will.

I sigh loudly, ensuring he knows I think he's being dramatic, and tap my foot impatiently next to him.

"Are you giving up?" I ask.

"Would you judge me if I did?" he says, a tone of resignation in his voice.

"I don't think it's a secret that I judge you for pretty much everything," I pause. "But I wouldn't judge you for that."

His fingers brush against my ankle, and it feels like every nerve ending in my body's been electrocuted.

It's a strange feeling; not bad, just foreign.

Nobody's ever reached out to me like this before, just to touch me. And that makes me feel things, and not the unbridled glee over the defeat he's experiencing like I should be.

I'm sad for him, feeling the frustration and self-judgment radiating off of him. If anyone gets to be dick to Joshua Henry, it's not him.

It's me.

"One more time," I tell him, my voice a little huskier from his touch. "Let's try to get to seven feet."

He groans, sitting up slowly, his legs still splayed out in front of him like a disgruntled toddler. I want to ask him to touch my ankle again, like I'm one of Jo's regency romance heroines and my ankle is a very sexy, very tempting part of my anatomy.

"Goddammit, Nicoletta, you're bossy." He grumbles, getting to his feet.

I put my hands on my hips and raise an eyebrow at him. "Okay, Mr. Dominant. You can't let the woman tell him what to do?" I bend over to double check the sandbag and make sure he's safe to climb.

He's silent, but I feel him behind me. He steps closer and suddenly his front is pressed against my ass. While I'm bent over. Considering how hard he is through his shorts, I know his dick is extra angry looking right now.

"If you're going to tell me what to do, Buttercup," he whispers, his beard brushing my earlobe, "I think I might like to be praised for doing it."

I straighten so fast I lose my balance, stumbling forward.

Josh chuckles and grabs my arm, steadying me. "So, eight feet?"

"I actually said seven-"

"Eight feet," he says, nodding his head as he tilts his head back to look up at the wall. "Let's go for eight feet."

And so he begins to climb as I stare up at him from the ground, my mouth hanging open.

He's going to kill me. Joshua Henry is going to kill me.

Maybe that was his plan all along.

"Nine feet!" Josh excitedly announces to Nellie as we leave the gym. "I made it *nine* feet."

It's like I'm not here. He's excitedly recounting his success to Nellie and Tyler, and even though I know it shouldn't, it stings. Why do I care if he's not paying attention to me? I shouldn't. It's nothing.

"Ready to go home?" I ask Jo.

"Actually, I'm grabbing drinks with Nellie and Tyler to discuss some visions they have for their wedding. We're hoping to find a venue that can accommodate November availability, so it's a rush. Are you good to go home alone?"

I swallow the lump growing in my throat, trying to push down the complex emotions and thoughts swimming in my head. "Of course, yeah. That's great."

Jo wraps her arms around me, giving me a tight squeeze that, in the past, has felt like it was putting me back together.

It doesn't tonight.

I feel a meltdown building. And the fact it's happening mere feet outside my happy place is simply unacceptable.

Nellie, Tyler, and Josh are still talking, so I turn around and start walking as fast as I can in the direction of our apartment. I don't even make it a block before I hear my name.

"Nic!"

Not again. Not. Again.

I walk faster, head down as I try to breathe as deeply and keep the tears streaming down my face out of view.

Of course I'm forced to stop at a traffic light, and he catches up to me.

"Nic, I just wanted to—" Josh freezes when I look up at him, tears streaming down my face.

"Please don't," I whisper. I hate that this is happening in front of him again.

"Shit." He looks so panicked, and it reminds me of how I felt when I brought over the wine, the fear he wouldn't be okay, that I'd hurt him.

But he couldn't feel that way.

It's Josh. It's me.

"What's going on?" Josh asks.

I shake my head and open my mouth, but all that comes out is a loud, shuddering sob. I cover my eyes with my palms, my shoulders heaving.

"Can I—can I hold you?" He asks cautiously.

I want to shake my head, to tell him to leave me alone, but I find myself nodding yes instead.

Immediately, his arms wrap around me, one around my waist and the other around my shoulders, pulling me tightly into his body. He's so soft, and he smells so good, like vanilla ice cream and a bonfire on a perfect summer night. Like comfort and safety.

He holds me as I sob into his shirt, forgetting for a moment he's Joshua Henry, the evil goblin who terrorized my childhood. He's just Josh, the man who, since coming back into my life, only touches me like I'm worth handling with care.

After a few minutes, I feel the waves begin to subside, and I'm able to regulate my breath and emotions. It hits me that I'm standing in the middle of a busy sidewalk weeping into someone's shirt. I make to pull away from Josh, but he doesn't let go, instead tightening his hold on me.

And god, it feels good. How does he know it feels good?

"I'm sorry," I mumble into Josh's shirt. "I need to stop making a habit of melting down in front of you. It's decidedly un-sexy."

He doesn't laugh. "I'm not going to say seeing you hurting is a turn on because it's obviously not, but this doesn't turn me off to you, either. You're a person, having a human experience." I feel him shrug his shoulders. "It's life."

I swallow. "That's a nice thing for you to say. Didn't know you had it in you."

He chuckles. "Right? I watched a YouTube video after you left last night on how not to be a complete jackass. Glad to know it worked."

I smile into his chest, inhaling his scent again. Safety. Comfort. Josh. And then my stomach sinks. I duck out of his arms and reach into my bra.

His eyes widen. "What are—"

"I lied," I admit. "There's no charge for guest passes. Nellie and I were just messing with you."

He blinks at me, and I wave the money at him.

"Take it. It doesn't feel right to take it from you anymore."

"I know it didn't cost anything, Nic," he says, and it's my turn to blink at him.

"You...what?" I stammer. "Then why didn't you say anything when I asked for your money?"

His cheeks flush the sweetest shade of pink, and *why* am I fighting the urge to lick that hue right off of him like it's icing on a cupcake?

"I didn't want to make it a thing."

I scowl and take a step forward so my nose brushes against his chest. I hear his breath stutter as I lift the hem of his NYU t-shirt and move my hand along the edge of his shorts before slipping the money into the waistband. "There," I say, stepping back.

He's staring at me like he's never seen me before, and it's unnerving. "Are you okay?" he asks.

"Are you asking me if I'm okay because I just gave your money back? Because that's a little rude."

"No, I'm asking if you're okay because you—" He rubs the back of his neck, like he doesn't know the right way to finish his thought.

"I had a meltdown," I said. "You can say that. It's a clinical term for a pretty common autistic trait."

"You had a meltdown," he finishes.

I should tell him I'm fine. Just smile and tell him I want him to make me come again at some point this week.

But I'm so tired.

"I—I'm always wiped out after this happens. Like achy and exhausted," I admit. "But I'm only two blocks from my apartment, and I'll take care of myself when I get home, so you don't have to worry."

Josh frowns at me and turns around, bending his knees. "Get on."

I eye the back of his head skeptically. "I beg your pardon?"

He sighs. "I'm giving you a piggyback ride back to your apartment, Buttercup."

My eyes widen. "No, you are *not*," I protest. But god, not having to walk right now sounds incredible. My legs feel like they might give out at any moment.

"Nicoletta," Josh says slowly and calmly. "Don't think I won't throw you over my shoulder if you don't get on my back."

I swallow hard, finding the image of Joshua Henry tossing me over his shoulder like a sack of potatoes far hotter than it has any right to be.

"Fine," I say, stepping toward him and wrapping my arms around his shoulders. He hooks his arms under my knees and straightens his back, lifting me off the ground. "Wow," I say, trying to keep my voice flat to hide my delight. "The air quality's better up here."

Josh chuckles. "Where do you live?"

I point in the direction of the apartment I share with Jo. As Josh treks down the street with me on his back, we're both relatively quiet.

Until my traitorous stomach growls.

Josh looks back at me over his shoulder. "Are you hungry?"

"No," I lie.

My stomach growls again. The traitor.

I can't see his face, but somehow I know he's trying to hide his smile. "Okay, you're not hungry. I, however, am famished, so I'm stopping at this hot dog cart to buy myself something to eat with this very nice extra forty dollars I recently came into."

"Hey," he says to the vendor. "I'm gonna have a dog with the works, and she'll have—" He squeezes the side of my knee.

"The same," I mutter. "And a can of Coke. Also three soft pretzels." If Josh is paying, I'm getting all of the free comfort food out of him that I can.

"Make that four pretzels and two Cokes," Josh says, sliding the cash across the surface. He gets the goods put into a plastic bag and passes it to me.

"You're in charge of these," he tells me as he starts to walk again. I spend the rest of our short trip wanting to eat my hot dog but knowing that would probably be rude, considering Josh paid, and then *panicking* because since when did I care about being rude to Joshua Henry?

He climbs up to the third floor with me still on his back, bending down so I can unlock the door and let us in.

"Are you—are you going to stay and eat?" I ask as I climb off his back, trying to come across as disinterested and aloof. That's new, having to intentionally act like I don't care.

"If it's okay with you," he replies, rubbing the back of his neck. I think he does this when he's feeling nervous, and I hate that he feels that way. The fact that I suddenly care about Josh's feelings is disorienting.

What is *wrong* with me?

"Sure." I pour our sodas into glasses with ice while Josh takes a seat on my couch. Holy shit, Josh is sitting on my couch. In my living room.

This is not how I thought I'd spend my night. I clear my throat as I walk into the living room, handing him his soda. "Here you go."

"Thanks."

I sit at the other side of the couch and immediately start spiraling. Am I sitting too close? Too far away? What should happen tonight? Should we just sit here in silence and eat our food and pretend we weren't screaming each other's names in ecstasy last night and that I didn't just meltdown?

Why isn't there a rule book about what to do after you and your enemy masturbate together and then he sees you have a sensory meltdown twenty-four hours later? I might be the only person who would get any use out of it, but it sure would be helpful right about now.

"Are you okay?" Josh and I both blurt out at the same time, looking at each other.

He grins at me, and I notice his eyes brighten when he does.

How despicable.

"I'm okay, Nic. Are you?" he prompts.

I nod and swallow the bite I had just taken while he was speaking. "I'm okay. Just worn out after that. But that's pretty much par for course."

"Do you want to put on *Ted Lasso*?"

And then I ask something I have absolutely no reason to care about. "Do you have a comfort TV show?"

"No, I don't," Josh says.

"Oh—" I start to say.

"I do have a comfort movie, though."

Chapter 14

Josh

Playlist: "Lay All Your Love On Me," Dominic Cooper, Amanda Seyfried

If you told me I'd be spending my Monday night eating hot dogs and pretzels with Nic on her couch while we watch my favorite movie, I would have thought it was a set-up to a weirdly hyper-specific joke.

"I can't believe your comfort movie is *Mamma Mia*," Nic says as the movie begins.

"Hey, it's a delightful movie. One of Meryl Streep's best roles," I argue. "*I* can't believe you've never seen it."

Nic takes a bite out of her hotdog and shrugs her shoulders as she chews. "I'm not really a musical person. Most straight men and I have that in common."

"I'm not straight," I say easily, taking a sip of my soda before leaning back. I see her freeze in my peripheral vision.

"That's- I shouldn't have assumed. I'm so sorry," she says, tripping over her words.

"It's fine," I tell her. Because, honestly, it is.

"It's not fine, Josh!" she insists, rotating her body so her legs are curled up and she's facing me. "I'm bi, and I was just no better than any homophobic—"

I grab her hand. "I know you didn't mean it. And now you know, and you don't care, do you?"

She looks at me, a horrified expression on her face. "Of course I care! Sexual identity is a vital part of one's personhood!" We blink at each other before she seems to understand. "Oh. No, it doesn't change the way I see you, if that's what you're saying." Her voice is soft, her eyes focused downwards on our hands.

"That's exactly what I'm saying." My thumb rubs firm circles on the back of her hand. I can feel her stress radiating off of her body, and I want to do whatever I can to help her relax.

"I'm not offended." I promise. Her eyes fill with tears, and my heart skips a few beats. "Nic, it's okay."

"I'm sorry this keeps happening."

"You have no reason to apologize."

"I—shit," she whimpers.

I don't know how I know what she's trying to say, but I do. I reach out for her, and she falls into me, turning so her back is pressed to my front. I tightly wrap my arms around her and pull her against me.

I hear her exhale and feel her body slowly begin to relax. "What's this movie about, anyway?" she asks after a few minutes of silence. "I think I missed the set up."

"That blonde who's singing is Sophie. She's currently telling her friends she sent wedding invitations to three different men she read about in her mom's diary. Given the timeline, she knows that one of them is her dad, but no one knows what she's done."

"Wild," Nic breathes, her eyes fixed on the TV. "So she just...invites them to her wedding?"

"She just invites them to her wedding," I confirm.

"But why not call them or visit or—?"

"She wants her dad to walk her down the aisle."

"But she doesn't *know* him, so it'll just be some stranger who happens to share her DNA walking her down the aisle. It doesn't make sense."

"It's a musical, Nicoletta," I sigh. "If it made sense, Colin Firth and Meryl Streep would not have agreed to be in it. It's nonsensical, and that's what makes it genius."

"I can see how it can be comforting," she says. "The music is fun, and Amanda Seyfried's hot."

"My grandma went to see the show on Broadway, and then introduced it to me when the movie came out. I was able to surprise her with tickets to it before it closed on Broadway a few years ago, too," I shrug, and my heart tugs at the memory. "It's important to me."

"You should get a *Mamma Mia* tattoo."

"I have a *Mamma Mia* tattoo."

Her head whips around, and her eyes widen as she looks at me over her shoulder. "You *do*?"

I blush and lift a hand to my t-shirt shirt sleeve, pushing the fabric up until it reveals the tattoo on the front of my shoulder. It's three envelopes with the names Sam, Harry, and Bill on them.

"Oh my god. That's amazing."

I narrow my eyes. "I can't tell if you're being sarcastic or not."

"No, no, I'm being serious. I think it's so cool that you love something so much you want it with you forever."

I smile shyly, caught off guard by her compliment. "Thank you."

She falls silent, and we watch the movie. It's nice. Normal.

But after forty-five minutes or so, when Sophie and her fiancé are pretty much doing a strip tease on the beach, Nic places her hand over mine and slowly drags it down her chest until I'm cupping her breast. "Is this okay?" she asks quietly, squeezing my hand.

I should probably hesitate, think rationally about this, but I don't.

Instead, I groan as I brush my thumb over her nipple. Her hand falls from mine as she gasps and leans her head against my shoulder.

I pluck at the taut peak, savoring the whimpers and breathy sighs my ministrations pull from her lips.

"More," she demands.

I groan and drop my forehead to hers as I slip my hand beneath her bra. "Like this?"

"Like that."

I gently run my fingertips over her hardened nipple. Her breath is so heavy, and I tighten my arm around her waist.

"What do you want, Nic?" I murmur, and she grabs onto my arm. Her nails are short, but that doesn't stop her from digging them into my skin, making me hiss from the sensation.

"I want you to touch me," she replies.

"Like this?" I ask, lifting my head and pressing my mouth to the pulse point on her neck.

"I want you to—" she stops, her heavy breaths filling the silence between us. I nip the sensitive skin of her neck with my teeth before chasing it with my tongue.

"Want me to?" I prompt in between wet, open-mouthed kisses.

"What you did last night—" she freezes again, and I move my hand from her breast to cup her cheek and gently turn her to me.

"Breathe," I tell her. She blinks at me, like she doesn't understand what I just said to her. "Do you want to come?"

She blushes and bites her lip. "Yes."

"How?" I prompt her, running my hand up and down her bare arm. "With my mouth? My hands? By grinding my cock against you or using your vibrator on you?"

She gasps, and narrows her eyes. "How did you know I have a vibrator?" she asks accusingly.

She's so flustered and annoyed, and it's fucking adorable. I chuckle and tap the tip of her nose with my fingertip. "So angry."

"How did you know?" she repeats, pushing my arms off of her and turning her body so she's sitting on her knees and facing me.

"You said so in the survey."

She blinks at me, "Oh. Right."

"Plus, since you said you've never come with another person, it made me feel better to think you at least took care of your pretty pussy with a good vibrator."

"You took care of me last night," she says. "You helped me. Can you do that again?"

"How, Nicoletta? I need you to tell me how you want me to take care of you tonight."

She doesn't respond, but her eyes are fixated on my mouth, her lids heavy and pupils dilated. "Has anyone ever gone down on you, Buttercup?" I ask gently.

Her eyes meet mine, and she swallows hard. "A few times. It didn't really feel like anything."

I frown. "I hate that no one ever made you come."

"Don't you dare feel bad for me," she snaps, eyes narrowing again. "I don't want your pity."

I look at her, bewildered. "I don't pity you, Nic. I pity every person who touched you and never got to feel you clench around them, because now that I know how that feels, I know exactly what they missed out on."

Her mouth drops open on a gasp.

"Lie back," I instruct, and she leans back, her head propped against the arm of the couch. I stand up and walk to the opposite end of the couch, bracing my hands on the arm and leaning over. "You want me to make you come like last night? All shaking and moaning?"

Her eyes are wide as she nods. "Yes, please."

"You've gotta ask, Buttercup."

She rolls her eyes. "Please make me come," she grumbles.

In one swift move, I lean further down the couch, grab her hips, and pull her to my end of the couch as I straighten. She squeals as she slides down to me, and I easily lift her hips and place her ass on the arm so her legs dangle. "Holy shit," she breathes.

I smirk at her before kneeling between her thighs and putting her legs over my shoulders. I press my mouth to her inner thigh over her shorts, sucking firmly.

"Oh fuck—*Josh*," she gasps as her hands tangle in my hair, scratching my scalp.

"Can I kiss you here?" I ask her gently, cupping her pussy with my hand, gently grinding the heel of my hand into her. "I'd love nothing more than to taste you."

"Yes," she sighs, arching her back and lifting her hips to make it easier for me to slide off her shorts.

Her panties are plain white cotton today, and fuck, it's so simple and innocent, and I can see her curls through the fabric, already wet just over her entrance. I groan and tense my hands on her thighs, leaning in and licking her over the cotton in one firm stroke.

Nic's hips jerk. "Fuck!"

I grab her hips, tight enough my fingers dig into her soft flesh. I indulge my selfish need for more of her sounds and flatten my tongue to stroke up her covered slit again, fastening my lips around her clit and giving her a long, firm suck.

"Josh!" she cries, her heels digging into my back as I hold her hips down. I've heard Nic say my names a dozen different ways. She's said it in annoyance, frustration, and anger, but this broken, needy way is by far my favorite.

"Panties off?" I ask, pressing featherlight kisses to her inner thighs.

She answers by lifting her hips and beginning to frantically peel the fabric off. I grab her ass to support her as she shimmies them off, kicking them somewhere behind me when they reach her ankles.

I gingerly run my fingers through the curls covering her entrance, and she shivers. "I'm going to need you to tell me if something's not working," I say, and she lifts her head to meet my eyes. "If it's not, it doesn't mean there's something wrong with you. You just need something else, and I want to be able to give that to you."

"Okay," she says quietly, her hand making its way into my hair again.

I part her and stifle a groan. She's so wet already, her clit swollen and pink. I lower my head and press a firm, closed mouth kiss to her. "No freckles down here," I muse.

"Disappointed?" she pants.

"No. Because there's so many other places for me to kiss. Like right here." I part my lips and suck her clit between them. She cries out, fisting my hair as she arches her back. She tastes better than I'd dreamed, sweet and musky and familiar and yet also brand new...so Nic.

I break contact with her skin, and she immediately whimpers and fists my hair, attempting to push my head into that place between her thighs again. "In a minute, pretty girl," I murmur, massaging her thighs. "Can I put a finger inside you?"

"Can you do two again?" Nic asks, her breath heavy and labored, her eyes screwed shut and tangled tendrils of curls spread out around her.

I do as she asks, fucking her with my fingers while flicking my tongue against her swollen clit, both of us lost to her pleasure.

"I—I—" Nic cries, her hands tightening in my hair, pressing me somehow even closer to her.

I want to be closer to her, need to be as close as I can be to this beautiful, menacing woman.

My name escapes from her lips on a rough, hoarse cry as she tightens around my fingers, a rhythmic pulsing I swear my heartbeat somehow matches.

"There she is," I murmur against her, before sucking her throbbing clit again.

"Fuck shit damn fuck motherfucker fuck fuck," she gasps, forcefully shoving my head from her. "*Fuck.*"

I straighten and wipe my mouth with the back of my hand. She lifts herself on her elbows, and her eyes meet mine, glowing and warm with satisfaction. I look deeply into her eyes as I suck her orgasm off of my fingers, one at a time. Her eyes widen and she whimpers. "Fuck," she repeats. "I'm sorry I pushed you. My clit is so sensitive right after I come, it almost hurts."

I pull my finger out of my mouth with a pronounced *pop*. "You don't have to apologize. I told you to tell me if something wasn't good, and you did." I pause. "Could you feel that?" I surprise myself at the depth of my voice, how husky and raw with my arousal it is.

Her brow furrows. "What?"

"Before, you said that it didn't really feel like anything when a partner went down on you. Did that feel like anything?"

She groans in annoyance as she drags the arch of her foot onto my shoulder, using her deceptively strong legs to push me away. "Goddammit," she grumbles. "You ruined it." I bite my lip, as I sit back on my heels, and she moves her remaining leg from my shoulder. "I like you so much better when your mouth is doing other things that don't include making cocky comments."

I raise an eyebrow. "What kind of other things?" I ask.

She groans again, loud and dramatic, as she throws her arm over her eyes. "Don't make me say it," she whines.

I chuckle and stand up, my eyes catching between her thighs. I want to make her make those noises again. Her cries, her whimpers...they're the best sounds I've ever heard. "I won't make you say it. Tonight," I tease gently.

She sits up again, and reaches toward my erection. "Do you want me to—"

"I have to get to Port Haven early tomorrow," I lie, taking a step away from her. As I bend over and clean our trash from the coffee table, I feel her eyes on me.

"I'm not bad at it," she says softly. "I've gotten positive feed-back before."

I stand up so fast I almost get dizzy. "No, that's—I have no doubt about your ability to give pleasure, Nic."

Her curls are mussed, and she has a hickey on her neck, which I love, but she looks sad, which I hate.

"Can I sit down?" I ask carefully. She nods and pulls her legs to her, resting her chin on her kneecaps. I sit next to her, and try so fucking hard not to dwell on the fact she's naked from the waist down. "Did you read the syllabus?"

She looks at me from the corner of her eye. "Yeah? Oral isn't listed for a while, but I'm a fast learner."

I bite my lip in an attempt to hide the delighted smile that wants to escape. "You are. And I just—sex isn't always reciprocal. I'm not doing this so you'll get me off—I'm doing this to help you learn about your body and desires. I don't want you to touch me because you think you have to. We can explore it in the future, but first I want you to just focus on yourself and what makes you feel good."

I reach out and grip a curl between my forefinger and thumb, gently pulling it and watching it bounce back into shape. "Are you okay if I go home?"

"I'm okay," she says, and I lean toward her, pressing my lips to her forehead. Her breath stutters as I touch her, and for a moment, I indulge myself, believing it's because she likes me.

"I'll text you in the morning," I say, my lips moving against her forehead. I don't want to separate from her just yet. "Nellie would have my balls if I didn't."

Nic is silent, and I force myself to break the kiss and stand up. After I throw the trash away and load the dishwasher, I open the door to leave. "What are you doing?" she asks suddenly.

I pause and look back at her. She's kneeling on the couch, her arms resting on the back as she looks curiously at me, "I'm going home."

"I know that. Why are you doing *this*? Why are you acting like this? So kind?"

It feels like she's accusing me of having some ulterior motive, but her head is tilted, her eyes light, so maybe she's just genuinely curious.

"I don't want to hurt you, Nic," I say, rubbing my knuckles over my jaw. "I'm gonna do what I can to keep us safe."

Nic bites her lip. "That's—thank you. I'm too tired to be angry or suspicious right now, which I'll probably regret in the morning. But not now." She yawns as if to illustrate her point. "Text me when you get home?"

I smile softly. "I will. Goodnight, Buttercup."

"Goodnight, Joshy."

I close the door behind me and let out a long breath. This was the first time I've had sex with the same person twice. I've always avoided it.

Then Nic Quinn came along and made me rethink everything I thought I knew.

And then she called me Joshy.

After sleeping with some past partners, they began calling me Joshy. As if having access to my body meant they knew me well enough to call me a name that only my parents and a select few others have ever used.

Nic saying it feels different than anyone else. Like I got to a part of *her* that makes her open up to me, makes her feel the same intimacy and closeness between us that I do.

I don't hate it.

Chapter 15

Josh

**Playlist: "Soon You'll Get Better," Taylor Swift,
The Chicks**

> **Josh:** Nic- Attached is a link to a survey.
> I want to do a check-in since we're two
> weeks into class. Please send it back at
> your earliest convenience. -J.H.

> **Nic:** yes, daddy.

Josh: Respectfully, fuck off. -J.H.

Josh: Take the damn survey and keep Daddy out of your mouth. -J.H.

Nic: well considering i haven't given you that blowjob yet…

Josh: Jesus Christ.

Josh: Can you wait until I'm back in the city to be a complete menace? Thank you.

Nic: wowww i pissed you off so much you didn't include your initials. who even is this?

Seen by Josh Henry at 3:23pm

"Who are you talking to that has you smiling like that?"

I jump and fumble my phone, face flushing. "No one," I say way too quickly to come across as even a little bit believable.

Grandma raises her eyebrow from the hospital bed we set up for her when she came home a few weeks ago. The e-reader I bought her so she could easily have her favorite historical romances on demand is settled on her lap. "Bullshit," she says simply, replacing her reading glasses and bringing the e-reader closer to her face.

My cousin Tara, who is sitting on the other side of the bed, snorts, covering her mouth with her hand. I scowl at her and flip her the finger, since Grandma's busy reading. "I saw that, Joshy," Grandma says, not looking up from her historical romance.

Tara sticks her tongue out at me, and I roll my eyes. Tara and I are the black sheep of the family, me the kid with dead parents, and Tara being, well, a flaming lesbian.

Black sheep we may be, but we're the only ones who've consistently visited Grandma since she got sick. Even since she moved home for hospice. Tara and her wife, Belen, visit multiple times a week, and I come every weekend, spending as much time with her as I can. Today though, it's just Tara, Grandma, and me.

I notice a bouquet of flowers on the windowsill, pretty daisies and carnations with sprigs of baby's breath. "Those are nice." I nod toward the flowers. "Who sent them?"

"Oh! Do you remember Aria and Sean Quinn? They go to Our Lady of Hope, too."

My feet, which I'd propped on the end of the bed, fall to the ground in my shock. Grandma doesn't notice, smiling brightly at the flowers.

"They came to visit a few days ago, and Aria showed me how to pull Bridgerton up on the Netflix if I want. Isn't that nice? They actually said they're going to stop by this afternoon before dinner."

First, it was Nic making a comment about not giving me a blow job. Now her parents are supposedly showing up?

Just my luck.

"So nice," I wheeze nervously. I see Tara side-eyeing me from her perch on the recliner. "I'm going to grab a snack. Do you need anything?"

"No, dear," Grandma says happily, her eyes running over her e-reader screen. "I'm feeling just peachy."

I mean. I'm not sure how one feels peachy while living through the late stages of metastasized lung cancer, but I let that little detail slide. She's been sick for over a year. More than a year of ups and downs, hope and despair, with no end—good or bad—in sight. Until that day two months ago, when the doctor told us treatment was no longer working, and Grandma made the decision to enter into hospice. Tara and I begged her not to. At first it felt like she was giving up, but she wanted to go home. She wanted to spend whatever time she has left in the place she'd lived and loved for most of her life. I shake the thought out of my head and get up from my chair, stopping at the head of the bed to kiss Grandma's forehead before leaving the room.

Of course, that's when the doorbell rings.

It feels like hives break out all over my body as I open the door, hands shaking. On the doorstep stands Sean and Aria Quinn.

Sean is tall with auburn hair sprinkled with gray throughout, deep green eyes that are crinkled in the corners and freckles all over his face. Next to him is Aria, short with shoulder length curly dark hair. She and Nic have the same brown eyes, and so much of her face reminds me of her daughter.

Hey guys, good to see you. I know your daughter, and was actually making her scream my name, what, forty-eight hours ago? Anyway, thanks for visiting my grandma while she slowly dies. Means a lot.

"Are you Myrtle's boy?" Sean asks after I greet them, shaking my hand.

I try to smile, but I am one thousand percent certain that it appears as more of a grimace. "Yep. Josh Henry."

Sean smiles at me, and dear god he has the same smile as Nic. *Fuck fuck fuck.*

"You're all grown up!" Sean says, beaming. "I remember when you were just a kid." He looks at his wife. "Ari, wasn't he in someone's class?"

Aria laughs. "Nic's, I think." She beams at me. "We have eight kids. It's hard to keep track of who's who sometimes."

I laugh awkwardly and shove my hands into my pockets. "Yeah, Nic and I went to elementary school together. If you'll excuse me, I'm just going to run to the kitchen and grab a bite to eat," I say, hoping I can escape. "I know you've visited her before, so you know your way around?

"We're all set, sweetie," Aria says kindly, her warm brown eyes kind, and I wonder if Nic has ever looked as friendly and non-threatening. "Take all the time you need for yourself. Take this to the kitchen and put it in the oven at three-fifty for forty-five minutes." She shoves a tray of food that seemingly appeared out of nowhere into my arms. "We're looking forward to spending some time with your grandma."

We exchange hugs, and I walk away, frustrated that Nic is living in my mind rent free, especially as my grandmother is dying.

That night, I'm on a late train back to the city, attempting to read a chapter of a Tessa Dare book, when I get a text from Nic.

Nic: I did your survey thing.

Nic: [Link]

I open the link, but instead of the survey I sent out, the "Never Gonna Give You Up" music video plays.

I guess I deserve that after doing the same to her on my birthday.

Josh: Nic- Very Funny. -J.H.

Nic: ooh, i got a VERY funny. that feels monumental to me.

Josh: Whatever helps you sleep at night. -J.H.

Nic: actually, orgasms help me sleep at night.

Nic: do you want the actual link.

Josh: After that, not particularly, no. -J .H.

Nic: ok.

Nic: [link]

Despite my annoyance, my curiosity gets the better of me and I open the survey. It's pretty basic, just checking in with her satisfaction levels, making sure she's comfortable with how things have been going between us and seeing if she has any comments or suggestions for what to do next.

She does.

I'm not sure *why* I have the audacity to be surprised by her strong feelings, but here we are.

In all caps, she responded to my question about future lessons with four words: BONDAGE AND BLOW JOBS.

Josh: Well, that's educational. -J.H.

Nic: <tongue out emoji>

Josh: I'm not getting paid enough for this. -J.H.

Nic: are you free on monday?

Josh: Not Monday, but Wednesday? Bring something that you like for dinner. -J.H.

Nic: yes, daddy.

Josh: I'm going to block your number. -J.H.

Nic: no you won't.

Nic: see you wednesday night <kiss emoji>

I sigh and scrub at my eyes with the heels of my hands. Nicoletta Quinn has shaved years off my life.

But honestly, my mind is already swimming with ideas of bondage and blow jobs.

Maybe an expedited demise is worth it.

Chapter 16

Nic

Playlist: "You Matter To Me," Drew Gehlig, Jessie Mueller

Quiblings Group Chat

Alex: nic when did you stop going to sunday dinner.

Ren: almost two months ago, i think.

Nic: wow, okay, judas??

Ren: <shrug emoji>

Kat: can't this be done outside of the group chat so we don't all have to get notifications for something that doesn't involve everyone?

Izzy: nic suddenly not showing up for dinner def involves all of us.

Millie: shut up, kat.

Jo: yeah, shut up kat.

Kat Holt has left the group chat.

Leo: what's her problem?

Jo: her husband probably.

Alex: can we focus? nic. why aren't you going home for sunday dinner anymore?

Nic: kat was onto something, why does this matter????

Ren: because mom gets sad during grace when she prays for you.

Millie: cuz no one laughs at dad's lame jokes anymore so he's telling even worse ones.

Alex: because mom asked me to move home because she misses me and i think she actually just misses you???

Izzy: because i got a new goldfish and you haven't met him yet.

Nic: I'm busy, okay? No one gets on jo's case and she only goes biannually.

Jo: dragging me into this seems like super unnecessary but ok.

Nic: i can't do this right now.

Nic: i'm sorry.

I wake up late on Wednesday, meaning I'm not able to get to the gym before heading into the office. Considering today is awful and movement always makes life feel a little less overwhelming, it's extremely unfortunate.

"Nicolette," Brooks says as he walks into my office without knocking. I clench my teeth as I pull my headphones off. "Danny and I are going to take care of the project Mitchell assigned you, okay? The one with the data from Florida?"

Until last week, all of my coworkers had called me Nic, which makes a lot of sense. It is, after all, how I introduce myself, what my desk plate says, and how I sign my emails.

For the past week, however, Brooks and Danny have been doing this cute thing where they call me Nicky, Nicolette, Nicole, even Nickel one time. Basically anything that isn't my name but kind of sounds like my name. I know they're doing it to bother me because Alyssa laughs behind her hand every time they do it.

Technically, I'm their boss. I don't act like it a lot of the time because asserting myself isn't my forte, but this sucks.

I swallow. "I asked you to look further into the discrepancies from the study done at Columbia," I say, my voice wavering.

He waves his hand at me dismissively. "Don't worry about it. We'll do it after we take care of the Florida case."

"The Columbia data is time sensitive, and I asked you to do it a week ago," I say, my voice not much louder than a whisper.

"Thanks, Nat," Brooks says, winking and shutting my office door behind him.

I lean back in my chair and take a shaky breath. The Columbia data is important. The basis of a lot of the projects we have planned for the rest of the year are based on the results.

However, it's not necessary for me to be the one who works on it, which is why I assigned it to my team. As a supervisor, my time and expertise are better spent elsewhere.

Like on the Florida data, which my boss, Mitchell, asked me to analyze. I'm sick of coworkers undermining me, thinking they know more than I do, despite my experience, education, and long history of success in the field. It makes me feel inferior, like what I do doesn't matter when I know it does.

It used to, at least.

I'm fighting back tears when I look at the clock and see that it's 4:30. I'm supposed to work until 5:00, so I pull my phone out and shoot a quick text to Mitchell, asking if it's okay if I duck out thirty minutes early. His response is immediate and encouraging, so I grab my bag before hustling out of the office, not saying goodbye to anyone.

An hour later, I'm standing on Josh's doorstep for our lesson tonight, shopping bag in hand. As much as I hate to admit it, Josh indeed is very skilled in the bedroom. If anything can get me out of my head, it's an orgasm from him.

He opens the door moments later, his face spreading into a smile. It makes me feel all warm and gooey inside, like a fresh baked chocolate chip cookie.

How embarrassing.

"Hey," he says.

"Hello," I reply, shoving the overpriced bag of food from Whole Foods into his chest as I push past him into the house. "We're cooking tonight."

"Uh," he says, closing the door behind me, as I continue deeper into the house. "That's fine. We can cook, what do you—"

"Pancakes. I want pancakes," I interrupt, stopping once I reach the kitchen. "It hasn't been a good day, and pancakes always made me feel better when I was a kid and—" I take a deep breath, frustrated at how shaky it is. "I just want pancakes."

Josh steps into the kitchen, standing across the island from me. He puts the bag on the counter and pulls out the pancake mix and other ingredients I'd brought. "Are you okay?" he asks suddenly.

"I don't matter," I say, surprising myself with my honesty.

He doesn't look at me, but his shoulders tense as he separates the ingredients on the island. "That's not true."

"No, it is. My family's upset that I'm not coming home as often because I'm an absent sibling, not because they appreciate, or hell, even know me as a person. I matter to them because we share DNA." I wrap my arms around myself and squeeze, feeling an overwhelming wave of sadness that I fight to keep inside. "Not because I'm...me. It's despite me being me."

Josh hasn't said anything, so I continue. "And then at work—" I scoff and roll my eyes. "God, anyone could do my job. I'm a pushover and I—"

"Nic," Josh walks around the island so he's next to me, pulling me into his arms and squeezing me tightly to his chest. The pressure is calming, but the fact that he knew what I needed and did it without me having to ask sends me over the edge.

I begin to cry and bury my face in his chest. Apparently this is just what I do now. He smells so good, like the best candle, all smoky and vanilla and, god, he's so soft. I want to sink into his body because for some reason, I know I'd be safe there.

"You matter," Josh says, pressing his lips to the crown of my head. "And I'm so sorry people haven't done a good job of showing you, because, fuck, Nic. You're a thorn in my side, but you're my favorite thorn. Like the kind on a rose."

I laugh through my tears. "You're just saying that."

"Why would I just say that?"

"So I'll have sex with you."

I know he's rolling his eyes, despite not being able to see it. "I'm saying it because it's true. And the fact that you don't know it's true isn't fair."

I wrap my arms around his center, and his hands find their way to my hair, softly caressing my curls and grounding me. I turn my head and press my ear over his heart, the gentle beat calming me as I try to match my breaths to his.

"I have chocolate chips. If you like chocolate chip pancakes," Josh tells me, his voice thick.

I sniffle. "I do like chocolate chip pancakes."

"Nic," He tilts my chin up until our eyes meet, and he moves his hand to tuck a curl behind my ear. "You're really fucking important," he says, his voice husky and low. "You matter a lot. To a lot of people." He pauses, like he's trying to decide whether or not to continue. "To me," he says, air whooshing out of him, like he's confessing to a heinous crime.

My embrace around him tightens. "I do?"

He leans down and nuzzles my nose with his, and *oh god* his mouth is so close to mine. Does he taste like vanilla too, or is he minty?

Jesus, Nicoletta. Keep it in your pants.

"You do," he affirms. "Do you really not know how much I enjoy spending time with you?"

My head is swimming. For over twenty years, I'd thought Josh Henry was the worst person to ever exist. And now that I'm actually getting to know him, I'm learning that he's kind and genuine. I don't know what to do with that. How to accept that I could possibly be wrong and to truly let him in.

"That's just because you like making me come," I answer, deflecting and sticking out my lower lip.

He chuckles, cozy and vibrant, and it somehow warms me from the inside out. "I *do* really like making you come," he agrees. "But I also like Rickrolling you . And hearing about your job, and how much you love climbing and *Ted Lasso*. You're funny and smart and—" He inhales deeply. His breath is hot against me as he cups my cheek, shaky and possibly as unsure as I feel.

I stand on my tiptoes, wrapping my arms around his neck. "Thank you," I whisper. "I don't know if I believe you, but those are all very kind things for you to say."

His hands stroke down my back and wrap around my waist, squeezing me against him, just the way my body screams for. "I wish you believed me, but I'll just keep saying it until you do."

"It's pretty fortuitous you happened to have chocolate chips tonight. These are good," I say, dipping a forkful of chocolate chip pancakes into Josh's homemade chocolate sauce.

"Yeah," Josh agrees, eyes focused on his plate. He takes a bite of pancakes, and I don't miss the blush that colors his cheeks like cherry blossoms.

He's such a damn goober.

The most thoughtful and kind and gentle and sexy goober that ever goobered.

What is happening to me??

Josh clears his throat as he looks over at me. "So, I read your survey."

I shift awkwardly. Joshua Henry has seen me pretty much naked and touched me all over my body. He's said the filthiest words to me and made me unravel with his mouth and his hand, but knowing he read that I liked it all? It's anxiety-inducing.

"Oh?"

"We don't have to do anything tonight," Josh adds, his voice softening. "Not if you don't want to. I think, or at least I hope you know that by now. But If you want to—" He trails off.

"Do you still want to?" I interrupt. "Or did me crying turn you off?"

"Nic," he says, his face serious. "You being human and having human experiences is not a turn off. I promise. That's something else I'll keep telling you until you believe it."

Why the fuck does that make me feel giddy? Like lie on my back on my bed and kick my feet in the air like I'm in a 90s rom-com giddy?

Something else to unpack in therapy with Maria, some other day.

"Do you want me to make you come? Would that help you feel better?" he asks, his eyes burning into mine. Something about his eyes are hypnotizing, making me want to let him into every deep, dark corner of myself I've tried so desperately to keep people out of.

"How many times are you planning on making me come?" I bite my lip, proud of myself for being a little dirty.

A wicked grin spreads across his face as he understands what I'm asking. "I'd like to see four. I really, really like making you come, Buttercup."

I swallow hard. "Four? That—that's twice as many times as I've ever come in one go."

His smile widens diabolically, and he nods his head. My stomach flutters in response, and I don't hate it. "I know."

I lick my lips, rubbing my thighs together in a fruitless attempt to relieve the ache he's responsible for. He valiantly attempts not to look but fails almost immediately. His Adam's apple bobs, and god, how is that lump in his throat so fucking sexy? I want to touch it, to lick, to bite it.

"So," I say, shifting in my seat, trying to get myself under control. "How do you plan on making me come? What does the syllabus say? Your tongue? Your fingers?"

His expression changes quickly, becoming serious again. "I wanted to talk to you about that."

My stomach sinks and my mind spirals. He's changed his mind. He wants me to leave and go home and make myself come with my vibrator and-

"In your initial survey, as well as in the updated one, you expressed interest in bondage. In, uh, in being tied up. Is that still something that you want to try?"

My breath becomes strained and heavy, like breathing is an Olympic sport I haven't trained for.

"Yes," I respond, my voice low and nervous. "I've never tried it, but I'd like to."

I stare at his throat as he swallows. God, what the fuck is wrong with me? Why am I so attracted to his damn throat? It's literally just a throat.

"Before we begin, you know I take communication and consent extremely seriously, but bondage is on a different level. Constant communication and consent is mandatory, for both of us. I like to use a rating system, to check in with my partner periodically. It's like a stop light: 'Green' means all is well and we can continue as is, 'yellow' means to readjust, and 'red' means to immediately stop. Does that work?"

"Yes," I affirm.

"This applies to both of us, so if either of us says 'red,' we stop. No shame, no fear. We cuddle, get chocolate milk, and maybe I'll make you watch *10 Things I Hate About You* if you feel up to it."

This makes me smile a little. "Okay," I agree, twisting my hands in my lap, "How...um, how—"

"How would this work?" he finishes my thought, and I nod. "If you're done eating, I'd love to take you upstairs and show you."

I am indeed done eating, so I stand up, gathering the plates and silverware we'd used. "Okay, let me take care of—"

"I'll take care of it after you leave, Nic," Josh says, placing his hand over mine. His voice seems strained, and a quick look at his pants confirms my suspicions—he wants me like I want him. It's all part of our arrangement, but will I ever get used to us wanting each other like this? "Come upstairs with me. Please."

I take his hand, intertwining my fingers with his, and let him lead me to his bedroom on the third floor. As we walk through the doorway, I freeze as I see what's laid out on the bed. He lets go of my hand and goes in before me, picking up the wand vibrator from the foot of his bed. I gulp, and whether it's out of anxiety or pure thrill, I don't know.

Before Josh, sex was just something I did because I felt like I was supposed to. It was basic and quick, sometimes penetration was involved, and other times just fingers or tongues. No one seemed to care how I felt during sex or prioritized my pleasure or wellbeing.

I thought that's the way it was, and maybe it is for most people, but Josh sending me surveys and putting my desires and curiosity first is—well, it's a lot.

"You've only used toys alone, right?" Josh asks gently, sensing my unease. He runs his grip up and down the handle of the wand, my eyes tracking his hand.

I nod, my eyes following the movements of his hand. "Only alone."

He nods. "And you haven't used restraints?"

"No." Velcro straps are attached to the bed. A smoldering heat spreads throughout my entire body, settling in my lower belly as what he has planned for me sinks in.

"Do you want me to restrain you tonight?" he asks softly.

I worry my lower lip between my teeth. Fantasizing about it is one thing—seeing that your fuck buddy has a whole thing planned is another. Glancing up at him, I ask, "Can you explain what you're thinking, please?"

"I'm thinking about how fucking pretty you'll look tied to my bed, blindfolded while I make you come over and over again with this," he says casually, tapping the wand against his open palm, like my panties aren't drenched and I'm not struggling to keep myself upright after those words.

"I think I'd like to try," I say.

His eyes search mine. "Are you sure? You aren't going to upset or disappoint me if you say no."

I can't find it in me to look away. "Yes." My voice is a little stronger, a little more self-assured. "I'm nervous, but I trust you. I want to try."

A sly smile lifts his lips, and he tilts his head to the side. "Why don't you go ahead and take your clothes off then, Buttercup?"

Chapter 17

Nic

Playlist: "Chains," Nick Jonas

I hate how hot Josh is when he tells me what to do. To his credit, he definitely knows better than to tell me what to do outside of sex. I didn't ever know consent could be as hot as he makes it. I know it's necessary, and everyone says it's hot, but I'd never understood it that way until now.

I obey wordlessly and pull my blouse over my head before reaching behind me to unclip my bra. The way Josh's eyes dilate as the fabric falls to the ground makes me think everyone who made fun of my small bra size was wrong. Maybe my breasts are just fucking right.

I feel Josh's eyes on me as I bend over to slide my pants and confidence underwear down my legs and over my feet. After I take off my socks, I straighten up, completely naked in front of his searching eyes.

Josh looks at me like I'm the greatest thing he's ever seen, like he can't quite get enough of me. I'm breathless knowing he wants me as much as I want him.

"Is this okay?" I ask, shifting my weight between my feet.

"*So* okay," Josh murmurs, lifting his eyes to mine again. "You're exquisite, Nicoletta."

His voice is husky, and god, I'm so embarrassingly wet right now. He takes a step toward me and cups my waist, such a soft gesture it makes me want to cry. I almost don't notice that he calls me by my full name, but I do notice how right it sounds when he says it, how different it feels now.

He tilts my chin up with a knuckle. "Do you want to lie down for me?" His voice is the perfect combination of firm and soft, of demanding and asking, and my knees tremble from the effect.

I nod, backing toward the bed. Josh stands at the edge as I sit on the side and swing my legs onto the mattress. I lie on my back, a pillow beneath my head, and fold my hands over my belly as I gaze up at the ceiling. I tilt my head to the side as I realize it's covered with the same stick-on stars I had as a kid. I want to ask but don't, allowing this to be another mystery of Josh that...makes me like him even more?

Who even *am* I anymore?

I stare up at the stars, and I wonder if this sense of calm washing over me is similar to the way Josh feels when he's fixated on my freckles. If so, I get it. I take some deep, centering breaths, and damn, my therapist would be so proud of me.

Josh is standing next to the bed on the side closest to the door, fluffing the pillow beneath my head. "Are you comfortable?" he asks. "Do you need another pillow, or want me to get rid of this one?"

I try to ignore the fluttering fruit flies in my stomach, making their way to my heart. "This is good."

His breath is heavy. "I'm going to restrain your left hand first, okay?"

"Okay." Josh covers my hands with one of his, strong and solid and warm. He squeezes my hand and gently moves my left arm, extending it and slipping my wrist through the restraint before fastening the velcro.

"Is it too tight?"

"No," I answer. He releases my wrist, and I look to my left, taking in my arm extended up and to the side, restrained so my movements are inhibited.

It's kind of hot.

No, that's not right.

It's *extremely* hot.

Josh continues to restrain my limbs, moving to my feet first and ending with my right hand. I feel so exposed, spread out like this, in the most thrilling way. He can see all of me.

He strokes my hair and looks down at me, his eyes dark with lust and bright with something I can't identify.

"So goddamn pretty," he praises me, his eyes scanning up and down my body, drinking me in. "Are you feeling okay?"

"Green," I respond immediately.

Josh chuckles, playfully pulling on a ringlet. "You're an eager little thing, aren't you?"

I bite my lip and feel my face heat as I duck my head to the side to hide myself. Josh clasps my chin in his hand, gently turning my face back to the side and up until our eyes meet. "Don't be shy, Buttercup," he says gently. "I want your enthusiastic consent."

He holds up a blue satin scarf that matches his eyes, and it feels like the fruit flies are dancing the Cotton-Eyed-Joe.

I nod. "Yes. Please."

"Lift your head," Josh tells me, and I oblige. As he ties the scarf over my eyes, he asks me to tell him what our agreed upon rating system is.

"Such a good girl," he praises when I answer correctly, rolling my right nipple between his fingers roughly. I squeal and jolt in response. Not knowing where his hands are and what he's going to do next makes my head spin.

"I'm going to check in with you consistently, but I need you to say 'yellow' or 'red' whenever you need to, okay? It won't change things between us or disappoint me. We'll just figure something else out that works for us. Promise me, Nic."

"I promise," I answer. He reaches over my body and pinches my left nipple, surprising me again, and my body arches off the bed. "*Fuck!*"

I hear a click and something liquid being squeezed out of a tube.

He parts me gently with his fingers, and presses the lubed wand right over my clit. He turns the vibrator on at a low vibration, and I mewl at the sensation.

"Fuck, Nic," Josh curses, his free hand somehow tangling in my hair. I'll never understand tall people and their freakishly long limbs. "I wish you could see yourself right now. All spread out for me, a vibrator on your swollen cunt. Blushing and wet, just for me."A whimper in response is all I can manage at the moment.

"I'm going to turn it up two levels. You know what to say if it's too much."

I nod my head eagerly and hear the buttons click again as the vibrations get stronger against my already throbbing clit.

"Color?"

"Green," I moan, grasping the arm restraints and pulling against them as my back arches off the bed.

"That's my girl," Josh says, and I can hear the smile in his voice, despite his ragged breathing. His fingers are still playing with my hair, his nails dragging gently across my scalp, twirling and pulling my curls so they bounce back into shape. It's soothing.

But I don't want soothing from him. Not right now.

"More," I gasp. "Please, Josh. I need more." My whole body feels like it's on fire, desperate for relief.

Josh groans, a broken, aching sound, and god, I love that I'm doing that to him. "Fuck me."

He presses the buttons twice more, and I grind myself against the wand. His fingers stroke down the side of my face until his index and middle fingers are pressing against my barely parted lips. I open my mouth, and he moans as I suck and twirl my tongue around his fingers. "Fuck, Nic," he rasps. "You're so good. So, so good."

I whimper, skin blazing from chasing the feeling that's so close, yet still beyond my reach.

"Do you like having your hair pulled?" Josh asks, slipping his fingers from my mouth.

"Never. Tried," I gasp. I'm close. I just need—god, I don't know what I need.

"Would you like to try?"

"Yes!" I cry, pretty much willing to try almost anything if it might help me come right now.

At my consent, Josh's hand is in my hair again, this time taking a fistful of curls and tugging right at my scalp.

I scream, my body thrashing against the restraints as I completely and totally free fall. He removes the vibrator from my body and presses his hand firmly on my pelvic bone. I'm gasping and crying, twisting and contorting in ways I never knew possible.

"You're magnificent when you come for me, Buttercup," Josh murmurs as I catch my breath and begin to come down from my high. He eases his grip on my hair. "I want to watch you fall apart like that all night."

"Ohmangyoddhg...," I garble incoherently.

He chuckles, running the backs of his fingers up and down my arm. "Once you're able to form words, can you give me a color?"

"Yellow-ish green," I gasp, a few moments later, words finally feeling possible again.

"Okay," Josh says. I feel him kneel on the ground, right next to my head, as he begins to stroke my hair so gently and attentively it would be irritating if it wasn't exactly what I needed after orgasming so hard I could smell sounds. "Talk to me, pretty girl."

"I want to keep going," I tell him. "I'm always so sensitive after coming, to the point that clit stimulation is painful, like I told you. I need some time to recover before you do that again."

"You did such a good job telling me what you need," Josh murmurs, pressing his lips to my temple. One of his hands finds mine and knits our fingers together. He firmly massages and squeezes my hand as he kisses my face, using his other hand to play with my hair. He's murmuring quiet words of praise and validation, and it's perfect, just the right combination of stimulation, tenderness, and rest.

Naturally, it only takes a few minutes until I ache for him again.

"Josh?"

"Mmm?" he responds, his nose nuzzling the side of my head.

"Green."

Josh reacts immediately, getting to his feet and using the wand to part the curls between my thighs. "We'll start at the lowest setting and build up again, okay?" he asks.

"Oka—oh *god*," I moan as the vibrations begin. I feel it everywhere in my body, in my tender breasts and lower belly, in my curling toes and fingertips grabbing onto the sheets. "Oh, fuck, Josh. Fuck, that's good."

He keeps his hands busy, between pinching and pulling at my nipples to lovingly stroking my face and hair, to pulling my hair. Despite the vibrator being at such a low setting, the stimulation has me screaming his name in minutes. Stars are sparkling behind the blindfold, and I feel disoriented in the best way possible.

Josh presses his lips to my temple as I come down from another soul-sucking orgasm. "You're doing amazing. *You're* amazing."

"Ungh," I reply.

"Think you can give me two more?" he asks, nuzzling his nose into my neck. He's so fucking soft when I'm with him like this, even as he has me tied up and spread open for him to do whatever he damn well pleases. His softness makes *me* feel soft.

I don't like feeling soft.

But I do like his praise.

And I do like him.

Oh, god. I *like* him.

"I'll try," I choke out as he softly cups my breast. My thighs are sticky from my orgasms, and I'm still too sensitive. "I just need to recover first."

Josh presses his lips to my neck, my head falling to the other side as I gasp his name. "We have all the time you need, Buttercup." He drags his lips from my neck to my cheek, his hand cradling my head.

And if I were to turn my head toward him, we could kiss. I could kiss him, and maybe that would be enough to tell him how soft and broken and strong and vulnerable and worthy being with him makes me feel.

There's not really a reason not to ask him to kiss me. Not anymore. I could taste him and admit I find him so beautiful and wonderful, but that's not what this is.

That's not what we are.

I swallow hard. "Green," I grit out through clenched teeth.

His movements still. "Nic-"

"*Green.*"

He suddenly takes my nipple between his teeth, tugging before soothing the ache with his tongue. He kisses his way to my other breast and repeats his ministrations, my heart pounding beneath my skin. He kisses down my torso to my stomach, kissing in a seemingly random pattern before I realize he's kissing the freckles he's obsessed with. I hum and wiggle happily against his mouth.

"You're stunning, Nic," he murmurs against my tummy before kissing me again. "I can't believe I get to do this with you."

"You should do it, then," I tease, surprising myself with the newfound confidence.

Josh chuckles. "So impatient," he teases back, spreading me again and pressing the wand against me. I'm even more sensitive than last time, but he knows my body and what I need, keeping it at a low setting to begin with.

And god, it's good.

"Josh," I whimper, bracing against the restraint. "Josh, Josh." I'm chanting his name like I'm worshiping a deity, and right now, that's exactly who he is.

"I'm here," he says, softly.

"Your fingers," I grit out, grinding myself against the wand.

"You want my fingers inside of you?" he clarifies.

"I want your fingers to fuck me!" I cry out.

"Atta girl," he says, and I hear his cheeky smile in his voice.

We both groan as he presses a finger inside of me, and it feels so good. He curls his finger, hitting my G-spot and I jerk violently against the restraints.

Closer, but still not enough.

"Do you need another finger, Nic?" Josh asks.

"Please," I gasp, desperate to be full as my hips thrust up into the wand.

He curls another finger into me. "You look so fucking gorgeous with my fingers inside of you," he growls, all primal and possessive, his need dripping from his words.

When I've adjusted to him, I'm just horny and wild enough to try something new. "Another?"

Josh curses under his breath. "Fuck, Nic. You're killing me."

The stretch of his fingers is so perfect, and I feel so full as I clench around him and find my release. Skydiving but never hitting the ground, just falling, and falling, and falling.

He removes the vibrator at the perfect time. "Leave your fingers," I choke out as my orgasm subsides. Josh must have put the vibrator somewhere because his free hand grabs my thigh firmly enough that his fingers dig into my skin.

Firmly enough that I know that tonight will be marked on my body for days to come.

Josh does what I ask, leaving his fingers in me and stretching me to the point I think I might break.

"One more, Buttercup. Give me one more." He thrusts at just the right angle, and before I know it, I'm falling again, all stardust and fireworks in the night sky as I sob his name, my body thrashing as the sheets are drenched in my orgasm.

And then, it's too much, far too much. I'm so overstimulated, my body engulfed in flames. But before I can say anything, Josh pulls his fingers from me, knowing what I need so well. He takes the blindfold off and kisses me all over my face, soft fleeting pecks, as his hands rub firm trails up and down my body, while I twitch from the aftershocks of my orgasm.

"I'm here. Stay with me, Buttercup," he's telling me, his voice sounding distant, like he's in another galaxy, as he cradles my head to him. "I've got you."

"Did I do a good job?" I ask hopefully, our eyes meeting.

Josh laughs, almost disbelievingly as he kisses and then nuzzles the tip of my nose, his breath hot on my lips. "Such a good job, pretty girl. Do you feel good?"

I nod. "Yeah. But I feel weird. And tired. Don't touch me down there for a while."

With my face cradled in his hands, I can feel my arousal on his hand. My god, it's incredible. Josh presses a gentle kiss to my chin. "I won't."

He's taking such good care of me, being so gentle and reverent with me. Even though I'm such a dick to him sometimes, he makes me feel good and beautiful and sensual and—

And his monster peen is right at eye level.

"Josh?" I say, a devious plan forming in my mind. "Can you put the blindfold back on, please?"

He pulls away, his brow furrowed. "What? Why?"

"Because I want to suck your dick with it on."

Chapter 18

Josh

Playlist: "Feel Your Weight," Rhye

I stare at Nic, eyes wide. This has to be an elaborate, super horny dream. "You what?" I croak.

"I want to suck your cock while wearing the blindfold," Nic repeats, her eyes on my aching boner as she licks her lips. She's saying it like it's casual, like she gives me head while blindfolded, naked, and restrained on my bed every day.

I haven't wanted her to feel like she had to give me a blowjob or make me come when we've been together. It's about her. And I'm pleased as punch to make her unravel with my tongue and fingers over and over again.

But she doesn't look pressured right now. Her eyes are dilated, and her nipples are peaked as she stares at me.

"Nic," I say. "You don't have to—"

"Joshua Charles Henry, kindly shut the fuck up," she interrupts brightly, her gaze lifting to meet mine. "I want to go down on you. I want to make you feel the way you just made me feel and hear you moan my name and make you fall apart." Her eyes widen. "Shit. Unless you don't want to? Am I coercing you into a blowjob?"

"No, no, no," I assure her quickly, probably too quickly. "I want it." My cock twitches dramatically in my pants, as if attempting to illustrate my point. We've only fucked a few times, but watching Nic come out of her shell, in more ways than one, and finding her voice makes me so damn proud. "I really, really want it. I've never actually received a blowjob from a blindfolded *and* restrained partner before, though."

Nic smiles either very diabolically or very serenely. I really can't tell in this situation. "Ah, so I get to teach *you* this time."

"You also haven't given head while blindfolded," I remind her.

"So we get to learn together," she amends.

"So we get to learn together," I agree, holding the blindfold out toward her. "Lift your head."

I adjust the blindfold so it's secure and then stand, my eyes going glossy while observing Nic before me. Her body is flushed pink, a sheen of sweat covering her from her pleasure.

And then that menace licks her lips.

"Fuck," I growl, feeling feral, uncontrollable. I frantically unfasten my belt, my fingers clumsy with excitement. "If you need us to stop, knock on the headboard, okay?"

"Yep," Nic replies. She's smiling slyly, and despite her legs being restrained to opposite sides of the bed, she's trying to rub her pretty, strong thighs together. "Pull out before you come, okay? I can't handle the feeling of cum in my mouth."

"I remember from the survey. Knock now, for practice," I instruct. Nic easily knocks on the headboard. "Good girl." Nic turns her head toward me, her breath heavy. She licks her lips again and god, I can't take it. She's too fucking much, in the absolute best way, overwhelming and enveloping me.

I groan as I pull my cock out of my briefs. "You're not going to bite me, are you?"

"No. I mean, not unless you like being bitten. Or you come in my mouth. I was serious about that. It's a sensory nightmare, and it very likely could cause a meltdown so come on my tits or something instead," she tells me. Despite not being able to see her eyes, I know they're that challenging fiery golden brown color I've come to love so much.

"I do enjoy a nice bite," I tell her, fisting the base of my cock. "But not on what will be in your mouth."

I cup her cheek with one hand, caressing her blush with my thumb as I kneel on the mattress. I move forward until my cock is just in front of her slightly parted lips before sitting on my heels, my knees framing her head.

Nic's tongue darts out, tentatively licking me, and I clench what feels like every muscle in my body. "Can you open your mouth, pretty girl? Nice and wide for me."

She wordlessly opens her mouth, and I thrust my hips forward until the head of my cock breaches her soft pink lips. She sighs and swirls her tongue around me, like I'm something worth savoring, worth enjoying.

I push in another inch, burying my fingers in her tangled curls and massaging her scalp. "You're taking me so well, Nic," I choke out, despite all the blood in my body now being concentrated in one very specific area of my body. "You look so pretty with my cock in your mouth."

Nic makes a happy little humming sound, her mouth vibrating around me deliciously.

I slowly pull out of her, and I swear to god, she pouts. Nicoletta fucking Quinn sticks out her lower lip when I take my cock out of her mouth, and hell, I don't want to make her sad.

"Open," I tell her, and her mouth opens, her tongue stuck out. This time, I thrust in another inch or so, pulling out quickly before doing it again, over and over.

She's moaning around me as I thrust into her talented mouth and what even is my life? How am I fucking Nic Quinn's face? How are my fingers tugging at her curls? How—

She gags on one particularly deep thrust, and I panic, pulling out of her "Color?"

"Yellow-ish green," she says. "Too deep."

She adjusts her head and presses her lips to my inner thigh, and I nearly come from how she can be the sweetest and most sensual person in the world at the same moment. "I'm okay, Joshy," she says, answering my unspoken question. Her voice is so soft, so reassuring, and I only want to hear that previously grating name from her. I want to hear her call me Joshy over and over and over again. "Can I make you come now?"

Don't kiss her don't kiss her don't kiss her don't kiss her don't kiss her.

I guide my cock back to Nic's mouth, slipping it in. She hollows out her cheeks and sucks hard when I thrust and *fuck*.

"You feel so good, Buttercup," I choke out. I'm so close, so quickly. I pride myself on my stamina during sex, but she's so gorgeous with me in her mouth, and she's so good at this, I can barely stand it.

I pull out and frantically fist myself, shaking with release as my cum lands on her perfect tits.

"Fuck," I groan, voice shaking. I get to my feet before sinking to my knees, laying my head next to hers, "Fuck, Nic."

"Told you it would be fun," she says, a hint of smugness in her voice.

"Shut up," I grumble, my breath and body still shaky and needing grounding. Nic giggles girlishly, a lovely, foreign sound I haven't heard from her before. Our mouths are so close, and her breath is so warm, and goddammit, I want to kiss her so badly. What's wrong with me? She set her boundary, and it's not like I haven't kissed anyone before—

But I've never kissed Nicoletta Quinn before, and every part of me feels like I'm missing out on something important. Something special.

Instead I lift my head and kiss her cheek again, my lips lingering against her blushing, freckled skin. I tuck myself back into my briefs and slide the blindfold from her face. Her wide brown eyes immediately find mine, like she's been waiting to look at me, and she smiles, so radiant and crooked and perfect.

"Hi, Joshy," she says softly, and my heart stutters.

"Hi, Buttercup," I respond, breaking eye contact because I'm afraid that if I don't, I'll grab her chin and kiss her, and, more practically, because I need to get her out of her restraints.

I unfasten the velcro on her left wrist first, and Nic's gaze follows my movements as I unfasten her ankles and other wrist. "How are you feeling?" I ask her.

She sighs as she sits up, "Good." She pauses for a moment. "Sore."

I wince. "I'm sorry. I didn't mean to hurt you."

"I know you didn't. You didn't do anything wrong. I loved every minute of it," she says softly, cupping my face in her hands.

"Let me draw you a bath," I murmur. *Stay the night. Tomorrow. However long. Just stay with me.* "Before you go home," I add.

It's not lost on me that really, I'm just trying to keep here with me as long as possible.

Chapter 19

Nic

Playlist: "Snow On The Beach (feat. Lana Del Ray)," Taylor Swift, Lana Del Ray

Josh draws me a lavender-scented bubble bath with extra epsom salt. He doesn't really seem to be a lavender scented bubble bath guy, and I hate that he continues to surprise me. Even more than that, I hate how pleasant those surprises have been. The way he treats me, the way I feel with him, is overwhelming.

I wiggle my toes happily, enjoying the feeling of my body being submerged in hot water.

"I'm going to give you some privacy," Josh says softly, pressing his lips to the crown of my head before rising to his feet.

I grab his wrist and frown up at him. "Privacy? I was just strapped to your bed spread eagle. Get in here."

He blushes, and how is this the same man who talks so dirty when I'm in his bed? "I don't want to impose."

"Josh, impose. Please."

He pauses. "I'm a big guy."

"It's a big tub."

"We'll have to let some water out so I can fit."

"Okay."

"You don't mind?"

"I want you in here with me," I tell him.

He bites his lip. "Will you drain a few inches of water while I get undressed?"

I pump my fist and hiss, "Yes."

Soon, Josh is propped up behind me and I'm in between his legs, reclining into his chest.

"How are you feeling?" Josh asks me.

I crack one eye open and tip my head back, peering up at him. "I feel like someone fucked me five ways to Mercury."

"Is that a saying?"

I shrug. "I just said it, so it is now."

Josh is quiet for a moment. "Should I have stopped?"

I shake my head before straightening my neck, looking forward. "No, I liked it. Maybe I'd even want to try it again sometime." I wince. "Not for a while, though. Maybe in a few millennia."

I can't see him roll his eyes, but I can feel the energy, and it makes me smile. He dips a washcloth into the water. "Will you let me take care of you?" he breathes into my ear.

Why am I fighting back a giddy giggle? I can take care of myself. I'm a strong, independent woman who is self-sufficient and—

And Josh takes really good care of me, too. It goes against everything in me to let him, but is it really such a bad thing to want him to sometimes?

"Okay," I reply, and he runs the washcloth over my skin, gently washing me. "You know, I'm surprised your bath shit doesn't smell like vanilla," I tell him, shivering as he gently washes my breasts.

He hums. "Why?"

"Because you smell like vanilla, you goon. Don't tell me you just roll out of bed smelling like a damn ice cream cone." He's silent, so I rotate my neck and look at him over my shoulder. He's avoiding my eyes, that adorable blush having deepened beneath his beard. "What?" I ask.

"You smell like lavender," he says quietly. "I thought if you ever took a bath here you might like lavender scented bubbles. I know with your sensory issues, taking a gamble on scents might not be the best thing I could do—"

I stare at him, my mouth ajar. "You bought lavender bubbles for the unlikely possibility that I took a bath here?"

"I mean, it's happening now so it wasn't that unlikely," he mutters.

I sniff, trying to get rid of that annoying feeling you get in your nose when you're about to cry.

I'm *not* going to cry, even if it's one of the most thoughtful things anyone has ever done for me. Even if I'm so overcome by the fact that he thought about my needs in such a kind, nonjudgmental way. I thought I'd regret telling him about my autism diagnosis, but he's simply shown me that he sees me, the me I thought no one could see. Who I thought no one wanted to see.

"Thank you," I whisper. "That's a really nice thing for you to do."

"I told you, Buttercup. I want you to feel safe here with me."

I lean my head back and press a quick kiss to his throat. "I do. Thank you," And I mean it. I feel safe with him. I don't know how he feels about me, but he's shown me time and time again I'm safe with him. I can trust and be myself.

It's the last thing I expected to happen.

Or it was, until the very last thing I thought I would ever say comes out of my mouth.

"I think I'm going to kiss you now, Josh Henry."

His breath hitches. "Why?"

I look back at him, meeting his soft blue eyes. "Because I'm safe."

I cup the back of his head and press my mouth to his, my whole body relaxing into his. Kissing Josh is like coming home.

I feel his lips open in surprise, and his breath is chocolate syrup and so him—safe and welcoming—and I need more.

I moan into his mouth as my fingers tangle in his hair, slipping my tongue into his mouth and gently stroking his.

He breaks the kiss, his eyes burning into mine. "Nic."

"Josh."

He growls, and then his lips are back on mine, desperate and needy, and goddammit, of course this man is a good kisser. He's good, period, and he's ruining my life in the best way.

He's not gentle. Our teeth are clashing, and he's loud, moaning and sighing into my mouth. The water sloshes between us as our mouths move together and it's both comforting and annoying as hell that nothing has quite felt this right before.

I'm the first to pull away. "Hi," I say.

"Hi," he replies, cupping my cheek and stroking my bottom lip with his thumb.

"Did you know?"

"Did I know what?"

"That kissing was going to be this good?"

A slow, cheeky smile spreads across his face. "Would you be upset if I said yes?"

"A little," I tease.

"Then no. I'm just as surprised as you are that this is the best kiss I've ever had." He searches my eyes. "I've wanted this so damn much, Nic." He runs his fingers up my side, over my shoulder and clavicle until he reaches my neck. "The whole time."

"Since the first night on the couch?" I ask, my voice wavering as he strokes my throat with his thumb.

"Before that."

"When I broke into your house on your birthday?"

"Since the train, Buttercup. I wanted to kiss you to know if you tasted as spicy as the words coming out of your mouth."

"And?"

He leans down and presses a kiss to the corner of my mouth. "I think the spice was you playing pretend, Buttercup. You're all sweet."

"This isn't the way things are supposed to go, is it?"

"What do you mean?"

"This. Whatever this is."

He moves the washcloth down my belly. "Do you remember what you told me when you made me pay to climb with you? That everyone has a different journey to get to where they need to be?"

"Yeah?"

"This is your journey, and even though it doesn't match what you expected, it doesn't mean it's wrong." He leans down and presses his forehead to mine, his eyes fluttering shut. "I'm simply grateful to witness it."

We stay in the bath until the water is cold and we're wrinkled and pruny. Josh takes my hand as I climb out of the tub, and I tell him that it makes me feel like a regency heroine climbing out of a carriage. He throws his head back, a deep, lovely laugh bubbling out of him, and I decide it's my new favorite sound. We dry each other off and find ourselves sitting on the edge of his bed, wrapped in towels as he tells me about his favorite historical romances. Because of course he reads historical romance.

"Tessa Dare is my favorite author," he tells me. "But Lisa Kleypas is amazing too. And Beverly Jenkins, obviously."

"Obviously," I agree, a lopsided smile lifting my lips up, as if my knowledge of historical romance extends past the sex scenes.

"I'm sorry," he says, blushing. "I'm probably annoying you."

I shake my head. "You're not. It's kind of fun listening to you be a giant-ass dork."

He sticks out his lower lip in a pout, and I lean forward, capturing it between my teeth.

"Menace," he growls, cupping the back of my head and pressing his mouth to mine.

I find his free hand, and our fingers automatically knit together, like a new reflex.

"Touch me," I whisper against his mouth. "Please."

"You're sore," he reminds me.

"I don't care. I need you," I whimper.

"Fuck," he growls, and he adjusts us so that we're both kneeling on the bed, my back against his chest again. His legs are spread wide, and I kneel between them. One of his arms wraps around me, his thumb and forefinger plucking at a nipple as his other hand slides between my thighs. "Lean back, Buttercup," he says, his breath hot against my ear.

I do as he instructs, my hand snaking up to wrap around the back of his neck.

"What do you need from me?" he asks, his touch light against my center.

"Slow. With two fingers," I gasp. He kisses my temple and pushes his middle finger inside me. We both groan, loud and rough. He presses another finger into me and strums my clit, causing me to wince. "Less pressure on my clit."

I can feel him smiling against my temple. "Such a good girl, telling me what you need."

God, his mouth. His words. I shudder.

"Harder," I manage to gasp. "Not faster, just harder."

"Anything you want." He thrusts his fingers into me with more force, and I cry out, uninhibited, unashamed. "Oh, you like that, don't you? My girl likes being fucked hard and slow?"

I whimper, unable to manage much else, and honestly, it's pretty rude of him to expect anything more of me right now.

I can feel his erection pressing into my back, so I lick my hand and reach between us, wrapping my hand around him. He moans in my ear as we touch each other, desperate and greedy.

"Nic," he breathes. "You're so good, Nic. So beautiful and so wonderful. What do you need? I'll give you anything."

I turn my head until our eyes meet. "You," I choke out, my body climbing higher and higher. "This."

His mouth is on mine again, and I grab at his hair as everything inside me falls apart, spiraling down, down, down. He whimpers as I clench around him, and I feel him come, hot spurts on my hand. Everything feels muddled in my head, my vision is blurry, and I have no idea how it happens, but Josh is laying me down, slowly lowering himself onto me.

"Fuck. Yes," I groan, wrapping my arms around his shoulders and pulling him into me.

"You okay?" he asks, nuzzling his nose into the side of my neck.

"My legs might not work again, and walking home will be a nightmare, but that's a sacrifice I'm willing to make."

"Stay here tonight," he says simply. "You can sleep in the bed, and I'll take the couch in my office."

My heart drops. I'd thought things had changed for us. That there was a new level of trust.

It changed things for me.

But he won't share a bed with me unless it's to fuck me. That's his choice, and I agreed to it going into the arrangement.

So why does it hurt so damn much?

"Oh. I mean, I might as well go home—"

"I have nightmares sometimes," he blurts out, avoiding my eyes. "I never share a room, or a bed, because of them. But if I were ever to share a bed with anyone, it'd be you."

I swallow thickly, overwhelmed by what he's told me. He hasn't given any details of his nightmares, but I know telling me took courage.

Maybe things have changed for him, too.

"Stay with me until I fall asleep?"

"Of course I will."

Josh gets me an extra toothbrush and goes downstairs to his study to make up the pullout couch while I brush my teeth in his bathroom.

"Do you want a shirt to sleep in?" he asks me when he comes back.

I meet his eyes in the mirror. "No," I say simply, my mouth full of toothpaste. "I happen to really like being naked in your bed."

He rubs a hand over his face. "For fuck's sake, you menace."

For someone who thinks I'm a menace, he sure holds me like I'm something good when we're in his bed.

"You have stars on your ceiling," I mutter, my eyelids growing heavy.

"I do."

"I had them when I was a kid. They're pretty."

"I did, too. When I moved in with Grandma after my parents' deaths, she put them on the ceiling to help me be able to sleep alone. When I moved out, I put them up again. It makes me feel less alone on the bad nights."

I yawn obnoxiously. "That's really lovely."

He chuckles. "Go to sleep, Nic."

"You're just saying that so you can get away from me," I mumble.

He's quiet, but right as I feel myself losing consciousness, his lips press lightly to my temple. "Getting away from you is the last thing I want, Buttercup."

Jo: i'm going to bed early, love you.

Jo: are you home yet

Jo: nicolettaaaaaaa

Jo: you're not in your bed

Jo: are you dead

Jo: can i have your iPad

Jo: okay for real where are you?

Chapter 20

Josh

**Playlist: "Every Little Thing She Does Is Magic,"
Sleeping At Last**

Nellie: hey, jo just texted freaking out because nic never came home tonight.

Josh: She's here. She fell asleep.

Nellie: OMG ARE YOU SHARING A BED IS THERE ONLY ONE BED

Josh: I'm sleeping in the office.

Nellie: honestly fuck you.

I wake up early the next morning with the sole goal of surprising Nic with breakfast in bed.

I don't know if she was joking or not, but I'll do whatever I
can to prove to her that getting away from her is the last thing
on my mind.

Which is obviously terrible for this entire operation.

After I make her pancakes and a glass of chocolate milk, I
place everything on a tray.

Look at me, all domestic and shit. It's almost sickening.

"Nic," I whisper, sitting on the edge of the bed. How the hell
is this tiny woman sprawled out across so much of my bed that
I have to sit perched on the edge? "Wake up. You don't want to
be late for wor—"

"Joshy?" Her soft caramel eyes fly open and meet mine,
blinking rapidly as a slow smile spreads across her lips. God, this
woman. She has such a hard and sometimes, frankly, intimidating exterior, but she's all soft inside. I want to wrap myself
around her and protect her from everything that makes her feel
the need to hide herself from the world. From everything that
makes her feel ashamed, like she's anything less than the brilliant
woman she is.

"Hey, Buttercup. I made you—*shit*."

She launches herself onto my lap, knocking the tray off and
wrapping her arms and legs around me.

"It wasn't a dream," she breathes into my ear.

"No." I look disappointedly at the spilled food on my sheets.

But Nic is naked and on my lap, inadvertently wiggling against where I ache for her.

Life could be much worse.

She seems to realize what just happened and looks around, a sad look spreading across her face. "Shit, Josh. I'm sorry. I was so excited to see you and—"

I cup her chin and turn her face to mine, shutting her up by kissing her.

I'm really enjoying the newfound freedom to kiss Nic whenever I want to. She kisses me like she wants more of me but is savoring what she has, too. She kisses me like she's amazed to be touching me, to be near me. Like she's been waiting to kiss me, the same way I've been waiting to kiss her.

"What was I saying?" she asks, a little dazed, when I break the kiss.

"Dunno," I lie. "But it's seven thirty, and I don't want you to be late to work."

Nic rests her cheek on my shoulder. "What if I don't go to work today?"

"You can do that."

"And what if you don't go to work."

"I'm listening."

"And we kiss and remake breakfast and get cleaned up in the shower instead?"

I pretend to think about it. "You make a convincing case, Dr. Quinn. Let me make a phone call."

One hour and one very steamy shower later, the two of us are in the kitchen, cooking up the rest of the pancake batter. Well. I'm flipping pancakes, she's sitting on my counter wearing my old NYU t-shirt and sleep shorts that I had to tie to the side with a rubber band so that they'd stay up on her. She's humming something as she scrolls through her phone, her feet kicking along to the rhythm.

I catch myself thinking that I could get used to this. Nic, in my space. In my clothes. In my life. After losing my parents, I've lived my life with a lack of permanence. I'm beginning to think of Nic as permanent, which is why I should have said no to her request in the first place.

But I can't find it in myself to regret saying yes to her.

"Your clothes should be ready to move to the dryer in another five minutes. Wanna switch them over and then put the bedding in?"

"Mmhmm," she says absentmindedly. "Can I log into my Amazon Prime account on your TV?"

"I think so. Why?"

A few minutes later, Nic is excitedly beginning *Twilight*.

We spend the rest of the day watching the *Twilight* movies, and once we finish the third, we take a lunch break and re-make my bed, immediately sullying them with a particularly hot makeout session.

I can't get enough of her.

"This was nice," Nic muses as I walk her out. "I'm sorry we didn't get to the last two movies. Or *She's the Man,* like you'd wanted."

"It was nice," I agree, shoving my hands in my pockets. What the hell do I do now? Do I kiss her goodbye or—

She kisses me, standing on her tiptoes, her hands gently placed on my shoulders.

I melt into her, cupping her waist in my hands as I kiss her back.

"Thank you," she whispers, breaking the kiss.

"What for?"

"Hanging out with me today."

I smile at her and take one of her curls between my fingers, pulling just enough to straighten it so it bounces back into shape. "Thanks for being a terrible influence and encouraging me to call out of work."

"Getting introduced to Charlie Swan made it worth it, right?" she asks, waggling her eyebrows knowingly.

"Obviously. Fuck the police, but he's hot."

She kisses me again, and I reluctantly watch her leave, waving to her when she looks back at me over her shoulder.

When I go back inside, my home feels a little less like home. I see and feel Nic everywhere, and now that she's not here? It doesn't feel right. It's like she's left a Nic-shaped-hole in my chest.

Twenty minutes after Nic leaves, I get a text.

Nic: hi.

Josh: Hey, Buttercup.

Nic: i liked kissing you.

Josh: I liked kissing you, too.

Nic: we should do it again sometime.

Josh: Did you text me just to tell me that you liked kissing me?

Nic: kind of, yeah.

Josh: Huh.

Josh: That's pretty cool.

Nic: you're not going to sign your initials?

Josh: I think you know who I am now.

Nic: you know who i am, too. not that i ever signed my initials like you did.

Nic: do you want to climb with me tomorrow?

Josh: I'd love to, Buttercup.

The next evening, Nic waits for me outside the gym. She's wearing a pink workout set that looks so goddamn pretty against her complexion. I try not to notice how her eyes light up when she sees me, and I know mine are lighting up the same way. Whatever emotion this is, it's brand new, never having existed before she did.

God, I'm fucked.

Chapter 21

Josh

**Playlist: "Build Me Up Buttercup (Acoustic),"
Callum J. Wright**

In the past two weeks since our first kiss, Nic and I have gone climbing almost every night, followed by us curling up on her couch to watch a few episodes of *Ted Lasso*. I've seen and enjoyed the show before, but it's different watching it through Nic's eyes. She's so excited and points out when masculinity, sexuality, and mental health are portrayed in a positive way.

"You never see mental health talked about like this in mainstream media," she says, her mouth full of chicken nugget. "Especially for cis men. But here you see men being vulnerable and showing emotion, and that's so important."

I have to fight to keep my eyes on the screen and not on her. She's so damn pretty when she's passionate.

"That's really cool," I agree. "It opens the conversation and makes it a safe discussion to have."

"Yes!" she says excitedly, her hands moving animatedly in my peripheral vision. "Are you in therapy?"

I freeze. "Uh—"

"Shit. Sorry. That's inappropriate isn't it? It's just my job and my own experience—"

"I'm not offended," I tell her. "The question just caught me off guard."

She snuggles into me, resting her chin on my shoulder and blinking up at me. "And?" she pushes gently, placing her hand over mine.

"Did you make me watch this show just so you could question me about my experience with therapy?"

"Nope," Nic says brightly. "Just a happy coincidence. Why don't you go now?"

I look at her, confused. "I don't need it."

The look she gives me immediately tells me that she disagrees. "Josh, everyone needs therapy. You still struggle with trauma-induced nightmares, right?"

I nod.

"Therapy can help you process what's causing them, maybe leading to them being less frequent and intense. And therapy can help you learn the skills to cope when they do happen, which can make them a little less horrible and all-encompassing.

You deserve that, you know? To not be completely tormented by your past. To be able to do things and not worry about how your trauma can ruin it."

I swallow hard, thinking about how much I'd wanted to sleep next to her two weeks ago. "Really? You think it'll help?"

"If you find the right therapist for you, I know it will. You just gotta give it a shot."

"I don't know where to start," I admit, feeling foolish.

Nic slips her fingers into my hair, massaging my scalp with her nails. "Lucky for you, you're sleeping with someone who knows not only where you should start, but what you should look for."

For the next hour, *Ted Lasso* plays in the background as Nic shows me different websites and tells me about different therapies that could be beneficial for my trauma. It's strange hearing her refer to my past as traumatic at first, but I realize she's right. Losing my parents was a traumatic experience.

"Are you going to Connecticut this weekend?" Nic asks after we'd screenshot a few potential therapists' contact information.

I nod. "Yeah, I'm visiting my grandma."

She nods, face falling a bit, and I know she's disappointed that we won't be able to do this tomorrow. I am, too.

"I was thinking," I continue, gently rubbing my hands up and down her arms. "If you're feeling up to it—and I need you to tell me if you're not—maybe on Tuesday you can come over to my place? Instead of me coming here?"

She tilts her head. We'd been coming back to her place because it's closer to the gym. "Why?"

I swallow. "Well, I don't have a roommate. And my bed is bigger."

She blinks adorably a few times before her eyes widen with understanding. "Oh. *Oh.*"

I bite my lip, saving the joke I want to make about the multiple O's I'm looking forward to giving her for another time.

"Yeah. That," I say.

Nic's period started last week, and while I'd enthusiastically insisted I had no qualms about penetration while she was on her period, she had cramps and asked to take it easy for another week.

It's been the hardest week of my life. Especially for my poor dick.

Except it actually hasn't been, and I've loved the intimacy I've gotten to share with Nic, the conversations and laughs we've had, the kisses we've shared.

It's terrifying.

"I think that will work," she laughs nervously, her eyes meeting mine.

I brush a curl back from her face. "Are you nervous?"

"A little. It's been a minute, and I want it to be good for you, and I worry it won't be."

I pull her into my chest. "I know it's easier said than done, but don't worry about that. Let's just enjoy what we have right now."

She nods against me. "I'll try."

"Good." I kiss the top of her head before resting my chin on her and closing my eyes.

That's the last thing I really remember before being woken up.

"Can you assholes shut up? He's sleeping," Nic hisses. The weight of her body lifts off mine as she sits up to quiet the alleged assholes.

"No he's not. Josh doesn't sleep in front of people," Nellie yells loudly, making me wince.

"I know he doesn't, but he is, so shut *up*."

I blink awake, confused as to when or how I fell asleep.

They're right. I don't sleep in front of people.

But I slept in front of Nic, and now she's trying to keep it that way. God, she's great.

"I'm awake," I mumble, opening my eyes. Nic is glaring at a very drunk Nellie, and less drunk Tyler and Jo.

"Great, you woke him up. Good work team," Nic says, voice dripping with sarcasm.

I sit up and wrap an arm around Nic before kissing her temple. "Thanks for trying, Buttercup."

The three newcomers gasp in unison. "Did you just kiss her temple?" Nellie screeches. "That's the cutest shit I've ever seen."

Nic winces, and I think about how Nellie's volume, which is objectively loud, must sound to someone with noise sensitivity.

"Penelope. Shut. Up," I say through clenched teeth. "Use your inside voice."

She ignores me. "You slept in front of her before me! That's not fair."

I glance at Nic, whose scowl should be immortalized in art. Who somehow made me feel so safe and secure that I fell asleep while holding her. "You'll get over it," I tell Nellie.

Jo's eyes are frantically darting between Nic and me, and I just hope she's not concocting a murder plot that will make my death look like an accident.

"People. Why don't we have a group chat? Best friends should have a group chat," Tyler says suddenly, their eyes growing wide.

"Are we all best friends, though?" Jo asks, narrowing her eyes at me.

"I'm starting a group chat," Nellie pulls her phone out of her pocket and creates a group chat. While she chatters about wedding favors and appetizers for a few minutes, Nic looks up at me. *Sorry,* she mouths.

I shrug and smile at her, hoping that she understands she doesn't have to apologize. "I should get going," I say.

"Can I walk you out?" Nic asks, and I agree. She kisses me as soon as the door closes behind us, wrapping her arms around my shoulders before I lift her up.

"I wanted to make you come tonight," I mumble against her mouth. "If you were feeling up to it. You have no idea how much I miss you on my fingers, Buttercup."

"Ah, damn," she hisses as I grind into her. "Guess you owe me an orgasm, then."

I give her one last kiss before lowering her to the ground, a grin on my face. "It would be my pleasure."

"I think that went well," I tell Tara as Grandma's doctor leaves the house. We just had a meeting with her in the living room, and at this point, we're not getting any good news, but we didn't get any terrible news either.

Tara eyes me. "She told us Grandma's probably going to die in the next two months."

"Could have been one month," I say, feigning an optimism I don't really feel.

Tara rolls her eyes as her wife, Belen, squeezes her hand.

Grandma knows she's dying, and the priority is keeping her pain-free and comfortable as her body continues to shut down. In a way, I think it's easier for her than the rest of us.

We go into the bedroom, where Grandma is reading a Julia Quinn book on her e-reader.

"Ah, look. I didn't die while you were gone," Grandma says brightly, lowering her e-reader to her lap.

"Stop making that joke," Tara whines as Grandma cackles. "It's not funny."

"I'm sorry, dear," she replies, wiping at her eyes. "How are you feeling about what Dr. Howard said?"

"I mean. Everything's terrible and you're dying, so not great," I tell her, sitting on the edge of the bed. Grandma places her hand over mine and squeezes. How much longer will she have the strength to do that?

"Do you want me to call Dad? He blocked my number so I'll have to use someone else's phone," Tara says, looking between us. Tara's dad, my Uncle Ray, disowned her when she came out in high school. She ended up moving in with Grandma and me, something that fractured his relationship with his mother. He accused Grandma of 'enabling Tara's harmful phase' and she accused him of being 'a hateful, ignorant bigot.'

Grandma makes a face, like she just tasted something sour, making the rest of us laugh. "No. He can read about it in the obituary section like everyone else. He knows I'm in hospice and hasn't visited. He can come at any time and chooses not to. So, I'm choosing not to call him."

"Don't do it because of me," Tara says. "I can put up with seeing him if you want to."

"Oh, Tara. What hurts you hurts me, too," Grandma says, reaching out with her other hand to squeeze Tara's. "You and Belen and Josh are more than enough family for me. And I'm so lucky to have a few more months with you and my favorite romance books."

I force a smile, trying to swallow the lump in my throat. I just wish we were luckier.

Chapter 22

Nic

Playlist: "touch tank," quinnie

Since it was the Fourth of July, I went home for Sunday dinner for the first time in weeks. And while it was still challenging, it didn't completely suck.

Mom and Dad stayed pretty surface-level with questions, asking about work and climbing. I helped Mom with the potato salad, caught up with Leo and Izzy, and asked Millie if she'd watched *Ted Lasso* yet. She hadn't. I ignored my older sister, Kat, and her douchebag husband, Steve, as much as I could. I even stayed until the fireworks, watching them from inside.

It was still loud, and my parents had too many goddamn children, but it was nice, too.

"Hey, kiddo," Dad says, coming up behind me and putting his hand on my shoulder. Everyone else is watching the fireworks, so I'm not sure why he's inside. "You doing okay?"

"Yeah," I say, smiling up at him, "I'm okay."

"You know," he says, staring out the window. "You've always hated fireworks, ever since you were a kid. The pediatrician told us you'd grow out of it, that all toddlers hate loud noises for a while, but you never did."

I bite my lip. "It's more than just the loudness. I can feel it in my entire body."

Dad nods, still looking out the window. "You used to beg us to let you stay home when we used to go down to the beach to watch them, and we never let you."

I wince. "Dad—"

"We didn't know how much it hurt you. I would've stayed home with you if I understood," he says, quietly.

"Dad," I say softly, wrapping my arms around him. "You didn't know. And I didn't know. We did the best we could."

"I hope you know how proud I am of you, kiddo," he says, kissing the top of my head. "Not only for your professional successes, but for the fact you came home and stayed inside for something that hurts you."

"I'm sorry I haven't been coming home as often."

"I am too, but you're an adult with your own life. I only hope you know you're missed."

I swallow the lump that's formed in my throat. "It doesn't feel like it most of the time," I admit, tightening my hold around him. "Most of the time it feels like if you guys really knew me, you'd be glad I stayed away."

"Are you a serial killer?"

"No!" I gasp. "Why the hell would you think that?"

"That's the only thing I could see that would make us not want you around, Nic. And even then, I have a lot of classmates who went on to be criminal defense attorneys—"

"I'm autistic," I blurt out. "I was diagnosed a few months ago. And I'm bisexual. I've been out to Jo, Millie, and Alex for a while, but I've been too nervous to tell you and Mom." I bury my face in his shoulder, too afraid to see his reaction.

"Okay," he says simply. "Thank you for telling me that. And I'm sorry you haven't felt safe to share until now."

I didn't expect this. I open my eyes and look up at him in surprise. "Sean Quinn. Are you in therapy?" He's acting like someone in therapy would act.

He grins. "As a matter of fact, I am," he says proudly. "Your mother and I are both in therapy individually, and we're seeing a couple's therapist together."

My eyes widen.

"We're fine," he says before I can ask. "But we can always be better, you know? It's been good. You know we started because we have a doctor in the family." He gently punches my shoulder.

Tears fill my eyes, and I hug him again. "I'm not ready for anyone else to know," I whisper to him. "Please don't say anything."

He squeezes me tightly, with just the right amount of pressure. "I won't, kiddo. And I'll be with you, whenever you're ready."

"Thanks, Dad," I say, kissing his cheek.

"Your brothers agreed to drive you to the station, since Leo needs to practice. Does that work for you?"

I nod. "Yeah. That's perfect."

An hour later, Leo is slamming on the brakes at every stop sign, his red curls bouncing each time.

"You know, you can always ease to a stop," Ren says from the backseat, much more gently than I would. His wavy, dark brown hair is longer than mine right now, and his green eyes match Dad's.

"I am easing to a stop," Leo argues, slamming on the brakes as he pulls up in front of the train station.

The three of us all climb out of the car, and Leo throws his arms around my neck while Ren jumps in the driver's seat to put the car in park when it starts rolling. Despite being nine years younger than me, Leo towers over me. He and his twin, Izzy, are the babies of the family, so the fact that he's over six feet tall now is disorienting. At least Izzy got the short genes, too.

"So, Nicky," Leo says, firmly thumping me on the back. "Mom mentioned that you and Jo have an extra room in your apartment. And I thought it would be soooo romantic if I brought Stella—"

I roll my eyes and shove him off me as I understand the ulterior motives behind his hug. "Ew. Get off me, Leonardo. Get a hotel room for your sex vacation." Ren barks out a laugh as he joins us.

Leo scowls at me. "I'm broke. And Dad's walked in on us twice now."

Ren and I shudder at the image. "That's horrific and definitely sounds like a 'you problem,'" I say.

Leo grumbles and stomps back to the car, slamming the door as he climbs into the driver's seat. I wince at the loud noise.

Ren looks at me. "How is he old enough to be trying to weasel his way into a sex vacation in your spare bedroom?"

"I don't know what mom fed the twins, but it needs to be taken off the market."

Ren chuckles, rubbing the back of his neck. "I'll send a strongly worded letter to the FDA."

"Are you happy it's summer break?" I ask him. Ren is a music teacher at the elementary school in town, and though I've never seen him teach, the mental picture of my little brother teaching a group of kids is the cutest thing in the world.

He shrugs. "Not really. I'm teaching more private lessons this summer, and honestly, I like teaching classes so much more. Parents are incredibly particular about private lessons, and it feels like it's more about the parents than the kids. I miss teaching kids the pure joy of music, not teaching them because their parents are making them do something over the summer."

"Ugh. Stop," I whine. "That's so cute. You're probably their favorite teacher."

He blushes, fighting a smile. "They call me Mr. Q."

"Lorenzo! That's adorable."

"It really is. I want to cry from the cuteness multiple times a day."

"Why do you teach private lessons if you don't like them?" I ask.

"My salary is shit. I can't survive on it alone," he admits. "I do what I have to so I can keep doing what makes me the happiest." He tilts his head. "Is everything alright? You're acting weird."

"I'm trying to be nice," I scowl.

"Right. You're acting weird."

Leo lays on the horn, and I grit my teeth, leaning around Ren to give him the finger.

"I'm gonna miss my train if I don't leave now." I reach up to hug Ren, who awkwardly pats my back. Have I really been that distant with all of them?

"Text someone when you get back to let us know you're safe."

I walk up the stairs to the platform, and for the first time in longer than I can remember, I'm glad I came to dinner this weekend.

As I think of the progress I've made, I see him, illuminated in the dark night by the lights on the platform. He's wearing a tweed jacket and chinos, like it's not July, and for some reason, seeing him in what must be his professor's getup makes my knees tremble. Like a magnet, I'm pulled toward him. He turns in my direction before I reach him, his eyes widening with recognition.

"Nic," Josh says, pulling his earbuds out of his ears and putting them back into the charging case. "Hey, I didn't know you came home.""It was a last minute decision," I say. "Decided while climbing this morning to come for dinner."

He smiles. "That sounds nice. I bet your family was happy to see you."

I return his smile. "Yeah, it was really nice to see them."

The train screams its arrival, and I wince at the whistle, pulling my earplugs out of my bag and plugging my ears as Josh watches.

"Will you sit with me?" he blurts out.

I smile and nod my head eagerly. I feel like I'm in high school and the quarterback just asked me to prom. But I'm twenty-nine years old, and Josh Henry just asked me to sit next to him on a commuter train, which is infinitely better.

The train slows to a stop at the platform. Josh takes my hand, leading us onto a car and we choose a row with three seats, where we can both sit comfortably. I take the seat by the window, and he takes the aisle seat after putting his duffel bag in the overhead rack. I put my back against the window, and stretch my legs out on Josh's lap, earning a grumpy scowl from him.

"Really?" he says, his voice flat.

"Mmhmm," I say. "You told me you owed me an orgasm, and I'm cashing in by using you as a footrest instead."

He blushes. "You don't want me in orgasm debt?"

I pull out my tablet and smirk at him. "Like you'd let yourself remain in any sort of orgasm debt."

Josh raises his eyebrow rakishly, and I blush, ducking my head down so my curls hide my face. "Who told you the orgasm could be traded for something else?" he asks, rhythmically massaging my calves in his lap. His hands are so big I bet they could completely wrap around my calf if he put his mind to it.

"Nobody," I say, lifting my eyes to his. His pupils are dilated. "I thought I'd be nice and forgive your debt."

His dilated eyes search mine. "Maybe I like being at your mercy, Nic."

My breath hitches.

The conductor comes by and checks our tickets. It's another quiet evening, and it reminds me of that first night all those weeks ago. Except tonight, my earplugs are in, and I'm not disgusted being in Josh's proximity. In fact, I almost want to take the earplugs out so I can hear the sound of his breath.

I bet if I did, it would be heavy.

"Have you ever done anything in public?" Josh asks, seemingly out of nowhere.

I blink at him. "I've most definitely done things in public."

He rolls his eyes. "You're a goddamn menace, you know that?"

"I do," I confirm.

"I meant—" He cranes his neck and looks around the car. "There are very, very few other passengers in this car, Buttercup. And if you're very quiet..." he trails off, his fingers sketching patterns on my ankles as he raises his eyebrow expectantly.

My eyes widen cartoonishly. I peer over the seats around us, and he's right. There are only a handful of people in the car, and at least an empty row around us on every side. But *still*. "Are you out of your mind?" I hiss. "We can't do that, we'll get arrested!"

"Only if we're caught," Josh says casually.

I roll my eyes because of course he's casual about this. "We can't, Josh."

"We can't because you don't want to, or because you think you shouldn't want to?"

I bite my lip. Damn him, I don't *know*.

"If you really don't want to, you know I'll respect that, Nic," Josh says gently, squeezing my calf. "But if you want to, I'd love to make you come right now."

"Have you done stuff like this before?" I ask nervously, my cheeks flushing pink as I worry my bottom lip between my teeth.

Josh, being a whole six-hundred feet tall, is able to reach over and gently pulls my lip out from between my teeth. He brushes his thumb against my lip, his touch featherlight.

"Yes," he answers honestly. "I've had public sex before. I don't want you to feel pressured, though. I just want us to have fun. If it doesn't sound fun, we don't do it."

"That's the problem," I admit. He cups my cheek with his hand. Before I can even register my movement, I'm leaning into him. "It does sound fun, and that scares me."

"Come here, Buttercup."

At his urging, I swivel my body and legs so that my back is pressed against his side and my legs are extended toward the window. Josh wraps his arm around my torso and pulls me closer. "You pull away or tell me to stop, and I will."

I tilt my head up, meeting his eyes. "I trust you." And it's true. Of course there should be a certain level of trust with any sexual partner, but this feels like more.

He feels like more.

I'm not sure if the twisting feeling in my stomach is from the nervousness and excitement I feel about what is going to happen on this train, or what will happen between us when we get off it.

Josh bends down and kisses me. His kisses are filled with the same need and yearning I feel. His hand moves mindlessly down my belly, and I moan into his mouth. The fruit flies in my stomach match his movements.

Fuck. Who am I kidding anymore? Josh Henry gives me butterflies.

"Spread your legs for me, Buttercup," Josh murmurs into my mouth. I oblige, and his hand cups me over my shorts. I whimper into his mouth, and he rakes his free hand through my hair. "You're wet for me already, aren't you?" he asks.

"I don't know," I answer honestly. "Probably."

He chuckles against my mouth, and he quickly looks around us. "Can I check?"

I let my leg fall off the seat in answer.

He groans as his hand slides under the waistband of my shorts and then into my underwear. He stops when he feels my curls, combing his fingers through them, and I can't help but grin. "You like my bush, don't you?"

"I like everything about you, Nicoletta," he says, his movements stopping when he says it. I wonder if he said it without thinking, if he's as confused and overwhelmed by these big, scary feelings as I am.

That mushy shit is something for later Nic and Josh to worry about. He parts my labia, and with one firm stroke with two fingers, touches me from my entrance to my clit. I jolt and gasp.

"You have to be quiet, Nic. This is for us, not for anyone else on this train."

I whimper, his words making me that much more aroused. I turn my face and bury it into his neck, hoping it will muffle the sounds of my pleasure.

I'm not a quiet person, not when I'm feeling this much at once.

"Good girl," he praises, the hand in my hair moving to cup my breast and thumb my nipple through my tank top. "Christ, Nic. No bra?"

"I'm an A-cup," I mumble into him, inhaling his scent. "Nobody knows."

"Nobody except me. Fuck. All for me." He kisses the crown of my head, and I whimper, clutching his shirt as he presses his middle finger into my pussy. "Two fingers, pretty girl?"

"Mmhmm. I love how good it feels when you stretch me." Jesus Christ, when did I start talking like this?

"Fuck," Josh breathes, curling his finger inside me so it strokes my G-spot. "You make me so goddamn hard when you tell me what you like, Buttercup."

I wiggle, a strange feeling of delight blooming inside of me. I like it when I do something Josh likes.

He quickly looks around. "We have a stop coming up soon. Do you think I can make you come before then?"

I freeze, and then my body is relaxing as Josh curls another finger inside my body. "That's a lot of pressure."

"Well, that won't do," Josh murmurs. "There's never any pressure on you. The pressure's on me." He thumbs my clit. "Am *I* going to be able to do just the right thing to make you come?" He plucks at my nipple, and I gasp.

"Keep doing that, and I might."

Josh strums at my clit, alternating between circles and vertical strokes, and *fuck* he's touching me perfectly. Screw Shakespeare, this man is an expert on my body and how to make me come undone.

Before I know it, before I can name or recognize the feeling, a wave of pleasure crashes over me. I bite Josh's shirt as I fight back a scream from some primal part of me, deep inside. He stays inside me as I ride out my climax, though he stops touching my clit. His hand moves from my breast to my head, cradling me to him and running his fingers through my hair. He's murmuring the sweetest words, but my brain is too muddled to be able to understand them.

I just know they're the sweetest.

When I start to come down, Josh pulls his fingers out of me, and my body immediately aches for him, like he's an integral part of my anatomy. He wordlessly brings his fingers to my mouth, and I turn my head. I meet his dark gaze before I part my lips, sucking him in and tasting myself. I savor the taste, bitter, musky, and sweet, as I clean his fingers. When he removes his fingers, he opens his mouth, the last words I'd ever thought I'd hear from him.

"I want to take you on a date."

I blink at him, stunned. "You—*what*?"

"I want to take you on a date," he repeats, his face reddening. "If you want to go on a date. With me."

If I could see myself, I know I would see the biggest smile on my face. "I'd *love* to go on a date with you, Joshua."

His returning smile is so spectacular that it overwhelms all of my senses to the point I almost don't hear the announcement:

"Stamford is next."

Chapter 23

Josh

Playlist: "Somethin' Stupid," Frank Sinatra, Nancy Sinatra

After I made her come on the train, Nic cuddled into me, all soft-limbed, satiated, and affectionate in a way I want to experience every day. I shared my earbuds with her, and we watched an episode of *Ted Lasso* as she ran her fingers through the hair on my arm and hand.

We took the subway back to Brooklyn, and I walked her home, savoring our kiss goodbye and the little sounds she made when I stroked her tongue with mine. She invited me to stay over, but I declined, knowing I got lucky when I fell asleep at her place last week. I wasn't ready to push my luck again.

When I woke up this morning, almost a week after the train ride, the first thought in my mind was: "Nic's coming over tonight." The brownstone hadn't felt right since the last time she'd been here.

Then I remember why she's coming over—so I can be inside her. The idea of being that close to her makes me breathless.

It needs to be perfect. I want everything to be perfect for her.

I've had sex plenty of times, and I know she's no stranger to it either. Hell, she and I have had enough non-penetrative sex that this shouldn't feel so important, but it does. I want *her* to feel important.

So I do something impulsive during my morning Zoom meeting with the rest of the English department.

> **Josh:** Jo, hi. This is Josh Henry. I got your number from the Group Chat Nellie made. I was just wondering if you know Nic's favorite food?

> **Jo:** hey, she's been talking about your chocolate oat milk a lot.

> **Josh:** what about a meal? I know she likes pancakes.

Jo: oh yeah she's a big fan of breakfast for dinner, and anything our mom likes. oooh, especially her gravy

Josh: Like biscuits and gravy?

Jo: you poor, simple man.

Jo: it's pasta sauce, basically. we've always called it gravy, dunno why.

Josh: How do you make that?

Jo: you'd have to start NOW. it's a whole day thing. wanna be cute and woo nic? homemade pasta and homemade gravy. you'll thank me later

Josh: Oh, it's not like that.

Jo: <disbelieving GIF> sure, jan.

Jo: anyway, i'll send you the recipe, i just have to get it from ma. fabulous grand gesture to show your love <heart emoji>

Josh: We're not in love.

Jo: keep telling yourself that, buddy.

I scowl down at my phone, apparently quite obviously, because Nellie, who's also in the meeting, texts me.

Nellie: okay babes, what's THAT face about.

Josh: I'm not making a face.

Nellie: <eyeroll emoji> ok nevermind.

Josh: Do you think I can order a pasta maker and get it delivered today?

Nellie: joshua. baby. it's new york.

Nellie: of COURSE you can.

Nellie was right, of course. I'm able to have a pasta maker delivered, as well as the ingredients for pasta and "gravy," sparkling cider, a pint of Phish food, and extra condoms and lube—just in case. Jo sent me the recipe right away, and since I only have a virtual class in the afternoon, I have time to spend the morning preparing the gravy, which is a goddamn marathon.

The sauce has to simmer on the stovetop for multiple hours, but Jo told me that if I really wanted to impress Nic, to wait to make the pasta until we can do it together.

At 5:01, there's a knock on my door, and even though I expect it, my heart jumps to my throat.

When I open the door, I swear, my eyes bug out of their sockets. Nic's wearing a fuschia sundress that I'm honestly shocked she owns. But, my god, it looks incredible against her freckled skin.

"Holy shit, Joshua," Nic yelps, whipping her sunglasses off her face. "You look hot as hell."

I look down at my outfit. I'd changed into chinos and a light purple button down. The sleeves are rolled up to right below my elbow, and the top three buttons are undone.

I look up at her, baffled. "Do I?"

Nic throws her arms around my neck, and I catch her, her legs wrapping around my center. "You always do. But your chest hair is really, really hot," she says, kissing my jaw.

I roll my eyes and stumble backward into the house with her still in my arms, balancing her weight in one arm to shut and lock the door. "It's not that hot, Nicoletta," I say teasingly as I put her on the ground.

She scowls up at me. "Oh, so you're allowed to find my body hair hot, but I'm not allowed to ogle yours?"

I blush, immediately thinking of the delicate curls between her legs. "You make a good point, Dr. Quinn."

She bites her lip. "Dr. Quinn. That's hot, too."

I clasp her chin in my hand and press a kiss to the freckle right on her jawbone, to the left of her chin. "Dr. Quinn." I move my lips another inch up her jawbone. "Dr. Quinn." I press a final kiss to a freckle hiding right below her ear. "Dr. Quinn."

"I've been told there's a freckle in my cupid's bow," Nic says, her voice shaky, fingers digging into my side.

I turn her head, looking intently at her mouth. "Huh. So there is."

"I think you should kiss that one next, Dr. Henry."

I capture her upper lip, where there's a freckle between the peaks of her cupid's bow, gently nipping and sucking, my cock hardening at her desperate mewls.

I break apart from her. "Not yet, Nicoletta. We have to cook."

Nic scowls at me. "You're putting me to work?" she asks as I take her hand in mine and lead her to the kitchen, reciting Macbeth's dagger soliloquy in my head in an attempt to get my cock to chill out a little.

When we get to the kitchen, Nic gasps excitedly. "Are we making pasta?" she asks as she bounces on her toes. "When I was really little, my mom made it for dinner every Sunday. Then she had more kids and decided there were too many of us, and we only get it for special occasions now." She beams up at me. "I can't believe you have a pasta maker! And is that Mom's gravy recipe?" she asks excitedly, bouncing over to the stove. "Oh my god," she says, spinning around to face me. "It *is*, isn't it?"

I awkwardly rub the back of my neck. "It's too much, isn't it?"

She throws herself at me without warning, the same way she did at the door. "It's perfect. Thank you, Josh." She squeezes me. "I know you're going to say it doesn't mean a lot—"

"It doesn't," I interrupt.

"Shut up, you silly man," she says, kissing my cheek with a loud smacking noise. "It means so much. Maybe you don't realize it, but a lot of people don't go out of their way to ask my sister about foods I like. With my food aversions, that means a lot to me." Her food aversions. I hadn't even thought of that. I just wanted to make it special for her. I squeeze her tighter around her waist.

"Did Jo tell you I asked her?" I ask, worried I overstepped bounds.

"Nah," she answers with a shrug. "I just know you wouldn't know Mom's gravy recipe without her help."

"Fair," I laugh, lowering her to the ground. "I want to be honest with you, Nic. I wasn't thinking about your food aversions. I just wanted to make tonight special."

"You don't have to think about my food aversions specifically, but you thought about *me*. You reached out to Jo to make sure you'd make something I'd eat." She turns and rifles through her bag, pulling out a glass bottle and a plastic bag. "I'd brought frozen chicken nuggets. Just in case."

I take the bottle from her hands. "Sparkling cider? Well, you won't be shattering this on the stoop, huh?"

Nic gasps dramatically, elbowing me in the side. "You're such an asshole!" She tries to spin away from me, but I catch her waist and pull her into me, her sweet lavender scent enveloping me.

"Thank you. The cider means a lot," I murmur into her hair.

She shrugs, wrapping her arms around my waist. "It's just cider."

"I made sure you had something to eat, and you made sure I'd have something to drink, Buttercup. We're looking out for each other. That's pretty cool of us."

"It is, isn't it?" Nic replies, a sense of wonder in her voice.

I want to look out for her all the time. Have her favorite chicken nuggets and food in my kitchen so she always has something she can eat. Keep a weighted blanket in every room and lavender bubbles next to my bathtub. Have *Ted Lasso* queued up and ready for when she needs it.

I don't know what that means, and I'm not sure I want to know.

At least not right now.

I clear my throat and pull away from her. "Now, you get to teach me how to make pasta."

A slow grin grows on her face, and it looks a little like The Grinch when he decides to steal Christmas. "I get to boss you around?"

My cock jumps. "Uh," I say, speechless.

"I'm in," Nic declares, grabbing my hand and pulling me to the island, where flour and eggs await us.

"No way," I laugh into my napkin. We're sitting at the dining room table, which Nic had insisted on setting with my parents' nice china. Nic played some Frank Sinatra from her phone while we cooked, and his smooth crooning continues to fill the air, lit candles flickering in the center of the table. "You're kidding."

"I'm not!" Nic insists. "I really thought that a virgin was someone who had a baby without being married. Like I thought what made the Virgin Mary so remarkable was that she had Jesus before she and Joseph were married! And so I told my Sunday School teacher, who was this little old nun, that I *never* wanted to be a virgin."

I laugh harder, tears filling my eyes. The fact that I can picture tiny Nic in some nun's face insisting she was right makes it even better. "What happened after that?"

She shrugs and picks up her fork, twirling the homemade fettuccine around her fork. "She called my parents, who laughed so hard, obviously. But then Mom sat me down to officially have 'the talk.'" She takes a bite of her pasta and chews. "I had a lot of questions about everything.""Of course you did."

"Like why would anyone ever want someone's penis in their vagina?"

Both of our movements still, the energy in the room changing completely.

"Do you still feel that way?" I ask.

She shakes her head. "I think I get it now."

"Are you done eating?" I ask roughly.

She nods, pushing her chair back from the table and standing up. "Yeah."

I follow her lead and stand from the table before taking two steps to pull her into me. I kiss her, one hand on her waist and the other in her hair, combing her soft curls between my fingers.

Our kiss is hard and needy. It's twenty years worth of bites and licks, of gasps and moans. "Let's go upstairs. Please, Nic."

"Yes." She jumps into my arms and wraps her legs around my waist, hands tugging at my hair. I start to walk toward the stairs, and she gasps. "The candles! Josh, the candles!" I stumble back to the table, and Nic leans over to blow out the flames, leaving wisps of smoke billowing from the table. "Okay, fire hazard eliminated. Take me upstairs."

"Upstairs," I agree. She presses her lips to mine, unbuttoning the next button of my shirt as I carry her to the third floor.

Chapter 24

Josh

Playlist: "Eat Your Young," Hozier

> **Josh:** I think I'm falling in love with Nic.

> **Nellie:** wrong.

> **Nellie:** you're past falling, you're splat on the ground, guts exploded everywhere, in love with her.

> **Josh:** Delightful imagery, thank you.

Nellie: am i wrong?

Josh: I guess not.

Josh: I avoided falling in love for almost three decades, and then it happens with the last person who would ever want to love me.

Nellie: i don't know, josh. you both look at each other an awful lot when the other isn't paying attention.

Nellie: don't sell yourself short. she's surprised you before.

I'm somehow successful in getting us to the bedroom without incident, and by the time I lay Nic on my bed, she's managed to unbutton my entire shirt and is frantically trying to push it off my shoulders. She's so fucking pretty, hair mussed and lips puffy from our kisses. I extend my body over hers, and though I know she likes it when I lie on top of her, I'm still so fucking scared I'll hurt her. I lean on my elbows, pressing kisses to her neck, gentle nips of teeth followed by long, worshipful strokes of my tongue. She wraps her leg around mine, rubbing her center against my dick.

"I want you," she whimpers. "Please, I've waited for so long."

"You've been such a good girl, letting us figure out what you like." I kiss her once more before pushing myself up and standing at the foot of the bed. Nic pushes herself up on her elbows and stares at me, eyes dilated and hooded. Despite my shirt being unbuttoned and half off, I still have an undershirt on, and she's still wearing that pretty sundress. "Come here, Buttercup."

Nic crawls to the edge of the bed before getting up and standing in front of me. I grab her hips and pull them into mine, my erection pressed against her as I kiss her again. My head swims, overwhelmed by her.

"I want you naked," she gasps, grabbing at my undershirt before I encircle her wrist with my hand.

"I will be. Soon. But there's something I've been wanting to do all night." I kiss her one more time before sinking to my knees. "You wore a fucking *sundress*. Do you know what you've been doing to me?" I lift her leg and kiss up her calf, starting at her ankle.

She giggles. "I think girls in sundresses are hot, so I was hoping you might think so, too."

"Fuck girls in sundresses," I say, widening her legs to fit better between them. "I'm into *Nic* in sundresses."

I lift her skirt up and freeze. "These aren't your confidence panties."

Our eyes meet as she peers down at me and blushes. "I wanted to try something new," she says quietly.

"I'll say," I run my fingers over the black lace that barely conceals her curls. "Are these comfortable?" "Oh, not at all," she says brightly. "I've been fighting a sensory meltdown all night. The thought of you taking them off was the only reason I kept them on."

I moan and kiss up her thigh, sinking my teeth into the skin just below the lace shielding her from my gaze. She squeals and jolts, and there's something about surprising her that I could get used to for my whole life.

Don't fucking go there.

She's magnificent from down here, all pink blushes and long lashes. I bite into the waistband of the flimsy lace and slowly pull the fabric down her hips. She whimpers and shimmies, helping inch down her panties. I slide them down her legs, the fabric pooling around her ankles as she puts her hands on my shoulders and lifts her feet to step out of them. I grab her panties and slip them into my pocket.

"I love that you want to try new things, pretty girl. But I hate that you were uncomfortable and didn't say anything."

"They were really itchy. And the tag was—" she shudders, and I shouldn't smile, but her vulnerability about her sensory issues is just so precious to me.

"You being happy and comfortable is the sexiest thing. Don't wear those again," I say, like I have any intention of her taking them home with her.

She bites her lip. "Or what? You'll check my underwear more often? You'll rip them off next time?"

I groan, pulling her left leg over my shoulder so she stumbles back against the bed with a squeal. "That was a dirty move, Joshua Henry," she grumbles, her thighs falling open.

"Right, because Nicoletta Quinn *always* plays fair," I say, raising a brow at her as she perches her ass on the edge of the bed and I continue to kiss her inner thigh.

She scowls at me, crossing her arms across her chest. "The sundress doesn't count."

I bark out a laugh. "The sundress absolutely counts."

She groans. "You're annoying. Shut up and kiss me."

"Where do you want me to kiss you?" I ask, running my hand up the inside of her leg.

"You know where," she says, her voice barely more than a whisper.

"I do. Tell me anyway, Buttercup."

"My pussy," she grumbles.

"Atta girl." I pull my undershirt over my head and use one hand to expose her where she's so wet and swollen and sensitive. I meet her gaze again just as I swirl around her clit with my tongue.

"Oh, fuck. Josh," she gasps, one hand fisting in my hair and the other grasping at my comforter. "More."

"Take it then, Buttercup. Show me what you want."

She moans, and her grip on my hair tightens, as her head falls backward. She grinds herself against my face. "Fingers."

I press both fingers inside her. She's so tight and warm, as soft as the most expensive lace she should be wearing. I suck her clit hard and curl my fingers into her, her cries and gasps becoming louder with each movement, each gyration of her hips. She surrounds me; all I can taste, smell, see, hear is her.

With one last desperate thrust of her hips, she comes, a broken cry from deep in her throat as she tightens around my fingers. Her hand falls from my head, and I lean back, eager to watch her ride the waves of her pleasure.

As she catches her breath, I get to my feet, grasping her face in my hands to kiss her. Her tongue darts out and licks across my lower lip, and I open to meet her, our tongues dance slowly, sensually.

"You taste like me," she moans against me, nuzzling her nose against mine as she touches my face. "Your beard's all wet," she says, pulling away and biting her lip.

"I don't really half-ass things with you, Nic."

She wraps her arm around my shoulders, pressing our bodies together as my hands rest on her hips. "You really don't, do you?" she muses, kissing me again. "Can we be naked now?"

I pull away and both of us fumble with my belt. She shoves my pants down my thighs, and I reach toward her, lifting the skirt of her sundress. "Arms up, Buttercup."

She raises her arms, and I pull her dress over her head in one swift movement. I kick out of my pants and pull down my briefs, feeling the heat of Nic's eyes on me. When I straighten, my eyes roam her body, and I try to swallow the lump which has grown in my throat. We've never been completely naked together before now. I feel exposed, like she can see everything—the grief, the trauma, the desire to be good enough. Like she sees all of that, and still doesn't avert her eyes.

"You're so pretty, Josh," Nic says quietly, almost reverently, as she reaches out to me. Her fingertips dance over the ink of my tattoos and through my chest hair. I cover her hand with mine.

"Is it okay?" I ask, suddenly anxious about how she's seeing me. I'm okay in my body most of the time, but being naked with a partner can sometimes cause anxiety. It's even more so with

Nic. I care about what she thinks of me, so much more than I should.

"You're perfect," she breathes before her eyes turn fiery. "Why? Who—"

I laugh, "Nic, no. I'm pretty good at distracting people when naked, making sure their mind is on other things. I don't know how to explain it."

"I mean it, Joshua," she interrupts sternly. "You're perfect. I love that your body looks as strong and as soft as you've been with me. I love how I can tell how much you want me, how wanted you make me feel. I love that your body on top of mine grounds me and helps me regulate. I love that you've made your body a shrine to the people and things that made you."

She intertwines her fingers with mine and brings our hands to her lips, kissing the back of mine. "Your body is so good, Josh, and I can't believe I get to know you."

I kiss her, knowing if I try to say anything, I'll cry. I'll say more than I should, more than she's ready to hear. I gently guide her to the bed, laying her on her back and then rolling her to her side, lying next to her so our chests are pressed together.

"I'm nervous," Nic whispers, her eyes searching mine.

"I am, too," I admit, rubbing her back. "What can I do?

She ducks her head and presses a kiss to a tattoo over my heart. "Keep touching me like this. Don't let me go. Please."

Doesn't she know? I couldn't let her go if I wanted to.

As we touch each other, I swear I can feel Nic's fingers tracing each of my tattoos.

"I need you closer, Josh," she tells me after a few minutes. "Inside me, please."

I groan and bury my head in her neck, kissing her sensitive skin before reaching behind me to grab the condoms and lube in my bedside table. Nic sits up and bites her lip, watching as I rip a condom packet open.

"Can I?" she asks. "I want to see if the banana lessons I got in middle school did me any good."

I laugh. "You're such a goober."

She smiles at me, all goofily and prettily. "Your goober."

Tenderly, Nic wraps her hand around the base of my cock, jerking it a few times and rubbing her thumb over the head and spreading the precum. I comb my fingers through her hair, trying to keep my breath even. She bends over, surprising me by swirling her tongue around me, looking up at me through her lashes.

"Fuck...Nic," I grit, my balls aching.

She smiles at me, taking me even deeper, and my hand fists in her curls, pulling the way I've learned she likes. She moans around me, the vibrations reverberating through my entire body.

"Nicoletta," I warn through clenched teeth. "I don't wanna—*fuck*." She's taken me impossibly deep, and I have less than ten seconds until I explode.

I pull her off of me and drop her on the bed. She lands on her back with an *oof* and scowls up at me. "I wasn't done, Joshua." I grab the still rolled-up condom from her hand and roll it down my cock. She gasps, "Hey! I wanted to do that!"

I press my lips to her, my body hovering over hers. "I was about to come in your mouth, Nic. You don't want that. And I want to be inside you so badly. Next time, okay?"

I feel her smile against my mouth. "There's a next time."

There is definitely a next time.

I sit back on my heels and spread her legs. Though her pussy is still wet and swollen from her orgasm, I want this to be perfect for her. I spread lube over her entrance before sliding my fingers into her again.

"You're pretty big," Nic says, propped up on her elbows as she watches me. "Have you ever not fit?"

I chuckle. "No, I've always fit."

"What if you don't fit in me?" Her voice is suddenly so miserable. When I look up at her, she's worrying her bottom lip as she avoids my gaze.

"Buttercup, look at me." She lifts her eyes tentatively. "I'm going to fit, okay? We'll go slow, and you'll tell me if you need to stop, okay? I'm not in any rush." My hand slides up to her stomach, gently massaging her soft skin. "I've waited this long to be inside you. I can wait a little longer and make sure you feel good."

"Promise?" she asks, her voice shaky.

I lean over her again and nuzzle her nose with mine. "I promise, Nic. You're not just a body to me, okay? I'm not just going to force myself into you."

She's quiet for a beat, and I realize something. "That hasn't been the norm for you?"

"It's been a while since I've had penetrative sex, but it always felt like they didn't care about my experience, and I wanted to get it over with. It's always been rough and fast and painful," she says, her voice dejected. "I knew what foreplay was, but I'd never had it, beyond a finger or two being shoved into me."

I try to control my breathing, control the anger I feel at how Nic's partners have treated her during sex. "No one should have done that to you. I've been paying attention in class, Nic, and I've learned the things you like. The way your breath hitches and your toes curl when you like something. You know more of what you like, too. I'm not going in without having done my research. And I'm not just doing this to get off. I want to experience this together."

She wraps her arms around my shoulders and pulls me to her. "You're too good to me, you know."

"You only think I'm too good because you feel like you don't matter."

"Well, who's the psychologist now?" she teases. I grind the heel of my hand into her clit and she gasps, "Josh—"

"Must be me. I knew exactly how you were going to respond to that." I smirk at her. "I'm going to make sure you feel so good, Buttercup." I curl my fingers into her, savoring that perfect hitch of her breath, the sound that haunts all of my best dreams. Her fingers dig into my arms.

"Do you want me to take the lead for now?"

She nods. "Yeah, and if something doesn't feel good—"

"Then you tell me and we fix it," I promise her, strumming my thumb up and down her clit, my touch featherlight.

"We fix it," she repeats, holding my eyes.

"You and me, Buttercup. Together." I reach over her and grab a pillow from next to her head, sliding my fingers out of her and sitting back on my heels again. "Lift your hips."

She obeys, and I slide the pillow under her ass, bringing her closer to me.

I put my hands on her knees and push her legs apart, gently lowering my body and hovering over her as I take my cock firmly in my hand and circle her entrance with the tip. I press myself against her and stroke up, pressing the head of my cock to her clit. She gasps and her eyes widen. She breathes my name and wraps her arms around my shoulders, pressing a kiss to my inner bicep. I line my cock up with her entrance, and our eyes meet. I could drown in her eyes, so soft and warm. Nic nods her head, like she's reassuring me.

I push into her, just an inch, and fuck, it's almost too much. She's so much, the best kind of overwhelming. Nic whimpers, that soft sound of pleasure I've become obsessed with earning from her, and my head falls into the crook of her neck. "Nic," I choke out. "Talk to me, pretty girl."

"More," she breathes. "I need more of you."

I groan and nip at her neck as I push deeper into her, and, god, she's so tight and warm and feels better than I imagined. "You're taking me so well, Buttercup," I gasp. "You're okay?"

"I'm okay." Nic's voice is strained, and I pull out, leaving just the tip inside of her. I wait a moment before pushing into her again, a little deeper than before. I wait for her body to adjust to me before repeating the motion. I kiss and whisper into her neck, stopping whenever I feel resistance to rub circles around her swollen clit before moving again.

And then I'm fully inside her, completely enveloped by her. I still as I listen to her breaths, which have steadied. "You're inside me," she says, peeking between us where we're joined.

I smile against her neck. "I'm inside you."

"That's so weird."

"Fucking bizarre."

She giggles, and I can't help but laugh with her. She adjusts her head so our eyes meet and noses brush. "I like this," she says quietly, her eyes warm and bright. I know she's talking about more than the sex.

"I do, too." I smile, kissing the tip and then the bridge of her nose. "We fit together perfectly, Buttercup."

And of course I'm talking about right now, physically, how being inside her pussy feels like a revelation, a prophecy fulfilled.

But then there's every other way, too.

The way that she fits perfectly into my home, sitting on my counter and drinking chocolate oat milk. How our bodies naturally fuse together when we cuddle.

She grinds her hips against me, and I almost collapse on her, overwhelmed with the feeling of Nic Quinn completely surrounding me, overtaking my senses.

I pull my hips back and slowly push back into her, tilting my hips, never breaking my gaze with her. Nic gasps, her mouth forming an "oh" shape as her fingers dig deeper into my biceps. "Is that the hip thing?" she asks, her voice husky and delighted.

I grin and pull my hips back again. "That was the legendary hip thing you heard so much about, yes."

Her eyes are wide, and she eagerly nods her head. "I understand the hype. Do it again."

And I do. I thrust into her, over and over again, more of my weight on her body. Her sweet breath hitches and moans show me the added stimulation of my body on hers only makes it better for her.

"I didn't know it could feel this good," she whispers, her fingers tangling in my hair as her other hand cups my jaw.

I didn't, either. I can't tell her that, though. But I never knew it could feel this soft, this safe. That my heart could feel like it's about to burst into sparkling sunbeams. That being inside someone this intimately could feel like all of my broken parts, all the parts of me that I try so desperately to hide, are being fused back together with dazzling golden light.

"Can I ride you?" Nic asks, and it's so sudden, so brave, that my legs buckle, and my body presses down on her even more. She hums appreciatively, wrapping her arms around me and grabbing handfuls of my ass.

My heart almost buckles too.

"You want to be on top?"

"I think so. I've only done it once, and the guy really seemed to like it—"

"Do you want to be on top because you want to, or because you think I'll like it?"

"Will you teach me how to do it?" she asks. "So it'll feel good for both of us? I want to learn."

Teach her. So she can learn. For the first time in too long, I remember why we're here, what we agreed on. I'm helping Nic figure out what she likes so she can express it with future partners. It shouldn't hurt. It's what we agreed on, after all. We don't hate each other any more, sure. But we're not together. There's no reason for her to be with me.

Even though I want her to.

So badly.

Shit.

I try to silence my thoughts and flip us over so Nic is straddling my hips, slipping out of her in the process.

"Put me back in, Nicoletta."

Chapter 25

Nic

Playlist: "Crashing Into You," Vance Joy

I whimper at Josh's words, at how strained his voice is as he looks up at me. I lift myself onto my knees and grip him at the base. I use my other hand to massage his balls, and he moans, tilting his head back. I line us up and slowly lower myself, ready for him this time.

We both groan when I sink down fully, and Josh grabs my hips. Any way he touches me right now feels like flames on my skin. I lean forward, pressing my hardened nipples to his chest, and bury my face in his neck, kissing where I know it makes him shiver, just below the edge of his beard. I want to touch him everywhere, for him to touch me everywhere, and maybe that's the problem. I want us to consume each other, to be everything, always.

I straighten my back wordlessly and slowly lift my hips before lowering myself back down on him, his fingers tightening their grip on my hips.

"Look at you, Buttercup," he says, a crooked smile on his face, his eyes on mine. He groans as I lift myself and sink down again. "That's perfect," he praises, his voice husky.

"You feel good," I tell him honestly, leaning forward and pressing an openmouthed kiss right above his pounding heart. "It's amazing, Josh."

"Good. That's—that's good," Josh chokes out.

I kiss up his neck and find his mouth, our tongues immediately fighting for dominance. His hands guide the movements of my hips, grinding me down on him to stimulate my clit. God, he's the absolute best at this.

He pushes himself onto his elbows, the adjustment making him hit somewhere new inside me. I cry out into his mouth and cup his face with my hands. Josh nips at my lower lip teasingly before chasing the bite with a soothing stroke of his tongue. He thrusts his hips into me, and I smile, loving how desperate he is for me.

He squeezes my hips, fingers digging into my skin, and I moan at the stimulation. I break our kiss and straighten my back, pressing my palms into his chest. I watch his Adam's apple bob as his hand runs up my side and cups my breast, his thumb running over my sensitive nipple. "Am I doing okay?" I gasp.

"Absolutely perfect, Buttercup. Touch your clit."

I tentatively stroke my fingers down his chest, pausing to trace the stretchmarks on his belly. I continue downward and explore where we're connected, causing him to hiss through his teeth. I hum and lean back, using his thighs to stabilize myself as I look down at us, and oh, god—seeing how we look makes me impossibly wetter. "Josh, look at us. We look so good." I touch some more, unable to look away.

"Yeah?" he asks huskily.

"Yeah," I confirm, lifting my hips and lowering myself back onto Josh's dick, watching him slide so smoothly inside me. "We fit perfectly," I whimper.

His eyes flutter closed. "Nic," he breathes.

I grind my hips against his pelvis as I bring my fingers from where he's throbbing inside me to my clit, rubbing circles around it. He thrusts up to meet me and *fuck*. "Josh," I groan, squeezing my eyes shut as my head falls back in ecstasy. "Do that again. Please."

He raises himself to his elbows, and we meet each other thrust for thrust. I shamelessly touch my clit and breasts, chasing my pleasure. My eyes open and meet his. I wonder if he's been staring at me like this the whole time, if his lips have been parted as he pants. One of his hands runs up my spine and grips the back of my neck. Josh presses me forward until I feel his chest hair rubbing deliciously against my nipples. I desperately grind my center against his pelvis, and he groans with pleasure, his eyes never leaving mine.

"Take what you want from me," Josh says, his voice desperate and raw. "I'm yours."

I moan and grab at his hair, adjusting our faces so that we're panting into each other's mouths. His eyes are the bright blue of an ocean I'd willingly drown in, but I know he'd never let me. I'm so close, and his hands are in my hair, pulling the way I like. I let out a broken sob, pressing our mouths together. I'm so close.

"I've got you," he gasps into my mouth. "Give it up, Buttercup." He tightens his grip on my hair as our hips move desperately against each other.

My back arches as I cry out his name, thousands of tiny lights exploding within me, one at a time, as I come around him.

Josh whimpers, and I feel his release pulse inside me. I collapse on his chest when I begin to come down, burrowing my face into the crook of his neck. It's too much. I'm feeling too much.

Josh moves under me, pulling himself out of me and gently flipping me onto my back as he hovers above me. He uses one hand to roll the condom off of him and tie it before his eyes appreciatively dance down my body, and I know I'm blushing all over. He presses his lips to mine, and I melt into him as he slowly lowers himself on to me, confirming he is far better than a weighted blanket.

When I feel regulated, he rolls to his side and pulls me into him, our chests pressed together. Our limbs are loose and tangled, and it seems like we spend hours in each other's arms, all gentle touches, sweet murmurs, and teasing kisses. Until he kisses down my body and roughly makes me fall apart against his tongue one final time.

"You never told me how you learned about sex," I say after.

"Didn't know you wanted to know." My back is to his chest, and his thumb is tracing soothing circles on my belly. I love when it feels like he can't keep his hands off of me, not just in a sexual way.

"Did you learn about it at St. Michael's?" I ask. While I went to the public high school in town, Josh had gone to the all-boys Catholic high school a few towns over.

"I mean, I had a health class where they talked about the importance of chastity before marriage and how birth control was a sin." He pauses. "But Grandma left condoms on my bed one day during my sophomore year. She wrote a note saying she wasn't ready to be a great-grandma, and I better use them."

I smile. "She sounds like the absolute best."

"She is." I can hear the smile in his voice, and he lifts his hand from my stomach, holding up his arm. "Her name is Myrtle, hence the myrtle tattooed on my arm."

I wrap my fingers around his forearm and study the ink that crawls up the length of his arm. "What's this bouquet?"

"The flowers Ophelia mentions in her soliloquy in Hamlet. It's my favorite play, and Ophelia is one of my favorite characters."

I run my fingers over the floral designs. "So you learned about sex at St. Michael's?"

He sighs and lowers his arm to wrap it around me again. "I really thought we had finished with this topic."

"That was very naive of you. It's like you don't know me at all."

"I had sex ed in seventh grade, too."

"At Port Haven?"

"Mmhmm."

"Did you have Mrs. Novack? Sixth period?"

He rolls me over so that I'm facing him, eyes wide and cheeks pink. "Oh my god. You were in that class too. I completely forgot."

I giggle and nod, biting my lip. "Don't tell me you're embarrassed."

He starts laughing too. "I was literally just inside you, but yeah. Remembering we had sex ed together and that you saw me put a condom on a banana is horrifically embarrassing."

He throws his head back and laughs even harder, and it's the loveliest thing I've ever seen. I want to make him laugh and laugh and laugh and laugh. "God," he says, when he's caught his breath. "Why is this so funny?"

"I think we've regressed to our middle school selves, so despite just having had sex and being naked in bed together, the idea of sex is now both hilarious and horrifying."

He chuckles, wiping a leaking tear from his eye. I love how when he laughs, his eyes crinkle at the corners. "Especially since I made countless penis jokes in front of my crush."

I tilt my head. "Who did you have a crush on?"

He looks at me in a way that makes me feel like I'm missing something. "Nic."

I blink at him. "Nick...Harrison?"

"No, Nic. Nic *you*."

I feel my heart stop for a moment. "No, you didn't."

"Yes, I did."

"Stop joking," I say. "It's not funny." I try to pull away from him, but he holds tight to me.

"I'm not joking. I always thought you were pretty, Nic. From my very first day at Port Haven, when I thought your name sounded like Nutella—"

"Stop," I say. "Fucking stop." I pull out of his grip, and fuck—I thought we were past this, but he's still laughing about something that hurt me.

"Buttercup, what did I say?" he asks as I sit up.

"All of it," I spit. "That shit hurt me, okay? You hurt me. And as much as I've healed, it's never going to be a joke to me."

I feel his eyes on me as I swing my legs over the side of the bed. "It's not a joke to me, either," he says softly. "I had a big ass crush on you, Nic. Have a big ass crush on you, as it turns out. And I thought it was *so* cool your name sounded like Nutella. When my parents died, my grandma let me have it with toast for breakfast, and it was pretty much the only good thing in my life at the time."

I freeze, my eyes filling with tears as I look back at him over my shoulder. He looks as confused as I feel, and I remember the past few weeks, all the other ways he's proven me wrong.

I'm safe with Josh. He doesn't want to hurt me.

"It wasn't a joke? You weren't making fun of me?" I ask.

Josh's brow furrows. "You could never be a joke to me, Nic."

"I was to everyone else," I whimper, a tear falling down my cheek.

His Adam's apple bobs as he swallows. He sits up and scoots to the side of the bed, cupping my cheek with his hand and wiping away the tear with his thumb. "Is that why you hated me? You thought I was making fun of you?" I can feel the hesitation in his touch and words, like he knows I could scare at any moment.

I shrug. "I hated everyone. You weren't exactly special," I try to joke. "But you could get under my skin like no one else could. Everyone was cruel to me, and no one ever tried to stop it. Not any teacher, or any classmate, or you. You saw, and you never said anything."

"I'm sorry, Nic," he says softly, his voice trembling. "I truly am. I saw the shit some of the kids pulled, but I didn't know the extent of how much it was hurting you. I'm so sorry."

I can't help it. I lean into him, and he wraps his arms around me, holding me against his chest. "We were kids," I murmur. "I was ignorant. I'm still ignorant, I guess."

"You're not ignorant. Who bullied you?" he asks, his voice suddenly protective, like he's ready to hunt down whoever hurt me.

I might let him.

"Oh, God. So many people. Bridget, Tommy, Lenore—"

"What did those shitheads do to you?" Josh grits out, his grip around me tightening.

"I didn't get my autism diagnosis until last year, so everyone just thought I was weird and rude. And they always said I had dirt on my nose, but it was just my freckles."

My breathing is heavy, and I squeeze my eyes closed, more tears escaping. He tightens his hold on me. "Sometimes it got physical, usually when I tried to ignore them. Pushing, tripping. It continued through high school, and I almost always had bruises."

"You tried to erase your freckles in second grade," Josh says.

"I thought if I could get rid of them, maybe it would stop. Obviously that didn't do anything but give me an eraser burn on my face. The school called my parents because I had disrupted class, so they wouldn't let me watch TV for a week, but no one asked why I did it." I try to laugh, but a choked sob comes out instead. " After that—"

"I remember," Josh says tersely. People had thrown erasers at me for the next month whenever I arrived at school. Our teacher had told them to stop, but she never actually did anything about it. "I didn't know—No, that's not true. I did know. I saw it happening, but I had no idea it went so deep. They did things to me, too."

I lift my eyes, and through my tears I see Josh, his steady blue eyes looking into mine. I see the little blond boy who had a purple cast on his first day. The way he laughed when I told him my name, the laugh I realize now was in delight, not maliciousness.

"You?" I ask, my voice breaking.

"I was a fat kid with no parents who lived with his grandma. There were fat jokes and dead parent jokes. It never got physical, but when I was finally able to convince my grandma I should go to St. Michael's for high school, I felt so much relief."

He strokes my cheek. "I thought everyone loved you. Sure, you were aloof, but you were so smart, and you always remembered everyone's name. I couldn't understand why you didn't try to stop it, and why you hated me so much. Do you remember that beach party when we were in high school?" "You threw your drink at me, so I threw my drink at you." "No, Nic. I came over to flirt with you. Some asshole bumped into me, and I spilt my beer on you. Then *you* threw your drink on me."

My head is swimming. I'm finding out that everything I held true about the man in front of me for the past twenty-two years is wrong. I was wrong.

"Josh," I whimper. I don't know what hurts more, finding out how wrong I was about Josh this whole time, or finding out that he was being bullied right alongside me. "I'm so sorry. I didn't know."

"You were trying to save yourself," he says gently, turning my head and nuzzling my nose with his. "I'm not angry with you. I'm only angry with myself for spending twenty years not knowing who you really are because you deserve to be known. And, fuck, if I could deserve anything good in this world, I'd want it to be knowing you."

"Me too. Knowing you is the best thing to happen to me," I desperately tell him. He presses his lips to mine, and I wrap my arms around his shoulders. I've always seen him as strong, but understanding more of what he survived makes him even more so. Our hands find each other, and I guide his hand to my breast.

"Nic," he groans against my lips.

"I need you, Josh. I have twenty years of not touching you to make up for."

He lays me down, kissing down and back up my body while I reach for the lube and condoms.

Minutes later, he's inside of me, his body hovering over mine as we cry out each other's names, our hurt and healing come together with our bodies.

"Nic—I—*Fuck*," Josh thrusts into me, one hand holding mine, another circling my clit as I weave my free hand in his hair. "I need to feel you come."

"Close," I whimper. "So close."

Josh's eyes leave mine, and he ducks his head down, taking my nipple gently between his teeth. He sucks rhythmically, swirling his tongue around the taut peak until I come around him.

A few more thrusts, and I feel him come, too. And then it's soft kisses and touches and promises of forgiveness and healing that come from a deeper understanding of each other.

"I have to go home," I murmur as we lie on our sides facing each other.

He cups my face with his hands and looks at me, searching my eyes. "You could stay," he stammers, his face reddening. "If you want to, that is."

"I know," I tell him honestly because I do know he'd let me stay; he'd sleep on his couch in his office again and let me take his bed. Maybe Josh even wants me to stay and would sleep in the bed with me if I asked, but I need to be alone tonight. I need to be cocooned by the familiar comfort of my own space to figure out why my heart feels like it's breaking and healing all at once. "But I can't. Not tonight. I—"

"You don't have to explain," Josh says, tugging at a curl, and watching with an amused smile as it bounces back into shape. "If you don't want to stay, you don't want to stay. But if you did want to stay, you could. Not just tonight, but whenever."

I smile softly and lift my hand to his face, letting the hairs of his soft beard run between my fingers. "You say that to everyone you make come." I tease.

He laughs, loud and lovely. "I definitely don't. Can I take you home?"

Part of me wants to argue with him, like it's in my DNA to be contrary to him. But a much larger, more reasonable part of me recognizes it is indeed quite late, so it's probably a good idea not to go alone.

I sit up and climb out of bed, finding my dress crumpled in a ball at the foot of the bed and slipping it over my head. As I search for my underwear, I can feel Josh's eyes following me from where he's still reclined against the headboard.

He snickers, rubbing his knuckles across his mouth in such a sexy way my knees tremble. "Looking for something, Buttercup?"

I plant my hands on my hips and scowl at him. "Joshua Henry, where are my sexy underwear? Those were six dollars at Target."

He winces. "Jesus, no wonder they were a sensory nightmare. Six dollars? You might as well have worn sandpaper."

I ignore him. "Josh, focus. Where are they?"

He grins at me, all trouble and mischief. *If* I had found my underwear and put them back on, they would have dropped right back down to the ground. "Aw, come on Nic. It's tradition that I get to keep your panties for a few days."

I roll my eyes. "That was one time so you could wash them because *you* made a mess. One time does not a tradition make."

"Two times might, though."

"You're such a damn menace."

Josh gets out of bed and walks to me, still gloriously bare, and bends down to press his lips to my cheek sweetly. "Looks like you've been teaching me, too."

I try to frown at him, but I physically can't right now. Josh Henry makes me feel like I'm all cotton candy clouds and starry skies, meteors and sunshine and first flowers in the spring. I've always been grumpy, but he makes me feel a deep happiness and contentment in the present. I've never felt like that before.

My inner grouch isn't sure how to feel about it.

Josh grabs some clothes from his dresser and throws them on before calling an Uber and walking me downstairs. He opens the front door for me, and I fight the urge to give him the finger for being so goddamn *kind*.

When we get into the car, I snuggle into his side, letting my head fall to his shoulder. He wraps his arm around me, pulls me into him, and presses his lips to my temple.

"If you still want to, I'd like to take you out the Friday after next," he says softly against my skin. "On that date I asked you on."

My heart is pounding between my ribs. I've never been asked out on a date that wasn't agreed upon over messages on dating apps and it feels nice.

"You still want to?"

"Very much," he tells me, and there's such a warm sincerity that it makes my heart beat even faster.

"I think I'd really like that."

It's quiet after that, and I find my eyes getting heavier and heavier.

"You can sleep, Buttercup. I'll make sure you get home."

As I fall asleep, safe in his arms, I know that as long as I'm with him, I'll always make it home.

Chapter 26

Josh

Playlist: "From the Start," Laufey

When I carry Nic up to her apartment, Jo is home. She takes one look at Nic, and then at me, her eyes narrowing. She points her finger at me and whispers, "You hurt her, you die." She pauses for a beat before whispering again, "Glad the pasta worked out."

"Thank you," I whisper back before carrying Nic to her room and laying her on the bed. She mumbles and turns on her side, kicking at me as I try to take off her shoes.

After I wrangle them off, I tuck her beneath her blankets, letting my fingers caress her cheek.

"I'm so fucking scared, Buttercup," I whisper. "I'm so scared it's just me."

I'm in love with her, and I almost told her tonight.

I know she's not ready, not just to say it back, but to hear and believe that I really love her.

"It's not," she mumbles, and my hand stills. "It's not just you." I know she's not awake, that it doesn't mean anything.

But it feels like something.

"I'm gonna wait for you," I vow. "I'm gonna wait till you're ready."

"Mm-kay," she agrees, smiling softly in her sleep before letting out a loud snore.

I bend down and kiss her cheek.

When I close the apartment door behind me a few minutes later, I can't help but feel like I'm leaving the best part of myself behind.

All the days that follow go by too slow. They're filled with classes, grading papers, talking about *A Midsummer's Night Dream* with students who don't want to talk about *A Midsummer's Night Dream*, meetings with colleagues, and having to go into the office *way* more often than I feel is necessary.

I'm only able to see Nic a few times to climb and then have orgasms after.

Just as the good Lord intended.

We talk in some capacity every day between texts and an unexpected phone call I'd only answered because I thought something was wrong.

"Hello?" I answered nervously.

"Hi," she said, voice soft.

"Nic?"

"Yeah?"

"What's wrong?

"Oh, sorry. Nothing. I didn't mean to scare you. I was just calling to say hi."

I exhaled slowly, a million pounds of anxiety lifting off my body and being replaced with tenderness. "You've never called before."

"I know," she said. "I, um, I wanted to hear your voice. I miss you." We were both silent for a few moments, as countless thoughts flew through my mind. "Josh? Did I lose you?"

"No," I said, shaking my head. "No, sorry. I was just thinking. You're not losing me that easily, Buttercup."

We talked for a few minutes before Nic promised that the next time we talked on the phone would be for phone sex.

She made good on that promise three days later.

Finally, it's the night before our date, and I send Nic a text before turning my light off to sleep.

> **Josh:** Hi Buttercup.

> **Josh:** How do you feel about surprises?

> **Nic:** i like the idea of surprises way more than i actually like surprises.

Josh: Hmmm. Okay.

Josh: I really wanted to surprise you, what if I give you a general idea of what we're doing tomorrow?

Josh: Like Thai for dinner and a museum after. Is it okay to surprise you with which museum and restaurant?

Nic: that's perfect. i know what to expect for the most part and how to prepare, but you still get to be annoying and surprise me.

Josh: How very annoying of me.

Nic: yes, exactly. glad we're in agreement.

Nic: i'll see you tomorrow

Josh: Can't wait.

I turn off my bedside lamp, smiling to myself. Part of me wants to panic over the fact simply texting her makes me smile this big, makes me feel this good. But is the panic even worth it at this point?

I'm done for.

I wake up a few hours later in a cold sweat, the blankets tangled and knotted around my body.

The nightmares have been happening since my parents died and are slightly different every time, which makes it difficult to prepare for them. I try to slow my breathing, inhaling deeply and rubbing my hands over my face.

Usually, I take a shower after, and sometimes I hop on Tinder and invite someone over or put on Mamma Mia.

Right now, however, all I want to do is talk to Nic, to hear her voice. But she's sleeping, and I'm not that much of an asshole, so I scroll through our texts, smiling as I reread her snarky comments and quips.

It doesn't fix everything. She doesn't fix everything. But despite her not being here and not knowing much about my nightmares, she makes me feel less alone. Her selfies giving me the finger and recent attempts at sexts make me smile.

She makes the after less terrible.

Eventually I fall back asleep, and when I wake up again, it's to my alarm.

I check my phone, and Nic's texted me a link.

Nic: buy these for me since you stole my sexy underwear.

Nic: [link]

I open the link and immediately roll my eyes as all-too-familiar music starts playing through the speakers.

> **Josh:** You're an asshole. You know that, right?

> **Nic:** okay, okay. here's what you should ACTUALLY buy me.

> **Nic:** [photo]

I gulp as I look at the screenshot Nic sent me. Soft black lace briefs. The model wearing them is beautiful, but all I can see is the fabric on Nic's full hips, begging to be dragged off of her.

My eyes widen when I see the price. It seems excessive for Little Miss 'Those Were Six Dollars from Target!'

> **Josh:** Did you Google "World's Most Expensive Panties?"

> **Nic:** ha ha ha. you're soooo funny, joshua. <unamused emoji>

Nic: no, i was looking through a face-book group i'm in for autistics and someone else had asked about sensory-friendly lingerie and this brand came highly recommended. Soft fabric, stretchy, tagless. i'm thinking about buying them.

Josh: I'll buy them for you if you let me keep the Target ones.

Nic: <eye roll emoji>

Nic: no you won't.

Josh: Ha Ha Ha. As my students say…

Josh: Bet.

Apple Pay is a godsend. I order her a lacy bralette with positive reviews mentioning sensory issues in a few different sizes as well as the panties in multiple colors and sizes. I even pay for overnight shipping to her apartment before sending a screenshot of the tracking number.

Nic: no you fucking didn't.

Josh: Yes, I fucking did.

Nic: why did you do that?

Josh: Because I want you to feel sexy and comfortable and because I can.

Nic: <angry emoji>

Nic: thank you. i'm annoyed with you. because of who i am as a person.

Nic: but thank you.

Josh: you're welcome.

Josh: I'll even let you keep them after you wear them.

Nic: jesus.

I smile to myself and roll onto my side. Spending the rest of my life both irritating and making Nic Quinn happy would be the greatest joy of my life.

The clock moves impossibly slowly all day. I can't stop staring at it, and when my last class gets out at 2:50, I don't know who's happier to get the fuck out of there: me or the students stuck in a summer Shakespeare class.

It's definitely me.

I get back to my apartment around four and immediately shower and trim my beard, using a new unscented beard oil I found.

I have every intention of getting on my knees again for Nic tonight, and she deserves the softest touches.

At 5:30, I'm knocking on Nic's door, holding a small bouquet of buttercups I picked from my neighbor's window box.

Nic opens the door, and I almost drop the flowers. She's wearing a black mini skirt with a black strappy top, fishnet stockings, and black heeled boots.

She's so fucking hot.

"Uh," I say, my mouth dry and my brain unable to generate any helpful words.

"Are those for me?" she asks, her eyes brightening when she notices the flowers.

I blush and rub the back of my neck, finally able to speak. "Yeah, it's silly—"

"They're buttercups, and you call me Buttercup!" Nic beams, taking the small yellow flowers from me. "I love it. Thank you, Joshy." She lifts herself on her tiptoes and presses her lips to my blushing cheek.

I am a millisecond away from melting into a puddle.

"Come in. I want to put these in water," she says, holding the door open for me.

I walk in, and she goes to the kitchen, getting a small vase from the cupboard and filling it with water before putting the buttercups in. I can't stop staring at her. Everything she does, from the way she has to stand on her tip-toes and stretch her arm above her head to reach the vase, to the happy little tune she hums while arranging the flowers, is so fucking captivating.

"You look beautiful," I blurt out, unable to keep it to myself.

Nic looks up at me, her eyes warm. "Than—" Her eyes widen as she takes me in. "What the *fuck*, Joshua?"

I look down at my outfit, anxiety rising. I called Tyler to get their stamp of approval, and they said I looked okay—

"That's the shirt you wore to your birthday party. The night I was drunk."

I meet her eyes. "It is?"

She's biting her lip. "Yeah. It looks good on you." She's talking with her hands. "It clings to all the places I like to touch and kiss, and it feels like you wore it purposely to torture me and—"

I take two steps toward her and clasp her chin in my hand, tilting her face up so I can kiss her. She hums against my mouth, and I wrap my arm around her waist.

"Hi, Josh," she murmurs against my lips, chasing her words with a teasing bite to my bottom lip, earning my moan.

"Hi, Nic," I respond, tracing her lips with my tongue. "You're breathtaking, Buttercup."

"No, you are," she says, fisting her hands in my shirt and pulling me into her. "We should just stay here. Order in. Stay in bed."

I groan against her. "I made reservations. And I really, really want to hold your hand in a museum."

She breaks our kiss and licks her thumb, bringing it to my mouth and scrubbing at what must be her lipstick around my mouth. "You can't say stuff like that, Joshua. It makes me all soft and mushy. And horny."

I smile at her and nip at her thumb, making her squeal before scowling at me. "I like it when you're all soft and mushy. And horny."

"Of course you do," she mutters, lowering her hand from my face. "Of course you fucking do."

I lower my hand and take her hand. "Can I take you on that date now?"

She smiles at me, all toothy and bright. "Yes you can, Josh."

Chapter 27

Nic

Playlist: "Comethru (with Bea Miller)," Jeremy Zucker, Bea Miller

Josh insists on taking a taxi for our date night, which I tell him is silly, but he ignores my objections.

I roll my eyes, but I love that while he's hailing the cab, one of his hands is in the air, the other is holding mine, not once letting go.

When we arrive at our first destination, I gasp and turn to him. "You're fucking with me. Thai Chef?" I always thought I hated surprises, but Josh surprising me by bringing me to my favorite restaurant in the city proves me wrong.

He grins bashfully at me, his hands shoved in his pockets. I can't help but admire how his shirt looks against his belly, and the skin and tattoos he's revealing with the top few buttons undone and sleeves rolled up to his elbows.

I might be dressed slutty tonight, but Josh Henry looking casual in a white button up is infinitely sluttier.

He bites his lip, and I want to yank it out from between his teeth with my own, remind him I'm the one who gets to bite him like that.

Instead, I reach out to him and pull myself into the softness of his body, tightening my arms around him. I feel him take his hands out of his pockets to wrap his arms around me, too, rubbing my back firmly with the perfect amount of pressure to keep my head clear.

"You talked to Jo again?" I murmur, inhaling the smoky vanilla scent of him.

"I think she almost doesn't hate me now," he jokes.

"She acts like that toward everyone," I tell him. "She's prickly initially, but she's actually a wonderful human."

"Sounds like someone else I know," he muses, burying his nose in my freshly styled hair, and it feels like he's breathing me in the same way I breathe him in.

I'm quiet for a moment. "Thank you. For this. For everything." *For taking care of me. And making me feel important and wanted and capable.*

"You don't have to thank me, Nic," Josh says softly into my curly tendrils. "I should be thanking you. I didn't expect to enjoy the summer term so much."

I smile into his shirt. "And here I was thinking you were enjoying *me*."

He pinches my side playfully, and I squawk, pulling away from him. "You evil goblin," he teases. "You must know I'm more than enjoying you."

My cheeks heat, and I want to ask him what that means. Tell him metaphors are hard, and I need him to spell things out.

But I don't let myself, too afraid of being wrong. Instead, I reach for his hand. "Come on, Joshy. Chicken Pad Thai and Shrimp Spring Rolls are calling my name."

I pull him through the entrance of the restaurant, noticing he was smart to make a reservation. I've never been here on a Friday night, but it's loud and busy and bustling. It smells so good, but it's also a little too much, and I'm starting to feel overstimulated. I dig through my bag, and my stomach drops as I realize I left my earplugs on my desk at work when I wore them earlier today. I've been meaning to get an extra pair to keep in my bag so I don't forget them and end up in a situation like this, but I've been putting it off. My heart starts to race, and I try to slow my breathing.

Josh squeezes my hand, and I look up at him. He leans in, his brow furrowed in concern. "Is everything okay?" he asks, the soft hairs of his beard tickling the shell of my ear as his mouth moves, and I twitch at the added stimulation.

"I forgot my earplugs," I admit. "And it's really loud."

"I have an extra pair," he says casually, like it's totally normal for him to have an extra pair of something he doesn't use.

I look at him skeptically. "You do?"

Earplugs are tricky. It took me a while to find a brand I like. Other kinds aren't as comfortable or effective.

Josh shoves his free hand into his pants pocket and pulls out a little, round black case I immediately recognize. After all, an identical case is currently sitting on my desk.

My eyes fill with tears, and my nose feels stuffy as I look down at his hand and take the earplugs, opening the case and breathing a sigh of relief when I see that they're the right size.

I put them into my ears, and the relief is instantaneous. The noises fade into a background hum, my brain settles, and I can think clearly again. But now I'm crying.

"Nic," Josh whispers, cupping my face and thumbing away a tear. "Please don't cry, I didn't—"

"How are you the best person I've ever met?" I ask as our eyes meet, my voice tight.

Josh pulls me into his arms, squeezing me to his body with the exact pressure I need, like he knows it by heart. "It's only because you haven't met yourself, Buttercup."

I order my usual Chicken Pad Thai. Josh and I end up sharing an order of Chicken Satay, and I steal a few bites of his Drunken Noodles. Josh agrees it's the best Chicken Pad Thai he's had, which I knew he would. Because it's objectively the best.

After dinner, Josh and I walk the two blocks to the Met. I look at him. "I didn't know you were an art snob," I tease.

He shrugs. "I mean. I appreciate art in all its forms. Performance, visual, literary...I don't know if you do, but—" He blushes and his hand brushes against mine. It's embarrassing how my breath hitches at such an innocent touch. "I thought it would feel nice to hold your hand in the exhibits. I've been thinking about it for a long time...fuck, this is ridiculous, isn't it? It is. I don't know why—"

I grab his hand and squeeze it, lifting myself on my tiptoes to press my lips to his cheek. "This is wonderful, Josh. Thank you."

He looks at me skeptically. "Really? Are you just saying that?"

"I haven't been to The Met since I came on a field trip in high school. I'm not very artsy, but I think it would be fun to get a tour from someone who is. While they hold my hand."

When did I go soft? Goddammit.

Josh and I walk into the museum and immediately argue over who's paying. He insists, saying he invited me on the date. I insist too, telling him to stop being so misogynistic and patriarchal, which immediately makes his skin pale, which makes me feel bad, which leads to my apology.

He ends up paying, and I whisper in his ear as we walk away, telling him I'll suck his dick to pay him back. My words make him sputter and blush in the most adorable way.

I like watching him blush. I like holding his hand and the way his hand feels on my waist when he steps behind me while walking.

I'm losing the very little street cred I possess as a five-feet-two-inch woman from suburban Connecticut.

"My parents used to take me here every month when I was a kid," Josh says as we move through the exhibits.

My heart jumps. Josh has barely said anything about his parents, and I haven't wanted to push him. I don't even know what we are, or if it would be appropriate for me to ask. I don't have a right to his past. "Really?" I ask. "You must have been really young."

Josh chuckles, pulling me back to a statue he's stopped near that I'd been ready to walk past. "Yeah. My mom was an artist, and my dad was sickeningly in love with her. Once a month, we'd get bagels with lox from their favorite Jewish Deli in Brooklyn and take a cab, which was pretty special in itself, to the museum." He nods at the statue. "This is one of my favorites."

Josh has walked us to the back of the building, and I allow my eyes to roam over the sculpture and placard. It's a nude woman with small breasts and wide hips, two characteristics I share, two characteristics I've always been self-conscious of.

"She looks like me," I whisper, taking in the curves and sharp edges of the sculpture. I feel Josh stiffen behind me, and I realize he hadn't made the connection. "Well. She's taller, of course," I say in what I hope is a casual tone that doesn't give away the panic I feel. "And she's also a statue."

Josh is silent, and I want to kick myself. Why did I say that? He was just showing me a sculpture he enjoys and I had to go and make things weird.

He wraps his arm around my waist and pulls my back to his front, resting his chin on my shoulder. "You're overthinking, Buttercup. I didn't make the connection before now. She does look like you, doesn't she? Those fucking hips..." He sighs, his hand leaving my waist and dropping to my hip, squeezing gently. I feel his breath blow my curls and shiver. "You're better than art, Nic. You're soft and warm and—" He breaks off.

I want to cry, and he's able to sense it. "Are you okay?" Josh asks me, gently turning my face toward his with his free hand.

I swallow, my eyes searching his. "I think so. I'm just over-whelmed. I'm suddenly feeling a lot."

He nods. "I am, too." His eyes are soft, so blue I want to dive into them and swim in them forever. "Want to look at more boobs?"

That perks me up. "Absolutely, I do."

Josh grins. "Fantastic."

He pulls away, and I immediately miss the feeling of his body against mine. He takes my hand and leads me through his fa-vorite exhibits, making a point to stop at every nude so we both get our fill of boobs. He tells me more about the memories he has of coming with his parents, how his mom would stare starry-eyed at every watercolor painting and how his dad would stare starry-eyed at his mom. He shows me his favorite paintings and tells me about the artists he begged his grandma to buy him books about.

"You were a strange child," I note, after he asks if I remember when he gave a presentation on Rembrant in fifth grade. I don't.

He chuckles, pulling me into him. He smells like leather and charcoal and vanilla, and I want to lick him, right here in the middle of the Metropolitan Museum of Art.

I can't do that, unless...could I call it performance art?

"You think I was a weird kid? You should have seen me in high school. I started reading Shakespeare for *fun*."

"Dork," I tease him as we stop in front of another painting. A naked woman, her back to us, is looking in the mirror, her nude front reflected in the glass. I stare at it, something about it intriguing me.

"I love this one. *Woman before a Mirror*," Josh tells me, rubbing his thumb on the back of my hand. "You can't see her facial expression as she looks at herself, and her body is realistic and human. It's been said she's simply acknowledging her body as it is, not judging or wanting to change it. Simply existing with it." His grip tightens.

"That's something you don't see a lot anymore," I say softly. "It's all about changing or loving your body whole-heartedly. Not just living in it."

"Yeah," Josh says. "It's one of my favorites. The technique and colors are powerful, sure, but she looks content in her body." He pauses. "It helped me a lot, as someone who always felt like I was supposed to be trying to change myself."

Before I can stop myself or think about it, I turn to him and wrap my arms around his center, my ear resting over his heart. He's so soft, so strong, and so beautiful. How dare he compare me to art when he exists?

"Do you still struggle with your body sometimes?" I ask him, looking back up at the painting. He doesn't answer at first, and it gives me enough time to realize my question might have been too personal. "Sorry, ignore me—"

"No," Josh says, his hand cupping the back of my head so his fingers weave through my curls. "No, I know you didn't mean any harm by your question. But you don't have to ask. I'm fine."

I tilt my head back to look up at him. He's gazing down at me, his face soft, and I believe him. "I want to ask, Josh. I want to know you, to hear everything you want to tell me."

His breath hitches. "I—yes. Short answer. I've come a long way, but for a long time, I'd look in the mirror and see something wrong, something bad. It's why I started sleeping around, you know? My body is good at making other people feel good, and I can forget about my insecurities when I'm focused on that." He searches my eyes. "But I was always nervous about putting too much weight on my partner, about hurting them."

"You were?" I ask.

He smiles at me. "Yeah. I was, but now someone gets cranky if I don't put my entire body on top of her after she orgasms."

I grin cheekily at him. "Damn straight, Joshua." I rub his back. "Thank you for telling me. Some of my younger sisters are fat, and I've heard stories about medical discrimination and fetishization. I don't know if that's your experience, but I hate that anyone's worth, or desirability, or level of health is considered to be directly tied to the size of their body."

We're quiet and look at the painting for a few more moments as we hold each other until Josh breaks the silence. "So what embarrassing things was Nic Quinn doing while I was reading *Much Ado About Nothing* for the fun of it?"

"I was hyper-fixated on psychology," I reply. "And *Twilight*. Obviously."

"Obviously," he agrees, and I feel his smile against the top of my head. "What interested you about psychology?"

"I never understood people," I tell him. "Why they act the way they do, why they are the way they are. Now I know that's just autism, but when I took a psych class in high school, it felt like I was getting a peek into a manual I'd never had access to. I was able to understand things I never had before through a psychological lens." I shrug. "Life and people began to make a little bit of sense for the first time."

When I look at him, he's staring down at me, and I feel my cheeks flush.

"That's amazing," he says, a look of admiration in his eyes. "You're amazing."

"Josh, stop. I was already planning on sleeping with you tonight. There's no need for compliments," I tease, waving my hand.

His expression changes. "Stop doing that."

I blink. "Stop doing what?"

"Acting like you're only good for sex. Acting like you and your interests don't deserve attention outside of it. I want to know about you, Nic, just like you want to know me, and everything I learn makes me even more amazed by you. You deserve to know that."

I feel like he just ripped my skin off of my body. I suddenly feel raw, exposed, and vulnerable.

I hug myself. "I'm not used to this. Sex has never been anything but casual for me."

"Come here," he says gently, pulling my body into his and wrapping his arms around me, squeezing me in a way that helps me be able to regulate and be okay in my body again.

"I don't know what I'm doing," I admit into his chest. "I usually know what I'm doing, but I had to consciously learn.

I have a routine and there's usually a right way to do things and I don't know what that is right now. That scares me."

"I don't know what I'm doing either," he says, pressing his lips to the crown of my head as he rubs my back with just enough pressure to relax my tensed muscles. "I have no idea where we're going or what this is. But I do know that I like this. I like spending time with you in all the different ways we have. And I want to spend more time with you. Is that okay?"

And for some reason, knowing he's just as confused by all of this as I am, knowing he's trying to hold on to me as desperately as I am to him, is reassuring. If I'm going to have no idea what I'm doing, at least I'm not the only one.

For so much of my life, I felt like I was missing something everyone else had, an innate understanding of life, of people. Like everyone else had an instruction manual for existing I didn't get. And it was so lonely, so damn lonely, to always feel like I was the only one who didn't understand what everyone else did.

But this time, I'm not alone. Josh is confused and scared and maybe missing a few of the instructions, too. For the first time in my life, I'm okay with there not being a set way to do things. Because I have Josh, the man who opened up about his parents and vulnerabilities. We have each other's backs.

"Okay."

Chapter 28

Playlist: "Glitch," Taylor Swift

I should be scared of how much I feel for Nic. Of how my heart feels like it's expanding so much it could pop like a balloon at any second. But I'm not. If I'm going to die because I've loved Nic Quinn too much, so be it.

She's so soft in my arms, her curls tickling my nose as I rest my cheek on the top of her head.

"Can we go home now?" Nic asks quietly.

"Are you okay?" I ask her, tightening my hold around her torso.

"Yeah, I'm fine. I just—I want to be home. With you."

Home.

The place that has never felt more like home than when she started coming over.

I'm so gone for this woman.

"Let's go home, Buttercup," I agree, loosening my hold on her.

Nic and I make our way to the exit and walk down the stairs at the front of the building. It's a warm night, Nic's holding my hand, and I spent the night showing my favorite pieces of art to my favorite person.

I'm on cloud nine.

Until some guy walking up the stairs bumps into me. I live in the city, and I'm a big guy, so I get bumped into a lot. I'm used to it. It's not a big deal.

At least not to me.

"Hey!" Nic snaps, pivoting her body and glaring at the man who bumped into me. "Aren't you going to apologize?"

The man stops climbing the stairs and looks down at us over his shoulder. "Are you talking to me?"

"Nic," I say, tugging at her hand. "Come on, let's go."

"Yeah, I'm talking to you!" she exclaims, pulling her hand from my grasp and firmly planting both of her hands on her hips. "Are you an animal? Or a kindergartener who hasn't learned how to apologize yet?"

I should definitely be embarrassed.

Instead I'm more turned on by Nic Quinn publicly reprimanding a stranger for not apologizing to me than I've been in my entire life.

And she's ridden my face.

Multiple times.

The guy turns to face us, looking at me and then back at Nic. "It was an accident, sweetheart."

My hands clench. She is *not* his sweetheart. Hell, she would probably say she's not even my sweetheart.

"Nic," I say as gently as I can manage, considering I want to punch this guy into outer space. "It's New York. It happens. Please, let it go."

Let it go so I can have my dirty way with you for defending me. Shut up, brain.

"He's a goddamned tourist!" Nic complains in my direction, tossing her hands up. "The 'it's New York' excuse doesn't work for people who aren't New Yorkers and you know it." I do know it. "He has a to-go box from Bubba Gump."

The stranger and I both look down at his hand, where he indeed is holding a plastic bag with the Bubba Gump logo. "He's probably from Florida or something," she grumbles, crossing her arms over her chest. "Fucking bigoted Florida Man thinking being a tourist is a 'get out of being an asshole free' card."

The guy's face flushes, and, god damn, her ability to profile him is hot as *fuck*.

"Jesus Christ," the guy snaps. "Fucking psycho."

"Yeah?" Nic says in a saccharine tone. "Buddy, you haven't *seen* fucking psycho."

Then Nicoletta Jane Quinn launches all five-feet-two-inches of herself at him.

I react immediately, grabbing her around the waist and lifting her off the ground as she frantically swings her limbs at Florida Man.

"Joshua, put me *down*," she growls, sounding and looking more like a feral kitten more than anything actually intimidating.

"Deep breaths, Buttercup. Orange isn't your color, and I don't particularly feel like spending my night bailing you out of jail," I tell her, tightening my hold on her as she squirms and claws at my arms.

"Control her!" Florida Man says, like I'm not currently physically keeping Nic from attacking him. Like I have, or would want, any control over her.

"Baby," I coo, pulling the nickname from my ass as I rock her back and forth. "It's okay. Let's go home."

"Fuck you!" Nic spits at Florida Man, her legs still kicking. "I just fucking asked for an apology!"

"Shut up, bitch!" he yells back, loud enough for several people to take notice and look over.

Nic's movements freeze, and my heart stops.

I slowly lower her until her feet are safely on the ground and push her gently behind me. I take two steps up toward Florida Man, until he's only one step above me and we're nose to nose.

Well, we're nose to chin. Despite being a step above me, he's still at least three inches shorter than me. I hear him gulp as he takes in my size.

"Orange may not be her color, but I'm willing to find out if it's mine," I tell him coolly. "I don't care if you don't apologize to me, but you sure as hell will be apologizing to that terrifying, somewhat violent, tiny woman behind me. And don't you dare call another woman that word ever again."

"Oh my fucking god," Nic breathes.

"Apologize," I demand, stepping up onto the step he's standing on so he has to take another step up, stumbling on the edge.

"This is so hot," Nic whispers excitedly behind me.

"Fuck, man!" Florida Man says. He leans to look at Nic. "I'm sorry. Happy?"

I give him a million dollar smile. "Immensely."

"*No*," Nic says, elbowing me as she steps in front of me. "He might not care if you don't apologize to him, but I fucking do. He's obviously willing to act out to keep me from acting out, so—"

"Fine! I'm sorry, both of you!" the man exclaims.

Nic's attitude does a one-eighty instantaneously. "Much better!" she says, praising him like the kindergartener she accused him of being. Her voice is bright and bubbly, like she wasn't about to do a stint in prison for assault. "Enjoy the Met. Take some of the culture back to Florida with you."

Florida Man turns and walks away from us, muttering under his breath. Nic is smiling, but her eyes are daggers as she watches him continue his climb to the entrance. Maybe I should be watching him too, but I can't take my eyes off of her.

Once Florida Man is inside the building and no longer a perceived threat, Nic turns to me and our eyes meet.

Then she's in my arms, and her lips are on mine, our kisses all clashing teeth and sucking tongues. Definitely not appropriate for our current location, but I can't find it in me to give a damn.

"That." *Kiss.* "Was." *Bite.* "So." *Lick.* "Fucking *hot*," Nic gasps, breaking our kiss to scrape her teeth just below the edge of my beard.

I groan. "We can't. Not here, Buttercup."

"Take me home, then, Joshy."

I hail a cab quicker than I've done anything else in my life, Nic still in my arms. When we're in the back of the cab, we're all over each other. The driver occasionally looks in the rearview mirror curiously, and I can't help but meet his eyes, hoping the look on my face tells him exactly what I'm thinking.

Yeah. She's mine. She chose me.

"You were gonna kill that guy for calling me a bitch, weren't you?" Nic asks with a gasp as she pulls her lips from mine.

"Of course I was, Buttercup. And you were willing to kill him for not apologizing."

"I was a little unhinged," Nic admits, her face flushing the same color pink as other parts of her body that I plan to worship tonight.

"Just a little. Sexy as fuck, though." I take her hand and place it over my erection, squeezing so she can feel just how sexy I found it.

She bites her lip. "Nobody's stuck up for me that way before. I think you know how it made me feel."

Her nipples are pebbled beneath her shirt, her lips swollen and breath heavy.

I know *exactly* how that made her feel.

"You do so much for me, Josh," she says, her voice softening. "So, so much for me. Can I do something for you?" "Don't sell yourself short. You have no idea how much richer my life is because I tried to sit next to you on the train, Buttercup." My throat feels thick because just thinking about how happy she's made me, despite how difficult everything this summer has been, makes me emotional. Knowing how easily we could have never happened.

"I want to do something special. You took me on this date and then defended my honor, which should have been annoying but instead was ridiculously attractive, and I want to do something for you."

"What kind of something?"

She bites her lip. "Anything. I'll do anything you want me to. Whatever fantasy you have."

The driver glaces at us in the rearview mirror, and I meet his eyes again.

That's right. Mine.

"Anything?"

"Anything."

I feel my cheeks flush as I bite my lip. "Well, there is something I've been wanting to try."

"I have to admit, when I told you I'd do anything you wanted tonight, going with you into your home office wasn't what I pictured," Nic tells me as I lead her into the room.

She's been to my place so many times, but this is the first time she's been in this specific room. There's a dark brown leather sofa and a dark oak desk which once belonged to my dad. My favorite vanilla-scented candle is on a coaster that Belen crocheted for me, and pictures of my family sit on my desk. There isn't much wall space, but what there is of it is covered in posters of various productions of Shakespeare plays I've seen on and off Broadway. The rest of the walls are lined with bookshelves packed to the brim with volumes of literary criticism, as well as dozens of editions of *The Complete Works of William Shakespeare* and individual plays.

But I watch Nic as, after taking in the rest of the room, her eyes settle on my absolute favorite part of the room. Her chocolate brown eyes widen as she takes in the bookshelf which is filled with mass market historical romances.

This is another part of me I've been cautious about letting anyone see.

But she isn't just anyone. She's everything.

"Holy *shit*," Nic breathes, dropping my hand as she crosses the room. "That is a *lot* of bodice rippers."

I laugh nervously and rub the back of my neck. "My grandma loves them, and I kinda just picked them up out of boredom and curiosity in high school, and I never stopped."

Nic bites her lower lip as she fights back a laugh, and I feel my shoulders relax slightly. It doesn't look like a mean-spirited laugh. She pulls a Beverly Jenkins novel off the shelf and examines the cover. "I don't know how you still manage to surprise me, Joshua Henry," Nic says softly. "And you know how particular I am about surprises. I like these."

I take a few steps forward until we're touching, my chest pressed against her back. I wrap an arm around her waist and pull her closer to me, inhaling her lavender scent. Mercilessly, Nic grinds her ass against my painfully hard cock.

I hiss through my teeth and use my other hand to dig my fingers into the soft flesh of her hip. "You surprise me everyday, Buttercup," I breathe into her ear, enjoying the way her breath hitches when mine touches her skin. "It's only fair that I have a few surprises of my own up my sleeve."

I reach my hand out and run my fingers along the spines of the books, my eyes searching. It takes me a minute or two to find what I'm looking for, and when I do, I take it off the shelf and loosen my grip on her as I step back toward my desk.

"Come here."

Nic spins around and walks to my desk, immediately hopping on the edge and kicking her boots off.

"Hold this," I tell her, letting my eyes roam down her body. Fuck, she's a masterpiece.

Nic meets my eyes and takes the book with a dubious expression. "What is it?"

"A book."

She rolls her eyes. "So helpful, Joshua, thank you."

I chuckle. She's so pretty perched on my desk, looking like she belongs there. Grading would be *so* much easier if Nic were to sit on my desk while I worked.

Or much harder.

At least I would be.

"It's called *The Duchess Deal*. It's about a really pissed off and misunderstood duke who enters into a marriage of convenience with a seamstress. He reminds me of you, actually."

Nic scowls. "A pissed-off duke reminds you of me? Stop, Joshy. You're making me blush."

I grin. "Especially when you frown like that." I tilt her chin up with my hand and thumb at her plump lower lip.

She playfully nips at my thumb. "Such an asshole."

"You really bring out that side of me."

She rolls her eyes, turning the book over in her hands and looking down to read the back. "Jo loves these and is always trying to get me to read them. I don't get the hype."

My stomach sinks. My plan isn't going to work if she's not into it. "You don't like them?"

Nic shakes her head, her curls bouncing with the movement before she freezes. "Well...maybe that's not quite true." The prettiest blush, the color of sun-ripened strawberries, starts to creep up her neck.

I smirk and lean next to her on the desk. "No?"

She bites her lip and, fuck, she so beautiful right now. "They're sexy."

"That's the best part."

I notice her hand between us is white-knuckling the edge of the desk, so I slip my hand under hers, flipping mine so it's palm up to intertwine our fingers together.

Her blush spreads up across her face. Even her ears are pink. "Sometimes..." She looks at me, her eyes searching and wide. "Promise you won't laugh?"

"I promise I won't laugh."

Nic takes a deep breath. "Sometimes I masturbate while reading them," she says quickly, like the faster the words are out of her mouth, the faster she'll be able to breathe.

I know the exact shade of pink her cunt is when she's turned on, what her clit looks like when she's aching and swollen. I know what she feels like when she comes on my cock, and I know what each noise she makes means. She's fallen apart at my touch so many times, and yet, she's still so embarrassed talking about masturbating while reading historical romance novels.

I take the book from her, flipping through the pages. "Nicoletta Quinn likes making herself come while reading about sardonic rakes and shy wallflowers passionately losing control?"

"Maybe," she answers in a small voice.

I stand from the desk and place the book back in Nic's hands after finding what I was looking for. "Read this."

Nic's eyes scan over the page, widening as she realizes what scene the book is open to. "Josh!" she hisses.

"Is that what you like to read? You read historical smut and touch yourself until that pretty pussy of yours comes?" I murmur, planting my hands on the desk on either side of her, leaning into her.

She lifts her eyes to mine with a sweet little whimper. Her *oh god I'm turned on and I don't know if I should be,* whimper. Her eyes are wide, wild, and oh-so-horny.

"Yes," she replies, her voice breathless and wanting.

"Do you remember when you said you'd do whatever I wanted? My biggest fantasy?"

"Yes?"

"What if I told you this was it?"

"What is?" Nic breathes, her voice heavy and laced with her arousal.

"You. On my desk. Reading a scene from one of my favorite historical romances while I make you come with my mouth."

Chapter 29

Nic

Playlist: "Don't Blame Me," Josh Rabenold

I stare at Josh, his ocean blue eyes hooded with desire. He can't be suggesting what I think he is.

"What?" I squeak, my grip on the book tightening. "Your fantasy is me reading a romance book on your desk?"

"And making you fall apart with my tongue, yes." He gently brushes back a rogue curl that had fallen into my face and leans into me, playfully nipping at the shell of my ear.

"Why?" It's hard to breathe. *This* is his fantasy? I told him I'd do anything he wanted, and he just wants me coming on his mouth.

"Because it turns me on when you say dirty words. It makes me so proud to hear you talk about pleasure and desire, and I want to taste and feel you while you do it. Do you know how fucking good you taste, Buttercup? It's like I was waiting to taste you my whole life."

"I—" I don't finish my thought, my head swimming and heart pounding as I whimper as Josh presses his lips to my neck. I feel him smile into me.

"Fuck, I love it when you whimper like that," he murmurs, pressing deceptively soft kisses to the sensitive spots he's learned on my neck. "That's the sound you make when you're just starting to get wet, when you want to rub those pretty thighs together to find relief for the ache in your cunt."

I moan in response to him, to his words and his touch. I tilt my head away, exposing more of my neck to him. His smile widens. "And that moan—ah, Buttercup. You've given yourself away. I know you're soaked."

"Josh," I whine, grabbing the back of his neck and urging his lips to mine. He groans as he kisses me, one hand guiding my leg around his hip and the other cupping my waist.

"I want to kiss you," he gasps as he pulls away. "I want to kiss you and make you scream my name over and over again while you read to me. Will you let me do that, Nic?"

I nod my head furiously. Fuck, if he asked me to read the Bible to him right now, I fucking would.

"Words, Nicoletta." His voice is husky and deep, and, fuck, my body *aches* for him. "You know I need your words."

"Yes," I manage to gasp. "Please."

Josh lets my leg drop as he falls to his knees between my thighs, his face inches from where I desperately need him. I spread my legs wider as he unbuttons a few more buttons of his shirt. He lifts them both over his shoulders, opening me to him.

If it were anyone but him, I'd be shy. But I know I can trust him. I know he listens to me, and he wants to make me feel good. Josh would never hurt me, which might be even scarier.

He palms my inner thigh as I lean back on my elbows, clutching the book to my chest. "These stockings...fuck. You've been driving me crazy all night. It took every ounce of willpower I have to not rip them off of you right in the middle of the Met and let everyone watch me make you scream."

"Then rip them," I gasp, trying to still my wiggling body. His eyes dart up to mine, and my flush deepens. "They're easily replaceable, if that's what you're worried about. I have multiple pairs."

Josh sighs, a light, airy sound as he hooks his fingers into the fishnets. "Thank god," he breathes before tearing them.

I squeal at the ripping noise, and my legs tense at the sting of the impact. Josh stills his movements and meets my eyes again, a concerned look on his face. "It's good," I gasp. "Keep going."

And he does. He tears through my stockings ruthlessly, like he can't get me bare fast enough. "I fucking love when you're at my mercy," he grunts. "But fuck, Nic. Sometimes I dream about you dominating me, making me beg for you."

I gasp, my arousal deepening at his confession. "I want to do that for you, too," I admit. "I want to try."

My stockings hang in tatters from my body, and all that remains between Josh and where I need him are my drenched confidence underwear.

"I love these on you," Josh says, a smile on his lips as he gently runs his index finger up my slit, and my hips reflexively jerk off the desk. "But I love them even more off of you."

I whimper, staring down at him. There's something about this man being on his knees for me that makes me feral.

"Nicoletta, I believe I assigned you some reading?" Josh says, his touch featherlight over my aching center. "I'd hate to have to fail you."

"Fucker," I grumble. His responding chuckle is deep and sweet as I lift the book above my head and begin to read the filthy scene on the page.

My breath hitches as Josh's tongue flattens against my underwear, the warmth and wetness of his worshiping mouth seeping through to my core. He continues to tongue me through the fabric, and it's a damn miracle I'm able to read aloud with how he's making me feel right now.

I'm trying to read, but I gasp and arch my back, book forgotten, as Josh parts me through my underwear with his tongue and sucks my clit into his mouth. He moves his mouth from me, and I prop myself up on my elbows and look down at him. He's staring up at me, brow raised.

"I thought you read books like this to make yourself come?"

I blush. "I do."

"Don't you want to come, pretty girl?"

I scowl at him. "You're a dickhead."

He ignores me, instead returning his attention to my under-wear. He crooks his finger into them, between my cunt and the fabric, and pulls them to the side. "Call me whatever you want, Nic. As long as you call my name when you come."

His mouth is on me again—now delivering fast, firm flicks of his tongue on my clit. My elbows give out, and I fall to my back, thighs squeezing his head as he makes me feel so good–the way only he can.

Trembling, I lift the book again, begging my mind and eyes to focus on the words.

I did promise him whatever he wanted tonight, after all.

I stammer through a sentence or two, and the words blur as pleasure builds in me.

Josh presses his finger into me and then, without prompting, another. He presses up toward my pelvic bone, and god, I'm so close.

"Skip ahead," Josh says suddenly, lifting his head. "Skip ahead to where he makes her come."

I flip forward and read.

Josh's mouth is on me again, and he moves his fingers, slow, hard movements into where I'm most sensitive. It's all building so fast, and I skip ahead even more to read the part he wants me to.

It's like magic, how just as I choke out the final words of the scene, everything within me tenses and explodes into a million little stars that surround Josh and me, illuminating and guiding me through my climax.

I ride out my orgasm, mind turning to liquid, as Josh continues to slowly move his fingers inside of me after moving his mouth from my clit.

He's so good. So good to me. He makes me feel better than I ever knew I could and *fuck,* it's terrifying and so right.

"More," I whimper, pushing myself up to my elbows as he rises to his feet. My legs fall from his shoulders, and he's slipping his fingers out of me. "I need more of you."

"You have all of me, Buttercup," he says, his voice thick as he leans his big body over mine. "I'm yours."

I take a fistful of the fabric of his shirt and pull him closer, our mouths colliding in a battle for each other, him fighting for me, and me fighting for him. I shudder because, *fuck*, he tastes like me, and he's right.

He's *mine.*

I gasp against him as he bites my lower lip. "I need you inside me. Now."

Josh breaks our kiss and straightens, his eyes dark and blazing into me as he undoes his belt. I can't take my eyes off of his hands as they move to his fly, deft fingers, still wet with me, freeing himself.

"Condoms and lube are in the desk drawer to the left," he says as he fists himself.

I lean back to open the drawer and grab an economy sized pack of condoms from it.

"Is there a reason you keep a ginormous box of condoms in your desk?" I ask as I hand him a condom and lube

"I told you, Nic. This has been my biggest fantasy. I'm a hopeful guy."

I sit up as he rips open the foil. I pull my top off over my shoulders, my nipples pebbling at the cool temperature. I reach forward and gently tug the condom from his grip, "Take off your clothes. I want your skin on mine when you fuck me, Josh."

In an instant, he's kicking out of his pants and briefs, and I'm lifting myself off the desk so he can pull my skirt, tattered stockings, and soaked panties off my hips, tossing everything to the side as his eyes run over my body. I lick my hand and grip his cock, pumping him twice before finally fulfilling my own fantasy and rolling a condom over him as he unbuttons his shirt, throwing it to the side. He pulls off his undershirt, exposing himself to me. It still feels like an honor to see him like this.

His expression suddenly changes, and his touch is tender as he brushes the same unruly curl from my face. "You're exquisite, Nic. I hope you feel that way with me."

"I do," I promise him. "I feel so beautiful when I'm with you. I hope I make you feel beautiful, too."

"You do." He leans forward and sucks softly on my lip. "I didn't even know I could be beautiful before you."

I whimper, so turned on and yet so sad that no one ever made sure Josh knows how beautiful he is.

Because *what the fuck*.

He hooks his arms under my legs and pulls me to the edge of the desk. He squirts some lube on his fingers, tenderly spreading it on my skin. "Put me inside you, Buttercup," he murmurs.

I line the head of his cock up with my dripping entrance, and we both tilt our hips as he pushes in. It's so easy, like my body knows exactly who this is, that I'm safe with him, and that he'll make sure I feel good.

"So fucking tight," Josh grits out, his voice strained. "You feel so good, Nic. I could stay inside you forever."

Then do it. Stay inside my heart and my body forever because I'm so much more myself when I'm with you.

His movements are hard and soft all at once, and my heart feels like it's breaking open. Tears fill my eyes, and I bury my face into his chest, clinging onto him like a lifeline.

Josh moves one hand to the back of my head, cradling me to him as tears fall from my eyes, overwhelmed by the emotional and physical sensations. "I know, Buttercup," he chokes out. "I know."

I'm so consumed by him that I have no idea where my body ends and his begins. He's a part of me.

"Stay with me. Please, Nic. I need you to come with me," he groans, slipping his hand between us and rubbing firm, hard circles around my clit.

"Josh," I choke out, my fingers digging into his flesh.

"You're right there, beautiful. Let go for me."

I come harder than I've come in my entire life. Fireworks and waves and every other metaphor don't come close to the way I feel in this moment, so safe, so...

So *loved*.

He yells my name as he comes, a string of curses and prayers and praise, as his body goes limp over mine. His breath is hot puffs of air into my mouth, his hands caressing me up and down my body as I tenderly hold his face in my hands.

"That wasn't in the syllabus," I breathe, voice shaking. I can't take my eyes off of him. Has he always been this beautiful? Even a month ago? Have his eyes always been this blue? Has he always been so safe?

"I think we both can agree the syllabus hasn't mattered for a long time, Nic."

My hands tremble as I stroke his face with my thumbs, slowly coming down from my orgasm. He's trembling, too, but despite that, Josh is holding me with a strength that can only be described as steady and safe.

He's steady, and he keeps me safe.

I don't realize I'm still crying until he lifts a hand to my face, brushing my tears away with his thumb as his deep blue eyes search mine. "Buttercup," he says, his voice shaky and a soft smile on his lips. "My Buttercup."

And that's when I realize.

I love him. I love Joshua Charles Henry and his steady strength and his soft heart and that damn smile and baffling, constant way he wants me.

I should be scared. I should be pulling away and running.

Instead, I start to cry harder.

"Nic—" I hear the panic in his voice as he pulls me into him, cradling my head in his hand. "Are you hurt? What—"

"I love you," I sob into his chest. "I love you so much, Josh."

I feel his body tense and arms tighten around me. Why isn't my fear instinct working? Why am I not throwing up because I just told him I love him? Because all the cards are on the table, and he could reject me?

Josh makes me brave.

The fucking asshole.

"Nic—"

"I'm not just saying it," I interrupt, looking up, his beautiful face blurred by my tears. He's frozen, eyes wide and mouth agape. "I mean it. And I'm telling you because I'm brave with you. I'm the Nic who is brave and who knows herself and says what she needs. And she needs you to know that she loves you."

Josh blinks at me wordlessly, and it suddenly occurs to me that he's still inside me.

What a terrible time to show everything I've learned from him.

"Say it again?" he whispers as his eyes search mine, his voice wavering, like he's unsure and disbelieving.

Be brave, Nic. Be brave for him.

I pull him down to me so our foreheads are pressed together. "I love you, Joshua Henry. I think I was bound to from the start."

He inhales shakily, and his eyes flutter shut. "I think I've loved you since the day you glared at me for telling you I thought your name sounded like Nutella. I've dreamt of you loving me since I ran into you that night on the train. And when I opened the door the morning after the party and saw you on my doorstep...the idea you wanted to be in my life, even just for sex? Even just for a little while? It's the greatest thing that's ever happened to me up to now. Nic, my life makes sense because you're in it."

I feel like my heart grew wings and is soaring away from the rest of my body. "You love me, too?"

"I love you, Nicoletta Quinn. With everything I am." Josh takes my hand and presses it over his pounding heart. "With everything I have, I'm yours."

I kiss him, and I know he can hear everything I'm saying in it.

I love you. I need you. Thank you. I'm yours. You're mine. I love you. I love you. I love you.

He pulls away, his cock slipping out of me. I whimper pathetically and reach out for him with grabby hands, needing his body against mine again.

He grins at me, all boyish and bashful and sweet, and I want to stand on the roof of this brownstone and scream for all of Brooklyn to hear that he's *mine*. That that's *my* smile.

That he loves me.

"I love you," he tells me again as he slips off the condom. I break out into the giddiest, goofiest grin.

Will it ever feel real? That he loves me? I hope it doesn't. I hope it always feels this incredible to hear it, to know it.

"I love you too," I whisper.

"Stay here tonight?" he asks as he throws the condom away in a small trash can next to his desk.

I nod in response. "Will you stay with me?"

"Yes." He hoists me into his arms, carrying me upstairs to his bed like a bride. And though it's not our wedding night, it feels just as monumental. Like the beginning of something new, something sacred.

Something good.

I hate change, and I hate surprises, but Josh surprising me by evolving from my enemy into my favorite person is the exception.

Josh is the exception to everything I've forced myself to believe.

He lays me in bed, and we lie side by side, staring at each other.

"Josh, is that a buttercup tattoo?" I ask, noticing the flower tattooed right beside his heart.

He looks down as my fingertips dance over it. "My dad called my mom Buttercup."

I burst into tears again as the meaning sinks in, and he takes me into his arms, holding me to him. "Why me?" I choke out. "Why did you choose me?"

"It just came out on the train. I could tell it annoyed you, and it was funny and then...then I understood why my dad called my mom that, and it wasn't funny anymore. You're my Buttercup."

I kiss his tattoo before tucking my head under his chin. I never expected to feel this loved, and my entire body is overwhelmed by how important we've become to each other.

I finally fall asleep in Josh's arms, my head against his heart.

Chapter 30

Nic

**Playlist: "A Sky Full of Stars - Piano Version,"
Danielle Leoni, Purple Lions**

Jo: spending the night at josh's again i see? seduced by thai chef?

Jo: strumpet.

Jo: hahaha kidding.

Jo: pls use condoms

> **Jo:** i'm not ready to be an aunt.

> **Jo:** don't be selfish

> **Jo:** use condoms.

I'm woken up in the middle of the night by Josh's body moving next to mine. He's restless, his body thrashing frantically as gasps and whimpers escape from his lips. My heart sinks as I realize what's happening, that he's having a nightmare.

I know from my education not to wake someone from PTSD episodes, but it's difficult when he's in such obvious distress and pain.

I turn on my side to face him, gently placing my hand over his and stroking his damp skin with the pad of my thumb as he lets out a shattered cry. It lasts for a few minutes at most, though it feels much longer, and finally his breaths slow as his body stills. I press my lips to his temple, and as I break contact, his eyes open and he stares at me.

"Nic," he breathes my name like I'm an answered prayer, water in a desert. "I—I forgot."

I shush him, caressing his cheek. "I didn't forget, you're safe. Can we look at the stars together? Count them?"

We both turn onto our backs and intertwine my fingers with his shaking hand. I lift my free hand to point out each star on his ceiling as he counts out loud. Slowly, his body relaxes and I turn back onto my side.

He stays on his back and scrubs at his eyes with his hand as he swallows harshly. "I never wanted you to see this. To see me like this."

I frown at him. "Josh, you've survived terrible, unprocessed trauma. I know it sucks ass when it happens and I hate that you deal with this, but it doesn't scare me. It's a part of your life, and you're a part of mine."

I pause, my thumb gently tracing over his full lower lip. "Do you remember when I came over that first time? When I asked you to have sex and had a meltdown when you didn't respond right away? You didn't look at me any differently; you just asked how you could make me feel safe. This is no different."

Josh's eyes flutter closed, and he turns his face, pressing his lips to the palm of my hand. His beard is scratchy against my skin. "I don't deserve you."

"Stop that. You deserve the absolute best, Joshua Henry," I tell him. "You deserve to be loved and cherished all the time, but especially when you're in the scary, dark parts of life. That's all I'm doing." He turns onto his side to face me and pulls me into his arms. "Do you want to talk about it?"

He exhales sharply. "They're slightly different every time. And it always starts normally, and then—" Josh's hold tightens around me. "And then I'm always in a car. Sometimes it's in the cab with my parents, and I watch them slowly die while I'm unimpacted by the crash. Other times, I'm driving or a passenger in the car that hits them, and I can always see their faces. And I always know they know it's me. That it's my fault."

"Josh." My heart shatters into a million pieces. "You know that's not true, right? It's *not* your fault. Your subconscious feels responsible, and your trauma won't let you forget, but it's a fucking *lie*."

He sniffles, and I look up at him, reaching up to wipe away a tear. "I logically understand that as a grown man, but sometimes it's like I'm still just a seven year old who broke his arm and whose parents were dead by the time they made it to the hospital where he was waiting for them."

"Oh, Joshy," I whisper, my own eyes filling with tears. When I look at him, I see the same little blond boy with a purple cast on his arm who stood at the front of the classroom as our principal introduced him. "I'm so sorry, that must be unbelievably painful."

He nods, his eyes distant. "It hurts so fucking much every time. But I don't want this to affect you or impact us so I think I want to try therapy again."

I cup his face and angle it until our eyes meet. "Please don't go to therapy because you think you're an inconvenience to me. Go for you. Because you deserve to find healing. I'm happy to help you ground after every nightmare and help you remember where and who you are in the present. But you need to want to heal for yourself."

"Do you think it's possible?" Josh asks, his voice barely above a whisper. "For me to heal?"

I kiss the tip of his nose. "I know it is."

Chapter 31

Nic

Playlist: "Crazy in Love (Acoustic Cover)," Girl in the Distance

Nic's Google Search (July 24, 3:42am)

- *How do you get your boyfriend to go to therapy?*

- *How do you know if someone's your boyfriend?*

- *If you tell someone you love them and they say it back are they your boyfriend?*

- *Is it weird to have your first boyfriend in your late twenties?*

- *How to get the guy you love and are sleeping with to go to therapy.*

The next time I wake up, sunlight is streaming across the room through the blinds. Josh and I had fallen asleep, our bodies tangled up in each other, after he told me his favorite memories of his parents. His mom, Larissa, always sang along to all the songs when they watched *The Lion King*, and every night. When he came home from work, his dad, Charlie, would have a brand new joke to tell him. He told me about his mom's art, how most of her paintings are still in the attic, and how he never goes up there because it still hurts too much. I held him and stroked his hair, listening to everything he told me. My imagination ran rampant picturing a tiny, gap-toothed Josh Henry in this same house, a boy who was forced to learn the horrors of the world far younger than he should have.

I thought we'd separate during the night, but Josh is still holding on tight to me. I look at him now, and the sun highlights the faint laugh lines around his eyes, the barely-there sprinkling of freckles across the bridge of his nose, the reddish undertones of his hair. How is he more beautiful each time I look at him?

It should be illegal, honestly.

I want to touch him. To kiss down his chest and his belly until he's moaning my name—

But he needs rest. Not his horny Buttercup waking him up for morning sex.

So I slip out of his arms and force myself out of bed, my body aching at the loss of closeness. Every inch of me knows Josh is good for me, that I should stay close to him.

For fuck's sake. Being in love is bizarre.

With a final look at Josh over my shoulder, I walk downstairs to his office naked. I know I'll find my outfit from last night bunched up on the floor somewhere.

When I catch sight of my skirt and the tattered netting that used to be my stockings, I bend down to pull the skirt on, but then I spot the white button up Josh had worn last night and get distracted. I drop my skirt on the floor, bringing the starchy fabric to my face. It smells like him, like home—warm and spicy. I pull it over my shoulders and fasten the buttons. Even with the sleeves rolled up, they still go down past my wrists and the hem goes all the way to my knees. The tag is worn and soft and doesn't bother me and I can't help but wonder how Josh will feel about never getting this particular shirt back. I want as much of him as I can have, to have a part of him with me always.

I go down to the kitchen, a new spring in my step that I don't hate. Humming to myself like some sort of lovesick loser, I pull two glasses down from the cabinets above the counter and fetch the jar with chocolate sauce and the vanilla oat milk from the refrigerator. I'm unironically singing to myself about never giving someone up, smiling as I think about Josh's reaction to me waking him up with breakfast in bed.

Or at least chocolate milk in bed.

I can be his breakfast.

After I mix the chocolate sauce into the glasses of milk, I take a sip to taste it, and the consistency and taste are both wrong. I wrinkle my nose and try again.

And again.

And again.

By the fourth attempt, I've stopped singing, and my dreamy smile has melted into a frustrated scowl. I'm just about ready to give up when—

"Nic."

I scream and jump a foot into the air, the spoon clanging on the counter. I spin around and see Josh standing in the kitchen doorway, looking like a fucking god. His hair is wild, standing in every direction, and his body is bare except for a baggy pair of sleep shorts.

He blinks at me, and my heart sinks as I realize I don't recognize the expression on his face.

Something's wrong.

"Josh?" I say cautiously. "What is it?"

He takes a few steps to close the distance between us, wrapping his arms around my body as his forehead falls limp to my shoulder, his back hunched over. I swallow and cup the back of his head, letting my fingers play gently with his soft strands of hair.

"You were gone. I woke up, and you were gone, and I thought—"

My heart sinks. *Fuck*. I didn't think about how he would feel waking up alone after the night we had. I'd assumed I'd be the one waking him up when I came back.

"I'm so sorry," I tell him, turning my head so I can nuzzle him. "I wanted to surprise you, since you surprised me."

He lifts his head from my shoulder and straightens his back, tilting my chin up so my eyes can follow his movements. He exhales harshly as he cups my face with his hands, his thumbs gently stroking my cheeks. "You're still here."

I lean into his touch, looking up at him. "I'm still here. I'm not going anywhere, Josh."

He bends down and kisses me, soft and slow and tender. He tastes like mint, and my heart shatters as I think of him waking up alone and then brushing his teeth before coming down to what he thought was an empty house.

Josh breaks our kiss and presses his forehead to mine, his breath shaky. "I love you," he tells me, his eyes fluttering closed. "I don't think words exist to express how much I love you, how much last night means to me. How much every moment I've spent with you means to me. I love you so much my mouth goes dry, and my heart hurts when I think about it too much. I spent tens of thousands of dollars becoming an expert in the most prolific wordsmith, and it means nothing when I'm with you. No story that's ever been written compares to the one we started writing when we ended up on the same train."

"Joshua," I breathe, my heart breaking and fusing back together with hot, liquid gold all at once. "Show me if you can't tell me."

He lowers his eyes, his gaze like warm sunlight on my body. "I came downstairs thinking you'd left without saying goodbye after the most emotionally vulnerable night of my life and instead I found the woman I love in my kitchen. Wearing my shirt."

He runs his thumb over my bottom lip. I dart my tongue out to taste him. He presses his thumb into my mouth, and my eyes stay on his as I wrap my lips around him and suck. "I woke up wanting you, Buttercup, fucking aching for you. I need you."

He pulls his thumb from my mouth with a pronounced *pop*. "Show me," I repeat, my voice breathy.

Josh's hands grab my hips and he turns us so my back is to the island. He spins me by my hips, and my hands grab the island surface.

"Hands on the counter," he breathes into my ear, goose-bumps rising on my skin at the feeling. "And tell me if I'm too rough."

All I manage is a whimper in response before he's lifting the hem of his shirt up, the fabric tickling the backs of my thighs as he exposes more and more of myself to him. He squeezes an ass cheek, his hand almost completely covering me. "You in my shirt...fuck, Buttercup. Do you know how hard I am right now? How it feels to see you in this? You're so fucking pretty." His hand slides between my thighs, where he finds the evidence of just how needy I am for him, too.

"Josh," I beg, my voice trembling and broken with need. "Please."

Josh wraps his free hand gently around my neck, his thumb stroking the column of my throat. I shiver as he gently turns my head until our eyes meet. "Please what, Nicoletta?"

"Please, fuck me."

His mouth covers mine, hungry and rough, and then he's pushing his fingers into my pussy.

"Oh, god," I cry out as he curls his fingers into me.

"Try again, Buttercup," he groans into my mouth, his hand moving from my throat to my hair, fisting a handful of my curls and pulling so perfectly my legs tremble. "God isn't the one who's about to make you come so hard you see fucking stars. Say my name."

"Josh," I moan, my back arching and knees buckling as the stars he promised are born. Sparkles of gold surround us, and hold me up through wave after wave of pleasure.

"That's my girl," he growls, his voice husky and primal. This is so different from the Josh who taught me over the summer. This Josh knows the extent of my ability for pleasure now, and he gives it to me without holding back. He pulls his fingers from my still throbbing pussy and brings them to my lips so I can clean them.

As my tongue swirls around his fingers, my heartbeat slows and I begin to return to earth. He kisses from my collarbone up my neck, nipping and sucking what I assume is a freckle below my jawbone.

I reach a hand behind me, cupping his cock through his shorts. He's so hard for me, and I need him desperately.

"Bend over." Josh presses a hand between my shoulder blades, applying pressure until I'm on my tiptoes, my breasts and palms pressed into the surface.

I whimper as he leans over me, reaching around to open a drawer. "Are you okay?" he whispers loudly, "Is this okay?"

I smile to myself and bite my lip. "I like it. I'll tell you if that changes."

"Fuck, yeah you will. You've come so far, Buttercup." Josh presses a sweet kiss to my blushing cheek, and the contrast of him finger fucking me roughly and bossing me around to these sweet kisses after checking in with me gives me the best kind of emotional whiplash.

"I love you," I croak.

"I love you, Nic. So much," he echoes. I hear a tear and look over my shoulder to see Josh rolling a condom onto his dick.

"You keep condoms in the kitchen, too?"

He meets my eyes, a guilty smile spreading across his face. "I keep condoms in every room. I think you underestimate how much I've dreamt of fucking you in every single room since I saw you in this kitchen the night of my party."

I groan, and my face falls to the counter, my cheek pressing against the cool surface. "You've loved and wanted me for so long, and I don't know what to do with that."

Josh leans over me, one hand on my hip. His breath is hot against my ear, and he circles my clit with the head of his cock. "Take it."

I cry out as he seats himself in me in one hard thrust, my body feeling as if it's on fire in the sweetest, most delicious way.

He pauses for a moment to allow my body to adjust to his sheer overwhelming size before moving his hips again. "I belong to you, Nic. You know that, don't you?" He grunts, breath hot and heavy on my skin as he fucks me hard and fast. "And you're mine."

"Yours," I gasp in response, my orgasm building quickly as he tilts his hips. All I want to do is tell all the people who think they know Josh Henry just because they fucked him that I'm the *only* one who really knows him. They can whisper to each other about their history with him all they want, but I'm the one he wants to fuck all over his house. The one he comes back to, again and again

He's *mine.*

"I wish you could see how good my cock looks fucking you, Nic. Your pretty little pussy was made for me."

Josh's hand back is in my hair, pulling, and my back bows as I come pulsing around him, all shooting stars and lightning strikes in my body.

He comes on a final thrust into me, roaring my name as he plants his hands next to mine and collapsing on top of me, pinning me to the counter.

"Fuck," I gasp as I come down. "Fuck, fuck, fuck—"

"Did I hurt you?" His voice is suddenly anxious, his hands moving over my body like he's checking for injuries.

"Not at all. I liked it. I liked it *so* much." I place my hand over his and squeeze gently.

He pulls out of me, and I wince slightly at the friction. I can hear him throwing out the condom. "It was—I've never felt this strongly before. About anyone. It's terrifying, and I don't know how to express it. It feels like the energy can't be contained in my body." He pauses. "That probably doesn't make any sense. I should just leave the big love declarations to the Bard."

I straighten before turning around to face him, the hem of his button-up fluttering down, covering me again. I can't take my eyes off of him. His eyes are filled with so much hope and vulnerability, and, *my god,* I love this damn man.

I lean into him, pressing my cheek to his bare chest and wrapping my arms around his waist. "It was perfect." I feel him exhale with relief and embrace me, cupping the back of my head and raking his fingers through the strands of my hair. "Thank you for showing me how much you love me, Josh Henry."

We hold each other in silence for a moment before he speaks again. "I'd never made love before." His voice is soft, reverent even. "I never knew what it was like to want to be this close to someone because you love them. I didn't know I've been making love to you this whole time."

Josh loves me twice more before noon, both of us giving everything we are to the other.

Josh Henry's Google Search (July 23rd, 11:53pm)

- *How to ask someone who used to hate you to be your girlfriend?*

- *Do adults have girlfriends or are they called something else?*

- *How do you know if someone still hates you?*

- *How many seasons of Ted Lasso are there?*

- *Is She's The Man on Netflix?*

Chapter 32

Josh

Playlist: "Iris," Kina Grannis

Nic and I are tangled on the floor, her legs woven with mine. I meant to get us to the couch—the place I first touched her, where everything started changing–but the extra foot and a half was too much.

"You should build me a fire," Nic murmurs, all satiated and sleepy.

I chuckle. "It's late July, Buttercup. That seems like a *terrible* idea."

"It'd be romantic," she argues, her eyes flying open to glare at me. "Be romantic for me, Joshua."

I kiss the tip of her nose and then the freckles covering her face. "Do you really want me to build you a fire? In ninety-degree weather? That's the worst idea you've ever had. But fuck me, I'll do it."

She lets out a long-suffering sigh, and I bite back a laugh. "Fine. But I expect the fireplace to be lit on a daily basis when fall hits."

I'm overwhelmed by the image of Nic coming over in the fall and letting herself in with her own key, her nose pink from the cold. Nic sitting on the kitchen island while I cook, kicking her fuzzy-socked feet as she hums whatever song's stuck in her head. Walking the city streets together, taking in the red and orange leaves, and marveling as the seasons change. Kissing her under the lights as snow falls over us, sticking to her eyelashes as she smiles that smile up at me that's reserved for me alone.

"You're sticking around that long, Buttercup?" I ask in what I hope is a casual tone, and not the over-excited way I'm actually feeling.

I feel her body tense against mine, and her eyes flutter open, her warm chocolate irises gazing up at me. "If you want me to stick around," she says shakily, eyes searching mine. "I think we still have a lot we can learn from each other. A lot of ways to love each other."

I swallow hard, emotion bubbling in my throat. "I want you sticking around more than anything in the world."

After I use my mouth to prove to her just how much I want her staying with me, we drag ourselves upstairs to shower.

Nic is in the bathroom, grumbling under her breath about being sore and the marks she's finding on her body, which makes me feel way more proud than I should.

I don't want to hurt her. But something about the fact that she can still feel me, even when I'm in a different room, makes me feel very caveman.

Me Josh. Her Nic. Her mine.

My phone is still on my nightstand from this morning. When I woke up and saw she wasn't in bed, and I hadn't received any texts from her, I slammed it facedown on the surface.

I couldn't believe she left without saying anything after all we'd shared the previous night, which makes sense, considering she didn't.

I pick up my phone, heart sinking to my stomach when I see dozens of missed calls and text messages from Tara and Belen.

"Shit," I hiss, tapping Tara's contact and lifting my phone to my ear.

"Where the fuck have you been?" Tara snaps in lieu of a greeting.

"I'm sorry. I left my phone upstairs and—"

"Josh. You need to come home. Now."

I freeze, my breath catching.

"We've been trying to get a hold of you all morning. Grandma couldn't breathe this morning, Josh. She was suffocating. You didn't answer, and I ended up calling my dad because Belen was at breakfast with a friend, and I was all alone, Josh. I was alone. They're both here now, and she's doing better. But she doesn't have much time left."

I sink to the edge of my bed, swallowing back the bile rising in my throat.

We're silent for a moment, and then Tara sniffs. "I'm really fucking mad at you, Josh. You promised we were in this together, and you didn't answer your phone. You know she's dying. I had to deal with that all alone."

Tears are burning my eyes. "Tara, I'm—"

"Just get home, okay? She wants you here. She's scared too." Tara hangs up her phone without another word.

My phone clatters to the floor, and I don't even remember loosening my grip enough for it to fall.

"Josh?" Nic's voice is soft, and I feel the mattress sink down as she sits. "Josh, what's wrong?"

My shoulders shake, and I begin to sob, covering my face with my hands. Wordlessly, Nic's arms encircle me as she soothingly rubs circles on my back and rests her cheek against my upper arm.

I cry into her, and she holds me, not saying a word.

Finally I catch my breath, inhaling shakily. "I haven't been completely honest with you about everything," I admit hoarsely, my hands clenched into fists in my lap.

I feel Nic tilt her head to look at me. "What kind of things?" she asks gently, without a hint of judgment or fear.

"My grandma's been sick. Really sick. Like she's in hospice. She's not getting better. She's—she's dying."

Nic doesn't say anything. She simply listens and rubs my back while I tell her everything about the past few months. How Tara, Belen, and I have spent most of our time in hospital rooms, how I bought Grandma an e-reader so she could still enjoy her romance novels when I wasn't there to read them to her.

I'm not sure why I didn't tell her before. Maybe I was trying to keep a wall of some sort between us still? Trying to keep her at arms' length and not let her completely in? Or maybe I just didn't want to tarnish this beautiful thing we built with my grief.

But here we are, all walls knocked into rubble.

"I wish I had known," Nic says, her voice cracking with emotion. "I wish I had been able—"

"I didn't tell you," I interrupt. "I made the conscious decision to keep that particular part of my life from you because I didn't want you to know. I'm sorry."

"No," Nic says firmly, grabbing my chin and angling my face until she can press her forehead to mine. "I know you were trying to protect yourself and do what you thought was right, and I don't hold it against you. We weren't supposed to matter. We weren't supposed to be...us."

I swallow. "I feel so fucking selfish. I didn't answer their calls because we were..." My chest feels like it's being pulverized. I had one of the most incredible mornings of my life, and now I feel guilty for enjoying it.

"I don't think Tara's truly upset with you for not answering your phone, or at least she won't be for too long. Give her time. She's feeling grief like you, and other things you're not because she witnessed something traumatic this morning. She might feel abandoned by you, and that's valid from her perspective, but deep down she knows you didn't abandon her. You just need to go to your family."

My train arrives in Connecticut less than three hours later. Nic offered to come with me, but I asked her to stay, knowing this was something I needed to face alone. I don't bother asking Tara for a ride because I can't hear her voice right now. I'm on my phone about to call for an Uber when a car honks. I lift my head and see a tall woman with dark, wavy brown hair past her shoulders wearing sunglasses and leaning on a black Prius. She's wearing a black pantsuit and red stilettos, and I'm immediately terrified of her.

I look around, certain she must be waiting for someone else, but not one person is walking toward her.

So I point to myself.

She nods.

She doesn't look like a serial killer, but can you ever be too careful?

I mentally shrug as I walk toward her.

"Josh Henry?" the woman asks, looking me up and down.

"Do I know you?" I ask, my brow furrowed.

"Kat Holt, Nic's sister. She called and asked me to give you a ride home."

I blink at her. "She...what?"

Kat chuckles and pushes her sunglasses off her face and into her hair. "She called me. I know, I was shocked too. It's the first time she's called me in her damn life."

She eyes me again, and I shift uncomfortably on my feet.

"You must be special."

I want to throw up.

"Oh, uh. Thanks for, uh, this," I say dully, feeling Kat's eyes on me as I shuffle to the passenger side.

"Do you want to put your bags in the trunk?"

I brought a full-sized suitcase, backpack, and my work messenger bag with me. I was stressed while packing, and Nic was incredibly helpful in making sure I got the essentials so I could call the head of the English department and HR to inform them I was going on leave for the foreseeable future.

"Yeah, that'd be great," I say sheepishly. The car beeps as she unlocks the trunk, and I load my stuff in. I can still feel her staring at me. I open the passenger door and slide the seat all the way back. This car was not designed for men my size.

I haven't been this scared of someone since I ran into Nic on the train.

"You know, Nic didn't mention how she knows you," Kat says.

Biblically. She knows me biblically.

"We knew each other as kids," I tell her. It's not a lie, and honestly, I don't know what we are beyond that, just that we love each other. That's as far as we've gotten.

"Hmm," Kat purses her lips as she puts her sunglasses on and pulls out of the parking lot. "Funny. From what I remember, Nic didn't have any friends as a kid."

That comment pisses me off. It might be true, but it still feels like a shitty thing to say about your sister.

"Didn't say we were friends," I mutter, just loud enough for her to hear. I can see her looking at me as we're stopped at a red light, but I don't elaborate.

It's the longest eight minute drive of my life, which we spend in complete silence. Normally I'd bend over backward to make her like me, but today I can't find it in me to care. Maybe that's not such a bad thing.

"Thanks again for the ride," I tell Kat when she pulls up in front of Grandma's house. "I appreciate it."

"Nic spoke very fondly of you," Kat says, her voice tight.

I swallow. "I speak fondly of her, too."

"She doesn't like people."

"I know."

Kat stares out the windshield. "The only reason I agreed to give you a ride is because she may or may not have threatened me. And I may or may not know for a fact she makes good on her threats."

I roll my lips, fighting back a smile. "Sounds like Nic."

She suddenly swivels her body so she's facing me. "She's sensitive. And she's book smart but goddamn, her street smarts are nonexistent."

I blink at her blankly. "I—"

"I'm not finished," Kat says, putting her hand up. "Don't you dare hurt her, okay? You're important to her. And I don't know what that means or what you two are, but," she says as she leans slowly toward me, "I know enough top defense attorneys to ensure whoever kills you won't serve much jail time."

I laugh for the first time since Tara's phone call.

Kat does not.

My eyes widen, and I nod. "She's really important to me, too. I don't want to hurt her."

Kat lowers her sunglasses down the slope of her nose, and eyes me. She's wearing an engagement ring with the biggest diamond I've ever seen and a coordinating wedding band, both of which sparkle so brightly they could blind me if the light hit just right. She has the same eyes as Nic. "Good," she says simply before sliding her sunglasses back up. "Now get out. I have to meet with a client in twenty minutes."

I get out of the car and open the trunk to grab my things.

"Wait," Kat says suddenly, and I freeze.

She sighs dramatically, and I refrain from rolling my eyes. "I'm sorry if that was a lot. I'm her big sister. This is out of character for her."

I keep silent, holding back the part of me that wants to ask her how well she actually knows Nic.

"We're all really protective of each other, but I'm especially protective of Nic. She's always been such a lone wolf, and I don't understand why she cares about you."

"Thanks," I say dryly. "Hearing you insult me and your sister in the same breath is super fun, but my grandma is literally dying inside, and I'd like to be with her."

Kat swivels around, swiping the sunglasses from her face, her eyes wide. "*Dying*? Nic—she didn't tell me that. What the hell? I came in here all Marlon Brando in *The Godfather,* and your grandma is dying?"

"So this isn't your normal disposition?"

"No, it is. But I could have pretended it wasn't for ten minutes. Did I scare you, at least?" She looks so hopeful, and it reminds me of Nic.

I sigh. "Yeah, I'm rethinking my plan to hurt your sister for sure."

She rolls her eyes at me. "Dick."

Yep. Definitely Nic's sister.

"If you need anything, let me know. I live four streets over."

"I will." *No I won't. Why the hell would I?*

Quinn women are *terrifying*.

I close the trunk and walk away without another word.

Jesus.

Chapter 33

Josh

Playlist: "I'm Fine," Ashe

Grandma makes it through the weekend. She's weaker than she had been, but she tries to keep her spirits high, despite her rapid decline.

Nic was at her parents' house on Sunday for dinner and asked if she could come over. I told her no, not wanting to have to explain to my family why she was there. She texted me that night to tell me to check outside, and I found a box with black and whites from the bakery by the gym that we love, a weighted blanket, and a handwritten note.

> *I love you, and I love Grandma, too. We're both lucky to have you.*
>   *-Your Buttercup*

She still feels too good to be true.

"Can you call my lawyer?" Grandma asks, voice hoarse on Monday. She hasn't been able to focus on reading, so I'd taken to reading her favorite books to her again. Sex scenes and all. "I want to make sure my will is all settled. And call Father Gilligan. I'd like to receive Last Rites."

Tara nods. She's kept it together since I arrived, but has barely spoken to me. I know she's hurting, but the thought of having to go through this without us talking is killing me.

I clear my throat and stand from my spot at the foot of Grandma's bed. "I'll come with you."

Tara looks at me suspiciously. "Fine."

"I'll stay here," Belen offers, looking between the two of us.

Tara and I walk into the living room, surrounded by pictures of us growing up, pictures of our grandparents as a young couple, my parents before their death; this was where I grew up, where I became who I am today.

"Tara," I say softly.

"I'm still pissed," she replies, scrolling through her contacts. "You don't know what it was like to experience that without you, and I never thought I'd have to."

I wince. "That's fair. I let you down, and I'm sorry."

"I hope it was worth it," Tara mutters.

And suddenly, Nic's in my mind's eye again, grinding and moaning. I love remembering moments like this, but it feels unbelievably inappropriate to be having dirty thoughts while not only is Grandma dying in the other room, but Tara's finally communicating with me after refusing to do so for the past forty-eight hours.

"You really don't want to know," I mutter, scratching at the back of my neck.

I feel Tara lift her eyes and look at me curiously. "Well now I do."

I look at her. "I don't want to dismiss the way you feel because it's valid, and I'd be upset if I were you." I pause. "I'm sorry I wasn't there when you needed me. I'm so, so sorry, Tara. You're practically my sister, and I hate not being able to hold each other up."

"Ugh, Josh," Tara's arms are around me, squeezing tightly. I blink away the tears filling my eyes. "Yeah, I'm pissed. But I know you didn't abandon me on purpose. I'm just hurting, and Belen's been telling me to talk to you, but I suck at saying how I feel and being honest about it—"

"Must be in the Henry DNA," I say teasingly, squeezing her back. "I'm so sorry."

"We're in this together, Josh. You and me. We always have been, and even though I'm pissed, I'm not letting it hurt our relationship. I promise."

We hug silently for a few moments until she speaks again. "Are you in therapy?"

I pull away, giving her a puzzled look. "What? No."

She wrinkles her nose. "Huh. You're talking like someone who's in therapy."

I rub the back of my neck. "I'm more in touch with my emotions now, that's for sure. And I do want to start therapy soon. I just haven't yet."

Tara beams up at me. "So. Who are they?"

"Who is who?"

"Whoever has you making you want to go to therapy," she says gently.

I feel my cheeks flush. "She's, um, she's Nic," I say simply, because how the fuck do I explain the complexity that is Nicoletta Quinn? "It's new."

"Must be pretty special," Tara says softly. "You look peaceful. Like, despite the absolute hell we're going through, there's this peace in your face, in your body. Can I meet her?"

I sputter. "Tara, I said it's new."

She waves her hand dismissively. "You met Belen after our second date."

"Right. Because I was helping you move in with her," I remind her. "I feel like it's not the same situation."

Tara rolls her eyes. "Does Grandma know?" I shake my head. "You should tell her, Josh. She'll be so happy."

I feel a bud of hope blossom in my chest. "Really?"

"Really."

Tara and I call Grandma's lawyer, who says he'll stop by later in the day. We also call Father Gilligan, who says he'll stop by for Last Rites and communion the next day.

It all feels too real. Too final.

I've been attempting to prepare myself for this for months. But now, the terrifying monster I've been dreading is finally digging its claws in.

Grandma gets weaker every day, and though we were told what to expect, nothing can really prepare you for it.

A week after Nic left the gift, Tara and I are sitting in Grandma's room with her and Belen, talking about our childhoods and reminiscing. Grandma seems to be feeling better today, but she's still tired, still declining. The hospice nurse told us during their visit this morning that she probably had another week or two, but to try to prepare for the worst.

What is the worst when the woman who raised you is dying? Is it the pain of waiting for the end, or is it the end itself? What's the real monster? Losing my parents was unexpected and sudden, and it fucked with my brain permanently. Grandma's decline has been slow, her illness taking her from us slowly, bit by bit, but her death is inevitable.

Loss sucks, no matter how you experience it.

Nic checks in with me every day with a phone call. I can't help but remember what Kat said about Nic never making phone calls, and I feel overwhelmed whenever I see her name on my phone.

I have no idea when she did it, but somehow she made "Never Gonna Give You Up" her personal ringtone.

Everytime she calls, she fucking Rickrolls me.

She rocks my world.

She hasn't called today, and I'm annoyed by how often I pick up my phone to see if I missed a call or a text or something, anything.

I miss her so damn much.

While we reminisce together as a family, there's a knock at the front door. I get up to answer, and when I open the door, I'm surprised to see Sean and Aria Quinn on the doorstep.

But not nearly as surprised as I am to see Nic behind them, holding an insulated bag nearly as big as her.

I want to grab her. Kiss her.

"Hi Josh!" Aria says. Both she and her husband are beaming, and seeing Nic in between them illustrates what a beautiful mix of the two of them she is. His smile, her eyes, his nose, her hair, his freckles, her lack of height.

"Hi," I respond, unable to take my eyes off Nic.

Aria throws an arm around my shoulders and pulls me down to her to press a kiss to my cheek. I hear Nic try to cover a snicker with a cough, and I want to glare at her. "I'm sorry we didn't call first, but I didn't want to give you the chance to say no."

Ah, so *that's* where Nic gets her absolute audacity from.

"Uh—" I say, lifting my eyes to meet Nic's again. Her cheeks are puffed out, and her lips pursed from fighting back laughter. I want to kiss that silly expression off her face.

Aria holds up another insulated bag that I hadn't even noticed was in her arms. "I brought enough food for ten people for almost a week, so you and your family have no excuse to not eat." Her eyes narrow menacingly. "I've been through this with both of my parents, so protesting is futile, Joshua."

I give Nic a panicked look, but she's looking at the ground, still making that ridiculous face.

Aria is simply an older, somehow even more terrifying Nicoletta Quinn, scarier than Kat and Jo combined.

How is that even possible? How does this damn family exist?

"Thank you," I manage to say. "This is really thoughtful of you, Mrs. Quinn."

She waves her hand dismissively. "Please call me Aria. And you remember my husband, Sean."

Sean waves at me, and I honestly wonder how his three children I've met barely resemble him. Italian genes are wild.

"And our daughter, Nicoletta."

"Nic," I say without thinking, and suddenly Nic's eyes meet mine, and she's not fighting back laughter anymore. "We were in school together and actually ran into each other a few months back on the train into the city."

I don't break our gaze. The pretty pink blush that creeps into her cheeks, creating a lovely canvas for her freckles, and the way she's chewing her soft pillow of a bottom lip, tell me that she, too, is remembering how she came undone on that exact train in my arms just a few weeks ago.

"That's right," Sean says, beaming and squeezing Nic to his side. I want to wrap my arms around her, ask her why she's here, beg her not to leave, beg her to stay with me. "Nic mentioned she knows you, and insisted on tagging along as an extra set of hands."

Knows. Right. Nic *knows* me.

In a way that somehow transcends religion and galaxies. She knows me intimately in a way I thought I'd never be known.

She *loves* me.

"Thank you for coming," I say, trying not to stare creepily at Nic. "I really appreciate it. Would you like to come in?" I ask, opening the door wider.

Aria and Sean both beam. "Yes, we'll put the food in the refrigerator, and you can go back to your grandma. Would it be alright if we popped in to give our love before leaving?"

I nod my head, but the Quinns are stepping through the doorway already, so they don't see my response.

Something about how self-assured they are is both disarming and comforting. Maybe because I feel like I'm floundering right now, like I have no sense of what to do, but they do. It's like they're a compass, guiding me in the right direction.

After I shut and lock the front door, I turn to see Nic still in the foyer as her parents continue to the kitchen.

I stare at her. She's here, and she's so wonderful it hurts.

Nic throws herself into my arms, wrapping her arms around my shoulders as mine tighten around her waist, lifting her off the ground so her feet dangle.

"You're here," I breathe, not fully believing it, despite touching her. "You came."

"I'm here," she responds, resting her chin on my shoulder. "I knew you wouldn't ask me to come, but I'm selfish, and I needed to hug you. To touch you."

I turn my head and nuzzle her cheek. Her skin is so soft, and she must have been spending time outside, because there are even more freckles adorning her face and, god, I've missed her.

"I've missed you. So much," I tell her.

Her hand is cradling the back of my head, and she leans back, her warm chocolate eyes searching mine. "I've missed you too," she breathes. "I don't want to overstay my welcome because I know you're dealing with things, but I want you to know you're not alone, okay? I'm here for you in the shitty times, too."

In the shitty times, too.

Would that be such a terrible thing to say during wedding vows? I tuck it away in my mind to revisit in another two years or so, when the timing's right.

Because I know the timing *will* be right one day.

I press my lips to hers, and it's quick, but it still says everything I want to tell her and don't know how.

That I'm so fucking grateful she saw through my "*I'm okay.*" That she's mine, and I'm coming back for her.

She breaks the kiss, and I lower her back to the ground, my arms immediately aching from the loss of her weight. "I should help my parents so they don't think I'm bothering you," she whispers, her eyes boring into mine.

"Keep bothering me," I say, and I mean it as a joke, but also, no, I don't. I want her to bother me for the rest of my life. "Meet my family."

Her eyes widen. "Wait, for real?"

I can't tell if she's terrified or delighted by the idea.

"I'm both terrified and delighted," she adds.

Well, that answers that particular question.

"We don't have to say we're anything," I amend. "We can just be us. Nic and Josh."

"Nic and Josh," she says slowly like she's trying the phrase on for size.

I drop one of her hands and entwine our fingers in the one that continues to hold her hand. "Come on."

I lead her into Grandma's room. Uncle Ray, Tara, and Belen are scattered around the room, while Grandma is resting in her hospital bed. Uncle Ray is in the corner, whisper-yelling into his phone, and Belen is giving him the stink-eye from her seat on Grandma's left side.

When Tara came out when we were in high school, Tara's parents kicked her out of the house. She came right to Grandma's and told us everything. Grandma and I drove over to Uncle Ray's the next day to gather her things so she could have what she needed with us. She was already the cousin I was closest to, but after that, and after I came out a few months later, we became more like siblings. I make sure to whisper in Nic's ear while nodding toward Uncle Ray, "That's my Uncle Ray. We don't like him."

"Got it," Nic says, nodding determinedly.

"He's homophobic."

"Gross." Nic scrunches her nose in disgust, still managing to look adorable. It's kind of amazing, really, knowing I have someone in my life who isn't related to me but who has my back, always.

Tara looks over toward us when she hears the floorboards creak and clears her throat obnoxiously to get Belen's attention. "Oh *hello,* Josh and strange woman," she greets, a diabolical grin spreading across her face.

On second thought, introducing two of the most terrifying women I've ever met might be a truly terrible idea.

But Nic simply raises her eyebrow. "Hello random woman who I thought was Josh's girlfriend when I saw a picture of her on his wall for the first time, but who I'm now assuming is related to him."

The entire room excluding Uncle Ray barks in laughter. Even Grandma laughs weakly before it turns into a wheeze.

But she looks delighted by Nic, the same way I feel delighted by Nic.

"You're a Quinn girl, aren't you?" Grandma asks quietly.

Nic blushes. "Yes, ma'am. I'm Nic. Josh and I went to school together, and I came to visit with my parents. They're putting three months of food away in your kitchen as we speak."

"Oh, I remember you, Nic. You frowned through your entire eighth-grade graduation."

"That dress was made of polyester, Mrs. Henry. I'd still frown if I had to sit for almost two hours in a dress like that."

Grandma waves her hand dismissively. "Please, Mrs. Henry was my mother-in-law. And she was *terrible*. Call me Myrtle. Or Grandma."

"Grandma," Nic says, a slow, sweet smile spreading on her face. "I'd like that."

"I'm Tara," Tara interjects, standing up and shoving her hand out to shake Nic's. "Josh's cousin."

"Not my girlfriend," I tease. Nic rolls her eyes at me as she takes Tara's hand.

"It's nice to meet you. I'm Nic."

"Oh, I know who you are, Nic Quinn. I've heard about you."

Nic shoots me a panicked look, and this time, it's my turn to roll my eyes.

"Tara Henry-Boyd," I chastise. "Stop trying to be scary."

Tara lets out a long-suffering sigh. "This feels unfair, you bringing someone home for the very first time *now*." Like I'd planned any of this. Like I saw Nic coming.

"Ignore Tara, dear," Grandma says. "We're all happy you're here."

"I'm happy to be here, too," Nic says, squeezing my hand.

And I believe her.

I really, truly believe her.

Chapter 34

Nic

Playlist: "The Great War," Taylor Swift

Quiblings Group Chat

Kat has been added to the chat.

Jo: people. there's bbq on saturday at mom and dad's be there or idk probably never see me again.

Ren: sounds vaguely threatening.

Jo: good. i wanted it to have nic vibes to scare everyone into showing.

Jo: except for kat.

Jo: i get it if you can't come boo.

Kat: fuck off

It's been a week since I last saw Josh and met his family. We haven't been able to talk more than a few check-in texts and "I love yous" since.

"So you're dating?" Jo asks as she bends into a forward fold.

I groan as I mimic her movements. I had been lying on the couch under my weighted blanket, Josh's button-up balled in my arms, an awful attempt at chocolate oat milk on the coffee table, with *Mamma Mia* playing full blast on the TV when Jo came home from a business dinner.

She took one look at me and ordered me to get up and join her in a YouTube Yoga video.

When I tried to tell her I didn't like yoga, she offered to go on a run with me.

So now we're doing a sun salutation at nine PM.

"Yes. No. Ugh, I don't know," I whine, lifting my chest into a half-forward bend.

"And you don't know because...?" Jo prompts, somehow able to talk and do the proper breathing pattern.

"His grandma's in hospice," I explain, trying to breathe the same way Jo is. I'm terrible at it. This is why I stick to climbing; there's no "proper breathing technique."

"I just—" she sighs as we lower our bodies to the floor in a half plank. "I don't want him dragging you along. You deserve better than that."

"If I thought that's what was happening, I'd agree with you." My arms are shaking, and the woman on the TV has a perfect cat eye, and I want to punch her pretty face.

Damn YouTube Yoga Gurus.

We press our legs to the ground and lift our heads and chests, arching our backs off the ground. "I didn't like seeing you like this, Nicky."

I groan at the physical exertion and at the nickname Jo knows I hate. "I miss him, okay? I haven't heard from him since Tuesday, and I'm not mad at him for it, but he's become a part of my life. A big, wonderful part of my life, and I miss him."

Jo groans and collapses on the floor. "I don't know how you talked and breathed and kept the proper form all at the same time." Jo wheezes. "I had two glasses of wine, and my body is *jello*."

I lower myself to the floor and rest the side of my head on my crossed arms. "You tricked me," I accuse, out of breath. "I was struggling to keep up with you."

Jo scoffs and flips over on her back. "Don't change the topic, Nicky."

I roll my eyes. "Okay, JoJo."

"I'm not sure I trust him," Jo continues. "It's so fast, and Nellie said she's never seen him date."

"He's not Kelsey," I say softly.

Jo snaps her head to the side, her eyes that match mine narrowing. "What did you just say?"

"He's not Kelsey," I repeat. "I'm not moving in with him anytime soon, and he's *actually* going through shit, not dragging me along."

Jo stares at me. "I—" She groans and presses the heels of her palms into her eyes. "Goddammit. I don't know what a healthy relationship, or potentially healthy relationship, looks like anymore, do I?"

"Jo," I say quietly. "You know you can talk to me, right?"

After Kelsey moved out, Jo withdrew and threw herself into work. She took on additional clients and started working seven days most weeks. Going to the climbing gym the first time Josh, Nellie, and Tyler came is the only social activity she's had since Kelsey left.

"She hurt me," Jo's voice breaks. "I really thought she was it, Nic. And she just fucking *left,* and I have to see her at work, with our boss who just announced their relationship."

My heart sinks at the pain in her voice. "You deserve better than that. And I *know* you know that."

She sniffs and wipes at her nose. "I do. And I've been going to therapy, and I've been trying to get my life back on track. I don't know what's wrong with me, Nic. It feels like she still has power over me, like she's stolen the life I thought I would have. The promotion, the relationship..."

"And that absolutely sucks," I interrupt. "Your feelings about the situation are valid, and just because Kelsey left you and continues to hurt you doesn't mean that's the only love you'll ever experience."

Jo's quiet for a moment before laughing shakily. "Sometimes having a psychologist for a big sister really is helpful."

"Wanna watch *Mamma Mia* with me? It's a great comfort movie."

She eyes me suspiciously. "Since when have *you* liked *Mamma Mia*?"

I blush. "Well, I've never actually seen the whole thing. It's Josh's comfort movie."

"Motherfucker," she groans, "That's a green flag."

"You sound disappointed."

"I am. Like yay, you're seeing someone who's not ashamed to say *Mamma Mia* is his comfort movie, but also I detest being wrong."

"Definitely a family trait."

"Oh, for sure."

At 4:16 the following morning, I'm woken by Rick Astley. Despite the fact I routinely sleep through all fifteen alarms I set for myself each morning, Josh's ringtone wakes me up immediately.

"Hello?" I answer groggily, my brain not recognizing the song right away.

"Buttercup-fuck. I didn't think you'd answer; it's so early. I shouldn't have-"

"Josh," I jolt upright, my head spinning from the sudden movement. I don't allow myself to wonder when he was able to change mine, too. I thought I had been so sneaky and clever when changing his. "Josh, what is it?"

He's silent for a moment before speaking again. "She's gone, Nic. An hour ago. They just came and got her."

My heart plummets. "I—fuck, Joshy." I swing my legs over the side of the bed. "I'm coming."

"Please—please don't. I couldn't live with myself knowing I burdened you."

"You can't burden me when I'm offering," I say softly. "I want to be there for you."

"Nic—" I can feel it, him shutting me out, and my heart sinks. "Don't. It's just going to be funeral preparations and—" He takes a deep, shaky breath. "I don't want you here."

I rest my elbows on my knees and lean forward. "Don't you dare, Joshua Henry. Don't you fucking *dare* shut me out."

"I'm not shutting you out. My grandma just died, and now I have to plan her funeral. Do you know what that feels like?"

My heart shatters, and suddenly I'm blinking back tears. "Josh, please. I know you're hurting, but you don't have to do this. Don't do this. Don't shut me out, don't make me wait-"

"Nic, stop." His voice is harsh, a tone I've never heard from him. "Stay home. I don't need you. I just—I thought you might want to know she'd passed." His breathing is shaky, and I know he doesn't mean what he's saying.

It still hurts.

"I'll be back in the city after the funeral, and we can talk then."

"Okay," I agree quietly, a single tear making its way from my eye down my cheek. He's not ready to be loved through this, and I can't force it on him. If he needs space, I'm willing to wait for him. "Okay. I'll see you when you're home. I'm so sorry for your loss, Josh. I'm *so* sorry. Remember to heat the lasagna at 350 for forty minutes."

I hang up the phone before he can say anything, before I break and beg him for what he can't give me right now. I crawl back beneath the covers which muffle the sound of my sobs until I force myself to get up to climb before work.

Josh doesn't text me until I'm at work hours later, after I've already left a voicemail for him.

> **Josh:** Nic- I'm so sorry. That wasn't fair of me to treat you that way. You're so much more than what I insinuated this morning. I love you, and I'm sorry. -Josh

I swallow hard. It's an apology, but I know he isn't ready for my forgiveness yet. I know he's not ready to hear he hurt himself far worse than he hurt me, and he needs professional help.

I'm in the office today, which is a terrible life choice. I should have worked from home and licked my wounds.

Instead I'm here, catching up on emails, when Brooks and Danny burst into my office without knocking, Alyssa standing behind them giggling behind her hand.

"Hey, Noelle?" Brooks or Danny says. Honestly they're both white former frat boys and are interchangeable at this point. I don't even blink when they get my name wrong. "When is the Florida report due?"

My stomach sinks. "Yesterday. Did you not email it to Mitchell?" I scroll through my emails, and yep. There it is: an email from Mitchell asking about the status of the project he asked me to do, the one I had let myself be steamrolled into delegating. The project and research I had been a part of from the beginning and care so much about.

"Oops," Danny or Brooks says, while the other snickers behind his hand. "We should be able to get it done by the end of the month."

I'm flabbergasted. "What have you been doing? You told me you had this under control."

"There were other projects—" Danny or Brooks begins.

"What other projects?" I interrupt. "Please send me whatever you've done with the Florida data. I'll be heading the remainder of the project."

They're not laughing anymore, and Alyssa is mysteriously gone from the doorway. "That hardly seems fair—" one of them says, surprised by my reaction. Honestly, I'm surprised, too.

"I have the necessary education and experience to do what is needed for this project, and I'll be taking over. You'll be doing what is assigned to you from here on out, understood?"

"I—"

"Do you understand?" I ask again, my voice firmer than it's ever been at work. I want to waver, to sit down and take it.

But I'm sick of it. I'm sick of just *taking* things. I deserve better in my sex life, in my career, in my personal life.

Josh showed me that.

Someone clears their throat from the doorway. I look over to see Mitchell leaning in the doorway, Alyssa behind him.

"I went to get Mitchell," she says. "I thought he should see what's going on." She glares at me.

"Nic, do you want to explain what's happening?" Mitchell asks, oblivious to Alyssa's stink eye.

"She's taking away our project and being a total bi—" Danny or Brooks says, complete disgust in his voice.

"Mitchell asked me, Danny," I interrupt, hoping that's the right name.

Honestly, I have no idea if I get it right or wrong. They're all glaring at me already and continue to do so.

I take a deep breath and explain what happened. How I felt pressured to give them the Florida project and how they've done the same with other projects. How I should have stood up for myself then, but I felt like I couldn't.

I'm doing it now, though.

"That's not—" Brooks or Danny starts to say.

"Thank you," Mitchell interrupts. "But I know for a fact the two of you had taken on the Florida project. You included me in emails, going behind Nic's back, or did you forget? Nic is your supervisor, and she was specifically assigned the Florida project because of her experience and seniority within the organization. All three of you have shown her substantial disrespect, and it's absolutely unacceptable. I'll be meeting with you individually this week to talk about your behavior and performance. You can go now."

I'm silent as I scrub my hands over my face. I went too far, and now I'm risking everything I've worked toward for literal years.

"I'm proud of you, Nic."

My head snaps up, and I blink at Mitchell, not comprehending the words he just said. "W—what?"

"You stuck up for yourself, and no offense, you should've done that *months* ago. But you advocated for yourself in a way I'd been hoping to see from you for a long time. Your work speaks for itself, but I've always hoped you'd speak for yourself, as well."

I sink down in my chair. "I wasn't too harsh?"

He shrugs. "They needed to hear it. They've been acting inappropriately for months, stealing projects and taking credit for your work. I know what you're capable of, Nic. It's why I hired you. You just need to know what you're capable of, too."

I blink away the tears that are suddenly filling my eyes. I laugh nervously. "I don't know when I became such a softie."

He smiles at me. "I don't either, but keep it up. You might be a softie, but you're a confident softie. You deserve to know your worth."

Before I leave the office a few hours later, I make a phone call. One I should've made a long time ago.

"Nic?"

"Hey, Mom," I swallow, my throat dry with nerves.

"Hi, sweetheart. Is everything okay?"

I laugh nervously. "Yeah, everything's fine. I didn't mean to scare you. I just have something I need to tell you."

"Okay, I'm listening," she says in what I recognize as her trying-to-cover-my-anxiety voice.

"I'm autistic. I was diagnosed earlier this year. And I'm bisexual."

I'm finally ready to let her see me. To really be *me* with everyone.

She's quiet for a moment. "Alright," she says slowly. "What does that mean for you?"

"Well, it means I like more than one gender..."

Mom laughs, really, truly laughs, and it feels like a million pound weight is being lifted off my soul. "I do know what bisexual means, darling. I meant the autism diagnosis. Are things different for you now?"

I think about it for a moment. "Yes and no. It explains a lot of things about me that I don't think anyone really understood, like my sensory issues and social anxiety. I'm not peculiar. My brain is wired differently. And that's so validating to understand and put a name to. I'm not broken—I'm autistic."

Mom's quiet for a moment before sniffling. My heart sinks.

"Oh, my sweet Nicoletta. I'm so damn proud of you."

I blink in disbelief. Aria Quinn does *not* curse. "You are?"

"You did such a brave thing by calling me and letting me know who you are, sweetheart. I've always loved you, and I've always been proud of the woman you are, but I can't imagine how nervous you were to get tested. And you did it and now I'm able to know and love you better."

I swallow the lump growing in my throat, "I—I'm not going to lie. I don't know what I expected, but this wasn't it."

She laughs again. "I'm glad I could surprise you. Now, how can I better love you with this new information?"

"I'm still me. I've always been bisexual and autistic. You just know the labels now," I tell her. "I can recommend some good books on autism and queer history, if you want."

"Oh, I would *love* that. You, Alex, Millie, *and* Jo," Mom says, her voice proud like she's listing her daughters that found the cure for cancer, and not her daughters who are out as queer. "I'm not sure what I fed you girls, but I'm so glad you're mine, just the way you are."

"You don't become queer by eating something," I say, confused.

"I'm sorry, sweetheart. I was trying to make a joke. I know that this is who you've always been, from before I knew you existed. And I'm so glad for it."

I recommend some books for her, and we exchange I love yous before hanging up. I send a quick text to my dad to let him know I came out and told Mom about my diagnosis *and* that it went well. He Venmos me $20 with a note saying, "I know drinks in the city are expensive, but hopefully this covers a beer or something. Love you, kiddo."

If I hadn't taken a chance and asked Josh to teach me how to enjoy sex, I'd never have found the confidence and self-worth to make any of this happen.

I'm finally, *finally* me, all because of him.

Quiblings Group Chat

Nic: hi. just wanted to let you know i'm autistic and bisexual.

Nic: that's all.

Jo: wait, since when have you been autistic? we've lived together for literal years?????

Nic: always been autistic, but was formally diagnosed in february.

Alex: HELL YEA BISEXUAL BITCHESSSSS.

Millie: yesss congrats on the bisexuality, boo. that makes half of us gay af <nail polish emoji>

Kat: am i the only heterosexual, neurotypical person in this family?

Jo: maybe, and yet you're still somehow the absolute worst one of us.

Ren: someone kick her out, i don't know how.

Izzy: on it.

Kat has been removed from the group.

Leo: can i make a cake to celebrate for the bbq? you're boring and like plain yellow cake, right?

Jo: she likes chocolate frosting.

Izzy: what color do you want the words to be, nic? light purple? i wanna make sure leo has the right icing color for the words.

Nic: yeah. that all sounds perfect. even a weird cake celebrating my neurodivergence and sexuality.

Nic: it all sounds perfect.

Chapter 35

Nic

Playlist: "Call Me If You Need Me," Vance Joy

"How does this look?" my tattoo artist asks, spinning her tablet on the table so it faces me.

I lean over, examining the fine-line tattoo I asked her to design. "Perfect."

"Great," she says, rising from her seat. Millie has striking green eyes and vibrant, long red hair cascading past her shoulders, pushed back by a peach colored bandana. She has a septum piercing, and whenever she wrinkled her nose while drawing, it would wiggle a little bit.

Nic left me a voicemail after we talked this morning, and I already know what it says. I can't find the strength to listen to her tell me I fucked up. I already know. I already know she deserves better than me, that she's walking away. So instead of facing my problems in a healthy way, I walked into Ink It Over, the tattoo shop on the beach. When I entered, Millie was sitting in a tattoo chair, squinting at her tablet.

"I'm going to print out the stencil, then you'll sign the waivers, and we can get started."

I have over a dozen tattoos all over my body. My arms and chest are covered in designs created by black ink, and I have a few scattered across my back as well. My skull tattoo, an homage to Hamlet, takes up the majority of my left thigh.

And yet, I still feel anxious every time I sit in a tattoo chair.

I lift my shirt off and over my head and show Millie where I want the tattoo on my right pec. She shaves the area before placing the stencil and then wrinkles her nose and tilts her head.

"You know," Millie says slowly, her eyes focused on the gun. "Tattoo artists are kind of like bartenders, but I'm sure you know that after all these bad boys."

I smile to myself. "I do, but I don't like putting my bullshit on anyone else."

"Okay, well, you're really tense right now, and when we're done and you relax, your tattoo will be distorted."

I blink at her. "Really?"

"Well, I don't know. But you need to relax, bro. My sister has a doctorate in psychology so I might as well be a therapist, honestly."

I force a laugh, but I'm thinking of Nic and her incredible brain, how she's supported me with resources and references in a way that makes me feel like she wants to help and see me heal. Not like she has to or sees me as too much to handle.

Fuck, I love her.

I remember the grounding technique she taught me: five things I can see, four things I can hear, three things I can smell, two things I can feel, and one thing I can taste. I go through the different steps and am surprised when I feel my body begin to relax.

"There we go," Millie says, sounding pleased. I hear her start the gun. "Just keep doing whatever you're doing. Deep breaths."

She begins tattooing me, and the feeling of the needle punching into my skin is both more and less painful than I remember. I keep my breaths slow and even.

"My grandma died. This morning," I say suddenly. I have no idea why I'm telling her this.

"Fuck, that sucks," she says simply, not even flinching. She's just focusing on the lines of the tattoo. "Is the lavender to remember her by?"

I sigh melodramatically. "No, I hurt someone I really care about. I said some really shitty things after my grandma's death and—and she's smart. She knows she deserves better than that."

"It seems like you're being really hard on yourself. Does this person know you well?" Millie asks. She doesn't look up at me once.

I exhale and lean my head against the headrest, my eyes fluttering closed. "Better than anyone."

It hits me then how true that is. I have lots of friends, plus Tara and Nellie who supersede all of that, but Nic sees me in a way no one else ever has. In a way I've never let anyone else see before.

"So, why the lavender?"

I slowly smile. "She smells like lavender. I can't smell it or see it without being reminded of her, and god, I'm selfish. I want to be reminded of her, even if she hates me, or I never see her again."

"You know, my sister with the doctorate says lavender has a calming effect on the parasympathetic system. She always has lavender perfumes, deodorant, laundry detergent, you name it. I'm not ashamed to say I borrowed her deodorant before a big test in high school." Millie chuckles, as my head snaps up. "She was so pissed."

Oh god. The nose wrinkle. The shape of their eyes. The way Millie is, as my students would say, a "yassified" version of Sean Quinn.

"Are you a Quinn?" I blurt out, equal parts horror and excitement growing in me.

Millie turns off the tattoo gun, and looks up at me for the first time since beginning the tattoo. "Oh god," she breathes, her eyes wide. "Which one of us do you know? I'm so sorry."

I smile. "Nic and I went to school together."

"Oh Christ, I'm *so* sorry," Millie says, grimacing. A need to protect Nic grows inside of me.

"No, no. Nic's my friend."

Millie looks over at my partially completed tattoo and starts the tattoo gun up again. I wince at the stinging feeling, but the pain is grounding. It makes all my emotions more bearable. "Huh. Nic has friends?"

I take a deep breath, reminding myself that the woman is not only related to Nic, but is currently in the process of permanently marking my body. "Why is everyone always so surprised by that?"

Millie shrugs, dipping the gun in the ink before bringing it back to my skin. "She doesn't like people. Like, at all. It's her biggest personality trait. That and having a Ph.D. in Psychology. Which is really ironic if you think about it, getting a doctorate in people's brains when you don't like people."

"She might not like everyone blindly, but she does like people who take the time and put in the effort to understand and give a damn about her. And not being friendly is *not* her biggest personality trait, nor is the fact she has a Ph.D. She's strong, tenacious, and compassionate, a good listener, smart and self-aware." I realize at this point I'm monologuing, but I don't care. "She's kind and willing to admit when she's wrong and—" I take another shaky breath. It hurts me so badly that her family can't see who she really is. All they see is the fact she doesn't have friends, like that's true or significant. She has Nellie, Tyler, Jo, and me.

If she'll still have me.

Millie makes a humming noise in the back of her throat, but doesn't look up, continuing to trace the lines of the lavender stalk. "So. You and Nic are *friends*, huh?" she asks, elongating friends.

My cheeks flush. "Yeah. Friends."

"Well, I'm just saying, if I ever talked about someone like that and also got a tattoo of what they smell like on my chest…" She lifts her eyes and meets mine as she dips the needle in ink again. "I wouldn't be so dense as to expect anyone to believe they're just a friend."

"I'm that transparent?" I ask, my cheeks flushing even more.

"Like a ghost, my dude," Mille says, bringing the needle back to my skin. "And everything you said about Nic? It's all true, and more. She's selective about people, so when she knows and cares about someone, she loves *hard*. She's understanding and compassionate and forgiving, probably to a fault at times. Unless, of course, you steal her deodorant."

I chuckle. "I fucked up, but maybe not that badly."

"Did you hurt her?"

I swallow. "I did."

"Are you going to do it again?"

"I never want to hurt her," I say, my throat becoming stuffy. Despite the pain I've always felt while being tattooed, I've never cried once.

The pain of losing Nic is exponentially worse.

"Listen. One of my siblings is in a toxic relationship, and we all know it, except for her. We've tried to talk to her, but she won't hear it. We've watched parts of her be chipped away over the years, to the point she's someone none of us know anymore. I don't know how long you've been with Nic, but she's been coming home for dinner again. And she's *happy*. Smiling and asking questions and playing board games with us. I didn't know she had it in her, happiness like that. Fuck, she told me she loved me a few weeks back, and I asked her if she was high.

My brother said she hugged him. Do you understand how truly bizarre that is?"

She looks up at me. "Nic is growing, not being shrunk like I've seen happen to other people I love. And while she's different, she's still Nic, just able to take on the world more courageously. Take that as you will."

I notice her eyes are teary, too. "But I hope you know by now, there are eight Quinns in my immediate family, not including Nic and myself, who *will* kill you if you hurt her again. All of us, except Alex, live in town or Brooklyn. We're all half-Italian, half-Irish, and my parents own their own law firm. Take *that* as you will, too."

Millie and I are silent for the rest of my appointment, and I mull over what she said. Mostly that I've now been threatened by four Quinns, one of whom I'm in love with and never want to hurt again.

After she finishes the tattoo, Millie rubs ointment over it and covers it with a bandage. As I pull my t-shirt back on, a light blue shirt with a picture of Shakespeare and the words "Prose before Bros" on it, she hands me a care instruction card.

"I know you're probably an expert at this, but I'm going to give it to you anyway," she tells me. "Don't be a fool and get an infection. I'll tell Nic what a loser you are."

It makes me smile. "I think she knows I'm a loser."

"You're gonna have to grovel, man."

Before returning to Grandma's house, I decide to walk around the seawall for a bit. It serves as our downtown area and has changed immensely since I moved away. There's a new combination bookstore and tea shop called Tea-riffic Books. I stop in to buy Eva Leigh's newest book and an iced London Fog Latte, and the woman who rings me up has bubblegum pink hair and a big smile. She throws in a chocolate chip scone with my order when I tell her I'm buying the book for myself. I want to tell Nic.

But I don't.

I walk back to Grandma's, with an hour to spare before Tara and I are scheduled to meet with the priest from Grandma's parish about the funeral. When I walk into the kitchen, Tara's taking some of the lasagna the Quinns left out of the microwave.

"Hey," she says, smiling softly. "Where did you run off to?"

"Went to that bookstore by the beach. It's cute—have you been there?"

"Yeah, it's by the tattoo shop, right?" she asks, putting a forkful of food into her mouth.

I flush. "Uh—"

"I knew it. I knew you ran off to impulsively get another tattoo," Tara shouts, food spraying out of her mouth as she points her fork menacingly at me.

"Okay, I definitely haven't done so enough times for it to become my brand."

Tara ignores me. "Just tell me it's not like Grandma's face or something. I know they're really good at what they do over there, but I don't think anyone can do that right."

I blush, shame over the fact I got a tattoo for Nic on the day my grandmother died washing over me. "I—it's for Nic, actually. Not Grandma."

Tara eyes me. "Wait, you got Nic's face tattooed?"

"Jesus, I didn't get anyone's face tattooed. Why would you think that? And even if I did, I helped you move in with Belen after your second date, so you have no room to criticize any of my life choices, ever."

She glares at me. "Okay, um, hella lesbophobic of you, but whatever. What tattoo did you get?"

"She always smells like lavender, so I got that."

"Aww," Tara coos before taking another bite of lasagna. "That's so cute."

"Please don't."

"She's gonna love it."

I feel ill. "I uh, I don't know if we're still together."

Tara freezes, eyes narrowing at me. "You guys broke up? What did you do?"

"Why are you assuming I did anything wrong? Maybe we just realized it wouldn't work between us," I argue.

She gives me a pointed look.

"Okay, fine. I said some really awful shit, and she hung up and left a voicemail on my phone—"

"Wait, so you two didn't break up?"

"I'm sure she broke up with me over voicemail," I explain.

"Who do you think she is, Joe Jonas? Come on, Josh. Give her more credit than that." Tara rolls her eyes.

"She *should* break up with me. I'm such a mess, Tara, and she deserves so much better than that."

"We're all messes, dumbass. I'm a mess, you're a mess, she's a mess, Belen's a mess. As long as we don't expect other people to clean up after us, messiness isn't a bad thing."

"She's not a mess," I argue. "She's perfect."

"She's not, Josh. She's a human being with flaws, and if you keep putting her on a pedestal instead of seeing her for who she really, actually is, of course you're going to think she doesn't deserve you. But that's not fair to either of you. You're both going to go through times when you need to support the other. Grandma did it for us in high school, and we did it for her when she got sick. Belen did it for me when I broke my leg a few years ago, and I did it for her when she got laid off. That's what love is, Josh."

"Maybe I don't deserve that."

"If you truly believe that and refuse to change your thinking, maybe you're right." Tara says, shrugging her shoulders. "But the thing is, you know it's not true. You know you deserve the same care and love you give."

I've never allowed myself to be anything other than my best in any relationship. Even with hookups. I'm the one who takes on the pressure, who makes sure everyone else is okay.

"Will you stay with me?" I ask shakily. "While I listen to her voicemail?"

She puts her hand on mine and squeezes. "I'm not going anywhere."

I open my phone and lift it to my ear, my whole body relaxing as Nic's voice fills my ear:

"Hi. It's me. I know you're hurting and avoiding me, and it sucks. It hurts. I'm not going to pretend that it doesn't because we're past that, aren't we? Past the bullshitting and pretending to be okay when we're not? I've never been able to pretend I'm okay with you, Josh. I've always just been me. As I am. And right now I'm hurting, and you're hurting, and I just need you to know that

you're not losing me that easily, okay, Joshua Henry? You're not. I love you so fucking much I left a goddamn voicemail. When was the last time you got a voicemail? Well, you probably get them all the time because you communicate like someone's weird great-uncle, but I don't. I love you so much that I'm leaving you this voicemail for whenever you're ready to listen, and whenever you're ready to let me love you again. However long it takes, Joshy, I'm waiting for you. I love you."

I let out a shuddering breath as I lower the phone from my ear, a tear sliding down my cheek.

"She's not leaving, is she?" Tara asks gently.

I shake my head.

"She's waiting for you?"

I nod.

She wraps her arms around my shoulders, squeezing me. "You're going to be okay, Josh. We both are," she says softly.

Nic stayed through the nightmare all those weeks ago. Maybe, when the nightmare enters the daytime, she'll stay too. Maybe she wants to love the things I try to hide as much as I want to love the things she tries to hide.

Maybe we'll both stay, both wait, through the shit times.

Chapter 36

Nic

Playlist: "The Most," Miley Cyrus

On Tuesday afternoon, Mom calls to tell me Myrtle Henry passed away Monday morning. I try to act surprised because, as far as they know, Josh and I are casual acquaintances. They're smart enough to know someone doesn't call a casual acquaintance in the middle of the night to inform them of a death in their family.

They text on Wednesday to let me know they're taking off from work Wednesday through Friday to be able to cook and go to the wake on Thursday. Sure, the reception after the funeral is being catered, but Aria Quinn lives in fear that the family will run out of food while they're grieving.

I don't tell my parents or Josh I'm coming in for the funeral, and I specifically ask Nellie not to say anything, either. I still haven't heard from him, and I don't know if he wants me there. I'm leaving right after Mass while Nellie and Tyler are staying through the reception, so he probably won't even see me.

The three of us take the train to Port Haven and Uber to the Catholic Church where the funeral is being held, the same church I grew up attending.

The church is crowded, buzzing with voices, and I flinch at the sound. I pause at the back of the church to put my earplugs in while Nellie and Tyler walk ahead, shameless in a way that makes me proud to know them.

Josh's family hasn't arrived from the funeral home yet, and I assume my parents are coming from there, too.

Fifteen minutes later, the hearse and limos carrying the family arrive. The procession of the casket and family into the church begins. I see Tara, Belen, and some others who look vaguely like Josh and Tara. When Belen sees me, she grins and tugs on Tara's hand. Tara peeks over, and I wave shyly. Through her tears, a broad smile spreads across her face, and I blush.

I look for Josh in the group and find him, but he doesn't look my way. I don't know if it's because he saw me and is avoiding me or if he doesn't see me.

My parents walk in after the Henrys, and parents must have a sixth sense for when one of their offspring is near because they turn their heads toward me at the same time, eyes widening in surprise. I wave awkwardly again and shrug.

The funeral Mass is a beautiful send off for Myrtle Henry, and I hope it comforts Josh, Tara, and the rest of their family. At the end of the liturgy, the priest announces that Josh will be giving the eulogy, and my heart starts pounding. I tear up a tissue in my lap as he walks up to the ambo.

God, he looks amazing. He's wearing a navy suit over a white dress shirt. I wonder if he had to buy a new one after I stole his other shirt. His pants and jacket cling to some of my favorite parts of his body, and I have to remind myself I can't lust after him in a damn church.

I mean, I suppose I can. But *should* I?

When he looks this handsome, how can the answer be anything but yes?

Josh puts a small stack of papers on the pulpit and braces his hands on the sides. He looks so self-assured and strong. Today is one of the most painful days of his life, and he still looks like he's conquering the world. I imagine this is what he looks like when he's teaching, and those damn butterflies are back.

He lifts his eyes, and it's like I'm a lighthouse on the shore and he's a ship caught in raging waters. His eyes immediately hone in on me, growing wide with surprise. I smile at him, fidgeting with the now-tattered tissue.

He blinks a few times, like he has to make sure I'm really there after closing his eyes. *I'm here.* I want to stand up and scream, *I'm always gonna be here.*

Josh finally breaks our gaze to begin his eulogy. "My grandma, Myrtle Henry, was the greatest person I've ever known. The greatest person I'll ever know," he says, his voice cracking, but not wavering. "Despite losing her son and daughter-in-law so tragically and unexpectedly, she never once hesitated in her own grief to love and raise their son. To love and raise me."

I'm already crying, and Tyler passes me another tissue, gently squeezing my hand. I squeeze their hand back as Josh continues to talk about his grandma, who raised three kids with her husband. How he always knew her as his beloved Grandma, a safe place for her misfit grandkids. I can't help but think about how brave he is for saying this, not just in church, but in front of his own family members who turned their backs on him and Tara. How proud Grandma would be of him.

Josh tells the congregation how, when Tara came out as a lesbian in high school, Myrtle had given her a big hug, and said, "I'm delighted to know the real you!" How, when Josh came out as queer a few months later, she laughed and made a joke about collecting queer grandchildren the way Josh had collected Pokemon cards as a kid. She then asked if he would help her choose an outfit for the Pride Parade in town.

As he speaks about the love his grandma showed to so many people, I cry and I cry because his strength and courage shine through his grief. I've never been prouder or more amazed by him.

When he finishes the eulogy, Father Gilligan gives the final blessings and the recessional hymn begins as the casket and family process out of the church. I'm not at the end of my pew, but if I was, I would reach out and squeeze Josh's hand. Instead his eyes meet mine again, and our gaze holds until he's too far from me.

I hug Nellie and Tyler goodbye and stay in the pew while everyone else files out to attend the graveside service. I want to wait until everyone else has left before catching an Uber back to the train station to avoid any discussion or explanation about why I came.

Josh saw me. That's enough.

After about ten minutes, the chatter from outside has faded, so I stand up and walk up the aisle and out of the sanctuary. As I'm walking through the vestibule, about to exit the church, someone grabs my wrist and pulls me aside. Despite the fact I should be terrified, I'm not. Even before his vanilla and smoky charcoal scent wrap around me, I know it's him.

"Josh," I breathe as he pulls me tightly into his chest. My heart is singing at being so close to him again. "Josh, you were so beautiful. So, so beautiful."

"You're here," Josh croaks, his fingers knitting in my curls as he holds me to him. "You came. And you took *forever* to come out of that damn church."

My skin flushes, and I wrap my arms around his middle, resting my ear over his pounding heart, right over his buttercup tattoo. His breath hitches. "I didn't know if you wanted me here or not, so I just came for Mass. I wanted to make sure you know you don't have to shoulder this alone, that I'm still with you. Are you mad at me?"

Josh laughs shakily, his hold on me tightening. "Mad at you? Not even a little bit. I'm only mad at myself for what I said. For pushing you away. For treating you with so much less love and respect than you deserve. I was an asshole, Nic. I'm so sorry."

"You were hurting," I say simply, rubbing his back. "It doesn't excuse it, but I understand."

He tilts my chin up, our eyes meeting and noses brushing. "If you'll still have me, I'm going to start therapy to deal with my grief and trauma, and I'm hoping to get referred to a psychiatrist to get medical treatment for PTSD and my nightmares."

"If you're promising to give yourself the care you deserve, of course I'll have you," I tell him simply. "I love you, Joshua Henry."

"I love you so much, Nicoletta Quinn," Josh breathes, pressing his forehead to mine as his eyes flutter shut. "I never want to hurt you."

"You're going to," I tell him. "And I'm going to hurt you. We're human. What matters is that we acknowledge our mistakes and do what we can to fix them. And you're doing that."

"Can I kiss you?" Josh asks me, like his lips on mine are the answer to his prayers, the meaning of life.

And god, after a week of not touching him, I feel it, too.

"Please."

His lips are soft and searching, like he's savoring me, taking his time to make sure I'm real. He slips his tongue between my lips, and I suck on it. He moans in response and pushes me against the wall, our kisses becoming more desperate, more frantic.

I untuck his shirt from his suit pants and slip my hand under his dress shirt and undershirt until I feel his soft stomach under my fingers. As I trace my fingers over his stretchmarks, Josh lifts my leg and hooks it around his hip so he can grind against where I'm so sensitive, so greedy for him and his touch. Right where it's *so* wrong to want him to touch me in a church.

I throw my head back, pushing it against the wall as my orgasm climbs so quickly. "Josh, I'm..."

"That's my girl," Josh growls, nipping at my neck. "Let it go for—"

A throat clears from behind Josh, and the speed at which we jump apart from each other has me lightheaded. I smooth my skirt down as Josh hurriedly shoves his shirt back into his pants.

"Joshua. Nicoletta," my dad says, his brow raised as Josh moves to the side.

Fuck fuck fuck fuck.

"Hi, Dad," I squeak, my hands flying to smooth down the curls Josh had tugged at.

"Mr. Quinn," Josh says, more fear than I knew possible etched on that handsome face of his. "I—I can explain."

I snort. I'd *love* to know how he plans to explain our very obvious dry humping in the vestibule of the church minutes after his grandmother's funeral.

Dad grimaces and waves his hand at us. "Listen, I left seminary to be with Aria. I've done worse things in a church vestibule."

"*Dad,*" I hiss, horrified.

"What? We have eight kids," he says, like that makes it any better.

"Oh my *god*!"

"Oh, I'm sorry. Are you uncomfortable?" Dad asks, his voice dripping with sarcasm.

Dad, one. Nic, zero.

"I'm so sorry, sir," Josh wheezes, about four seconds away from hyperventilating.

"Listen," Dad says. "I didn't super love walking in on... that."
All three of us shudder in unison. "But you're adults. And if I
were to walk in on Nic getting it on with anyone, I'd want it to
be Josh." He pauses as Josh and I stare at him in horror. "I heard
it. I was trying to be supportive, but I heard it."

Josh laughs, but I'm still too horrified to find it funny. My
parents have always been open about stuff, but this is the worst
thing I've ever experienced.

"I'm trying to say I like the two of you together." Dad looks
between us. "Are you together? Or, uh, do I not want to know?"
He grimaces, and I know the poor man has seen some shit
among my siblings.

I don't know how to answer Dad's question, if I'm being
completely honest. We're not *not* together, but we haven't defined what we are yet.

"Yes," Josh says suddenly, his voice so certain and confident
my heart soars. "We're together. Nic and I...we're dating."

I beam up at him, and though he's looking at my dad, he
squeezes my hand.

I'm so fucking gone for this infuriating, wonderful man.

And he's so fucking gone for *me*.

"Did my daughter know you were dating before you said it?"
Dad raises his eyebrow, and I roll my eyes at him saying 'my
daughter.' He's trying so hard to be intimidating.

And I guess it's working, because poor Josh pales. "N—no,
sir," he wheezes.

"Okay, I think we've overused the sirs, Josh," Dad says.
"Please call me Sean, especially since, if you're going to ask her if
she wants to date you, and she says yes, you'll be coming around

more often." He's fighting back a smile, and I both love and hate him for it.

"Nic, would you—" Josh begins to say, turning his body toward me.

"Yes," I blurt out, not letting him finish. "Yes. Very much so. I'd like to be together. With you."

My two favorite men in the whole world beam at me, and my grumpy ass can't help but smile back.

"You should probably know the limos left a while ago. We were following the processional before I realized I'd left my glasses in the pew," Dad warns.

Josh reddens and rubs the back of his neck nervously. "Yeah, I told them to go ahead without me."

Dad furrows his brow again. "How were you planning on getting to the cemetery?"

"I really didn't think that far in advance," Josh admits, and I want to kiss him all over his dorky, blushing face.

Dad eyes me suspiciously. "And you? Why didn't you ride with your mother and I?"

"I didn't want anyone to know I was here."

"At a funeral in a small church where everyone can see everyone else?"

I feel my face heat. "I also didn't think that far in advance."

Dad and Josh both laugh, loud and joyful, and the sound makes me feel like my heart is filled with helium, like I can float into the sky.

"Jesus, Mary, and Joseph," Dad chuckles, wiping a stray tear from his eye, his shoulders still shaking with his boisterous laughs. "You two really are perfect for each other. Bring him around more often, kiddo. We'll drive you to the cemetery, but we have to hurry. It's a thirty minute drive, and the graveside service starts in—" he checks his watch. "Twenty-six minutes."

We leave the church, Josh still holding my hand in his. It feels *so right* to hold his hand in front of my family.

"Ari!" Dad calls to Mom as he opens the driver's side door. "Look who I found canoodling in the vestibule. *Someone* takes after their mother." He gives me a pointed look.

"Please stop," I grimace. "I'm begging you."

"Just like your mother—" Mom slaps Dad on his arm, and I shriek and attempt to cover my ears, but I find I'm unwilling to let go of Josh's hand. Josh, meanwhile, just laughs, the fucking traitor.

"Sean Joseph," Mom scolds. "Behave. We don't want to scare Joshua off."

"Yes. We wouldn't want to scare *Joshua* off," I grumble.

Suddenly, Mom gasps dramatically, her head whipping toward us. "*Canoodling*?" she shoots out of the passenger side before I can pull the back seat door open. She rushes to our side of the car. "I knew it, I knew it! You owe me three hundred dollars, Seanny!"

My eyes widen. "You bet money? Three hundred dollars? That, what, Josh and I would canoodle in the church vestibule?"

Mom shoots me a look. "Of course not. That you'd date. Or something. Whatever. I won."

She throws herself at Josh and wraps her arms around his shoulders. "I've always known you're our family, Josh."

I'd never simultaneously hated and loved being Aria and Sean Quinn's daughter more.

Chapter 37

Josh

Playlist: "Sweet Nothing," Taylor Swift

Dealing with Grandma's funeral service is terrible, but Nic was right all along. Knowing she's by my side, that I'm not alone in this, makes all the difference.

After the burial, everyone goes back to the house for a small reception. Instead of going in the limo, Nic and I rode with the Quinns again. Aria and Sean joke and laugh, and despite how often Nic groans in embarrassment, this feels right.

For most of my life, my only family was Grandma and Tara. They're more than enough, but Sean and Aria immediately treating me like I'm theirs, like I've always been a part of their family is a surreal experience, especially after losing Grandma. They even open their arms to my weird little hodge-podge family, inviting Tara, Belen, Nellie, and Tyler to the barbecue they're hosting this weekend.

After almost everyone's left, Sean and Aria wash dishes in the kitchen and put away the plentiful leftovers. It's silly, but I'm grateful they insisted on bringing way more food than necessary.

Maybe that's what life is. Funerals and making sure everyone's fed after. Losing those you love, and finding something new and beautiful.

"Thanks for coming, man," I say, hugging my friend Brandon.

"Of course. I'm so sorry for your loss—your grandma was one of a kind," he says as we pull away. "But I have to ask, isn't that the girl who threw her drink on you at that party?"

I stare at him, not comprehending the quick topic change right away. "What?"

"Remember that night on the bluffs? We were going into senior year, and you said you were going to flirt with that girl and you spilt your drink on her so she threw her drink at you?"

I burst into laughter, and look over my shoulder, where Nic is deep in a conversation about autistic influencers with Belen. "Yep. That's Nic, my girlfriend."

A slow smile spreads across his face. "You're kidding me. That's a story to tell the grandkids."

I chuckle. "Yeah. She's simultaneously the greatest and most menacing human I know."

"That sounds terrifying."

"That's a great way to describe it."

That night, after everyone has left, Nic and I are in my childhood bedroom. We're breathless and satiated after making up for the days we were apart. She'd run to her parents' house to grab some stuff, since she hadn't planned to spend the night, and we fell into bed as soon as she came back.

"How are you feeling?" Nic asks after we'd made each other come. I've missed her and the way she tastes and the knowledge that *I'm* the one who gets to make her feel that good.

I shrug. "Feels like I survived a funeral today."

She nods. "Makes sense. How do you feel about the house?"

"That's...more complicated."

She hums. "How so?"

"There's what I know my family's going to say I should do, and then what I think Grandma would want me to do. What would be best for me."

"I'll support you in whatever you choose. But you deserve good things. Just for you. Not for your homophobic uncle or other shitty family members. Grandma left you the house to take care of you, not for you to take care of the house," she says, tracing her fingers over my chest.

Her head is resting on my arm, and her fingers still as they touch the bandage over my new tattoo. My heart stutters. "What's this? Did you get hurt?" The concern in her voice is palpable.

I cover her hand with mine. "So..." I say, drawing out the word. "You know Millie?"

She lifts her head, and I can just make out her bewildered expression. "Millie as in my *younger sister* Millie?"

I nod. "Yeah. I accidentally ended up in her chair at Ink It Over the other day. She's...slightly threatening."

"We all are," she admits. "We protect each other fiercely." She pauses, and I squeeze her hand. "Is it a new tattoo?"

"Mmhmm."

"What is it? Is it for Grandma?" It's just one word, but whenever she refers to her as Grandma and not "your grandma," it makes me so fucking happy. Like we're really each other's family.

"Promise you won't laugh," I say softly, squeezing her hand.

"I didn't laugh at your *Mamma Mia* tattoo," she says.

I scowl. "Because it's a fantastic tattoo."

"Show me this one?" she asks, moving her fingers over the bandage again. "Millie's an incredible artist."

I swallow and begin peeling the bandage off. Nic reaches over me to turn on the bedside lamp. When it's uncovered, she tilts her head. "Is it lavender?"

"It's lavender," I confirm. "Do you know you smell like lavender all the time? I don't know if it's your shampoo, or body wash, a perfume or laundry detergent..."

"Try all of the above."

"All of the above," I amend. "I thought I'd lost you when I said that shit to you. I didn't think we'd be together in my childhood bedroom less than a week later."

She's staring at the black lines, her body language and expression unreadable.

"I needed to keep you with me in any way I could. So I kept your smell." I pause. "That sounds creepy when I say it out loud."

"I feel like I should make some joke about being creepy, or about how silly you should feel because you got the tattoo for no reason." She cups my cheek with her hand and gently turns my face to hers. Her eyes fill with tears, one lone drop escaping and streaming down her pretty face. I thumb it away. "But I love you so much. And the tattoo is beautiful. You're beautiful. I just want to kiss you—"

I cut her off by pressing my lips to hers. "I love you more than you can ever know, Buttercup. I didn't know that my life was missing sunshine until you opened the blinds. I want everything with you Nic." My fingers trail down her body, each curve and edge so familiar now. "No matter what the future holds, I want to hold your hand through it."

I kiss her again, and for the first time, the present and the future make sense. Though nothing is definite, Nicoletta Quinn is steady and certain when I am hurting and broken. She's patient and forgiving with me when she's impatient and unforgiving with the rest of the world.

Knowing she wants to share herself and her life with me makes everything feel like it's going to be okay. She's helped my family and my heart expand, filling in pieces I didn't know were missing.

I'm going to be okay, all because she cursed me out on the Metro-North.

Chapter 38

Nic

Playlist: "Karma," Taylor Swift

Josh and I are late to the barbecue. We were getting ready in the bathroom when, inexplicably, I ended up on the counter while Josh was on his knees, arm pinning me to the surface while he made me scream his name.

Being in love with a man who loves eating my pussy just as much as I love him eating my pussy is kind of the greatest thing ever, even if it means we're late for family events.

I look around the backyard, and my heart warms. Everyone I love is here. My parents, Nellie and Tyler, Tara and Belen. All of my siblings are here too, except for Alex, plus some of their friends and significant others. But even with Alex living in LA, Izzy is still FaceTiming her as she and her best friend, Finn, sit at a table by the pool.

My dad waves at us from the grill with a spatula, wearing the apron I got him for Christmas, featuring an illustration of Ted Lasso, Coach Beard, and Roy Kent with the words "The Good, The Beard, and The Angry."

"Have you met everyone?" I ask Josh, taking his hand in mine.

He shakes his head. "No. Just your parents, Jo, Millie, Kat...and wait, does she work at the bookstore downtown?"

He points at Millie's best friend, Poppy, who's sitting on the edge of the pool, feet dangling in the water next to Ren. Kat is glaring at them from her lounge chair next to her asshole husband, Steve. She's probably mad at Poppy and Ren for bothering her perfect existence, though Poppy is quiet and Ren is a man of very little words.

Kat's just the worst.

I nod. "Yeah, that's Poppy. She's Alex's best friend. Her parents own Tea-Riffic Books."

We walk toward the fenced-in pool, and Leo is the first of my siblings to notice us.

"Hello!" he yells, leaping up from the lounge chair he and his girlfriend, Stella, had been sharing. He jogs over to us, his red curls bouncing and brown eyes shining with something diabolical, I'm sure. "I'm Leonardo Quinn, and who are you?"

"Leo!" Millie snaps, lowering her sunglasses. She's lounging on a pool floatie, feet crossed at her ankles, one of Jo's romance books on her tattooed chest. "Don't be an asshole!"

Leo scowls. "I'm being hospitable," he argues. "No one else came over to introduce themselves to Nic's new boyfriend."

It's silly, really, but it's also the first time someone has referred to Josh as my boyfriend, and I can't help the ridiculous smile that's on my face.

"Do you live in the city, too?" Leo continues, not asking Josh his name or anything else important, like the little shit he is. "Do you think my girlfriend and I—"

"Oh my *god*, Leo," I groan, planting my palm on his forehead and pushing him away. "You're so annoying."

"I'm Josh," Josh says, reaching his hand out to shake Leo's. "I do live in the city, but I grew up in Port Haven."

Leo's grin is so annoying, and I'm so close to climbing over the closed fence and pushing him in the pool to wipe it off his face. "Nic's never brought home a boy or a girl before," he says in sing-song tone.

"I'm going to kick your ass," I growl through clenched teeth.

He ignores me. "Sooo—"

"Leo!" Stella yells, sitting up and shading her eyes. "Stop being a dickhead and reapply your sunscreen before you burn."

I glare at Leo and point at his girlfriend. "I'm keeping her if you ever break up."

Leo rolls his eyes. "Yeah, yeah. We're not breaking up, so I guess you get to keep both of us."

"Nice to meet you, Leo," Josh says to Leo's retreating form.

The rest of the day is overstimulating, and I'm grateful that Josh has an extra pair of earplugs for me again, since I left mine in my skirt pocket yesterday.

He laughs with my parents and listens as Jo tells him about how Nellie and Tyler's wedding is coming along. He's officially the new Quinn family champion at ladder ball and plays root beer pong with us, too. When Leo and Izzy attempt to double team him with their weird twin antics and shove him into the pool, Leo's the one who ends up in the water instead. Izzy's smart enough to jump in before her turn. He and Ren discuss *Mamma Mia*, because apparently Ren is a big ABBA and Colin Firth fan. Who knew?

Leo did indeed make a cake celebrating my autism diagnosis and bisexuality, which makes me tear up. Maybe it's because his and Izzy's birthday is later this week, and the asshole still took the time to think about me, even if it is weird as fuck.

Josh and his family fit into my family. Like a spot no one realized was empty had been sitting there, waiting for them to fill it all along. It's one of my favorite days, watching Josh as he is showered with love, imagining what our future could look like.

When he notices my body begin to tense, he asks me to show him where the bathroom is.

I take him inside and point toward the half bath on the first floor. "It's that—"

"Take me to your room."

I don't ask questions. I just lead him upstairs, where my bedroom is still decorated with posters of the cast of *Twilight*.

"What do you need?" Josh asks, wrapping his arms around me and pulling my body into his.

I sigh and relax into him. "I don't know."

"Want me to paint your nails?" he asks, nodding toward a ten-year-old bottle of black nail polish.

For some reason, that's exactly what I need—him sitting on my twin-sized bed with me, painting my nails with clumpy black nail polish that has a questionable smell.

And I can see us doing this in my apartment when the weather is cold. In his home. In our home. With future members of our family.

The future looks good.

Chapter 39

Nic

Playlist: "Never Gonna Give You Up," Rick Astley

Three Months Later

> **Mom:** Hi, sweetheart! Dad and I are saving you a seat. We can't wait to see you. <kiss emoji>

Nic: hi mom!

Nic: thanks for saving me a seat. i can't
wait to see you and dad soon! love you!

Josh is late. His meeting finalizing the sale of Grandma's house ran later than expected, and my relentless texting has done nothing to clear up traffic on 95. Luckily, since my parents drove down together, Josh borrowed my dad's car and is driving to Jersey instead of dealing with the train. We'll drive back up to Connecticut tomorrow afternoon to return the car before taking the train back into the city. Most of my family is already here, with the exception of Kat and Steve, who weren't invited, Alex, who's in LA, and the twins who are a few months deep into their first semesters at college. Tara and Belen are also here, and it's incredible to see how my life and Josh's really have merged together in such a short time.

I've missed him so much. We've had to do long distance-ish for the past few months while he stayed in Port Haven and readied the house to sell. He took a leave of absence from work, and I visited on the weekends, and we never missed a family dinner. I'm pretty sure my family likes him more than me.

Josh took the train home once a week for therapy and to meet me for lunch and, more often than not, a quickie.

Despite the difficulties of being apart, the past few months have also been wonderful. Josh started medication to help with his nightmares and anxiety, and he has been going to therapy weekly to process his trauma. I'm his biggest cheerleader, and whenever I think I can't be more proud or love him more, he proves me wrong.

I used to hate being wrong.

"I'm going to *kill* him," Nellie says through gritted teeth. Her hair is done in an intricate updo, and she's wearing a silky, floor length slip-dress.

I don't know how Jo was able to plan this entire wedding in such a short amount of time. She survived off applesauce pouches and the occasional spoonful of almond butter, but she did it, and everything is perfect.

Even if she has a new eye twitch.

"He'll make it," Jo says, her left eye twitching as she gently pats Nellie's shoulder.

Just then there's a knock on the door, "Joshua, get in here!" Nellie roars.

The door opens, and a woman with long, curly blonde hair sticks her head in. "Sorry, darlin'. It's just me. Thought I'd get some pictures of the bride getting ready."

Nellie sighs. "Hi, Hunter. Sure, let's get pictures of me committing murder. Free evidence."

I look at Jo, who's staring at the photographer, mouth open and eyes wide. The photographer, Hunter, notices, and her eyes widen, too. "Giovanna?" she croaks out.

"Hunter," Jo breathes, looking like she's going to pass out.

I look between the two of them, trying to figure out why Hunter looks familiar until it clicks.

"Oh my god! You're the MacIntires' granddaughter who spent that summer with them! Jo, remember? She went to the party at the bluffs with us."

"I remember," Jo says, still staring at Hunter.

Weird.

"Nicoletta, where is your boy toy? He is our *officiant*," Nellie hisses. "He's a dead man." She looks at me, her gaze softening. "Sorry for your loss."

I wave my hand. "No, no. I get it."

"I'm here!" The door flies open, and Josh basically falls into the room, a garment bag folded over his arm. He's sweaty and breathing heavily, and it immediately makes me think about all the other times I've gotten to see him sweaty and breathing heavily, and I bite my lip. His eyes widen as he takes Nellie in. "Fuck, Nellie. You're so beau—"

"I know!" Nellie yells, pointing with her bouquet of light pink and burgundy roses and white peonies. "What the fuck are you wearing?" Hunter's finally stopped staring at Jo and is pointing her camera at her. I cannot *wait* to see those pictures.

Josh blanches and looks down at his flannel shirt. Poor guy isn't safe from any of the women in his life. "I didn't want to fuck up my suit—"

"I don't care. I'm getting married in seven minutes, and I'd love for my officiant to be there."

"Come on." I grab Josh's arm and lead him to the bathroom, closing the door behind us. I take the garment bag from him and hang it on the back of the door. When I turn back to him, he's already started undressing, and I audibly groan as he unbuttons his flannel.

"Keep your hands to yourself, you menace," Josh warns, his blue eyes sparkling. "Nellie doesn't seem adverse to committing a double homicide today." His hands unfasten his jeans, the dark wash ones that make his ass look delectable.

I roll my eyes and turn my back to him to unzip the garment bag. I hear him inhale deeply and grin to myself. The red satin midi dress I'm wearing with fishnets makes my ass look just as delectable. "Stop leering at me and take your clothes off, Joshua."

He grumbles incoherently, and I hand him the pieces of his suit. It only takes a few minutes, and then he's fixing his hair in the mirror.

"Now who's leering, Nicoletta?" Josh says, meeting my eyes in the mirror.

"Not my fault you're a total hunk in a suit," I say, shrugging. "You better hurry and put your dress shoes on or else you'll be marrying Nellie in just your socks."

Five minutes later, Josh is standing under a floral arch and I'm seated between Ren and Mom. When I sat down, Dad's hand was definitely steadily climbing under her skirt, and I almost turned around and walked away.

The wedding is perfect. Jo moves seamlessly around the venue, whispering into her headpiece, and Tyler looks hot as fuck in a fitted black suit. All the anger that had been on Nellie's face melts away as she walks down the aisle.

Josh tears up as he reads sonnets and poems and talks about how Nellie, and then Tyler, became his family after he moved to the city for college.

And when Nellie and Tyler kiss, we're all on our feet cheering loudly. I'm able to look between the people in front of me and meet Josh's eyes. He smiles at me, and I get butterflies in my stomach. Josh's love is familiar. It's safe, steady, *home*. But it's also thrilling and exciting.

I love you, Buttercup, he mouths.

I love you, too, I mouth back.

I didn't know I'd dreamed of loving and being loved by Joshua Henry for my entire life, but now that I do, now that I am, it's so obvious.

"This song's for Nic. Rick told us it's your favorite," the DJ says before an all-too-familiar melody fills the hall.

I look humorlessly at Josh. "Really?"

"Come on, Buttercup. It's our song!" Josh insists, standing from the table and pulling me up too.

I groan. "I danced with you like five times."

"One more. Give me one more."

I smirk at him. "You plan on saying that again later tonight?"

He grins back, unashamed. "You know me so well."

We end up being the only people on the dance floor. It's late and most guests, including my family, have left. Despite the tempo of the song, it all feels intimate.

"Remember when you Rickrolled me for the first time?" I ask him, burying my face in his shirt and inhaling him.

"When you broke into my house and asked to fuck? Yes, yes I do."

I roll my eyes. "You're so dramatic."

"Have I told you that was the best day of my life?" he says softly, lowering his mouth to my ear so only I can hear him.

I shiver at his breath on the shell of my ear. "You're lying."

"Maybe I am. Maybe it was when I saw you naked and over-come with pleasure for the first time. Or when you told me you loved me and made my wildest dreams come true. Or maybe it was a Tuesday, twenty-two years ago. You wore mismatched socks and a green sweater, your hair in pigtails. Aria had packed you a Fluffernutter for lunch, and you drank from a carton of chocolate milk."

I look up at him, our eyes meeting. "You remember that much? Why the hell didn't you say anything? That's romantic as shit, Henry."

"I was waiting for a romantic time to tell you."

"And after Rickrolling me at your best friend's wedding seemed like the right time."

"Correct."

I stand on my tiptoes, and he leans down, brushing our lips together. "You're an evil goblin," I murmur.

"I'm *your* evil goblin," he corrects, softly nipping at my bottom lip.

"My evil goblin who threw a drink on me on the bluffs ten years ago."

He pulls away. "We've gone over this, Nicoletta. I will always regret the two decades we spent hating each other." He dips me, making me squeal before he helps me stand upright again. "But

I'd do it all again if it meant that it would lead to where it did." Josh cups my cheek, running his thumb over my lower lip. "If it would lead to us."

"None of this was supposed to be real," I whisper, staring into his eyes.

"No. We were just two fools trying to figure out what you like."

I smile crookedly. "Turns out we like each other the most. We're the realest thing I've ever known, Josh."

He pulls me into him, and as we dance, I think about whatever's out there—god, the universe, whatever has a hand in our lives. I thank the stars on Josh's ceiling for guiding him through the dark and back to me, for the late night train that carried us home. For everything that went wrong, just so we could get this right.

Nic & Josh's story is far from over! Keep an eye out for them in the next Quiblings novel, Back to Me.

Acknowledgments

I'd always heard it took a village to raise a child, but I had no idea it took a small country to write, edit, and love a book baby.

Nic and Josh came to me, pretty much fully formed, one night in April, 2023. Since then, they're taken over my life. They both have so much of my vulnerabilities and loving them so deeply led to me loving myself in a new way, too.

First, to myself, at every stage of life. To baby Katie who dreamed up stories of talking lizards, to teenage Katie who worked tirelessly on her high school creative writing magazine to make it perfect, to college-aged Katie who majored in English because even though she had no idea what she wanted to do, she just knew she loved stories. Thank you for fighting, for dreaming, for staying. We fucking did it.

To my therapist, Val, for encouraging and listening to me through this whole process. Thanks for being just as excited as I was to find my fire again.

To Cheyenne, who was one of the first people I told about Josh. I knew he was fat from the start (hahaha), and as someone who loves fat representation as much as I do, she was the person I went to to make sure I got him right. Thank you for going above and beyond, for answering my unhinged, middle of the night texts when you woke up the next morning. For editing and sensitivity reading. *From the Start* only exists because of you, and I am forever grateful.

To Tara, Kristen, Izzy, & Megan. Thank you for your expertise and willingness to fact check my writing in regards to your lived experiences. It means so much to me.

To Paige. Your neck must hurt from all the hats you wore. Thank you for bringing Nic & Josh to life with your incredible artwork. I don't know how you took my descriptions and got it all right, but I'm so grateful you did. You made them real for me. Thank you for beta reading and editing, and just loving me, Nic, and Josh so much all this time. You're stuck with me for eight books now, sorry.

To my beta readers. Thank you for taking your time to tell me what worked and what didn't. I appreciate every one of you so, so much.

To my family. Sarah, I'm so sorry if you've read this far. But thank you for always asking about my writing, for being so excited for me, and for always championing me. You mean the world to me. Mom, again, I'm sorry if you read this far BUT I did give ample warning. Thanks for letting me live with you when life collapsed on me, for loving me with patience, and believing in me when I couldn't believe in myself. Dad, thanks for not looking at me funny when I spent all my time visiting you on a laptop. I hope you never read this.

To Allie. Thank you for being one of my first and biggest fans of Nic and Josh. Your excitement over them during such a difficult time gave me so much hope, and the thoughtful gift and texts will forever mean everything to me.

To the authors who inspire me. Thank you for having the courage to share your vulnerability and stories. I understand now how *brave* each of you is, and I feel so honored that you've shared your stories with the world, and in turn changed, and saved, my life.

To Ricki and Cait. Thank you for reading early, and texting me updates. I can't explain how much it meant to read that you loved it so much that you cried, that you couldn't put it down. You helped me rebuild my confidence, and I'm so grateful.

To you, reader. Thank you for reading *From the Start*. Thank you for taking a chance on a debut indie author and her story. Thank you for wanting to read stories about queer, disabled, and fat love and joy. Thank you for sharing and liking my posts, for following my social media accounts, and cheering me on along the way. My gratitude is endless, and I can't wait to thank you again and again for Jo's book, and every book that follows.

About the Author

Katie Duggan (she/they) is a New England transplant currently living in Northern Virginia. She writes romance novels that give fat, neurodivergent, and queer characters spicy happily-ever-afters. When Katie's not writing or being kept up at night by her characters, they can be found drinking root beer, going to therapy, convincing people to read her favorite books, and doing whatever hobbies give their neurospicy brain the most dopamine at the moment.

Email: KatieDuggan.Writes@gmail.com

Instagram & TikTok: @KatieDugganWrites

Also by Katie Duggan

The Quiblings Series

From the Start – Nic & Josh's story is available now!
Back to Me – Jo & Hunter's story coming August 2024

Made in the USA
Columbia, SC
14 September 2025

62017172R00253